The Keeper

MRC
Chicago, IL

Cover design by	Dave Robbins
Text design by	Brian Fischer
Author Photo by	Nick Bianco

Carr, Martha Randolph, 1959-

The Keeper: Second in the Wallis Jones Series; a novel / Martha Randolph Carr.

Printed in the United States of America
ISBN-10: 1620309904
ISBN-13: 9781620309902

The Keeper

A Thriller
Second in the Wallis Jones Series

Martha Carr

Dedicated to Don Allison, whose continued guidance in life and literature make so much possible.

To Dave Robbins, Nick Bianco and Brian Fischer for donating your time and your talents so generously.
Forever grateful for your friendships.

And to my son, Louie and his wonderful Katie who remind me all the time of what really matters and how wonderful life can be in any given moment.

CHAPTER
1

Harry Weiskopf was reading when he heard the quiet pops followed by something heavy hitting the floor. There was only one cry for help and it had sounded more like a yelp of surprise than anything else.

He had stood up, wondering if he should prepare himself for something but beyond that there wasn't much else he could do.

His room was in the basement and only measured twenty feet by twenty feet. A big square. Many of the houses in Central Florida were built on reclaimed swamp land and relatively few neighborhoods had basements. No one suspected he was there. That's what made it the perfect prison.

There were certain geographic features about the house that made the location desirable as well, given its purpose, and kept at least one side relatively hard for someone to casually stroll up and say hello. The house was on a lake, which kept any kind of passing traffic to a minimum. There was also a discreet camera and sensor system that showed when someone was entering the grounds. The inside of the house was wired from end to end as well.

Sometimes Harry took to talking directly to one of the cameras in the room, giving a lecture on whatever was on his mind.

He could only reason that there was good insulation and sound dampening material, maybe a good air filtration system for the basement because there were no windows. All the hours he had to observe the few details he had right around him led him to believe he was breathing air circulated by the filtration system.

His room was most likely largely isolated from the main house upstairs and had very heavy walls and ceilings reinforced by steel. A guard had even mentioned there was a generator in case electricity went out during the frequent thunderstorms or occasional hurricanes.

The downside to a lake style house would be that the neighbors would typically be out and would most likely mingle with the people occupying the house. Harry sometimes wondered how they dealt with that problem but he couldn't get anyone to tell him. He wondered if perhaps an entire family lived right above him.

The only time he saw his guards, though was when they brought him something or just randomly checked on him. They never said much of anything.

Maybe they were afraid he'd start yelling for attention and never stop. The thought had occurred to him.

For the most part, he had noted when they first arrived, for the few moments he was outside that the house blended easily into the neighborhood.

The basement was completely hidden from the outside world. No windows or obvious doors and the entrance to Harry's room was hidden inside of the house, accessible inside of what had seemed like a closet when they escorted him inside and shut the door behind him.

The room, his prison cell buried in the middle of suburbia was bare of anything but the essentials to let him sleep or sit at a desk and all of that was nailed to the floor or the walls. It was like being permanently entombed in a Motel 6 but without the complimentary newspaper at his door.

He wasn't to be trusted with anything more than an outdated paperback book or an old magazine and even those were all tagged and numbered.

Pop, pop. More sounds and feet moving quickly in his direction.

He glanced at the nearby wall where he had been keeping track of the days by marks, tucked back in a corner. Anger quickly took him over with the thought of how he had tried to pass so many hours knowing there would never be any real change. Not for him, not after what he had done.

"It looks like change has found me," he whispered, not wanting to get involved just yet in whatever might be headed his way. A small giggle escaped him.

"Get down," yelled someone and Harry fell to the floor behind the bed without even looking to see who had said it. He couldn't even be sure they had meant him.

The door splintered with the first shots through the reinforced wood and steel. When they built this fortress the creators had probably never envisioned someone getting this far. Just then, an enforcer, a long, solid battering ram came splintering through, quickly followed by four men who surveyed the room for a moment.

Harry was still on the ground, barely peeking over the bed.

"You alone?" asked one of the men. Harry nodded his head, unable to do much more. They quickly stepped toward him and scooped him under the armpits, pulling him to his feet and half-carrying him toward the remains of the door.

There wasn't time to grab a jacket. Harry Weiskopf didn't care. He was getting out of that room.

They were shoving him quickly along the hallway toward what he remembered as the front door. Once he was placed inside that room, 745 days ago, all he had seen beyond it were glimpses of the hallway when they had brought him food or done wellness checks. Now, he was whisking past the pale grey walls being carried along by new faces.

His makeshift prison, as it turned out, sat on a fairly busy street along what counted for a main street in Bartow, Florida, population 17,545 people, including the elderly snowbirds from much further north.

People who couldn't let go of their family or friends but had enough of trying to navigate ice or snow.

At first they had held him on an estate along River Road in Richmond, Virginia until the house in Bartow was ready for him. That place had been nicer, he thought. The window had a nice view of the James River and the decor was more thoughtful.

Old money chic. Everything was well-made and showed generations of careful wear.

Occasionally, the elderly owner had stopped by to talk to him about what had happened, asking him for more details about who he had talked to in Management.

Harry had enjoyed the visits with the old man, Thornton somebody. It was hard to remember anymore. At first, Harry had been reluctant to say much, in case he would have to look at how he had helped to plot something even he was unaware of till it all came out in the open.

Isn't that what Norman had kept shouting at him?

Harry's mind played a lot of tricks on him lately. Memories came and went and seemed to blend together with nothing new to really break them up anymore or distract him from just the passing of hours.

Thornton had been kind to him though, and over time Harry had started to trust him and told him everything he knew. He had even worked at trying to remember more details. Names, dates and things he overheard in case they were important. Maybe this was his way to not only redeem himself but get out of that room in Richmond and actually get to go back home to Florida. He looked forward to Thornton's visits and tried not to pepper him with too many questions about what was going on outside in the world. Thornton had seemed reluctant to say too much, anyway and Harry didn't want to ruin things. He lived for their meetings.

They had even talked a little about learning how to accept things and find some peace. It wasn't too long though before all of the visits from Thornton stopped and he was left with just the guards. That's when he was abruptly moved. He wasn't sure what day of the week it was when they came to get him, he never was. The guards had told him to get up and follow them. He tried to get his clothes but they said someone else would see that his things were moved, such as they were.

All he had were some toiletries, a small wardrobe and a picture of his family when the brothers were all in their twenties and their parents were still alive. A woman, Esther and her husband, Herman were also in the picture. Harry had known them his entire life. They owned a bookstore in Richmond now, at least he thought so. He had lost touch with them a long time ago.

He tried to ask about Thornton and where he was going but no one would answer him until they were on the plane. Bartow, Florida, final stop.

Someone must have decided he was too close to where so many people had died. Too close to his brother, he thought. That was probably the real reason.

He was just starting to feel a small amount of acceptance at his fate in the upscale prison when they had dragged him off to Bartow on a private plane.

Bartow, Florida, named for the first Confederate officer to become a martyr, thought Harry, just like me.

Harry knew a lot of facts and figures from the old magazines and books his guards would allow him to read. There was nothing else to do. He was seen as a threat to national security and wasn't allowed to have access to any kind of real-time news. Everything he knew about the world pre-dated the last two years.

He had felt some remorse when he was first deposited on that estate in Richmond. His mind kept whirling, stuck on what he had done to so many people.

But it wasn't long before the tedious days started to string together and he saw how they had decided to blame him for everything. No trial, no jury and worst of all, no visitors.

The thought made him bitter in equal measures with a sense of pride that he had finally shown his brothers, Norman and Tom that he could do something on his own that made a real difference.

"I have no family," he muttered as they hurried him along outside.

"Street clear?" asked the older man. He was clearly in charge, thought Harry. The oversized men that surrounded Harry looked nervous even as they kept moving efficiently through the large, Spanish style house that had been Harry's prison. Not much longer, thought Harry. He knew that he could be headed to something worse but he pushed the thought away. Anything is better than this small space for the rest of my life, he thought. "Even death," he whispered, surprising himself at how comforting the idea sounded.

As they pulled him outside, a large hand in the center of his back pushing him with a steady strain, he twisted around to get a good look at the house. It had been dark when they arrived and he had felt so beaten by all of his dreams that he didn't lift his head. He wanted to remember where Norman and Tom had left him to rot.

The house was a Spanish revival and looked like a cheap version of something that an American dreamed up who liked bling but couldn't stop himself from cutting corners.

Just inside the front door would have revealed a different story.

The two-story was really a fortress designed to quietly keep someone inside. The walls were reinforced and heavily insulated for sound. The windows were level-eight panes of polycarbonate surrounded in glass and could withstand early rounds from even an AK47.

That was all the Circle guards thought they would need to keep Harry Weiskopf secure. No one was even supposed to know he was still alive, much less his whereabouts. Fewer than ten people knew what had really happened.

His family held a funeral back in Richmond, Virginia and buried a John Doe from the local morgue. The church was full to overflowing with people who knew Norman and his wife, Wallis. Norman had wept as if Harry was really dead and had said a lot of nice things about the three brothers when they were little. Both he and Tom had even been pallbearers bearing the token brother out of the church on their shoulders. His stand-in was now resting comfortably in Hollywood Cemetery near the soldiers who had died in the War Between the States

A guard told him all of that but was overheard and quickly replaced.

That had been the end of any kind of real news and had hurt Harry the most. It was as if he had never existed and was easily forgotten. "I have no family," he said, this time with a little more volume. The leader seemed to smile a little but quickly went back to softly barking orders.

Harry never knew what they listed as the cause of death. He was hoping it was some kind of accident and nothing as boring as heart failure. His brothers had stopped by only once to say goodbye and never made contact again. They blamed him for all of the murders but that wasn't fair. That's not what he was trying to do, after all when he told a Management operative about Carol Schaeffer and the thumb drive she had in her possession. It had all gone horribly wrong and they had killed her. Nothing was really right after that and more people had died while everyone fought over that thumb drive. "Like a fumbled football at a championship game," said Harry, to no one in particular. It didn't matter, no one was really listening to him anyway.

He felt his stomach sour and he pressed his eyes shut, hesitating and trying to stop for just a moment.

"Move it," hissed the older man. The hand in Harry's back pushed a little harder. They pushed Harry into the back seat of a large, black SUV with dark, tinted windows. "I thought these were illegal in Florida," said Harry, as if that mattered. He could feel a steady stream of fear starting to creep up inside of him.

Suddenly, clear as day, a memory of Norman, Tom and Harry hanging out with their dad popped up in his head. It was one of those rare Richmond winters where the snowfall was heavy and the ground stayed cold. School closed for a few days and before long their mother was tired of seeing them draped all over the furniture, complaining about nothing to do.

They had all hiked to the Virginia Country Club with its wide, steep hill that would have made for a perfect ride. But the groundskeeper was watching out for interlopers and had shooed them away, saying it would hurt the golf course grounds.

Norman was starting to fade and said he was cold but for once, Tom had sided with Harry and insisted they had come too far to turn back. There aren't going to be many snowfalls like this, Harry had said. He felt a certain surprise of delight when Tom had agreed and told Norman to keep walking.

They had pressed on to Boatwright Lawn at the nearby University of Richmond and found a lot of their friends already happily throwing themselves down the hill on trays from the cafeteria, or on round plastic sleds and old-fashioned Flexible Flyers. The brothers had a long, plastic toboggan that could fit all three of them on one run if they squeezed together. Their combined weight made the sled tear down a hill and the air rush into Harry's lungs. He loved being in the middle where he could feel secure between them.

They had kept at it, trudging back up the hill so many times till his legs burned from the effort and the snow was jammed into his boots. The walk home seemed to take forever and by the time he was by the fire in the family room his fingers and toes were bright red and numb for what seemed like hours. Their clothes were soaked and hung on a makeshift line their mother had strung in their little laundry room.

"My Weiskopf men," their father had said, smiling broadly as Harry had drifted off to sleep in front of the fire. He had wanted to stay awake forever just to keep this day. It was the best day of his life.

A sadness settled over him as the car accelerated and he left the Florida prison behind. He turned and looked at it, wondering if this was going to be the last day of his life. "I have no family," he said, and shut his eyes, trying to rest up for whatever was coming next. Maybe he would see Thornton again.

Two cars trailed the SUV that held Harry Weiskopf and up ahead two more would quickly glide in front of that one till Harry was protected from all sides. George Clemente was in the car immediately following the SUV so he could keep an eye on his prize. Clemente was thought to be a rising star in Management. A comeback of sorts. He was rising even more than those who still stood above him could even realize. They would know soon enough when they were replaced.

He had almost died two years ago at the hands of an old enemy. A bothersome Episcopal minister, Reverend Michael had beaten him badly but he had managed to survive, even if his rehabilitation had taken months. That only gave him the time he needed to come up with a viable plan.

He gathered around his hospital bed the lieutenants who had come through what happened in Richmond and given them their orders. They were to keep working as a cell within Management, known only to themselves. The rest of Management had not discovered them so all was not lost. Not by a long shot.

Clemente had known for some time about a former Management operative, Mark Whiting who had successfully gone over to the opposing forces, the Circle and had risen in the ranks at the Federal Reserve based in Richmond. Whiting had run out of town not too long after Clemente's beating and just ahead of a hit squad from Management. No one really knew where he was anymore. Clemente didn't really care. He had other things on his mind but for a while Mark had proved useful.

He had discovered that Mark had also spent the last years of his career at the Reserve quietly stealing millions by shaving off amounts from Management accounts that no one would ever notice. They were so small, but so continuous that over time millions of dollars had been drained.

Clemente had tripped over the plan almost accidentally when he was looking for his own way to create an army. He had dreams that involved reshaping Management into the force it had once been in the world. That was going to take a real army and a lot of money.

He had piggybacked on Whiting's idea and taken larger amounts but still small enough to avoid notice, at least until he could take enough power that no one would say much of anything to him.

He was tired of being pushed around by Management operatives who had grown accustomed to a softer way of life. They had forgotten what it had cost to get this far and if someone didn't step in soon, the Circle was going to take enough away that it would become close to impossible to regain a footing.

Clemente wasn't going to let that happen, even if his methods were going to have to be a little harsh. They had already quietly purged a few of the weaker members from their cell. Such a disappointment but they were given a proper burial in a potter's field. Clemente had pulled the trigger himself on each one of them. Personal responsibility was very important to him.

They didn't suffer, he thought.

The car ahead slowed to let the two lead cars, a BMW and an older sedan glide in front of them. It was only a thirty minute ride to the private landing strip where a plane was waiting for them but Clemente wasn't going to relax till the son of one of the original twenty enemies was safely locked away under his command. Clemente had plans for Harry Weiskopf.

The thumb drive had eluded Clemente and he had taken a beating from that sanctimonious priest trying to capture it. The incident in Savannah had almost cost him his life but in the end, something good came of it all.

That's the way it generally worked, thought Clemente. Stay calm, look for the solution.

He was confined to a hospital bed for months as the bones in his back repaired and then more time in a rehabilitation facility as he learned to walk again and regained his strength.

Right from the start, even before he was off of the painkillers he had started to come up with ideas.

There was a Presidential election that was coming in less than two years but the incumbent, Ronald Hayes was a Circle operative and was most likely going to win a second term. Four more years of the Circle being in control of key moves was more than Clemente could stomach.

The key was to somehow unsettle the American public, who were unaware of the two world-wide giants and shake their faith enough in the current sitting President. Make them beg for change.

At the same time, the hidden Management cell could use circumstances to their advantage and take out enough Circle operatives to leave their side wounded and vulnerable, maybe even sloppy.

The bigger picture, the grand idea had come to Clemente all at once. Really, it was obvious once it had settled in and he could see how much good it could do for everyone, especially in Management. Even the unsuspecting middle class would eventually benefit, whether they would ever know the details or not.

They would start a civil war, a quiet war. They would organize and plan military operations exactly like an established country but carry it out in front of an unsuspecting American population. Most operations would have to be small in size and move through buildings or even subdivisions and the planning would have to be careful and well thought out. If the general public ever caught on to the plan, too much could be lost.

Their ignorance to the bigger picture of the two world powers was necessary so that Management could more easily wield their power. Perhaps someday Management could step out from the shadows and operate on a more transparent basis. The idea made George Clemente smile. Then he could name himself the President and stop all of this nonsense. Instead of one man, one vote he could finally parse votes out based on wealth.

It wasn't a new idea. For hundreds of years that's the way the civilized world had worked and had gotten along just fine. Frankly, democracy was in its infancy, thought Clemente and was proving to be mostly annoying.

The war was only part of the plan. The financial institutions would have to be consolidated so that they could more easily be controlled and manipulated. In order to do that Senators and Congressmen who were part of Management had pushed through enough legislation to deregulate the banks and trading floors. The two could now write their own rules and they wasted no time figuring out tangled ways to make more money that quickly became hard to trace to their sources.

It wasn't long before the economy was struggling to right itself and the problems quickly spread to the rest of the world. Sometimes a good plan just comes together, thought Clemente.

They pulled up to the airstrip and quickly loaded Harry Weiskopf onto the plane. If he wasn't so valuable as a trading chip with the softhearted Circle, Clemente would have killed him on the spot and left him for the Circle to find.

As it was, the roaring fire back at the Bartow house was going to be a problem for someone to explain to locals if they realized the interior of the house wasn't exactly burning down. The exterior would have come down by now, exposing the frame of the inner rooms. It would somehow get taken care of by local Circle operatives, Clemente knew that, but it would also slow them down just a little and time was what he needed most these days.

Time to get the war well underway and time to find the identity and whereabouts of the Keeper and the cell around him. Time to kill them all and finally destroy the Circle.

CHAPTER

2

A banjo, a machete, night vision goggles, a used Play Station. Detective Arnold Biggs liked to run lists through his head. It calmed him down, helped him to focus. He needed to focus if he was going to be able to pull this off and not end up dead.

His teenage son, Maynard had spent his first real paycheck on a big splurge. A banjo, a machete, night vision goggles and a used Play Station. Arnold smiled just thinking about it and felt his breathing get a little easier. He had been way too young when he accidentally became a father and still remembered what it was like when money crossed paths with youth.

The detective was standing on the edge of the three-story brick building, ready to run. He had mapped out the route and was playing it in his head over and over again. Go down the old black iron fire escape along one side of the empty tobacco warehouse. Take the turns as fast as he could on his busted knee. It would have to hold up long enough to let him take a few more steps, get down into the alley and along the old pavers.

The detective was only in his early forties and had only been made detective after putting together who had been responsible for a string of murders in the quiet West End of Richmond, Virginia just a couple of years ago, where he had been a patrol cop for years. He had really liked one of the victims, old man Blazney and the whole thing had felt a little personal.

It was unfortunate that it had turned out to be a deputy named Oscar Newman, a fellow law enforcement officer who just seemed to lose it one day and went on a rampage. In the end, he was shot down by an old lady, the mother in law of a friend of the detective, when Newman broke into their house and shot up the place.

When Biggs was made a detective they had immediately paired him with an older detective, Jason Busby, Buster to everyone else, who at first had mostly grunted out orders and made him drive.

Detective Biggs knew enough about how to get along with his elders to not ask too many questions and quickly carried out orders. Not only did he learn a lot and fast but he earned Buster's trust at the same time.

It was the only reason they had ended up standing watch for Rodney Parrish, against direct orders on a couple of flat rooftops. If the snitch was telling the truth that would put him right in the path of Parrish. Biggs long suspected Parrish of a lot of things but had been warned off of him. Parrish, though had finally crossed the line.

Detective Biggs was a hulking figure and at least twice Parrish's size. His meaty hands resembled a catcher's mitt and could easily throw Parrish around like a doll. He was looking forward to the satisfying thud Parrish would make when he hit the ground.

Biggs dropped his shoulders and let out the breath he was holding in a rush of air. Just a couple of years of being a detective and the entire thing was about to go to hell for all the right reasons.

He blinked his eyes hard to let go of the image of the woman's dead body so he could concentrate on the alley.

He tapped his gun again, a light tap. His heart was already pounding and the feel of the cold metal calmed his nerves just enough.

Something darted by the alley and his nerves gave into old training and immediately reacted.

"Now," he said in an excited whisper as he ran a few steps, the rooftop gravel crunching under his thick-soled shoes. "Dammit," he whispered. It was just a rat.

No one was around but the pressure was weighing on his chest. Doing the right thing seemed downright stupid but living with himself if he didn't would have been a long, hard road and he wasn't willing to walk it this time. He wasn't sure why but that was one dead body too much. He could figure out all of the reasons later.

Consequences were a hard thing to live with sometimes. That was something he was always trying to teach Maynard.

The rat that had suddenly darted out of the alley down below, startling Biggs, was followed closely by a lean yellow cat. It had been just enough to make Biggs jump. He was glad Buster couldn't see him from where he was standing down below.

He would have jumped too, thinking Biggs had actually seen something and then called him an asshole for shaking him out of his calm. No one would have even cracked a smile. Parrish was that much trouble.

Biggs pushed out the worry of what this was going to cost both of them and kept watch on the narrow backstreet that ran down between the old brick office buildings. He was standing on the roof of the old warehouse, determined to nab Parrish.

Most people thought of Parrish as a thief and a local numbers runner, even a sound guy for some barely talented hip-hop bands. Definitely not worth this much trouble.

Biggs had his own suspicions for a long time though that involved a lot more if he could just prove it. Only problem was that Parrish was protected by too many legit people and for reasons that Arnold Biggs didn't completely know yet. He had bits and pieces of the answers and that's what made all of this so dangerous. In the past he couldn't be sure if pursuing Parrish was only going to cost him his career and the start of a decent pension fund without yielding some kind of satisfying conclusion. The dead body had tipped the scales even if grabbing Parrish would set off some people.

Lieutenant Greevey had given a direct order more than once to leave Parrish alone but Arnold Biggs knew right away that the day would come and it wouldn't be possible. Buster knew it too. They did a nice impression of paying attention and without a word went back to work.

They knew better than to even try to have a conversation inside the police station. There were eyes everywhere and they couldn't be sure who was watching and who cared. Greevey was fond of saying that he was part of management, for what that was worth and they could be too if they would just follow orders. Detective Biggs decided he was as far into management as he wanted to be and was just fine staying a detective.

"Buster," he said, "Come on, let's get going. There's still a few more people we can talk to about the Queen's thing."

He had started the day with the idea of just working a case. Parrish was not on his radar, not really.

There was a string of robberies that were bugging him, mostly because he couldn't make everything fit together.

A growing list of small mom and pop stores had been broken into through air vents followed by a quick smash and grab of mostly cigarettes and baby formula. Both could fetch someone a quick profit on the local black market and not leave much of a trace. Several of the stores had security cameras but they were always disabled before the thief entered the building. The latest break-in was in the Queen Stop 'N Shop.

Somehow by late afternoon that trail wound itself around and had led both detectives to this place, standing watch for Parrish on the top of old brick warehouses in what was still known as the tobacco district, in the hot sun with no shade. It didn't matter that it was fall in Richmond. The sun was relentless.

Biggs kept watch on the alleys below as he ran the pieces of the case through his head again, trying to see where Parrish fit in but the trail wasn't clear.

That didn't mean it wasn't there. If Parrish was a part of it, there was something larger going on with all of it. Both detectives were sure of it.

Looked at separately, the robberies didn't form much of a pattern and seemed at best, random attempts to make some quick cash.

However, Biggs approached every new case by laying out everything he knew about the crimes in long lists. He loved lists.

Where the victims lived, if they went to the same diner, even their religion and if they showed up anywhere on a Sunday. Things like that mattered in a small town like Richmond, Virginia.

"Always go local. Even a crook has to lead some kind of life," said Buster. It was one of the best things Biggs had ever heard him say.

That's how he started to spot the beginnings of a strange pattern. All of the robberies stretched neatly across only two police precincts and all of the owners belonged to the same men's civic club, some kind of circle. Biggs still needed to ask more about that.

There were other stores in the area, stores that had more merchandise or had locations that would seem to make better targets. None of those owners though had the same connection. Someone was targeting these particular stores.

A pattern could be as telling as a fingerprint even if Biggs couldn't tell what it was just yet.

Biggs suspected the Browning brothers who were always getting into trouble and were known for just this kind of heist. Only catch was that they weren't smart enough to make up a plan and they wouldn't have thought to take care of the cameras.

They usually acted on impulse and hoped everything would turn out alright. That's why they were constantly being caught and charged with something but just as often evidence would go missing or a witness would lose their nerve. They were being protected. Both detectives suspected they were doing favors for cops on the side, whether it was of their own free will or not.

"They're in someone's pocket," said Buster, in that gravelly voice that only years of smoking could produce. His wife worked for nearby Phillip Morris and still got the company perk of a free carton a week.

"That part is obvious," said Biggs at the time. "The question is whose and do we care?" Biggs learned early in life that every town has its lines that you don't cross.

They stopped the younger brother, Paulie Browning as he was coming out of the free clinic run by the Episcopal Diocese that was set up in an area just across the dividing line of Main Street. On one side sat St. John's Church where Patrick Henry made a famous speech about liberty or death next to rows of carefully renovated houses that had been constructed just after Sherman's march.

On the other side, not too far past the rows of old businesses that fronted Main Street sat one of the largest housing projects in the country, Gilpin Court, named for an actor who had been born there on Charity Street. Its other nickname was Apostle because so many of the streets had been named after St. James, St. Luke or one of the other original twelve men. Things hadn't quite worked out the way someone had hoped for most of the residents. The choice between liberty or death seemed to have already been made.

Paulie was at the clinic on a regular basis to get help for his diabetes and was known to stop by every week at around the same time.

They caught him coming out and he had startled for a moment when he saw the detectives but the small spark of fear was quickly replaced with a little bravado.

"Doesn't matter what you want today. Even you two are not stupid enough to take on Mac and Rodney. Nobody takes on the combinating of numbers. It'd be like Batman and Robin thinking they could take down Lex Luthor and the Kracken combined. Suicide," he said, smiling and leaning back on his heels.

"You seem to already know why we're here, genius," said Buster. "And we're that stupid," added Buster, his deep rumble making it sound menacing.

The mention of Rodney Parrish's name had made Biggs a little more interested in the conversation. There it was again and somehow connected to the robberies. It bothered Biggs that he couldn't see where the trail was taking him. He possessed a certain amount of confidence, though that more would be revealed. Call it a common man's faith.

"Me too," said Paulie, smiling and putting up his hands. "Me too and everybody knows it. Say stuff all the time without knowing what it means. My little sugar problem keeps me in the bed anyway so I don't know anything about anything."

"That's not going to do," said Biggs. "We'll be needing a little more. Start with how you and your brother suddenly got enough for an above-ground pool." One of the first things the detectives had done was to check out the living conditions of the Browning brothers and see if there were any new, shiny objects. The pool kind of stood out.

"Living a little large for someone who's always in bed, aren't you? Free clinic is all you can afford but you have a pretty nice backyard going on."

"I think it's got to be some kind of illegal to be hanging over people's eight-foot privacy fence without a warrant of some kind," whined Paulie. "That pool was paid for in full, you know."

"Stop making our point for us," said Biggs.

"And if we look in the trunk of your car?" asked Buster.

Paulie backed up until he was resting against his car. "You have no cause," he said, lowering his voice to a whisper. He knew it was pointless.

Richmond had its own set of rules and they all started with who was related to whom. Sometimes a name made a business deal a lot easier and sometimes a different name took away a few basic choices.

Biggs didn't press the point. He didn't like feeling like he was taking advantage of anybody but if someone was already there he could be quiet and listen.

"So, it's gonna be like that," said Paulie. "Alright. I'll give you a little something and then we all get on with our day." The detectives didn't move.

"Look for Ralph, he knows more. He's been hanging out with Parrish, saying he's learning the business from him. Not too sure what that means. Ralph's an even dumber brick to not be aware there's no business to be learned. Geez, Parrish will keep him around until Ralph's a problem and then we all know what might happen. Come on, you two statues cannot be that white."

That actually got a smile out of Biggs. "Where do we find Ralph?" he asked.

"Try Franklin Street, that neighborhood, near Willow Lawn. I saw him last night, hanging out poolside and he said he had business over that way. He's got no car so he should probably still be there. Town doesn't care about the walkin' man, not too big on buses."

"We know, Paulie. We're from here," said Buster.

Paulie shrugged his shoulders. "Just sayin'."

They had kept their side of the bargain and let Paulie go on his way. They didn't really have anything on him anyway and they always knew where to find him if the lead turned out to be completely useless. Better to keep moving for now.

When they had left Paulie the detectives still weren't planning on looking for Parrish. Not directly at least. Both of them liked what they did for a living and weren't planning to boldly disobey their Lieutenant. Let the pieces all fall into place first, maybe work themselves out.

And yet, here he was hours later on the top of a building keeping watch for Parrish, the details of the robberies more of a way to pass the time. All of the pieces of this day had led to the top of this warehouse and Parrish. Biggs wiped his face on a clean, white handkerchief. His father had always carried a handkerchief and small things like that mattered to Biggs. He pictured the body again, stiffness already setting in to the joints. It pissed him off to think he'd been a little too late.

"Think about that another time," he whispered, spitting sweat.

The sun was finally getting a little lower in the sky and was at least no longer beating directly on the top of Biggs' head. That was something even if the wet heat would hang on long into the darkness.

Biggs position was a little higher than the surrounding buildings with a clear view of a short side street not too far over from Grace Street. Just beyond that was the governor's mansion that looked like a smaller version of the White House but with far less security. Nearby, office workers could sit on the green lawn during their lunch hour and gaze up the small, rolling hill at the large front portico.

Biggs usually ate his lunch in the front seat of the older Crown Vic he was issued, running the details of whatever case he was working on through his head, looking for the pattern.

He was standing on the rooftop, wondering what it was about these owners that made someone want to rip them off.

He settled back into a comfortable stance, ready to run. The dense humidity in Richmond was hanging well into October and making his shirt cling to his back as he stood up straight. The winters were always mild here but the summers could beat a man into the ground and were known to slide into the fall, some years.

He looked across the buildings and gave a small wave to his partner who stood down below where he could see most of Biggs' blind spots. The older detective got the lookout that came with fewer stairs.

They were working off of the tip they got out of Ralph who always liked to talk too much. He was the last person who should have been hanging around someone like Parrish but Biggs figured that was their problem.

They had stopped Ralph on Franklin Street, wandering down a narrow section where it picked back up again between the Fan neighborhood and the West End. He was balancing a large speaker on his shoulder trying to make his way in the direction of Broad Street, the only place where the buses would be running.

"What you doin', Ralph? Can we give you a lift somewhere?" Buster asked, taking on a casual tone as he leaned out of the car window. Ralph had glanced back and seen them coming. They had noticed his pace slowly quicken, as much as it could with a large speaker clearly weighing him down.

"Prefer walking," he said, like he was trying to be indifferent to the whole thing. It was hard for such a round man to look so indifferent in this heat. The heavy speaker wasn't helping and his suit jacket was soaked through with sweat. The combinating house insisted all of their workers wear a suit.

"Nice day for it," said Buster. Biggs was driving, keeping the car at a pace with Ralph's footsteps. "Where'd you get the electronics?"

"Made a trade for it. Fair and square. You got nothing today, gentlemen," said Ralph. Biggs stopped the car and quickly got out.

"Traded who for what?" Ralph looked startled. Biggs had heard the mistake even before Ralph realized what he had given away. He stopped and stared at Biggs like he was measuring out what to say next.

"Don't go with, none of your business," said Buster. "You know that never plays well with us." Ralph looked over at Buster and shifted the speaker, letting a long trail of spit loose that landed between them.

"Shit, you know you're gonna' get me killed one of these days." Ralph shook his head and set the speaker down. "What are you trading for my information?" he asked, trying to look determined. "When they beat my ass later I'd like to know I got something out of it."

That made Biggs smile. "You have a point, Ralph. How about we let you keep the speaker and we don't ask too much about the original owner? Who did you trade for what?"

"The Dark Lord," said Ralph, raising an eyebrow. "Parrish. Scary son of a bitch. Don't really like to have anything to do with him but he wanted something from me and I happened to be in need of a speaker, for no particular reason."

"We heard you were working with him," said Buster.

"Mac's idea," said Ralph, scowling.

"Not yours?" said Biggs. Ralph gave out a laugh that sounded more like he had lost a bet.

"What did he want from you?" asked Buster.

"I know, I was as surprised as you gentlemen to hear there was something Rodney Parrish would need out of me. Turned out to be nothing. He even paid me a little something for it," he said, nudging the speaker with his toe. "He just wanted an address for some old broad. Alice Watkins. Said he had unfinished business. I do small fixit jobs for her, keep her lawn. She paid me extra to keep that quiet. Rodney found out and paid me more, plus the speaker. Fair and square."

That made Biggs' stomach churn. Parrish was a numbers runner for Mac and the gambling house on Broad Street and notoriously cheap. Everyone knew he made most of his money doing odd jobs, mostly for cops. If Parrish wanted an address badly enough to pay for it, then somebody bigger needed a favor.

Nobody asked Parrish to do anything unless they thought a little violence might be in order.

"What's the address?" asked Buster. Ralph let out a sigh. "Just off Patterson Avenue, not too far from here. You know, one of those little bungalows. Nice little place. She's only had it about a year. Moved out of the suburbs where she was living with that family. Can't blame her though, crazy family. You remember the place. Deputy went buck wild or something, shot up the place. The grandma took him out. Jones something, I think. That was a couple of years ago but still, you have to wonder. That was you that figured it all out, wasn't it?" asked Ralph, pointing at Biggs and smiling.

Biggs didn't return the smile.

"He tell you why he wanted it?" he asked.

"Nope," said Ralph, "but I can't say I really pressed him for much of an answer. Not a good idea. There was one thing, though. He did say the two had met before and they were some kind of friends. Funny, kind of when you think of it. Parrish being friends with some old white lady in the suburbs. Not his usual traffic. Makes you wonder why."

CHAPTER
③

"Go!" Biggs practically yelled it into the radio. Parrish was coming down the alley, exactly where Ralph had said they would find him. He was on his way to make some pickups for Mac. There were always a few people every week whose old debts had come due. Tuesday was when Parrish would go hunting for them. Ralph had learned the usual route from hanging out with Parrish.

The same people were always getting into the same trouble, every Tuesday. Parrish had perfected scaring most regulars into paying up on time without having to do that much anymore but there were some stubborn holdouts who seemed to believe that somehow this week would have a different ending for them. Ralph not only knew where the debtors were but when Parrish would pounce.

Ralph talked too much as a rule but he wasn't worried about the two detectives busting up Parrish for the numbers. No one got in the way of Mac's business. Too many people benefited one way or the other from what Mac was doing whether it was from the chance to win a few dollars or get paid off with a few more. It wasn't even something that too many judges would be happy to see on their docket. Best to pick a different battle. It never occurred to Ralph there might be something more and that made him chatty.

He coughed up Alice Watkins' address and was relieved when the two detectives let him go on his way. His day was going pretty well.

Biggs insisted they swing by the little bungalow on Malvern, over Buster's complaints about getting mixed up in any of it. They were supposed to be heading over to Queen's to ask the owner some more questions. Buster was always more pragmatic and didn't see the point of getting that far into other business.

That is, until they went inside the little bungalow. That changed Buster's mind for good. It just wasn't right.

Biggs covered the few steps to the fire escape in seconds. The radio crackled and spit. He could hear his partner breathing hard and the sound of running footsteps. The detectives were using walkie talkies they had gotten from a local big box store in order to keep their chatter to themselves.

Parrish was in one of his trademark skinny-leg suit and ties, swinging his briefcase. He even looked like he was dancing just a little.

Biggs took the thin, metal steps down the side of the building as fast as he could, each step rattling and shaking from the heavy thuds as he threw his weight forward. He wanted to get to Parrish ahead of Buster for the privilege of pitching him on the ground.

He came spinning around the corner, sliding to a stop just as Buster got to the end of the alley, staying just out of view. Parrish stopped in mid-stride and cocked his head to one side. The two men were well acquainted. Richmond was a small town, after all.

"Detective Biggs," said Parrish, nodding his head.

Biggs took a step forward and Parrish straightened up but made no move to run or turn away, until he saw Buster step out into the open holding a weighted flapjack.

Something about the way they were moving seemed to let him in on all of it. They weren't going for their guns or pulling out handcuffs right away. If they were there to arrest him, that would be only an afterthought.

No one was going to be able to protect him in this alley, either. They had stopped on Malvern Avenue at the little bungalow.

In one graceful move he swept the briefcase up, under his arm and turned to run, already in mid-stride. Surely, with his short, lean frame he could outrun two old bulls.

Biggs was on him before he had gotten very far. He even lifted Parrish a little in the air before he shoved him hard into the solid, stone pavers.

His head gave a nice bounce, thought Biggs.

The detective felt the anger rise up in him again and fought the urge to lift Parrish back up over his head, to see if he could crack him in two against the pavement. He sucked the air in between his teeth, trying to calm down as he thought about the case. Narrow area, owners all belong to the same men's club, planned jobs, no fingerprints. It wasn't helping.

He watched Parrish's teeth rattle and clack together. It was a good hard tackle, worthy of what was surely going to follow for the detective from taking down Parrish.

Parrish finally lay still, his hand clutched around the briefcase. Buster came around Biggs, shaking his head. "Don't know if it'd be better if he was alive or dead."

Biggs kicked Parrish hard in the ribs and Parrish groaned but didn't move.

"He's alive."

The dead body flashed through his head. He kicked Parrish again, hard.

By the time the two detectives had gotten to the little bungalow what blood there was, was already congealing.

The front door was locked, no sign of forced entry. But Parrish had a style and was considered the best at breaking and entering without ever leaving a single clue. Anyone who had a reason to get tangled up with him knew that about him.

People who were robbed by him generally didn't even know they had been robbed. He was very good at cleaning up after himself.

Biggs looked in the window, cupping his hand around his eyes with his face pressed up to the window pane, hoping to see anything that would give him probable cause for what he knew he was going to do anyway.

There was nothing, and in the end he told himself that was the reason. Everything appeared to be exactly where it was supposed to be and who really lives that way. He broke a couple of the small panes in the narrow window that ran alongside the front door and pulled his sleeve tight around his hand so he could reach in and unlock the door. He still managed to knick one of his knuckles on broken glass.

They found the body of Alice Watkins lying in the bathtub, her throat slashed and a look of surprise still on her face. Buster pointed out the bruising on her knuckles and Biggs nodded, hoping he'd find matching bruises on Parrish when they found him.

There was no mess to clean up, no blood splatter. Her death was probably quick and whoever had done it had cleaned up everything.

"Parrish," Biggs spit out. "I knew it."

"Let's go hunting," said Buster.

They called in the murder but didn't stay on the scene. The radio dispatcher came back with orders from Lieutenant Greevey to return to the scene, oversee the case. He must have suspected what they were about to do.

There was really only one reason they would have left Alice Watkins by herself, even if she was dead. It wasn't right.

Still, as Parrish lay there in the alley, the only marks on his suit was the little bit of blood from what Biggs had done to him and dust from the alley.

Buster kneeled down and broke open the briefcase and found tools carefully rolled up in soft grey felt. They appeared clean but Buster knew that a little testing in a police lab might reveal traces of Alice Watkin's blood. Maybe even a little of Parrish's blood as well.

Biggs nudged Parrish with his toe. "Come on, get up. You're coming with us."

Buster looked up at his partner. "You sure about this?" he asked.

"You really feel good about just letting it go?" asked Biggs.

Buster didn't answer him but took out a plastic tie and rolled Parrish over, pulling his wrists together to restrain him. Parrish was starting to regain consciousness.

"You think he broke anything?" asked Buster, as he hauled Parrish to his feet. Parrish groaned and sunk back down to the ground before Buster roughly lifted him quickly to his feet again.

Parrish let out a yelp and opened his eyes wide.

"Maybe," said Biggs, not feeling any real satisfaction. "We need to make a stop."

"Seriously?" asked Buster. "You putting off the inevitable? It won't help. It's going to be hard as hell to get him booked as it is, without someone intervening. The faster, the better."

"I know, I know. We still need to make a stop."

Biggs pulled the car neatly up to the curb, parking just outside the police tape that now surrounded almost the entire block of Malvern Avenue that contained the little bungalow nestled between two Colonials.

They could see their Lieutenant arguing with a man and woman just outside the taped-off area. Both the detectives recognized them from the courthouse. They were fairly popular lawyers in Richmond, especially the woman.

"She's like family to us," yelled Wallis Jones. "We're all she has, we have a right to go in there," said Wallis. Her husband, Norman Weiskopf was holding onto her arm.

"Maybe you should take your wife home," said the Lieutenant, "she seems a little hysterical." The officer turned away for a moment and whispered something in Wallis' direction that no one else could hear. She jerked back around and looked like she wanted to start a fight. Her hands were balled into fists.

That's when Norman let go of her arm, even seemed to nod in her direction like he was giving her the go ahead. Either way, he suddenly stepped between the Lieutenant and his wife as Wallis ducked under the tape and kept running toward the house.

"Bad time to get out of the car," said Buster, watching the determined woman rush by a startled officer and go quickly into the house.

There was a high-pitched shriek, "Alice!" that came from within the house.

"You might as well let me go in and get her," said Norman.

"Won't be necessary," said the Lieutenant. Moments later, a uniformed officer was leading Wallis out of the house. She wasn't resisting and even seemed determined to get back to Norman.

"Determined broad," said Buster.

"They've finally killed Alice," said Wallis. "It's just like Lily Billings, just like her and it's our fault, we should have made her stay with us. I knew this would happen." Wallis was quickly walking away with Norman keeping pace beside her. "They're finally getting around to tying up loose ends."

"You don't know that, Wallis," he said.

"Don't ask me to believe in any more fairytales, Norman. We can't go back to random anything. You know they did this to her. It's starting again. We have got to get home and check on Ned."

"What did that cop say to you?" asked Norman.

"He called me Black Widow," said Wallis, repeating the old nickname used around the courthouse, mostly by lawyers who were tired of losing to her. Even beat cops knew it. It was also well known by everyone that Wallis hated the name even if they said it more out of a respectable fear than anything else.

Wallis seemed to suddenly notice Biggs and Buster sitting there quietly taking it all in and she glanced behind them at Parrish in the back seat. Biggs turned around for a moment to see Parrish smile and nod in recognition. The color drained from Wallis' face and she looked like she wanted to say something.

Biggs could barely make out what she said and it made no sense. Wallis had turned to her husband who was also staring at Parrish and said in a lowered voice, "You need to call your brother."

"None of this is really making sense," said Buster.

"It will," said Biggs, looking back at Parrish again, "it will. Give it time, more will be revealed."

"Yeah, well it's alphabet soup until then."

"Where we going next?" said Parrish, who seemed to be enjoying the way things were going.

"We're going to see a man about a booking," said Buster. Parrish let out a snort. He had been inside a precinct many times without ever having his pictures or prints preserved for the record.

But both of the detectives knew they had a window of about an hour when they could rush him through and at least get Parrish into the system before the Lieutenant returned. If they could get him into the system they might find allies who could help them keep him there.

There was nothing incriminating on the surface of things that would let them haul in Rodney Parrish, except for the word of a petty thief. Both detectives knew that Ralph was probably going to change his mind anyway about everything he said once he realized it was all connected to some white woman's murder.

That didn't matter anymore.

Sometimes it wasn't about right or wrong, even for a cop. It was about the damned consequences. "What do you think Wallis Jones meant when she said, 'they killed Alice?" asked Buster.

"I have no idea," said Biggs, "but it's a part of this pattern. I knew that poor slob they pinned Lily Billings' murder on didn't do it." Parrish let out another snort and a howl of laughter.

CHAPTER

④

The pain in his side was getting to Staff Sergeant Leonard Kipling. He shifted the M249 machine gun to the front, strapping it down tighter to keep it from jostling. The pain was rattling down from his waist and into his hip with every step he took. There was no open wound but he was sure he had torn something in his abdomen, maybe even broken a rib. It was gradually getting harder to take a deep breath. The skin was already mottled with crimson patches of red but it didn't matter. He had to make it up Haskill Mountain before the enemy squads found him.

Sergeant Kipling had never been completely comfortable with using the term, enemy when referring to the other side. They had all grown up in similar neighborhoods after all.

Maybe even some of the same neighborhoods. It wasn't the country that was dividing them.

That had all changed today when he saw how focused they were on drilling them all full of holes. He was all that was left of his squad.

Kipling had no more doubts. He was an Army Ranger in the Circle, fighting in a very real civil war that was only sanctioned at the top because everyone in the middle knew nothing about it. There were the politicians elected to pass laws and that kept the lesser wheels of a middle class life running smoothly. But the real power had always belonged to others.

Soldiers from both sides, whether it was the Circle or their enemy, the larger menacing Management, knew better than to say anything when they went on leave, back to their suburban homes along quiet streets and cul de sacs.

On the battlefield men and women went on missions to hunt down the enemy, who could be their neighbors back at home. When they were in their communities they made a point of giving everyone a wide berth until new orders came in and they set out again.

If someone came back injured it was from an unfortunate vacation mishap or a car accident. If they were dead the family might suddenly move without an explanation to avoid having to explain at all.

There was talk in the upper levels of the Circle that plans were underway to congregate the families of soldiers in neighborhoods, like open bases hidden in plain sight so that all of this would become easier to keep under wraps.

But for Sergeant Kipling that was all going to have to wait. He was going to have to figure out how to live through today if he wanted to see his family again. He knew that the casualties his battalion was taking were already the worst of the civil war. Something had changed.

The mission for his squad was straightforward. Not easy but very simple. Get a message to a former Circle operative living in Montana. The only known operative to have ever been a part of both sides and left it all behind without having to be put in the ground. He was living a quiet life in the wilderness with his boys and little girl. There were whispers about him on both sides with stories about how he had pulled it off. Some even said he had never really existed but the Sergeant knew that was just folklore.

He had met Whiting once when he was younger and a foster father had introduced them at a Circle meeting back in Richmond, Virginia. It had been a small, quiet gathering of the descendants from the remnants of the original Circle. His father had said Mark Whiting was a very smart man who knew how to think for himself. The Sergeant had never forgotten how in awe his father looked when he said those words. Not too long after that his parents had died in a car accident, leaving just Sergeant Kipling and his brother Dennis. He pushed the thought aside.

After that, there were too many foster homes to count till he had finally landed in an orphanage run by the Circle. That had been his salvation. He was finally surrounded by people who treated him like family again and he had an entire campus to roam that felt like a small town full of kids who all had something in common with him.

It was only natural that one day he would end up working in the Circle's system trying to be of service to his country.

"Get to Mark Whiting," mumbled the Sergeant, licking the blood off of his lip. It was his mission imperative.

He was moving fast across the terrain and didn't stop to use the satellite phone to let someone know what had happened. It wouldn't matter anyway. No one was going to try and rescue him. Everyone in his squad had understood that before they set out. No communication until after the mission was complete and they had made it to the next post in Billings.

The Sergeant and his squad of six men had left the Circle base camp that was located in Calgary, one of the largest prairie provinces of Canada. They headed for a soft spot along the U.S. border where they could cross into Montana without being detected by Management drones. The war made it harder but there were still places where Circle held the terrain and could keep out enemy drones and block certain satellites from seeing too much.

Their urban base camp was typical of what had evolved during the combat that was less than a year old and was quietly moving across North America. The war was a new style started by Management and being waged between two old forces who wanted to win at any cost but were hoping to never have to tell the general public.

Everything was contained to small areas so that it could be explained as an industrial accident or if necessary, a terrorist plot that was stopped before it got too far. A body count was tolerable but exposure of the inner workings of either side was not.

The idea of a common man's democracy meant a lot to most people. If the general populace knew that the lines were drawn in different directions that crossed traditional borders, fear could cause order to break down.

Panic among the middle class might cost both sides to lose too much power. If the infrastructure could stay hidden then neither side, Circle or Management had to give up the idea that they could were right and knew the best way to provide a better life.

Once the war was decided there would still be a prize worth keeping.

It didn't matter that one side, Management thought that force was occasionally necessary for the greater good. In order to be happy for any length of time in Management it was necessary not to look to hard at what everyone was doing or ask many questions.

People in Management learned how to smile 'up' to their superiors and crack the whip to anyone below them. It was a very comfortable life but with fewer choices and generally no out clause, other than death.

The Circle was much easier to get along with but they were idealists and that left them open to almost being wiped out only a couple of generations ago. Only twenty of the original Circle had survived the earlier slaughter but they had instituted a new plan to gather recruits by operating children's homes, called the Schmetterling Operation and their numbers had been growing and were rumored to be in the thousands.

Things were changing rapidly and for now, the Circle was in the White House. Both sides knew that President Ronald Haynes was likely to win reelection.

Management was apparently taking notice. They were pushing back.

At first it had only been a few direct and deadly hits against suspected Circle operatives. They were ones that Watchers had been keeping track of for years and were just high enough to cause harm without declaring war.

The Watchers were Management's spies in plain sight who kept track of their neighbor's movements and over the years had come to know who was most likely working for the other side. Someone within Management had pulled the trigger on a different plan and things had escalated. Recent events had caused the Circle to make a change.

Sergeant Kipling was entrusted with a message to inform Mark Whiting of that change. Alice Watkins had been killed and no one could be sure what she had said before her death. The Sergeant didn't know who she was and didn't need to know other than Richmond, Virginia was causing problems for the Circle, again.

The Keeper could be in danger and needed to be hidden away. Mark Whiting was the only person that anyone could think of who had ever outwitted Management. Someone at the top of the food chain had singled him out and now it was Sergeant Kipling's duty to get the message to him. The Keeper was on his way and needed to be protected. Mark would need to know ahead of his arrival.

Two years ago when a key Circle player, Carol Schaeffer was murdered Management had turned Harry Weiskopf, the son of one of the Circle's original members, and his betrayal almost cost the Circle their plans to rebuild. The Schmetterling Operation was almost exposed. Thousands of children's lives were at risk.

The Circle had managed to recapture the thumb drive with the Circle's long-range plan and the list of up-and-coming operatives they were grooming from childhood but not before both sides had counted up losses.

That was when Mark Whiting had disappeared and taken his family off of the grid, along with a few million dollars of Management's carefully embezzled funds.

The Schmetterling Operation, or the Butterfly Project, and its system of orphanages also gained a few new members. The day Mark Whiting left his old life he helped rescue a few others. Carol Schaeffer's widower Robert and their two boys, Trey and Will had fled to the Midwest to an orphanage where they could blend in and finally be forgotten.

Schmetterling was the Circle's plan to raise their own population to finally have enough members to invade every area of the good life across the Western world, diluting Management's stranglehold. They would do it right under Management's watchful eye but in places where no one ever paid much attention.

Carol, the murdered Circle member, had once been a part of the operation, raised on the grounds of one of their bases. Now, her husband, Robert and their children had run to the safety of another base, just ahead of Management hunting them down. They wanted the list and would do anything to get it back. But Robert Schaeffer was never in possession of the thumb drive and it wasn't long before it had fallen into the attorney, Wallis Jones' hands.

The new orders had also carefully explained to Sergeant Kipling about the strange confluence of family lineage in the Jones household. Wallis Jones was a descendant of the original creators of Management, daughter of the legendary Walter Jones who was known throughout all of Management's ranks.

Her husband, Norman Weiskopf was like the Sergeant, a descendant of the Circle's precious twenty. That made their son, Ned, now a young teenager the most precious commodity of all to both sides. The Sergeant was informed of what had happened just a couple of years ago, because if he survived he was told they would need him in Richmond.

They were moving him up to a higher cell, but that was only if he could survive getting to Mark Whiting. He was either going to be promoted next or honored posthumously.

Wallis had managed to finally, safely deliver the thumb drive back into the hands of the Circle, Sergeant Kipling had been relieved to see, but not until after someone tried to run her off the Nickel Bridge into the James River.

It was all at the cost of her not knowing about her own family lineage, her husband Norman's own family tree and what it would all eventually mean to their young son, Ned. There was no going back into ignorance.

Fortunately, the Circle's operation plan, their OPS was finally coming to fruition and perhaps Wallis and Norman would never have to face Ned's unique lineage. Not much chance of that, thought the Sergeant, trying to focus on the startling story he was told, instead of the pain radiating around his middle.

However, it was true that the numbers of the young men and women in the ranks of the corporate world, the armed services and political office was climbing just enough to finally sway the balance. If they could stop Management from always moving their new recruits upward into a better life they could take some of the shine off of Management's lifestyle. Then waving a cushy middle class life in front of parents who were desperate to see their children succeed in a world that had become harder to just stay middle class wouldn't be so easy.

A previous attempt by Circle to create their own society had ended in carnage just a couple of generations in the past when Management had killed millions, leaving only the twenty. But this time they were within a few years of seeing it all succeed.

All of it almost came to an end a couple of years ago and just as they were starting to create trouble for Management. A lot of brave Circle people had paid with their lives, one of them Sergeant Kipling's own brother, Dennis.

The traitor's life, Norman's older brother, Harry was spared but only because he was the son of one of the original twenty and the brother of Tom, the current Keeper. That news had made the Sergeant angry for a moment till his training got him to focus back on the mission at hand. He was taught that revenge was always a wasted effort that only led to sloppy mistakes.

Besides, Harry was locked away in solitary confinement for the rest of his life. Only a handful of people even knew of his betrayal or of his continued existence.

The thought that the man would only know four bland walls for the rest of his long days made the Sergeant feel better about how his brother had died holding back Management from ever finding the Schaeffers.

Sergeant Kipling had always known that Dennis had died in service to the Circle but it wasn't until he was read-in for this mission that he learned just how important his brother had been to the survival of their side. He had left for the mission with a heightened sense of pride and duty to the country and his family.

It was a comfort to know that the Keeper, the only one who knew where all of the Circle's cells were and all of the plans, was safely back in Wisconsin with only a handful of people who knew his real role. Too many knew, really, but still they had managed to keep it between the family, Esther Ackerman, a local bookstore owner who knew how to keep secrets and a family friend, Alice Watkins.

The Circle had struck back and used their advantage of finally having key players in the military and in the White House. But the margin couldn't last, making it necessary to keep going until the next phase of their plan could begin.

That was when the war broke out, slowly at first as Management used force to try and take over the old fashioned way by grabbing territory that flanked key areas of North America and Europe.

The Canadian Circle army base was hidden in plain sight in one of the most populous areas of the suburbs. Their cover was as the executive sales team for a software company, hiding their true intent even from the other people who worked in the ten-story building. A thousand people moved up and down the elevators every day, nodding hello or looking the other way as they held on to their coffee or checked their email.

The army unit could come and go without anyone questioning their movements and if someone new suddenly appeared in the elevators on a more regular basis or another person suddenly left, no one thought much of it. Salesmen were known to chase a deal and change their loyalties.

Another squad was based in the corporate headquarters just outside of Chicago in the upscale suburb of Northbrook. They were just far enough away from where the fighting was taking place that their families weren't in harm's way. It would have been too much of a distraction.

In both locations the buildings sat off by themselves with large parking lots that made it difficult for anyone to walk up to the building without being seen from a long ways away. That's where Sergeant Kipling had been based till he was called up to Calgary.

There was a fair amount of sales people in the bigger population areas, but in more rural areas it was harder to hide them. Instead, the Circle had worked squads into different parts of society, using the skill sets that the recruits had to place them in regular employment. Regular communication in the remote area was done mostly through civic or alumni groups where they could congregate to watch a basketball game or grab a beer without drawing too much attention.

They made sure they had enough of a diverse life that there were multiple reasons to seek out other members of their patrol.

The more spread out over different walks of life, the potential for more interaction and information gathering across a larger spectrum was possible, keeping the organized war a secret from the population that was living on the battlefields, ignorant to the danger.

A few Circle members were already placed in positions of power and responsibility in politics, business, and even religious roles and could not only gather information but were useful to push forward agendas that could help them fight the growing war.

Sergeant Kipling and his brother were the grandsons of one of the original twenty who had survived the slaughter in Europe and because of their parents' early demise, they were even Mercy men, raised on the grounds of Mercy Home in Chicago. All six members of his squad were raised at different children's homes as part of the Schmetterling Project. They were the beginning of the new wave and a new day for the Circle.

Each of them had volunteered and then learned part of the background of the mission. They all understood how important the directive was and Sergeant Kipling had set out determined to get everyone safely to the next encampment.

But a Management squad had been waiting for them when they moved across the border. The seven men in his command broke into a 'V' formation pushing out in all directions. He had counted eight men before gunfire had pushed them back.

Now he was the only one left from his squad, wounded but still moving. He didn't want their sacrifice to not mean something. He didn't want to let Dennis down either.

The Circle had tried to get in touch with Mark Whiting for months. None of the encoded radio signals had been answered and time was running out. Encrypted messages had been randomly mailed from different people and different locations, mostly as spam but those had garnered nothing as well. They were down to having to get to him face to face.

Two patrols were moving through the mountains right behind Sergeant Kipling and if they caught onto his trail his instructions were to pass by the target. He couldn't lead them to the ranch up on Haskill Mountain. That meant the Keeper would arrive on his doorstep unannounced.

Mark Whiting was being entrusted with the safety of the Keeper.

It was a necessary move so that the leaders of the Circle could focus on the war.

The battle between the two old organizations was growing deadly and no one could be sure that the Circle could win and keep the war from spreading beyond the North American continent. If they couldn't there was always the chance the warfare would spread to the general population, even if it was referred to by Management as terrorist activity. Even if they were really the terrorists.

So far, the battles had been in remote locations and the casualties were noted only by the two sides or were reported in the news as a random act of violence. The pieces were not forming a picture, yet.

"Read 'em and weep. The dead man's hand again," he sang quietly, telling himself, one more step, one more step, occasionally tapping the small pin affixed to his parka. A tight circle of twenty stars against a dark blue background. One star for each survivor, including his own grandfather.

Sergeant Kipling was fighting to keep the Circle alive so that more of the children of the Schmetterling Operation could be given time to finally blossom and a new system to pay off for everyone.

So much had been lost the last time the Circle had tried to take down the older, darker structure and so many millions had died. Only the twenty had made it and after they had immigrated to the United States to start over it had still taken two more generations to finally be back in a position to threaten Management. His father had told them the stories of coming to America so many times that Leonard had started to see them as fairytales. Now, he knew they were all true.

Just two years ago it had all come so close to being extinguished again. The Keeper had to be moved to safety.

Kipling stumbled forward, noticing the small drops of blood in the snow. His nose was bleeding and his breathing had become labored.

If the people who lived along the suburban streets and commuted the vast ribbons of highways to the clusters of cubicles all along the Northwest knew there was a civil war running past them, they would at first mark it down as just another conspiracy theory. Both enemies would help with the illusion, making up plausible reasons why there was an increase in bloodshed.

But if things got out of hand, no one would be able to keep denying it. The war would spread like spidery veins out toward the coasts.

Panic would quickly break down into mayhem and looting. Then, everything the two sides had built and were now fighting to control could be destroyed.

Some skirmishes had already moved past the Canadian border and were pushing into parts of Minnesota, land of ten thousand lakes.

"You know it's gonna' be the Ace of Spades," Kipling sang. He spit and saw more droplets of blood in the snow. No point in worrying about that right now, he thought. If he made it to the property on top of Haskill Mountain then he could rest.

He was moving through the tall quaking aspens in the Salish Mountains of Montana and was making better time than he had expected. He had been moving all night, crossing from Canada into the States under a new moon, not stopping to do anything but pee at the base of a tree and check his side to see if there was any blood. The bruising had deepened and turned black but he could still move and that was all that mattered.

He was getting sloppy around the edges though and snow had gotten into his boot where shrapnel had torn the Gortex. But it was still more important that he move as fast as possible, away from the Management operatives that were searching for him.

There was no time to stop and take anymore inventory.

They couldn't be sure that he was still alive but their search of the area would be thorough. The SERE training, typical for an Army Ranger was keeping him alive. They had drilled a basic message into him at the camp and it was helping him to keep going. He had lost just enough blood though to be lightheaded and his attention was harder to focus.

The light of the one house up on this side of Haskill Mountain was just ahead and he hadn't seen a trace of the squad hunting him for at least the past few miles. He could complete his mission. Mark Whiting's house was only a mile away when he felt the bullet rip through his shoulder.

"Survival, resistance, evasion, escape," he whispered, fragile snot bubbles forming on his lips. It was a strange prayer, he thought as he fell forward into the snow. "Save the Keeper," he said. The snow felt good against his cheek.

CHAPTER

5

Mark stood in the center of the small stand of trees and looked up through the branches of pines at the small patch of blue sky that was barely visible through the branches. The letter he was holding fluttered in his hand as the cold wind made a whistling sound higher up in the trees. He had left his hat sitting on the kitchen counter and his close-cut afro was doing nothing to protect his head from the cold.

It wasn't so easy to shake the conservative way of dressing he'd known most of his life as an employee of the Federal Reserve in downtown Richmond, Virginia.

Mark was doing his best to let the new information settle comfortably into his bones.

The trees were close to seventy feet tall and had been seedlings back when Management was first formed with the idea of bringing a little more order to society. Mark didn't like thinking about an organization that had been growing over the past two hundred years until it stretched into every corner of the world. It made it harder for him to believe he had finally escaped the entire game.

It didn't matter to him that years earlier he had changed sides and was playing for the Circle, trying to keep Management in check. In the end, Management had wanted him dead and no one in the Circle would have been able to stop them. He wasn't even sure anyone would have tried very hard.

Someone inside of Management had even figured out how he had used them for a little bologna slicking and stolen millions right from under their noses. The only thing that saved him was probably that whoever they were, he had been able to tell they were stealing in far greater amounts.

He glanced at what was on the letter. He had gotten another letter with another short missive. It was Amendment III from the Bill of Rights. 'No Soldier in a time of peace, shall be quartered in any house, without the consent of the Owner, nor in a time of war, but in a manner prescribed by a manner of law.'

Every letter had a small star stamped on the front of the envelope. Someone from within the Circle, he didn't know who, was letting him know that things were getting worse.

Whoever was sending them had taken a chance that he had held onto an old OTP. The message was easily decoded with the only out of date list that he had kept. Usually they were updated once a month. Someone had done their homework.

He was being asked to take in an important cell member, someone either high up or important to the Circle. The frequency of the letters made him wonder if it was really a request.

The previous ones had only mentioned lines from the Constitution that were a body count of some kind. Translated they read, 'four just outside of Detroit on several floors. News sites said it was workplace revenge.' The letters had a series of circles and x's. That one had meant one Circle, three Management were dead. He burned all of the letters as soon as he had read them.

He was sure it was a steady recitation of the dead to let him know there was a quiet war already underway. A civil war was spreading across the map that no one outside of the two giants had figured out was all connected. At least not yet.

Mark was surprised a war hadn't started sooner. There were rumors of it all the time even before he had left Richmond in the middle of the night.

Once or twice since the letters started he caught himself analyzing what might have finally caused the tipping point but he quickly stopped himself and went in search of his kids to go do something else.

But someone was trying to draw him back into what he had successfully left just four short, calm years earlier. It was just long enough to lull him into thinking maybe he had pulled off the impossible. Then, a few months ago the letters started.

Mark had made a point of not watching any news. Whatever he needed he'd gather at the local diner and that was plenty.

Anything more than that, anything that reached out to even statewide news would cause his old training to kick in till he was looking for the connections and reading the currents, forming a picture. Knowledge wouldn't be power for him. It would only keep him from sleeping at night.

He worried for just a moment that he had created the same watchful eye inside of his oldest, Jake. He was constantly carrying around the small Sony Action camcorder filming around the property. Mark caught him taking it to school with him and Jake had insisted it was to film his friends for a class project but he didn't believe him. He had seen Jake's light on late at night, often enough as Jake scanned the footage on his computer as if he was searching for something. Jake had become his own surveillance team and Mark wondered if he was searching for signs of Watchers. He wasn't sure that it wasn't after all a good idea but the thought of his teenage son working so hard to protect the family was a little hard to bear.

Mark pushed the thought aside, trying not to feel the regret wash over him.

He shuddered and felt the cold wind across the back of his neck. It was getting harder to hold on to a sense of ease that he had only been able to claim in the past year.

Mark had just recently started to relax and let the older boys, Jake and

Peter wander into town on their own. Ruthie was still a little too young to go without him. All of that would have to end.

Jake would know right away something was wrong and demand an explanation. Mark had also found evidence in Jake's room that the young teenager was keeping a surveillance log. Mark told himself that training Jake and Peter had been a necessity back in Richmond to ensure their safety. That never completely sat very well with him but the other choices were worse. Management could have used them for their own purposes.

Mark had to protect his children, particularly since he was all they had anymore. His wife had cut and run a long time ago and they had lost touch. She had been a Management operative and was disgusted with him when he switched sides.

The whole point of getting off the grid in Montana had been to let the kids be kids. Maybe it was too late for Jake. Still, he was willing to do whatever it took to give them a better life than the one he knew.

"Hard ground," he mumbled to himself, feeling the frozen ground beneath his boots, "smell of sap", he said as he turned in a slow circle taking in the small spots of muddy green and brown visible through the snow drifts. Down below in Flathead Valley he could see through his binoculars the ribbon of gravel roads where they had plowed and the smoke winding up from chimneys spaced out across the landscape. He liked this part of the world, even if he did miss his old hometown of Richmond, Virginia. There was no going back though, not if he wanted to live past his forties.

The fall weather had been brutal and there was already a thick layer of snow on the ground. The wind was blowing in from the north and was making the trees sway and creak as if they could snap in two at any moment.

He felt the anxiety lift for just a moment as he labored to breathe in and out. A thin trickle of cold sweat crept down his arm as he grasped the letter more tightly. He looked out over the valley from his perch on the mountain and wondered if he was as well protected as he thought.

He had destroyed all of the letters, he reminded himself. The first few he had burned without really reading them, but they kept coming. Temptation got to him eventually. Besides, he had to know if they were all a warning that something was creeping closer to his sanctuary in the mountains.

He heard what sounded like a familiar whistle that he couldn't quite place but still some part of him knew and his entire body tensed with the effort of listening for what was coming next. It was gunfire of a certain kind. Long-range and quiet, professional.

There was a very small chance that it was someone illegally hunting for deer out of season and on his property but he knew most of the hunters in these parts. None of them would be shooting so close to a house where they knew there was children, no matter how much alcohol or weed they had ingested.

He strained to see if he could tell if the gunfire was coming closer to the house or moving away. The wind was making it difficult to accurately identify the direction it was coming from.

Another faint whine. That one seemed a little further away, a good sign but he couldn't be sure. He turned to run toward his house wondering if he could get picked off before he even got there. He was suddenly glad that Jake was still so watchful. If he didn't make it back Jake would hesitate before heading out to look for him. He knew better to respond than react to any given situation.

He came up the last hill toward the house and heard another faint, high-pitched whistle and realized the direction had changed. Someone was firing back. Mark wondered for just a moment if the war had spread to right outside his door and everything was in far more chaos than he realized.

"Dammit," he said, as he ran the last few yards. Unplugging from all of the news had seemed like such a good idea. It had felt like a relief until those letters had started coming.

It had never occurred to him that the country could unravel in just two short years while he was out of touch.

Jake came running out of the house, breathless, looking like he was about to take off for the woods. His son was already taller than his father and the wind was making his long hair that surrounded his face in a large halo, blow straight back. Mark had tried to get him to cut his hair shorter, blend in more but Jake was always explaining to Mark that this was the current trend. Cutting his black curls short would actually make him look like he was a newcomer to town and only draw attention. Mark had let it go.

"Jake, Jake," Mark yelled as quietly as he could to get his attention. Jake stopped in his tracks and turned toward his father. The boy was already six feet tall and only fourteen years old.

"Where are your brother and sister? Are they secure?"

Use the least amount of words as possible, Mark thought. Only ask for information, leave any emotions or worry for later.

"They're in the safe room, locked in," said Jake. He looked like he was waiting for further instructions. "The go bags are with them."

Mark winced. Jake was thinking they'd need to run again. He's been waiting for this day, thought Mark.

"Get the long guns and a tarp," said Mark. "Not the Remingtons," he added. Their shorter range would make them useless. "But do not fire unless absolutely necessary. They may be passing us by and we don't want to get involved if there's any way we can avoid it."

Jake spun around and bounded back up the stairs to the wide porch. It wasn't long before he was back with two rifles, AR-15 semi-automatics, the civilian, hunting versions of the military M-16 that could reach out a few hundred yards. He passed one to his father.

The other belonged to Jake and had been a present on his last birthday.

A rifle is put together based on the job it has to do and the ammunition and accessories that are available for it. An advantage to being in the wide open spaces of Montana was that the same scope that was needed to see game at a distance could double as a sniper scope without standing out. Mark had hoped he would never need to be grateful for the dual purpose.

The AR-15 shot a .225 round that was also widely available, and Mark knew from his days of training with Management, was one of NATO's standard rounds. It blended easily and was a popular weapon that Mark had been able to get a class three license for as a fully automatic weapon.

In an area full of hunters going for the most firearms legally possible didn't make someone stand out at all.

"Tuck the tarp into your jacket. You have your binoculars with you?"

Jake pulled out the Barska Blackhawk binoculars just enough to show his father. "Go out forty paces and only survey the area. We'll meet halfway back, understood?" Jake nodded and took off in a run toward the woods, making almost no noise. Mark wondered if the boy had been practicing for something just like this. He moved like it was second nature to be quick and silent.

Mark headed off in a quarter direction away from his son calculating when he had gotten to a hundred feet and crouched down, carefully looking for any signs of human beings trampling through the woods. Whatever he heard could have been miles away and headed in another direction. It was what he was praying for, over and over again.

There was no sign of anything but a buck and probably his doe that must have startled and run at the same sound of gunfire he had heard. He went back twenty paces on an angle in toward where he knew he'd find his son.

Jake was already there. The blood had drained out of his face and he was trying to steady himself and remain calm. He looked like he was fighting back tears.

"What, what?" hissed Mark.

"There's a body," said Jake, his body shaking. "It's a soldier. I'm not sure he's alive, about thirty paces in that direction. Come on."

Sergeant Leonard Kipling was wearing fatigues that did a good job of blending in with the snow and mud. It only made the thin trail of crimson near his mouth stand out even more.

"He's a Sergeant," said Jake, pointing at the three stripes on his shoulder. "But who's he fighting for? Is he one of us?"

He must have seen the puzzled look on Mark's face. "A Circle, is he a soldier for the Circle?"

"Stay back," whispered Mark. "I don't know, son. I don't know for sure that we have soldiers." He rolled the Sergeant over and noticed there was no movement.

Pinned to his lapel though was the circle of stars. Whatever he was doing, it was for the Circle. Mark wondered for a moment if this was the visitor the letters had mentioned or had they given up on letters and were that desperate to get him to acknowledge the message.

"He's one of us," said Jake. "We have to help him."

"We don't really have a side anymore and we don't know who else is in the area."

"We have to help him, Dad," said Jake, almost yelling.

"Okay, okay, we'll help him because it's the right thing to do but we're going to have to hurry. Keep watch," he said, trying to give Jake something to do, to distract him from the body.

Mark knelt down and felt for the carotid artery in the Sergeant's neck. He was still alive but the pulse was thready.

"He's alive," he said. Jake stopped for a moment and looked at the body. Suddenly, he looked more like the little boy that Mark usually could barely remember.

"Go, check out the perimeter and get back here, double time but don't fire on anyone."

Jake quietly ran through the woods and his father watched him disappear between the trees. He didn't have the luxury of wondering whether or not a fourteen year old boy should be drawn into a battle. The war was here and Jake needed to know he could defend his family if he had to, it was alright.

Jake came running back, his eyes wide. "A small squad about a mile away, headed in our direction. What do we do?"

"Get out the tarp and lay it flat on the ground right next to the body."

Jake did as he was told and helped his father quickly move the Sergeant onto the tarp. The Sergeant let out a low groan but didn't regain consciousness. Mark wrapped it around him and tucked the edges in tight.

"We're going to have to run while we carry him, you understand? There isn't much time and we have to be careful not to lead them straight up to the house. You notice their firepower?"

"Hard to tell," said Jake. He looked worried.

"It's good that you're afraid, Jake. Let it work for you. You ready to lift on your end? Grab the man by his ankles. He's going to be in a lot of pain and will probably resist. We don't have time to be polite. You're going to have to ignore that and keep up with me. Do you think you can do that?"

"Yes sir," said Jake. Mark felt his heart break just a little at the curt reply but there was no time. A mile could be crossed in just minutes even by a squad loaded down with equipment or minor injuries. They had to move out of the way.

They covered the blood in the snow and Mark quickly cut down a small branch from a nearby fir, lightly brushing over the trampled area so it would appear more normal, at least to someone looking through a scope from a distance.

"Are you ready?" he asked Jake, who nodded and picked up two corners of the tarp. Mark led them in a slightly zig-zag pattern being careful to step on roots whenever he could to hide his footprints. He knew Jake would know to do the same thing. It made it even harder to run quickly but adrenaline was helping.

The Sergeant cried out in pain and tried to struggle but they had a tight grip on him and kept moving.

"Not a good time to come to," said Jake, breathing hard.

"We're going around back," Mark said over his shoulder as they got closer to the house. They went to the door that opened into the basement and put the Sergeant on the ground. He let out another groan and seemed to be trying to sit up but the tarp had his arms trapped by his side. Jake knelt down by his ear.

"You're safe, we're with the Circle too. Don't struggle, we're trying to get you inside."

Jake looked up at his father and Mark nodded. "Good job, son," he said. They moved Sergeant Kipling to the room that was hidden behind the far wall and had been built for something just like this. Even if the Sergeant had decided to start screaming, no one would hear him in there and no one on the outside would be able to tell there was even a room in there.

"Leave your gun in here. There's plenty in the house and we can't be seen running around the outside of the house with guns in our hands."

They went out the way they came and headed for the front of the house.

"Walk slowly," said Mark. "We're out looking at the property, that's all. Slow your breathing down and get a positive image in your mind. Hold it there. We're going to come into their view now and we need to look bored." Mark slowed his pace.

"Don't look for them, son. They'll stay hidden unless we give ourselves away. Come here," he said and gathered his son under his arm. "I'm here," he whispered and gave Jake a quick kiss on the top of his head. "You don't even fit under my arm anymore," he whispered. "Let's go start dinner," he said, trying to bring things back to a more normal level.

They would take shifts that night checking on the Sergeant and watching for patrols. Peter and Ruthie would have to sleep in the safe room, just in case. If the Sergeant lived long enough to regain consciousness they could get some answers. Then they'd know if they needed to cut and run.

CHAPTER
6

Wallis took Joe, the family Bichon out for a walk in the early morning hours. Her mother, Harriet had stopped by for a visit and Wallis' choices were to argue or get out for a little air.

She'd already been outside for a few minutes just pacing back and forth in front of the taller bushes by the road where she couldn't be seen as easily from the house.

There were always a few kinks in her relationship with her mother, especially in the years since her father died. Both of the women were strong willed and loved their families. The only real difference as Wallis saw it was that she wanted to help her husband, Norman or her twelve year old son, Ned figure out what they wanted to be in life. Harriet was sure she already knew better and was willing to say so, every chance she got.

Somehow it was never quite what Wallis had in mind.

Harriet even knew who Wallis would be from the moment she was born. Harriet started telling her before Wallis was out of a crib. Her daughter was to be someone in this world. She was to be a force that caused others to tremble, according to Harriet. It was ironic, then that she named her only child after the former royal consort, Wallis Simpson.

The idea of the overly formal Harriet Jones choosing a woman who made a king resign made Wallis wonder just what her mother had seen in her.

Not a family court attorney, apparently because she was always finding different ways to let Wallis know that she could still aim a little higher, become a judge.

Norman was fond of saying that Harriet was misunderstood.

"You never hear her saying I will end up a judge," he would say, "she's ahead of her time promoting women."

"Yes, that's what it is," Wallis used to say, trying to keep any kind of edge out of her voice. But that was no longer as easy. Not since the shooting a little over two years ago. Not too many people had to forget on a daily basis that their house had been a crime scene.

Lately, she just didn't give an answer and instead would take the dog out for another walk. It was all she knew to do to avoid saying what she wasn't even sure was true.

Norman noticed the silence and caught her hand once before she could maneuver her way out of the house. "I get it," he said. "It's a lot to absorb and we are fix-it kind of people with a situation that doesn't remotely have one. Take all the time you need to get to some peace but don't leave me out of it. Okay?" he asked, squeezing her hand.

She had said, "Deal," but wondered for just a moment if she even knew how to explain what she was feeling.

They were stuck inside of a massive conspiracy that crossed borders and involved people more powerful than Wallis could comprehend or had ever met. Yet, somehow Ned, her young son who was more interested in Comicon and D.C. Comics over Marvel than real world domination was the most important player of all.

She had seen for herself what they were capable of doing. Wallis had met people she feared or admired and still it was hard to believe.

Harriet took it all in as if it was a course correction that involved a few unfortunate mishaps. Her mother seemed to easily bend with whatever horrible circumstance was laid at her feet.

Wallis knew one truth, more than ever, about her mother. Harriet Jones believed in the power of bloodlines. That left Wallis wondering what she might be capable of doing under the right circumstances. So far, Wallis had been able to right herself by sinking back into a renewed faith but she knew in the right moment all of that could be forgotten. Then it could be possible to go too far.

"I don't even know what that would look like," she said as Joe barked at a nearby squirrel, pulling on the leash.

That wasn't what dug so deep under Wallis' skin and kept her up some nights, staring at the ceiling. It turned out that Norman also knew all along the real story behind everyone's family tree. It took a misplaced thumb drive for the truth to come spilling out.

Wallis was born into some kind of dynasty. Her father, Walter was descended from the original founder of Management but he had never said a word about it to Wallis. Harriet had sworn him to secrecy. No one had told her anything.

It was conceivable that Harriet would do exactly as she had decided was best, Wallis got that completely. For some reason that bothered her a lot less than Norman's silence. She thought they were a team.

"Norman," whispered Wallis, sucking in a breath of air to try and steady her nerves.

"And Harriet, of course," said Wallis, as if she was talking to the dog. "Joe, how is it possible to admire and at the same time, look down on someone who gave you half your DNA? That's right. I think she sold out, a long time ago. All of this royalty bullshit. She's just mad at herself for what she never did." She rubbed her temples, trying to will away the beginning of another headache.

Wallis looked over at the old Blazney house at the end of the short street. New people were moving in and there were painters setting up outside the house. The familiar purple door was being painted forest green like most of the other doors in the neighborhood. Mrs. Blazney had moved into a retirement home since her husband was murdered and his body found alone in a field. He was still in his pajamas.

Wallis caught herself trying to picture that morning, wondering if she could have done something to prevent such a sweet old man from being a casualty in a fight he never knew anything about. "I wish I still didn't," said Wallis, kneeling down to give Joe a kiss on his head. He rewarded her with a sudden lick of her face, knocking her back till she was sitting on the ground.

A wave of anger came over her for just a moment, surprising Wallis and left as quickly as it came. "I can't keep going like this, Joe. I can't keep acting like it's everyone else's fault. There has to be something I can do."

Joe rested his head in Wallis' lap as she watched the purple gradually disappear and she had to make herself take in deep breaths. The ground was icy cold underneath her thin jeans but it felt good to have any kind of distraction. "I should talk to my mother," she said, smoothing out Joe's fur. "Stop asking myself the same damn questions and see if I can stand getting a few answers. Couldn't get more frustrated with her, could I?" she said to Joe, who gave a short bark. The painters turned around to look and Wallis gave a friendly wave.

They waved back but stood still until she stood up and brushed herself off.

"Okay, enough already. I can't take it anymore. I've felt sorry for myself long enough. Alice Watkins would not approve." She choked up trying to say her friend's name. "I can't save you, Alice or Larry or even poor, old Ray. But maybe I can do something and find some peace. Right?" she said, giving a gentle tug to Joe's leash.

Joe stopped and let out a low growl, gazing in the direction of the main road. Wallis felt herself tense up and had to make herself look in the same direction. Joe rarely ever growled at anything except squirrels or rabbits.

She saw an older sedan sitting a block away with a man behind the wheel. Nothing about it seemed off but she trusted Joe's instincts. He not only loved everyone he ever met, he usually wanted to get them to play with him. He was straining at the leash, jumping up on his back legs and barking.

Wallis kept looking at the man to let him know he had been seen. He returned her gaze with no expression at all on his face. Definitely one of those damn Watchers, she thought. It's like he's on the job. She turned toward the house and pulled Joe along behind her. He kept trying to move toward the car, still barking.

First Alice, now this.

Something was definitely starting up again. "Time to get some damn answers out of my own mother."

The woman could annoy Wallis with a look but it was also true that she had demanded from some pretty scary people that her daughter get to choose for herself even if Wallis never knew till recently about the deal Harriet made with Management. Wallis still couldn't get the details out of Harriet.

Harriet meant what she said about Wallis getting to choose even after Wallis chose Norman Weiskopf. Harriet did keep her comments to their usual level. She told Wallis what would be better but she never actually did anything to stop her. It was a kind of approval.

Maybe if Harriet had actually known that Norman was a second-generation survivor from the original Circle she would have done something to prevent the marriage but it was too late now. There was Ned to think of and Harriet had proven just how much she loved Ned.

Two years ago, Deputy Sheriff Oscar Newman had broken into their house, hell bent on finding the thumb drive that Wallis had in her possession and had shot up the place. In a desperate attempt to escape being killed off by someone from Management he had tried to prove his worth but none of it went the way he wanted or expected.

He had grabbed Ned and held him at gunpoint for a moment until Wallis had shown Oscar the thumb drive that held the Circle's plan to rise from the ashes. Ned had escaped and Wallis had squeezed her eyes shut, waiting for Oscar to finally kill her.

Harriet Jones still had other plans for her daughter, and they didn't include dying. She had made her way into the house and shot Oscar in the gut, chatting with him while he died, telling him how much no one would miss him. Wallis tried to get her wits about her and call for an ambulance. It was too late though and Oscar died but not before Wallis saw the lengths her mother was willing to go to make sure no one bothered her family.

She may have looked as cool as could be as Oscar grunted and slowly bled out in their bedroom but Wallis saw the anger barely perceptible in her mother's face. Harriet was angry enough to kill and would do so whenever necessary.

It wasn't too long after that, Harriet had strongly suggested they redecorate the room as if that would be enough to loosen the grip of the memories.

"Mom?" Wallis called out. "Are you upstairs?"

Wallis heard the quick, careful steps of her mother's heels. She rarely wore flats.

"Stop yelling like a fishwife, please. What is the matter? You never call me 'mom'." Harriet's eyes narrowed. "What is it?" she asked again.

"There's someone outside that may be watching the house. You know anything about that?" Wallis took Joe off of his leash and he immediately ran to a front window and started barking again. Harriet looked at Joe and her mouth became a determined straight line of deep red lipstick.

"No, but I will," she said, quickly grabbing her purse that was resting on the front table. Wallis noticed there seemed to be a certain heft to the leather bag.

"Are you carrying a gun with you all the time?" she asked, "Even in my home?"

"Successfully growing old in Management with any sense of dignity requires the occasional target practice," Harriet said.

"Not at people, not as a way of life and definitely not in my home," said Wallis, grabbing her mother by the arm. "No gunfire in my neighborhood, not one single shot."

"I'll do my best, dear."

"When did you become Annie Oakley?"

"You're dating yourself, dear. I'm more like… Who am I, Ned?" she yelled toward the stairs.

"So I got these lungs from you," said Wallis.

"Robocop," came the answer from somewhere upstairs. "Not all of your parts are original."

Wallis was sure she heard a short laugh and a gurgle from someone in the kitchen.

"I should go check on Norman," she said.

"Hmmm," said Harriet, raising one of those perfectly drawn eyebrows. "I'm going to let that one go because it's true," she said, patting her artificial hip, "and because it's the first time I've seen you even attempt a smile in a very long time."

"The car is to the right, across the street about a block down. You can't miss it," said Wallis.

"It's probably some fool Watcher," said Harriet. "I'll set him straight."

She watched her mother walk quickly up to the top of the driveway and survey both directions.

"Be careful, Mom," whispered Wallis.

Wallis knew that Harriet really didn't care for Management and their tactics. That only added to her frustration when Harriet would go on about the importance of honoring your roots. They had gotten into an argument the last time her mother stopped by the office to drop off a set of commemorative dessert plates of the newest royal, Prince George.

"What roots, Mother?" Wallis had blurted out, when Harriet had insisted that their roots were just as good as the British royal family. "The ones that have thought up more than one way to kill every one of us? I'm pretty sure the Windsors gave all of that up well over two hundred years ago. What's our problem?"

"You're a Jones, they're good people, and you're also a Carter from my line. My side of the family is English, from royalty."

"Management royalty, Mother."

"Yes, well, maybe that's true and the more obvious kind of royalty too. That matters, you'll see."

"How do you manage to overlook all of the rest?" Wallis asked, exasperated.

"I have no choice, dear. They're my kin. You don't get to choose who shows up for Thanksgiving dinner. You just set another place at the table. Trust me, I'd have all kinds of ideas if that wasn't true."

"I can't do it. I can't overlook what they've done."

"Some," Harriet said firmly. "Some of them have done, Wallis, and they were punished, all of them. I saw to that," said Harriet, her voice rising with every word. Wallis had touched a nerve. "It's very easy to be so idealistic, dear when someone else is keeping the peace. It's okay, even better that you go on about the business of living. But don't disrespect those who do all of the heavy lifting that makes it possible to make a little meatloaf without having to actually kill the cow."

"I've heard the other stories. I heard what happened years ago," Wallis said, quietly, not willing to let it go completely.

"That was another time, another place. It's different now," said Harriet.

"Then explain to me how Alice Watkins died," she said, the tears rolling down her cheeks.

Harriet was about to say something when Wallis' assistant, Laurel had interrupted and said there was a phone call for Wallis. Harriet slowly put down the small plates and quietly left, gently shutting the front door to the office without another word. Wallis wasn't sure her mother was angry or thought it better to give things a little time.

Wallis didn't hear from her again till her mother stopped by this morning, unannounced. Harriet rarely ever called first.

"She's too smart to warn us first," said Norman, when they saw her cream colored Cadillac pull into the driveway.

She had brought by a small wooden bowl for Ned, big enough to fit in his hand and was telling him it came from a tulip poplar that had been started as a sapling on the grounds of the first Jones to come to America.

"He helped bring a sense of order to a new country," said Harriet, holding the young man's chin in her hand. Ned was still as thin as a reed but he was already taller than his grandmother and Wallis could see how much he loved her.

That's why she decided a walk was the best choice.

Ned never really got over the shooting. He had immediately stopped sleeping in his bedroom at the top of the house and slowly migrated all of his things into the guest bedroom closer to his parents. Sometimes he would cry out in the night like someone was chasing him and Norman would have to hold him tight to convince him it was only a nightmare. None of it was real.

Wallis hated that part because it was a lie.

Most of it was real.

They were just doing their best to hold the barbarians outside of their lives. There was no way to ever know if today was the day they would no longer be able to do it.

Wallis stood in the doorway, trying to hear anything that sounded out of place, wondering if her mother was okay.

"What's going on?" asked Norman. He was drying his hands with the dish towel from the kitchen.

"My mother has become our one-woman neighborhood watch. Did you know she carries a gun?"

"I assumed she did," said Norman, looking uncomfortable.

"That was two years ago. I didn't think she carried one all the time. She should have been back by now. Why is it I feel a little better with a senior citizen as our muscle?"

"Because she has small firearms training and not much restraint when it comes to her family," said Norman, trying to smile.

Wallis let out the breath she was holding. "I'm going to go check on her," she said.

"We'll go together," said Norman. "A family stroll to check the property," he said, trying to make a joke.

When they got to the street Harriet was standing in the road by herself looking in every direction like she was trying to see every corner.

"What is it, mother?" Wallis asked.

"He gave up a little too easily," said Harriet. "There must be some kind of backup," she said, as she looked over to the Blazney house.

"No way," said Wallis. "You think the new residents are Watchers of a more permanent variety?"

"It would be a lot easier to keep an eye on things if someone could take a walk around their own neighborhood," said Norman.

Wallis looked at the two of them and realized she had been missing the opportunity.

"We need to talk," she said. "The three of us have to start working together and come up with a plan."

"That's my girl," said Harriet. Wallis noticed Norman trying not to smile.

CHAPTER

7

The new numbers were due back to the agent who acted as a courier for Maurel by the end of the day. The issues weren't on the end of the older systems manager who was known around the office as Maurel Samonte but the program wasn't cooperating. The entire computer system was frozen and even seemed to be deleting newer information.

Maurel wasn't her real name. It was only the latest role she had been given as an operative for the Circle. There had been countless names in the thirty-five years she had assumed different identities in order to help further the cause. Frankly, for Maurel it was about trying to keep a certain balance in the world and she had seen enough of how Management did business to know that if they ever were able to operate without any checks the planet would be divided up into a modern form of monarchies. It would appear as if there was an entire middle class that was living a fairly decent life but it would come at the price of being able to choose to opt out or dream bigger. Life would become very defined.

That was already the fate of families who put their children into the private feeder schools that supplied Management and grew up to take their place in the corporate, political or military rank and file. They were even spilling into the media and sitting on early morning talk show couches. It wasn't a bad life, unless someone had a different idea about how their life ought to look or wanted to openly express a different kind of opinion. There was no out clause except openly joining the opposition and hoping no one cared enough not to kill them off.

In her latest assignment with the Circle, she had been the document manager for the Kroton system within Westin Fullerton, Incorporated, for almost a year. She walked in knowing how the corporate game was played. The larger the corporation, the more narrowly defined someone's role was and they were expected to stay within those lines.

Management operatives who had sipped the Kool-Aid did particularly well in large corporate settings.

People were rewarded with lives that played out a lot like roadmaps with very few surprises.

Maurel at least knew how to play the part.

Previous roles in her years as an operative had put her in a cubicle before and she knew that time didn't change the way humans got along in close quarters. She was sitting at her desk, waiting for the technician on the phone to fix the problem so she could get back to work.

The off-site technician was mostly trying to placate Maurel. He wasn't really concerned with whether or not the problem was fixed today or even tomorrow.

He had no way of knowing a simple computer glitch was getting in the way of a Circle operation or that he was talking to one of their oldest agents.

Maurel Samonte was on a schedule and needed to get the information on enemy troop movements in the escalating civil war from the files where it had been left by the eyes and ears the Circle had in place to different locations on the server where it could be found by the officers in the field who needed it. Sooner rather than later.

The war was mostly being played out only a couple of states to the north.

There were rumors that it was starting to spread into the heartland of America.

From the information that was gathered, Maurel could see that was true but it wasn't her job to confirm gossip for other operatives or to even comment in any way. Her main focus was to be a modern version of a digital telephone operator right under the nose of Management.

Maurel was the only one the Keeper trusted enough to be able to stay calm while sitting among Management's people all day and still focus on what needed to be done. The orders had been delivered by an agent in person and told to her verbally so there would be no record. She was given the background on her new role and placed in the position by a temp agency that knew how to sell her to the company. After that, Maurel made herself invaluable and before long she was absorbed into the company. She didn't know if there was a backup plan in case they had let her go after a few months. That wasn't part of her job and Maurel knew that to be a good agent meant to always have a singleness of purpose.

The purpose might have looked to outsiders like a moving target with every new set of orders but once the path was set, she followed them to the last line. This time it was to keep the information flowing in the right directions behind the scene.

To follow the new orders though, she had to take on a new life again with all that entailed and let go of any sense of schedule or order she had managed to create for herself. It had taken her awhile to even find a decent cup of coffee. There was a cafeteria on the first floor but Maurel thought that the coffee they brewed in large urns lined up against a wall, tasted like swill. It was one of the few things that she was unwilling to just go with the flow to blend into a crowd.

Fortunately, being snobby about coffee had become an American pastime. She found a small hole-in-the wall run by a young couple from Panama that had a much better brew.

She was used to being moved around like more of an asset to a cause than a human being who might mind picking up everything and changing her identity, the way she looked and even her name. She was an expert at appearing friendly at work without revealing too many details while learning the small things about others.

There was one real friend she had managed to make on an old assignment. It was a very rare occurrence and Maurel was hoping to see her again someday. Wallis Jones was special and had done what was necessary to keep her family safe. She wasn't tied to a cause or trying to prove something even after she found out about her own legacy. Maurel respected that, maybe even admired Wallis.

One day Maurel hoped their paths would cross again but until then there would be no contact of any kind, no mention of being from anywhere other than Central Illinois and farmland. No long conversations about it that might lead to too many questions. Just a short answer and a nod before getting back to work. If necessary, Maurel would retreat into what looked like a bad mood and put on her ear buds till the person found someone else to bond with and moved on.

That was protocol.

An operative was always set up to be from somewhere not too far away from where they were currently stationed that was populated enough so that not knowing everyone wouldn't be seen as odd. That way if someone had a cousin or an old friend who was from there, there was a natural cover.

The childhoods of the Management people around Maurel were vetted to make sure she wasn't building a past that came too close to anyone who was already there.

Then her background was slipped into the database of an old high school and the appropriate civil records in case anyone wanted to look. When the assignment was finally over the same material would be erased as if she had never been there. Her real records were wiped clean a long time ago and even Maurel rarely thought about the memories that once belonged to her.

It was all just a label anyway.

"Hey, how long has it been like this?" asked the young technician. Maurel thought he looked bored. He kept trying different things to fix the system and to get her computer to work again.

Maurel made a point of not offering too much assistance. He couldn't know that she knew more about how the system worked than he did and was a specialist of sorts, trained by the Circle to do more than one related job.

At the same time that Maurel was compiling a digital history of the thousands of documents and presentations that flow through any corporation, she was also tasked with being a monitor at one of the six world-wide locations where the Circle maintained servers. Each monitor was to ensure the safety of information that was gathered from all over their territory. Most covered several countries.

Maurel's territory overlapped a nearby system that went from the Carolinas and included Kentucky and Ohio as it cut through North America from the mid-Atlantic stretching throughout Canada. Each server gathered a different set of data.

All but one of the locations were located in favorable geographic areas where the Circle had the political and legal clout to help protect their assets.

They were more secure than the Federal Reserve and contained assets far more valuable than money. The online clouds were full of metadata gathered on thousands and thousands of subjects sent in by various Circle operatives all over each region. Phone records, troop movements, family histories, GPS records from cars and smart devices and even shopping habits. All of it had a special tag included that denoted Management, Circle or no affiliation and affected how the data was sorted and then mined.

The other locations were the ones that sat in neutral areas that looked far more nondescript and were mostly surrounded by Circle families or no one at all. The one exception was where Maurel sat every day for at least eight hours. She was the only operator at risk monitoring the only information reserve that sat in enemy territory. It was all deemed necessary because of the value of the special category of information that she could steal from her employer.

Only the Keeper and the top cell in the Circle knew the location of this particular server or the identity of its operator. The records that were kept on the other locations only listed five areas. Maurel's region, number six, was kept hidden from almost everyone.

The other servers' locations were known to a horizontal group of cells, high enough in the Circle's hierarchy so that if something happened to one cell, one network of agents, another could laterally move over and keep the server operational.

Only Maurel's would fall silent if something were to happen to her.

Each of the servers had a secure communications link set up to allow only authenticated users to log on to the system and each location's link was unique to that location.

A firewall had been set up around each network that didn't allow any traffic to come into the network from outside the users but it was all still connected to the internet. A user, or agent in the field who was pouring in the information they'd gathered, entered by a port in the firewall that had to be opened up with a series of encoded steps to allow communications to flow.

It was called port knocking and involved the user knowing first how to locate the online ports, or doors in the cloud system set up by the regional server. The user would then initiate a connection with a closed port through a set of sequences that would open the right ports for the information they were going to import, or export.

But the first set of sequences would still not give the person access to any information stored on the valuable server. The agent would have to have a current encryption key to then access the contents on the system.

There were two distinct steps. First, knowing how to tell the port to open up, and second to be able to validate with an encryption key and password that changed every week before an agent could log into the cloud. The encryption key or certificate was a digital signature algorithm set up with multiple layers as well. The first layer had an encrypted signature that would allow an entire group to get closer to the information. The second layer had a constantly changing random signature quotient that was unique to each user and allowed the agent to only access a very narrowly defined area. The last step, a pass phrase would determine if they could enter information or take any away with them.

Someone using the system correctly would only be able to access his content. Even then, they would still not know where the ultimate servers existed in the world.

Separate servers had been set up in even more locations where agents could port knock into the data with links to an intermediate set of servers that eventually connected to the six main locations.

The system made it possible for anyone, anywhere in the world with access to a smart device and wifi to gain access to the portal that they needed.

Maurel was one of six agents who hovered over a segment of the system and made sure nothing peculiar suddenly appeared or disappeared.

She had been with the Circle for so long that it had become her entire life. No real family to speak of anymore outside of the contacts who came and went.

She was in her sixties and too old to be running through the woods or anywhere else in pursuit of someone or even worse, from someone.

The last assignment had been easier. She lived on the campus of an orphanage posing as a Mother Superior. Before that she had been in Richmond posing as a psychic, Madame Bella. No one ever paid close attention to psychics who set up shop. They didn't want to be seen as taking any of it seriously. That assignment had lasted a few years and had put her directly in Wallis Jones' path. It had also cost her a couple of fingers when Maurel had to save her own life but she had managed to hand out a few wounds herself.

Playing a Mother Superior turned out to be one of her favorite roles. Faith was the only thing that kept her from nagging little desires to be like everyone else. The people who sat around her were always talking about what they might have been or hoped to become and it always involved something with a little more flash.

Maurel wanted to be a little more average. Not the average details of finding a husband or a little house but just the consistent backstories of childhood and the tiring struggles that everyone else had to tell. All of hers were written for her by copywriters within the Circle and they had changed too many times for her to try and remember. That would have been too dangerous, even in her daydreams. For better or worse, in this day and time she was Maurel Samonte and worked at Westin Fullerton, an enormous insurance management company, as a data information manager. Any other thoughts were devoted to her role in the war.

For a little while though she had tasted some kind of normalcy but it was just by chance. The assignment as a Mother Superior had placed her in the center of Circle operations and given her the best chance at being herself that she had known since first joining the cause so many years ago.

Her role was to appear as a spiritual leader and that made everything easier. Pieces of her real personality got to peek through in conversations. Occasionally she had even let herself believe that she could retire right there in that role and live happily ever after.

Then the war broke out and as soon as the first casualties were reported something inside of her knew that nothing was going to stay the same. She had made a mistake to ever let herself think that retirement was going to be something she could design or even have as her own.

None of it turned out to be divine destiny after all. It was just one more assignment and when the new orders came, Maurel dropped her old name and started studying her new background.

Her current assignment gave her another title as the manager of the Kroton system for Westin Fullerton with corporate campuses all over the world. They were listed as a Fortune Sixteen company, with several foreign subsidiaries and were one of the largest pharmacy insurance companies in the world.

It was an almost perfect cover for data mining. Almost everyone who carried around an insurance card had their prescriptions processed by Westin, whether they knew it or not. Medical insurers, third party administrators, corporations that were self-insured and even the new health care exchanges set up in the United States created for the millions of uninsured, all needed someone to manage the prescription claims.

Westin Fullerton took it one step further.

Strategically located across the world were large, non-descript, warehouse-sized buildings that did nothing but process bulk orders for medications for chronic conditions. Everyone with a chronic condition that had to take medications on an on-going basis eventually ended up doing business with Westin.

Weaving over the heads of everyone who worked on the noisy floor of the mail order warehouse was a large, serpentine track that carried plastic green tubs, two feet by two feet squared, across squeaky little rollers. Each tub represented one person's prescription order. Most with a healthy profit margin.

A relationship was forged between the company and the customer that would last for years and was more important to most people than any other. Management had quickly learned that people would consider forgoing vacations or even mortgage payments before they'd give up on their medications.

The business was a cash cow with a partnership that only death could break.

A greyish-white, padded anonymous-looking bag full of drugs would show up in someone's mailbox in exchange for all the pertinent information about their health, their employment, their family and where they lived. All details that even helped Management to know who was most vulnerable to offers from a feeder school.

The company was better at gathering information than Google or Facebook, combined and were under dense regulations never to share any of it with anyone. That made planning the development of the war even easier.

Management could build demographic profiles to use as a basis for decisions about what areas of North America were worth taking by force and what areas could be absorbed more easily through gaining a family's trust. The upper cells had come to see there was no better way to do that than through the open door of someone's health and well-being. Westin Fullerton was one of their better creations and was helping them to infiltrate everyone's daily life.

The Circle was aware of what they saw as a problem and had come up with a simple solution. Piggyback on what Management was doing and steal the same information, including who was in the ranks of Management that they'd never been able to identify before now.

The company was infiltrated and run by strictly Management people right up to the senior levels. Management had seen the value of not only having access to the general population's information but the staying profitability of health care. It was one of the few things that would still be viable, even in a bad economy or a war.

There were a few known Circle operatives in the ranks but they were kept in low-level positions where they had no access to anything important. One of them was the man who delivered the mail every day, pushing around a cart.

Maurel was seen as neutral by Management and her background constructed so carefully that no one was able to detect how recently she came to exist in this identity.

There was a detailed background check before she was hired but all of her references were put in place for just such an occasion. Circle families whose direction was to live quiet lives within the middle class and never appear as if they took sides with anyone. Then when they were called upon, they could give a plausible reference and vouch for someone with just enough detail that didn't draw suspicion.

That way a high-ranking mole could dig their way into the center of a Management operation and create a hidden server.

Each of the Circle's six main servers were classified information so that hackers wouldn't know to even look for them. That's why the last one, the sixth one was known to even fewer people. The information that was mined on a daily basis was part of the bigger scheme to finally bring down Management or at least cripple them for generations to come.

The Keeper had devised the plan and would give the order to start the last phase when they had enough information on key Management people who were customers of Westin and in particular received a padded white envelope in their mailbox every month.

Even Maurel didn't know exactly what the last phase of the plan was exactly. It had been described to her as the failsafe and her part would come at the end of it, if it was ever necessary.

Further protocol had been put into place to fool Management in case they started to catch wind of any of the servers. There were other databases being run on the outside of the system that the Circle put a lot of energy into hiding, with just enough sensitive information to give the operation a sense of authenticity without risking any real harm if it was detected. Even the Circle people running that system were unaware they were acting as a front. They were defending misinformation with their lives but it was just as necessary in order to protect not only the soldiers in the field whose information was being kept through a backdoor in Management's own system, but the volumes of information that the Circle was able to steal from Westin Fullerton's records. The false operation was vital.

If it ever became necessary, Management would have something to keep themselves busy while never suspecting that the real prize was an older woman who sat in on of their cubicles and had lunch with them in the corporate cafeteria almost every day. Maurel usually settled for the salad bar except on Southwest Tuesdays when she would head down in the elevator early to get some of the popular chili. That always ran out early.

She found that it was always best to enjoy as many pieces of the role as possible and have some kind of life. She had learned that a long time ago. It was necessary to accept everything as normal, otherwise the imaginary questions of what might have been would creep up in her mind and might show on her face.

"Okay, I'm going to take over your screen for a moment," said Ed, the technician on the phone. "And see if I can't figure out why the data isn't syncing up with us."

"No, it's not on my end," said Maurel. "The data is getting to you just fine. It's not getting loaded into your system so that it can be released for use the next day. Does that make sense?"

"Sure, sure," said Ed. "Hold on, let me see something. Can you hold on?" Before Maurel could answer there was already the sound of Abba singing 'Waterloo' in her ear.

Maurel wasn't worried. She knew her system was still secure. There was a backup system Maurel had constructed that she could go to if Ed couldn't straighten things out in time for her to send a report.

However time was running out for even the secondary report. If nothing appeared within the appointed hour an automatic message would be sent to a different operative who would alert a Circle cell that a report had been missed. No one along the chain would know who had missed their report. They would only know to send a predetermined message till it rose up the Circle ladder to the appropriate person.

Systems would be put on alert, affecting a variety of operations, particularly battle strategies but no one would come to check on Maurel. They would wait to see if a message would appear at the next appointed time to find out if she might be dead or alive.

That was also protocol.

Fifteen minutes to go until the message would be sent and Maurel would let it go for the day. She could work on entering actual Westin information instead.

She had been in too many tight spots to let something like this get to her. The operation that brought her into contact with Wallis Jones had been just as important and that one had almost ended in disaster at the highest Circle cell. The Keeper had almost been killed. This was a momentary glitch even if officers in the field would have to come up with different strategies while the Circle waited to find out if one of their own had been betrayed.

"Okay, you were right. We see it. It was something simple. The code that turns the documents into pdf's and relays everything back to Kroton was hanging up the whole thing. Sorry about that."

"Not your fault, Ed. Glad you found it. Will I need to reload all of the data I sent in since yesterday?" His answer would determine if there would be a way to run a report today. If someone else reentered anything then Maurel would have to use the backup system after all.

When things ran smoothly, key officers in the field came back to their day jobs and sent data using certain program codes that determined what fields Maurel would enter into Kroton. Even though Maurel sat at Westin Fullerton, Circle officers were in every walk of life door knocking to send information straight into a Management system as Westin corporate documents. Even if the officers were just as unaware.

Checks and balances were in place at every level to protect against the entire operation being exposed or worse, brought down. Officers didn't know anyone in the cells above them or in other units. If they were ever captured in a suburban battlefield they would not be able to give up the next link in the command.

Modern torture that was officially known as thoughtful interrogation wouldn't yield anything. Someone might break and want to tell something to bring on a peaceful death but they wouldn't know enough for it to matter and eventually even their captors would understand.

In order to gain useful information someone would have to be able to see past all of the keywords like '30-day refills' or 'durable medical equipment'.

Besides, only nine minutes to go now. Time was growing short. She held her breath for a moment despite all of her years in the field.

"Nope, we got it. Once we fixed the problem the system kicked in and started picking up everything. Give it a couple of minutes and your stuff will all be there."

"Sounds good," said Maurel. "I've got a couple of minutes." She slowly took in a deep breath.

"Yeah," laughed Ed, with a snort. "Almost three hours till quitting time, what's a couple more minutes?"

There was still time to run the report so that it would be there for another operative who was buried even deeper within Management's ranks. They would take it up to the top of the Circle. Even Maurel didn't know who was on the other end, gathering her reports.

There was that other matter, thought Maurel.

There was another portal that only Maurel and two other agents on the outside knew about that could wait. Maurel had recently been ordered to start monitoring a small cloud in the database that collected information on a shorter list of people whose names were encoded to keep their identities anonymous. Maurel couldn't tell who they were, or even what side they were on, but she wondered what importance they played in all of this.

A group of salesmen passed by her cubicle talking loudly about how business was going. Maurel looked up for a moment as they passed by to see if she could tell if someone was limping or favoring an arm.

It stood to reason that some of these people were enemy combatants returned from the same open battlefields near the Canadian border and were nursing some hidden bruises or sutured wounds. It gave a new meaning to paid time off.

"Maurel, you want my popcorn?"

It was Farrell who worked in the cubicle next to hers and had to comment out loud on everything that happened during the day. Most people had learned to see it as background noise. The popcorn was free with coffee every afternoon. An odd combination and resulted in the entire building smelling like a movie theater every afternoon.

"Sure, Farrell, thank you."

"Can you hold it with your bad hand?" asked Farrell. Maurel smiled and held out her left hand to show him the remaining fingers worked just fine. "How did you lose them?" he asked, nodding at her hand. It wasn't the first time he had asked.

Maurel caught someone rolling their eyes as they walked by. A lot of people thought Farrell was a little odd because he had no filters and was bound to ask whatever he was thinking. Maurel found it refreshing most of the time.

"It happened a long time ago," said Maurel. "A different life," she said, taking the popcorn and turning her back. That was one good trait Farrell did have. When someone went back to work, he went back to talking to himself without any kind of fuss.

Maurel kept her back to everyone and let the report run across her screen as she scooped up a handful of popcorn and pushed it into her mouth. She thought about the one place she might have called home if only she could tell someone.

I miss Richmond, she thought. It's an odd thing to live without any kind of labels that you get to keep, maybe even defend.

She pushed more popcorn into her mouth, letting go of the thought. It would only make her days longer. Someday this assignment would end and she would be onto another place, new people. Perhaps that one would not be quite so lonely.

CHAPTER (8)

Wallis looked in the rear view mirror. Ned preferred sitting in the backseat most of the time where he could act like he didn't hear his mother talking to him. Sometimes Wallis made him sit up front with her but it didn't really change anything.

"You have your lunch money?" she asked, glancing back and forth between the traffic and the top of her son's head. He was buried in a book.

"Yeah," he grunted.

"You get all of your homework done?" She already knew the answer. He always finished his homework but she was about out of topics.

Ned was in the seventh grade and didn't like talking to adults as a part of being twelve but Wallis was convinced that being shot at had made it worse. She blamed herself.

"I like your new car," he said, his head still down. Wallis felt her heart jump a little. Ned was picking a topic and actually talking to her.

"Really? Thanks. I appreciate all of the research you did."

Her old car, a Jaguar had been practically demolished by the same murderous deputy sheriff and the car chase had almost cost Wallis her life. Wallis had loved the car because she felt it showed a certain amount of independence.

Lately, though she wanted a little more stability. It crept into all of her decisions lately. The red Subaru Forester made her feel like it would be a little harder to run her off the road the next time. She suspected Ned felt the same way. She knew it when he pointed out that it was voted the best small SUV in snow.

Richmond rarely got snow and when the city did, it only lasted for an afternoon.

"Sure, no problem," he said, and looked up for a moment, making eye contact with her before looking down at his book again.

"I've been thinking of moving back into my room. Back upstairs," said Ned.

"Oh?"

"Yeah, it's my space. You okay with that?"

"Sure, sure. Any reason you wanted to do it now?"

"No, I've been thinking about it for a while."

That was it. He didn't say another word and Wallis couldn't think of a way to keep the talk going. Her throat ached and she felt the same lingering sense of loneliness that draped itself over her more and more lately. It didn't matter if people were in the room or not.

It was so unlike her. She was used to life being black and white, right or wrong. You dealt with something and moved on to the next thing. That trait was most like her mother, even like Norman and she had always taken comfort in it.

Nothing was going to drag into the corners of her soul for very long and take up residence. Then a crazy man pointed a gun at her son and her mother fired back and everything changed.

Wallis learned how to second-guess herself and wondered if she had failed at the one thing that it turned out mattered to her most, Ned and his happiness.

It seemed like they had both taken a right turn just not in the same direction and she wasn't going to be able to fix it or to just leave it alone. Instead she tortured herself with small plots to draw him out that she never tried or attempts at small talk that were heavy with her desire to hear that he was okay in there.

None of it worked to her satisfaction and her restlessness was only growing.

"Knowledge isn't power," she said, risking telling the truth a little. She never knew if it was better to talk to him like he was a small adult or plaster over everything as if she could make it all right. Usually Wallis ended up feeling like she was wrong, no matter which way she went. There was a certain amount of freedom though in that too.

Easier to just do something when you're convinced that failure is inevitable either way.

"Whoa," she gasped, hitting the brakes.

She had almost slid through the yellow light at the busy intersection at Pemberton and Three Chopt. A car had jumped the green light and sped through just in front of her bumper. Her heart was pounding and she had to take in a couple of deep breaths to calm down. Ned's new school, Harrison Middle School was just up the steep hill, right next door to his old elementary school, which sat just above it.

"What," said Ned, raising his head. He looked concerned and immediately, Wallis regretted saying anything.

"Nothing," said Wallis, "talking out loud."

"Knowledge isn't power," he repeated, "I heard you. Maybe not by itself." He locked eyes with her as his hair fell across his forehead and he shoved it back across his head. A large piece stuck up from the top of his head, giving him a comical look above such a serious expression. Wallis noticed how long his hair was getting and wondered if she could change the subject to getting a haircut.

"Your hair's getting a little long," she said, glancing away from the rear view mirror. It was hard to hold his steady gaze and talk about nothing.

"Yeah, whatever," he said, and went back to his book.

Even my mother is better at this than I am these days, she thought, wincing.

"You're right," she said, trying to get him to look up again. "It takes more than knowing something. It's just that I'm not sure what that would be and I don't want to be wrong."

"Yeah, whatever," he said again, not looking up at all.

"I'm sorry, Ned," she said, catching herself tearing up and knowing right away that had been the wrong call.

"For what?" Ned asked, clearly angry. "Why do you always do this?" he asked, as she pulled into the large, open parking lot of the middle school. Ned flung open the door to the car. "Why do you always make me have to care about all of your worries? I'm just a kid, you know. And then you do nothing about any of it. Tell your Bunco friends. Don't you have one of those parties tonight? Tell them. Leave me out of it," he spit out as he slid out of the car and slammed the door. He marched off toward the building without looking back.

Wallis felt the familiar ache again and wanted to go after him and explain everything but knew it wasn't right. He was just a kid and she had no idea why she would tell him that there was no solution.

She watched him until the car behind her gave a short honk and Ned turned the corner where she couldn't see him anymore.

She turned up the radio and tried to listen to 'All Things Considered' on the radio and let go of the thoughts that just kept making an endless loop in her head. The drive to the office was uneventful and as she pulled into her parking lot she looked over at the new sign next door advertising an accountant.

"I miss you, Madame Bella," she said, tearing up again. "I don't even know the name you go by anymore." Wallis shook her head and gathered up her things. "Oh my God, I have got to cut this out. Enough already. I barely knew the woman."

"You talking to yourself again?" asked Laurel. It was Wallis' assistant who had seen her through every crisis and still seemed rock steady. She was standing in the doorway of the office, holding Wallis' favorite mug. The one that said, 'You win some, you lose some, but you get paid for all of them.'

"Got your coffee," said Laurel. "I saw you pull up. What are you thinking, or is that a thorny question?"

"More like a weepy, pathetic question," said Wallis. "I got into an argument with Ned that I started for no good reason that went nowhere."

"He's twelve. It goes with the territory. Of these things I know well." Laurel was raising two children of her own. "The only cure is time," she said, taking Wallis' briefcase from her and handing her the mug. "Your job is to keep him alive long enough to get older so he wises up. And try and have a little fun yourself in the meantime."

"Then I'm doing a poor job on both counts," she said.

"Wallis Jones, that self-pity is only going to fly but so much. You are not all that unique, my dear."

"Really feeling the job security, aren't you, Laurel," said Wallis, already feeling better. "Thank goodness for you."

"Was that all that got you riled up this morning? That's all it took?" asked Laurel. "Morning, Patty," she said, to the other paralegal. Patty was an older, heavyset woman who spent every break smoking out in the parking lot and as a result the waiting area always had a lingering odor of Pall Mall's. She was William Bremmer's assistant, the third partner in the law firm. Wallis and Norman made up the other two partners. William and Norman handled small businesses while Wallis focused on family law, where all of the real drama unfolded.

Wallis waited till they got up the stairs to her office.

"There was a Watcher outside of my house today. My mother went out and chased them off."

"She take a shot at them?" asked Laurel, raising an eyebrow. Wallis smiled despite how she felt.

"I made her promise not to."

"You're using AARP as your bodyguard?" asked Laurel.

"I said the same thing to Norman," said Wallis, smiling again. "My mother seems indestructible and she is packing. I wish I was more like her right at the moment."

"I think you are. You've just lost sight of it."

Wallis let out a deep sigh despite herself. "You know what it is? I've lost this idea that everything will work out okay in the end. It's like I'm waiting for the next punch and I'd prefer it took me out instead of Ned or Norman. But it's not working."

"I can imagine it's not."

"I told Harriet and Norman that we have to start working together. Yeah, that's right. The three of us. And you know, I think Harriet was actually proud of me."

"Your mother is proud of you more often than you give her credit."

"Yes, but for what?"

"You're determined to stay stuck in this rut today. I'm gonna just leave you there, if you keep it up and go find something more productive to do."

"Okay, okay. It's just, that short burst of bravado has already passed. Being around Ned used to fill me with courage or at least joy or peace or something. Now, I can pretty much guarantee that it will leave me feeling unsure of myself, the world and anything else you can name."

"Welcome to teen angst. It's their job to make you think it's you and they're damn clever at it."

"So, what do you do to not wish away the time?" asked Wallis.

"You ask yourself what am I supposed to be doing, and you go do that. You stop making everything so complicated."

"You ever think about what happened, Laurel?"

"Of course I do. There were people chasing us with baseball bats and guns. It was like something out of the movies. But I don't try to make sense of any of it. It doesn't make sense. All of it is someone else's game."

"How do I get out of the game?"

"Just don't play," said Laurel.

"I don't pay you enough."

Laurel took on a familiar determined look. "Don't insult me. I don't take that well. I am well compensated and the two of us are friends. I know you're trying to ease your own pain but try and stay with it. It won't kill you and you just might learn something."

She turned and left Wallis' office without another word. It was the usual way she ended conversations. She never felt the need to hang in with some tidy chitchat. It was a quality Wallis treasured.

"You're like a compass," she shouted after Laurel.

"Please," she heard back, noting the sound of mild annoyance.

The day seemed to pass slowly. A former client stopped by to start divorce proceedings with his third wife. Every new wife looked like a slightly younger version of the one before and they all turned out the same way. She had told Norman that morning that she should have an easy day, explaining another repeat was stopping by.

He suggested she start her own frequent flyer card.

"It would cut too far into my profits," Wallis answered, trying to zip up her dress.

"Come on," Norman said, pulling her into a tight embrace and kissing her neck. "All you have to do is pull out your notes from the previous years and repeat."

"Very funny," she had said, before she pulled away and turned around. "Could you zip me up? What?" she asked. "Ned's in the next room."

Norman had zipped her up without another word. That wasn't helping her mood either.

The client had stopped by with evidence from a private investigator that showed his wife was cheating on him. He looked genuinely hurt as he laid out the pictures.

"I want to make sure she gets nothing," he spit out.

"What about your children with her?" Wallis knew he had finally given in and started a family with wife number three. He was getting older and apparently had thought it was time to put down some real roots. Usually he was the one trying not to get caught at something.

"The bare minimum," he choked out. Wallis knew he didn't mean it. He wasn't an unfair man even if he was a little blind to his own behavior. It was pointless to go over a strategy with him yet. She tried to put her hand over his to offer a little comfort.

"It gets easier," she said, hoping that was true.

The man had abruptly pulled his hand back and slid back in the soft leather chair that faced Wallis' desk.

"Don't feel sorry for me," he said. He looked like he had tasted something sour. "I'm already moving on."

Wallis felt a little tired as she pulled back her hand. "You are not legally separated yet. Be careful or you could end up paying more than you hoped," she said, trying not to sound as exasperated as she felt. She gave him a half-hearted smile and sent him off to Laurel to make another appointment.

She stopped in Norman's office after she heard the door close downstairs but he was nowhere to be found.

"Norman around?" she asked Patsy.

"Went on an errand, is what he said," said Patsy. "You want me to call him?"

"No, I'll call him." She suddenly wanted a little fresh air even if the wind was biting and she stepped out the back door into the large parking lot that spread out over several acres until it ran into a strip mall with the usual Chinese restaurant, a dry cleaners and a drug store anchored by a Hallmark card store and a few other shops Wallis had stopped noticing a long time ago. A bank sat awkwardly in the middle making it hard for cars to maneuver through the parking lot.

Norman picked up on the first ring.

"Hey, how's your day going?" she asked.

"Not bad. None of my clients are in jail or being indicted. Slow day," he said with a chuckle. "How was your repeat?"

"Exactly as you thought he would be except this time the missus played the same game on him. He wants to make sure she gets nothing and he already has another one lined up. It's amazing how he misses the irony."

"You could even tell him and he'd look at you like you were speaking a different language."

"Hey," said Wallis, softening her voice, "sorry about this morning."

"What about it?" asked Norman.

"About turning you down. It wasn't fair."

"It's one morning in years' worth of mornings. You get a pass every so often, Wallis. It's okay."

"I'm having trouble letting myself off the hook for anything."

"I've noticed. It's not normally a Jones trait. You don't usually try to carry the weight of the world, you know. You don't even cook."

"Hardy, har. You knew that going into this arrangement. My contributions are more of the world domination variety."

Norman laughed and Wallis felt her body relax.

"See? There you go," said Norman. "Making jokes about the end of life as we knew it. That's my girl. Look, Wallis, I've said it to you before. I had years to get over being born into some conspiracy that had me by the short hairs before I even knew it existed and I spent plenty of time arguing with my father about how it was all wrong. Remember, I'm the one they originally tagged as the Keeper."

"Fortunately, you had me to keep you from that post."

"Seriously. I have not thanked you enough. That will take years. Can't have the Keeper being married to Management's princess, even if she doesn't know she's really a kind of old world blue blood."

"You know, I made that big statement about the three of us working together but I still have no idea what that really means. I'm all talk."

"You're not supposed to come up with the plan all on your own, you know. It's amazing how much of this you're willing to take on. That's how Ned gets you. Hell, that's how Harriet gets you. I'd do it too but I'm the bigger person."

"Thank goodness you're such a decent person or I'd be lost," she said, meaning it as more than just a joke. "You have any big ideas?"

"As a matter of fact, I'm working on that," said Norman. "Come home and I'll fill you in. Get Chinese from across the way, okay?"

Norman hung up and knocked on the parish door. It wasn't long before Reverend Donald was pulling open the old wooden door to St. Stephen's Episcopal Church.

"Come on in," he said. "He's already here."

CHAPTER

9

"He was easy to find?"

"Not really. Esther helped me find him," said the pastor, referring to the bookstore owner who was one of the last of the original twenty and kept watch over Norman and especially his brother, Tom, the current Keeper. The bookstore had to be rebuilt after Oscar Newman blew it up coming closer to killing Esther Ackerman and Tom and finally doing away with the Keeper than all of Management had ever been able to do. He had only been seeking a little petty revenge and in the end had failed.

The new bookstore was almost as packed full of books as the first version but was a little more updated with a computer system. Norman and Tom had convinced the older couple to at least try.

Norman and Reverend Donald worked their way back to the small room where brides usually got ready before they walked down the aisle. The furniture was all heavy wood with faded red velvet and a little uncomfortable.

Sitting on the edge of an ornate bishop's chair with carvings of small birds all the way down the sides and across the back, sat Helmut Khroll, the journalist who had become a friend to them since everything had come out in the open, at least for Wallis. Just at the top of the chair, framing the top of Helmut's head, were two keys carved out of the wood. It was the mark of the saltire with the left key of absolution drawn over the right key of excommunication.

Helmut was a journeyman's kind of storyteller and Norman had suspected for a while that he was more tied to the Circle than he was saying. Helmut never appeared to work for one particular news organization and went in search of stories that uncovered whatever Management was trying to bury. Norman sometimes wondered how he managed to stay alive at all.

"That can't be comfortable," said Norman.

"Point out a place that would be in this entire room," said Helmut. "Why are we meeting here?"

"Because my secretary can't hear a thing if we sit in here," said the pastor. "And she thinks it's in her job description to listen in on all conversations. Why do you think I had you come in the side door? I'll walk you out the front just so she'll know she missed something."

"Helmut, why are you even in town? It seems a little too convenient. First, someone is watching our house," said Norman.

"No, has been watching your house. They've been there all along," said Helmut.

Norman felt the color drain from his face. "Why do I still get surprised?"

"I really don't know," said Helmut, in his heavy German accent. "The patrols have stepped up but that's no wonder. The war is getting worse."

"What war?" asked Norman, trying to not sound anxious as he noticed the pastor and Helmut look quickly back and forth at each other.

"Someone want to tell me what's going on? What did I miss?"

"I thought for sure you would have been filled in," said Helmut, not taking his eyes off of Reverend Donald. "After all, I made a point of telling the good Father everything I knew. And…"

"And, they deserved a little peace for as long as they could get it," interrupted Reverend Donald. "There was nothing they could do, anyway."

"What war?" asked Norman again, a little louder.

"The civil war that has broken out between Management and the Circle. It's mostly along the Canadian border right now but it's spreading and it's getting worse," said Helmut. "Come on, you didn't notice the uptick in gun violence?"

"I noticed but I didn't see the connections," said Norman. "What exactly are you trying to tell me? That as a country, we're at war, whether we all know it or not?"

"Yeah," said Helmut, "isn't it a kick in the head? Who even knew that one was possible? If I wrote about it no one would even believe me. I'd be the weird nut who doesn't think we ever landed on the moon, sort of thing. And yet, I've been to one of the Circle's base camps. We have nifty uniforms and everything."

"We?" asked Norman, "so you've officially joined a side? That's new."

"At least for now," said Helmut. "That could fluctuate. Dammit," he said, suddenly standing, "this chair is God-awful. Feels like it's going to attack at any moment. Why do you people keep putting out these things?" he said, starting to pace the room. "What the hell was this room designed for anyway?" he said, sweeping his arm around to take in all of the velvet-covered furnishings. "Did you get a donation from the Presley estate?"

Reverend Donald quietly took a seat across the room.

"We had to have some way to make sure everyone knew who was in charge, without saying so, of course," said Reverend Donald. "The Episcopalian way of doing things. Bold statements without saying a word."

"I realize that neither one of you really likes to come at something directly," said Norman, "but if you could for just a couple of minutes focus, I'd appreciate it. A war?"

"Yes, a war. A war and all that goes with it," said Helmut. "Come on,

Father Donald, chime in. You know more than I do. You're part of the mother ship after all."

"Mother ship?" asked Norman.

"Well, the Episcopal mother ship," said Helmut, "we all know they're pulling a lot of the Circle's strings, for better or worse."

"We all know?" asked Reverend Donald, not looking amused. "Don't start rumors, Helmut. Look, Norman, there's been no official declaration of war. How could there be? Where would we send it and there's no diplomats to recall. Somehow it all just kept escalating until we ended up here."

"When did it start?" asked Norman. "What, no one wants to speak? Why the reluctance?" he asked, looking at the two men. "No, it didn't," he said, suddenly realizing what must have triggered all of it. "No, he whispered, sitting down on the tight, red tufted leather of the bishop's chair. He realized that his own brother, Harry's betrayal to the Circle and then inability to deliver to Management what they wanted, the name of the Keeper or the outline of the Circle's plan to rebuild their numbers had led Management down a much darker path.

"Alright, I'll go," said Helmut, "since no one else wants to," he said, looking at Reverend Donald, who looked like he wanted to say something but thought better of it. "No? Okay, so, maybe it was Harry or maybe it was coincidence, who knows. Suddenly, a few good Circle operatives ended up dead and without any kind of provocation. Very against the rules, these days."

"Am I late to the meeting?" Esther Ackerman came haltingly into the room. She was wearing her favorite mauve wool coat with the faux fur collar. Snow was clinging to the tips of the fur.

"Is it snowing outside?" asked Norman.

"I was in Hanover County," she said, glancing at Reverend Donald. Norman watched how they seemed to be speaking to each other without really carrying on much of a conversation. He wasn't used to being left out.

"It's snowing a little out there but nothing to speak of," she said, gradually dropping the Eastern European accent Esther had been using for years to hide her real German background.

"You ever get confused and mash the two accents together, German and, what is that other one, Serbian?" asked Helmut, as Esther laughed and gave him a hard swat on his back.

"You are a devil, Helmut Khroll," she said, still laughing.

"And a fellow German, lest you forget with all of your play-acting," he said, winking.

Esther laughed again and sat back for a moment, closing her eyes and taking in a deep breath.

Age was finally catching up with her and she was moving more slowly these days. Norman hated to see it. She was like his second mother. Being in the middle of a bomb blast two years ago with Tom hadn't helped anything, either.

"How did you get in?" asked Reverend Donald.

"Don't worry, I know all about the extra eyes and ears about this place. I used my church key," she said, smiling, pulling out a common can opener from her pocket. "That and you left the side door slightly ajar. Hello Norman, good to see you still in one piece, my love," she said, offering her cheek for a kiss.

Norman got up and let Esther sit in the prominent chair. He stayed standing and leaned against a wall for support.

"Helmut was starting to tell me about the war we're all in and once again, I didn't know anything about. Does Tom know?" asked Norman.

"Of course Tom knows, dear," said Esther, cutting off Helmut before he could answer. "He would have had to give the orders to actually form our side."

"Of course he would," said Norman, giving the back of his head a careful pat, pat.

"But that's not really why we're all here," said Esther.

"I thought I called this meeting," said Norman, suddenly taking stock of everyone who was there. "Isn't that why we're all here?"

"No, dear. Another delightful coincidence. Really helped us to cover our tracks, so thank you," said Esther. "We were going to have to meet with you anyway. Isn't it wonderful how things sometimes work out? There's been an incident. Harry has been broken out."

Norman practically shouted, "What?" as Father Donald tried to wave at him to quiet down. "When? How? Who?"

"All good questions," said Esther. "Too bad we don't know the important answers. Some very well trained people broke in the same night that your friend, Alice Watkins was killed. We have to assume it was Management. Who else would care? The really good questions are, how did they know where to find him and what do they want with him? They can't possibly think we'd bargain all that much to get him back. Sorry, dear but it's the truth."

"I know that," said Norman, quietly. "And?"

"And, we haven't heard a thing since they took him. So, why bother? Then Alice Watkins is suddenly killed and after all this time. Again, why bother? I understand the little ferret, Rodney Parrish did the deed. He really doesn't do much without a payoff. We have to wonder if they're connected."

"I don't know that name," said Norman.

"Better that you don't," said Father Donald, "he's like a paid serial killer, frankly."

"What's the difference between that and the usual kind of paid assassin?" asked Helmut, sounding annoyed.

"He's been known to kill for free. Some would say, for fun," said Reverend Donald, fingering the small silver cross hanging at his side.

"How do you know him?" asked Norman, looking at his old friend.

"I hear things," said Reverend Donald, "and in this town it doesn't take long before Rodney Parrish's name comes up, somehow."

"I don't see it," said Norman, walking to the window to try and gather his thoughts.

"Alice knew the identity of the Keeper, your brother. Unfortunately, there are Management operatives in the Richmond police force and they have kept Rodney Parrish on their payroll."

"The rumor is they've even paid him off by letting him amuse himself with a few burglaries, his other love. Only Circle storeowners, of course," said Helmut.

"You see, this is why we never wanted anyone to know the identity of the Keeper. No loopholes. It causes all sorts of problems. But then, circumstances come up that no one expected and what are you going to do," said Esther.

"Well said," said Helmut. "Alice was a good old girl, though. She could be trusted. But that Parrish fellow is a little monster and it looks like Alice went down swinging. I don't believe she said anything."

"But we can't be sure," said Esther. "And if the Keeper is captured."

"Then all of hell breaks loose into the open," said Reverend Donald.

"Do you think that's why someone has set Harry free?" asked Norman.

"We don't know that he's free and I suspect he's not," said Esther. "He's merely changed prisons, most likely. And to answer your question, no, we don't know if it's all a coincidence or somehow connected."

"I vote for connected. Too odd," said Helmut.

"Really," said Esther, rolling her r's dramatically. Norman saw the strain in her face suddenly. He wondered just how bad things had gotten.

"So, now what?" asked Norman. "What exactly does this have to do with Wallis and Ned?" he asked, dreading the answer.

"It's not exactly a state secret anymore who Wallis is or how Ned is related to everyone," said Helmut. "We can't tell what Management is up to so we can't be sure what they'll do next."

"Are you saying Ned is in danger," asked Norman, walking to the door to leave. Helmut put his hand on the door, holding it shut.

"Not yet," said Helmut. "I would have come and gotten all of you myself, if I thought that was the case. But there's something afoot. That's why the Watchers are becoming more obvious. And, they may be trying to get us to show our hand. Panic and run somewhere."

"This is all crazy," said Norman.

"That's why we didn't include Wallis in this conversation, just yet," said Reverend Donald.

"That's not going to fly," said Norman. "You know how it turned out the last time I decided to keep something from her for her own good. I'm not on board."

"We don't have enough answers and it would only worry her further. I know she's struggling still with everything that happened," said the minister.

"You're not?" asked Norman. "I'm not doing this without her. I'm just telling you."

"We're getting off track," said Esther, in a stern voice. Norman went back to the window and looked out over the small memorial garden below.

"A unit has been sent to Montana to collect Tom," said Esther.

"Tom is coming to Richmond," said Norman. "He can stay with me."

"Not quite," said Esther, "that is too dangerous. Just moving him puts up a red flag, so now we have to follow through and hide him. And, I have a theory about Harry. I don't believe that was a general plot, to take him I mean. I have come to believe that there is a master cell operating independently within Management's ranks that is attempting a coup. In fact, I believe they have orchestrated all of this, including the war."

"What war, exactly?" asked Norman

"It's really quite simple," said Esther. "There's a Presidential election in just over a year and while the real power may sit behind all of the pomp and circumstance that passes for a two-party system in America." She stopped for a moment and seemed to get lost in thought.

"Esther?" asked Reverend Donald, but Esther gave him a curt wave.

"Let me finish, it's nothing. A small worry for me alone." She looked at Norman, and wagged her finger at him.

"You haven't done that to me since I told you who I was planning to marry," said Norman. He loved Esther and was reminded just how old she was getting to be these days.

She let out a short laugh and dropped her hand, smoothing out the wrinkles in her dress. Norman knew that Esther put on a dress, rain or shine, work or play. He preferred women who could be consistent. So much of his childhood had lacked that quality.

"You have always been a charmer, Norman Weiskopf. Even more than that brother, Tom. Really, the election is more of a show to keep the masses occupied and it does a lovely job of that. But whoever is President has a few extra perks, particularly for the Circle that aids our cause."

"The tunnels," said Father Donald, quietly.

"Yes, the tunnels being one of the main advantages, which Management is still largely unaware of, at least to their full extent. That and it's easier to move around the more traditional civilian armed guards if you're President, than if you're not."

"The National Guard is fighting on our side?" asked Norman.

"No, not really dear, at least not those members who aren't already in the Circle. But when they're called out to at least occupy a certain area, it makes it harder for Management battalions to pass through unnoticed, and they know it."

"So what does this have to do with starting an entire war?" asked Norman.

Esther hesitated and bit her lip.

"The election will most likely go to the sitting President, President Hayes. No matter what Management does, he will likely win. They seem to have already accepted this fact. But a super cell has not and they have decided to pick a rather large fight."

"Their real aim seems to be to upset the election," said Reverend Donald.

"Or something we just don't see yet," said Helmut.

"Yes, that's what worries all of us," said Esther.

"Not to sound cold, but why don't they just kill President Hayes?" asked Norman.

"Oh, they've tried," said Esther, "they've tried a few times, but unsuccessfully. We have always had several different layers in place to stay a step ahead of assassination plots. But you make a good point. Why start an entire war if all you really want, is one dead man?"

"Instability," said Helmut. "Instability of some kind," he said, vigorously scratching his head, the thick greying curls barely moving. "Any kind of widespread, unchecked violence would do and it would only really harm whoever was sitting in power."

"Besides the people who are killed in the war," said Norman, once again, patting the back of his head nervously.

"Yes, besides that," said Helmut. "That makes the next question, what is to be gained from the instability. Usually the two sides like a certain amount of calm, even if it's only on the surface. Why risk all of that? And I think I have the beginning of an answer. To form a different enemy, a new terrorist that the ninety-nine percent would be willing to start a real war with, a world war."

"Who are you nominating?" asked Father Donald.

"China," said Helmut.

"That's a long way to go with your theories," said Norman.

"Not really," said Esther, "if the super cell is only trying to extort something and doesn't want another world war as much as anyone else."

"An extortion plan? What could be worth that much for someone to go to that much trouble? What does America have, or even China that would cause all of this?" asked Norman.

"No, you're looking in the wrong direction," said Helmut. "But we're off topic. We are here to talk about how to protect Tom and to make you aware that Harry may pop up to ask for a favor or two."

Norman suddenly felt a little unsteady on his feet as Reverend Donald put a strong hand against his back. His stomach turned sour and he wondered if he was going to lose his breakfast on the old horsehair carpet. "My own brother. Stop, I know what you're going to say. If he does show up, someone sent him. It's more of some kind of plot. Good God," said Norman. He caught his reflection in the window as the sun was starting to set.

The garden outside was now covered in shadows. He was wearing the Richmond uniform for lawyers. A slightly starched white shirt with a bright blue tie, grey slacks with a slight cuff at the bottom. Norman didn't see any real advantage to standing out in a crowd. His family neatly pulled that off just by their unique heritage, anyway. He looked at the dark circles underneath his eyes and it only made him feel worse.

"Stop feeling sorry for yourself," said Esther. She had always been able to tell what he was thinking. "Self-pity does not look good on anyone. Besides, I have you by at least twenty years and I'm still swinging."

"That's a dame," Helmut whispered to Reverend Donald, gaining an appreciative look out of Esther.

"Norman, we find it necessary to pause, at least for the moment. Better to take stock than make some grave error. We are all here so that we can share the little bits of knowledge that we have and to stay watchful. Unfortunately, for the moment we must wait to see what this hidden hand inside of Management is up to. Until then, watch over your family. Tell Wallis, if you need to," she said, "because I know you will, anyway."

CHAPTER

"It's started again," whispered Wallis. She always found it difficult to speak too loudly in the sanctuary of a church. The older Baptist minister, Reverend Adler sat in the pew next to her, not saying anything. He was wearing his standard uniform of a clerical collar that seemed to perpetually rest against an oversized Adam's apple. He had his jacket draped across the pew between them and Wallis could see the small metal clasps that held his rabbat in place. Focusing on the smaller details was helping her to get the words out.

"Did you hear that Alice Watkins was murdered? Murdered," whispered Wallis. "Before two years ago I don't know that I knew anyone, personally that had been murdered. Now I'm not sure I can count them all on one hand."

Reverend Adler didn't answer. The lanky pastor stretched his legs till his long, narrow feet disappeared under the pew in front of them. His long, angled limbs were bent to fit on the worn wooden pew.

"Faith is what matters to me most and if it doesn't weave through everything then I'm not being authentic and that will show through. And I need to walk the walk no matter what. However, this story of legacy, mission, purpose. I am in a unique position to talk about it or at least get people's attention. Frankly, I identify more with my mother's more humble roots and that's how I see myself. I don't know. I feel like I'm rambling. It's hard to get a clear thought."

"What are you trying to tell people, Wallis?"

"My message is that who someone is and what they have to offer counts," she said, slapping the wooden seat. "Actions count more when added up than the grand gestures. I have seen that in my own life and it's what makes it possible to create the kind of changes we all long for, one step at a time."

There was a hum from the slowly moving fans overhead. Wallis looked up at the familiar stained glass windows on the near side of the church in a stack of different sized rectangles. A local craftsman who had attended the Baptist church years ago had done all of the work. This was the church that Wallis had attended with her parents at Easter and Christmas and then all summer long when Harriet had dropped Wallis off at bible camp. Reverend Adler had been the pastor the entire time but was getting close to retirement.

"Those are all great ideas, Wallis, but without any kind of plan of action I've found that great ideas tend not to go anywhere."

Wallis looked down at her lap. It wasn't like her to be so unsure of what to do next. She had always had a plan in life. She knew she wanted to be a family court attorney, what kind of husband she was looking for and how life ought to look in general.

"None of my great ideas are working out," she said, barely above a whisper. "It's getting a little tough to keep making plans."

"Maybe that's because they're your plans."

"Didn't you just say, make a plan?" she asked, trying not to sound annoyed.

Reverend Adler sat up straighter and stretched his arms over his head before leaning forward, resting his elbows on his knees.

"It's like the simplest of concepts that is near impossible for most of us mere mortals to grasp. And when we do it's like a firefly in a bottle. Just a little bit of light that won't last if we don't just let it go."

"I'm not following at all," said Wallis.

"I know but keep listening. Some of this is bound to sink in. I've known you since you were born. You're stubborn but you go after something until you finally let go and it all comes together."

Wallis felt a smile creep across her face despite the low-level of anxiety that she was normally feeling lately.

"Look, for most people, God is fire insurance. They want to stay out of hell. They're willing to be nice to their neighbors, pay their taxes or at least most of them and not honk too much in traffic. They're good people. But when it comes to life in general, the plans for life, they're not willing to let go of how it ought to look. Wait right there, no interruptions," he said to her, making a little steeple with his long fingers.

Wallis had seen him make this gesture her entire life. It was always right before he was going to say something that she was sure she should write down and just carry in her pocket. Like a fortune out of a cookie but something that might actually be useful.

There was a faded strip of paper taped to her bedroom mirror that had scribbled on it, 'set the truth free, let it do its own work' in faded blue ink. Those words had saved her marriage at its darkest point two years ago.

Wallis had shown up at the church that night after finding out what Norman had kept from her because for the first time since she had met him, she wasn't sure she could stay. That had scared her almost as much as having a gun waved at her son. Church had been more of a convenience to her, especially after her father died. But she had been desperate to figure out how to forgive Norman.

"It's not the making of the plan that's the problem. Those are necessary. How do you drive to Asheville, North Carolina if you don't get a map? Love Asheville, have grandchildren there." He glanced at Wallis who tried to look patient. The pastor let out a small grunt.

"The problem starts almost immediately after that when we decide that the route we came up with is now the only route that's possible. If the road has been washed out we stand there and cry about it or shake our fist and then demand that the road be rebuilt. It doesn't seem to occur to us that the plan will have to change."

"I actually understood that but I'm not getting how it applies to this particular situation."

Reverend Adler raised a bushy eyebrow, which made him look twice as indignant.

"Okay, okay, I'll sit here quietly." It was somehow comforting to have someone so calm insisting on manners. Southerners, when confronted with chaos often start with manners to sort out what to do next.

"You have had a remarkable run of setting a plan in motion and then watching them all take place. Where you wanted to go to school, when you wanted to get married, what you wanted to be in life. I know your nickname among some of the less self-assured lawyers in town is Black Widow and I know you hate that name, as you should. But I'd venture to guess that you also took a certain amount of reassurance from it. Yet, one more sign that you knew what you were doing. That was your mistake, right there."

Reverend Adler sat back and shut his eyes for a moment. This was a standard part of his counseling as well and Wallis found it frustrating but knew she had pushed things far enough. She sat quietly and waited for him to start again, trying not to think about getting home and checking on Ned. That had become important to her lately, even if Ned found it to be just one more example of bad parenting.

"You made a plan and expected everyone to go along with it. After all, you're an educated, sound and reasonable person who generally thinks well of everyone, right?" The eyebrow shot up again as he steadied his gaze at Wallis. "And then, suddenly no one was listening and life kept on rolling forward, fair or not fair. Things started moving so fast there probably wasn't time to even make a plan. But then you thought the genie was back in the bottle and it was just a particularly bad wrinkle. You missed the point, Wallis. Life was never yours to design, just to be a part of with everyone else. You make a plan, include others and then take the step in front of you knowing full well, everything is open to change because you're not in charge. God's in charge. Like I said, very simple concept, difficult for us to just do but in that nugget lies a peaceful life."

"Not if people are shooting around you."

"Ha, that's a good one. But not true, dear, not true. Okay, time to go," said the pastor, suddenly standing up to his full height, well over Wallis' head. "The missus will have dinner waiting for me and you've got enough to chew on for now."

"When do I come back?" asked Wallis.

"I'm inclined to say Sunday would be a good starting place but short of that, let's just say, you'll know when the time is right. In the meantime, let everyone you love off the hook. Work on a little humility."

"You didn't really tell me how to deal with the Watchers," said Wallis.

"Actually, I did," said the pastor, as he held open the glossy red door.

Wallis picked up Ned from his friend, Paul's house. Wallis had handled the divorce when Paul's mother Sharon had finally gotten a divorce from her husband, David Whittaker.

Ned waved goodbye to Sharon, who came out to the front hall, wiping her hands on a kitchen towel.

"See you at Bunco later?" she asked Wallis. Ned brushed past her without a word and headed for the car.

"I'll be there," said Wallis. "It was my turn to pick up the prizes. Have to get him home to dinner first. Better run."

"Sure," said Sharon, "Hey, Paul is the same way with me. It's just a phase. Rumor is that it'll pass in about ten more years," she said, laughing.

The drive home was quiet but Ned had sat up front next to Wallis. She took that as a good sign.

"You have much homework?" she asked.

"No, and it's already done," he said, not looking at her. "I think I'll move my stuff tonight."

"Okay. You need help?"

"Dad can help me. You have Bunco."

Wallis felt a twinge and wondered if he had picked tonight because he knew she'd be out.

"It's nice to have a few minutes alone with you." She knew she was fishing for some kind of reaction. Something she would never do in court.

"Okay," said Ned, as he pulled out a book. Let everyone off the hook, she thought, as she let the silence fall between them the rest of the ride home.

Later in the kitchen she watched Ned relax more around his father. Wallis stayed in the kitchen after Ned went upstairs to start carting his things to the small bedroom at the top of the house.

"You don't normally stick around to watch me wash dishes," said Norman. "Something up?"

"I want to tell you but I've been told to mind my own business."

"Interesting. Tell me anyway."

"Ned can't stand to be around me. He tolerates being in the same room with me."

"He does the same things to me. He just saves it for when you're not around. He's a genius, you know. If he did it in front of someone else, we'd realize it's him, not us," said Norman, smiling as he stacked the plates back in the cupboard. "It's psychological warfare at its best."

"It's so painful, I find myself thinking about being nicer to Harriet."

Norman stopped what he was doing and came over to sit by Wallis at the kitchen table, flinging the damp, yellow dish towel over his shoulder.

He scooted his chair over till the yellow pine was touching Wallis' chair and he took her hands into his. "We're a team, Ned's a kid. Worse, he's a tween with a genius IQ. We're outgunned. But, we're still a team."

"Norman," Wallis whispered, "I really do love you."

"I know," said Norman.

"No, listen to what I'm saying. I get it even if I'm struggling right now." Wallis took in a deep breath and let it out slowly to give herself a chance to think for a moment. "I am unsure of everything right now. Every little detail. And for some reason I want to be right."

"That's understandable," said Norman, giving her hands a little squeeze. "You're singlehandedly trying to keep us all out of harm's way and you know it can't be done. It's driving you crazy. Ask me how I know that."

"Because you lived it too," said Wallis. She took in a deep breath.

"Still live it. My brother is the Keeper," he whispered, "and the other one is off the ranch, which brings me to tonight's things I have to tell you that you won't like."

"What?" asked Wallis, pulling her hands out of his grasp and sitting back in her chair. "Is it bad? Is someone dead?"

"Whoa, whoa, come on. Not dead bad but close," said Norman, giving a soft, pat pat to the back of his head. "Someone broke Harry out of his expensive, cushy prison of one."

"Do you know who?"

"There are ideas floating around but that's all it is. I got hoodwinked into a surprise meeting with Reverend Donald, Helmut and Esther this afternoon."

"That can't be good. The posse was rounded up," said Wallis.

"And, there's more."

Norman got up and started pacing the kitchen. "Apparently, a war has been let loose by Management. Not a typical war, although I'm not sure I know what a typical war is supposed to look like. No actual declaration." He stopped pacing and sat back down. "Did you realize there was some kind of war?"

"I knew there was a lot more people with guns randomly shooting up things but I thought it was some kind of trend. I don't know, when I say it out loud that doesn't make sense. Who said it was a war? Who is fighting who?"

"You always do ask the best questions. Apparently, the Circle is fighting a super cell within Management that has managed to get us to shoot back. There are even uniforms and regiments and ranks. I missed it all, which is a blessing in a lot of ways."

"Tom knew, didn't he?"

Norman let out a snort. "You are smarter than I am. I thought at first I'd have to tell Tom, till Esther reminded me that he would have to be the one to start the whole thing. My brother started a war. While sitting in Wisconsin. My hippie brother."

"Fortunately, I'm in on the whole conspiracy juggernaut or I'd be wondering right about now," said Wallis. "But why start a war? Surely, Management can't think they can just take over the country even if they can't win an election."

"How did you manage to catch onto all of this so quickly? I had to have it explained," said Norman.

Wallis laughed and folded her arms in so that she could lean into the curve of Norman's chest. He wrapped his arms around her and pulled Wallis into his lap. "How do you go grocery shopping for Cocoa Puffs and look out for your crazy brother who may be part of a plot to take over the country, all at the same time?" asked Norman.

"Apparently, you just do," said Wallis.

CHAPTER 11

Forty-five steps from the last tunnel till he reached the small, side room. Heel, toe, heel, toe. Nothing in the protocol to attend a meeting at the White House had changed in the three years he had been carrying out his orders except the meeting room. Fred Bowers still had to take the same precautions to hide his real initiative within the Circle. He was crossing through one of the oldest and largest underground tunnels lined with large clay bricks that cut from the Hay-Adams hotel toward the White House. They had originally been constructed for different purposes but now served as a useful way for people who didn't care to have their movements tracked, move around nearly two square miles of Washington, all underground and out of sight.

Both Management and the Circle were aware of the existence of the system of tunnels. Most of Washington not only knew of their existence but had seen parts of some of them. It was a mark of how important a Congressman was if he'd been able to take a few friends at least part of the way down the tunnel whose entrance lay the closest to the old swimming pool that was now covered over and was being used as a drafty holding pen for the press corps.

The Secret Service took naps on cots in the tunnel that was closest to the East Wing during State dinners. Usually, it was the large rats who also lived down there that would wake them up in time for their shift by running across the cot. But there was another tunnel.

Often, the underdog in any fight will look for ways to get around the more massive, violent machinery. The Circle had done the same and quietly created another tunnel that had proved useful many times. Halfway between what was known as the Hay-Adams tunnel and the White House, there was a smaller side tunnel that led to St. John's Episcopal Church. The church was a sanctuary, like most of the Episcopal Church, for the Circle as a means to keep Management's power in check and to act as a spiritual sounding board for Circle operatives.

No one in Management even knew of the last tunnel's existence. The sitting President determined who had use of the tunnels and for now it was the Circle's opportunity, which meant the Bishop kept the side tunnel open. If things were to suddenly change the tunnel would be walled off so expertly no one would ever suspect its existence. The tunnel would be ignored and wait for a better time.

For now, it was a way for Fred Bowers to still meet with President Hayes.

It was becoming more difficult for Fred to make the entire journey to the upper floors of the White House. Since the start of the war there had been a few attempts on the President's life that the Circle had managed to keep out of the press. No one in Congress or the Senate even knew about the incidents. So far, only the potential assassins had met with violence.

But Fred's role as a mole within the Circle who served only the top cell while being able to mix among crowds, all while going unnoticed, was too valuable. Fred was more valuable than even the President's life, and too valuable to risk someone seeing him so close to anyone that important.

Other Circle operatives saw him as a low-level flunkie who couldn't be trusted with anything of importance. Management saw him as so useless he wasn't worth following.

He had carefully crafted a persona as a constant worrier, a rule follower who worked in downtown Richmond at the James Center as a forensic accountant and was married to Maureen Bowers, his college sweetheart. All of it was created years ago. Even Maureen didn't know Fred's real backstory and he didn't know hers. They were both trained to never ask each other those kind of questions.

No one but the top cell in the Circle knew that Maureen was an operative as well. This year they would celebrate their twentieth wedding anniversary since an advisor had arranged the entire thing and copywriters had supplied them with their life stories. She was coming with him to visit the President this time.

They had been married by the Bishop of Virginia at St. James Episcopal Church, the year before the fire that took out the steeple. Quick thinking saved the old Tiffany windows along one side.

Fred often told a story about how his father, who had grown up in the Fan district that surrounded the church would play stickball on Franklin Street, just in front where the street began to narrow. One day in the 1930's while playing against a group of kids from a poor section of Shockoe Bottom, the ball had gone flying through one of those famed, priceless Tiffany windows. The other team, which was all black, had fled, knowing their fate would be far worse even if they had nothing to do with what happened.

This was the part where Fred would always choke up a little as he said, his father got everyone on his team to take the fall because it was the right thing to do. That they had to pay a dollar a week, an enormous sum of money in the 1930's to the church treasurer, all summer long to learn their lesson.

Fred would slow down at this part as he described how his father would say they'd have to climb the large, spiral staircase with the beautiful, wide oak railing to hand in their dollar. He'd always finish by saying, "My dad said it was worth it. Best money he ever spent."

Fred would point out that he grew up in Northern Virginia but most of his family had since scattered. They had come to Richmond years ago for a slower pace. Fred's father had apparently died years ago, and even had a headstone with his name on it in Hollywood Cemetery where all of old

Richmond was buried.

It was all a lie, except for the headstone, which marked the grave of an unknown homeless man who had died from acute liver disease behind the Food Lion on Patterson Avenue. The coroner was a Circle member and had called as soon as the body had been processed. No one would know one less body had been planted in the potter's field in the far reaches of Henrico County.

Fred had a few other stories that all centered around the church and his father that he loved to tell. There was no one left alive who could verify whether or not he was telling the truth and the fire that happened not too long after his wedding destroyed any records. It was all very convenient.

He wrote a large check to help with the rebuilding.

No one ever seemed to notice how little he talked about himself or his own childhood, or didn't care. But Fred knew it was important to Southerners to find a connection. They tended to trust someone outright if they thought there was a common thread of shared traditions that at least originated on Southern soil even if that was all there was to it.

The couple quietly got in the car and settled in as they pulled out of their driveway. Maureen smiled and waved at a neighbor, and turned to look lovingly at her husband. They both knew the small details mattered and this was touted to their friends as a second honeymoon. Besides they rarely took trips together.

Maureen was traveling with Fred this weekend as cover.

This time, though the President had asked to speak with Maureen, in person. If it had been anyone else who was asking but the President, the request would have been immediately turned down. There were too many risks, no matter how slight and there was a war going on, besides the recent assassination attempts on President Hayes.

But even if he was more of a figurehead than an American President with all of the powers that everyone thought went with the office, he was still a formidable figure who could demand something and expect everyone to listen.

They would be staying as usual at the Hay-Adams hotel directly across from the northern side of the White House. Maureen had let it be known at Bunco night with her friends and that the anniversary trip was a gift from Fred.

Finally, after twenty years, they would be spending the entire weekend using the spa inside the hotel and shopping along M Street in Georgetown. It was already on their schedule to stop and gather enough trinkets on their way out of town to make it all more plausible.

Maureen planned to pick up a few small things for Bunco prizes when the women gathered to play the next time. It would cement the story in everyone's mind. It was always the small details that made a story work and become a truth for everyone else.

Their hotel room had a clear view of the White House. Fred had requested it, saying they had stayed there when they were first married and they were coming this weekend to celebrate their anniversary.

The room selection was really just more protocol. Circle members who were assigned to protect the Bowers when they were in Washington would be able to see them remotely and protect them without having to get close enough to be spotted. It would mean leaving the curtains open just far enough at all times but Maureen had learned a long time ago to let go of any sense of real privacy. Her life had not been her own since she had agreed to a life perpetually undercover.

The room was decorated with fresh flowers and champagne. Someone at the hotel had decided to help the celebration get going.

"I plan to open this later," Maureen said, smiling at Fred.

"We have to be ready for a plan change," said Fred, grimacing.

"I know you're not a big fan of change, at all," said Maureen. "But we can mix in a little fun without giving away the Republic. Twenty years and you can't trust that I won't do something stupid. We really are an old married couple," she sighed, sounding annoyed.

A small smile came across Fred's face. The past two years were different for the couple. The murder of people right around them had seemed more personal, even if they weren't the first deaths they had seen in the field. They were innocent neighbors who over the years had become friends and had had the bad luck to get caught in the crossfire. Fred knew that Maureen had taken the death of Yvette Campbell, one of the Bunco ladies, particularly hard even if she never spoke about it.

He had held her hand as they sat quietly out on their back porch, and he had pushed her out the door to go to play with the ladies who had at first been her assignment but were now her friends. Watching her struggle to be a good agent while mourning the loss of her friend softened Fred despite all of his training.

It was not a good idea, given their real intention for everything they did in life, to start to care so much about anyone else's well-being. It had crept up on him anyway.

If he had been asked directly, he would have even had a hard time denying he was actually glad to have his wife along on the trip. She was the only person he could think of in this world who would appreciate what this life was like for him without any kind of explanation.

Everyone needed someone like that in their corner. Fred never let himself think about what it would be like if something happened to Maureen or the powers that be within the Circle did something as simple as reassign one of them. After all of these years that was still a possibility, especially given the war.

Fred was a little concerned that Maureen was told to accompany him so that the President could break that very news to both of them and soften the blow. He couldn't bring himself to suggest it to Maureen.

"Okay, you have a point. And, yes, we really are an old married couple, even if it's in service to our country," he said, grabbing Maureen around the waist and pulling her in closer. "Isn't that what most mothers tell their daughters anyway? Lie back and think of God and country? We just get paid to do the same thing."

"Then let's try out this room and our patriotism before we have to leave to meet the President."

"I was thinking of taking a short nap," said Fred, as he kissed Maureen's neck. "But I'm fairly certain you outrank me."

"And an order's an order," said Maureen, unbuckling his pants.

"An order's an order, ma'am," said Fred, as he kissed his wife of twenty years. He put the thought of a forced separation out of his mind and held his wife.

"Oh, you are a very good rule follower, Fred Bowers, if that's your real name," said Maureen. He laughed as they laid back on the bed and celebrated twenty years of being partners.

Later, they ordered dinner from room service and made a point of choosing from the menu what would pass for a romantic dinner. Both of them were wearing robes when the waiter came to the door and Fred tipped him heavily, in cash, setting the scene for the waiter to remember if anyone ever asked him for details later.

After the waiter left, they quickly got dressed and headed down to the basement using the elevator. From there, they found their way to the tunnels and quickly made their way to the door that opened to the St. John's tunnel.

The vestibule sat just behind the sanctuary and was designed for ministers who were about to walk out to the front of the church and address their flock.

"Good evening Mr. and Mrs. Bowers," said the President. He was already waiting for them, sitting on one of the small wooden chairs that was hastily pulled from a Sunday school room down the hall.

"Good evening Mr. President," said Fred. He grabbed his wife's hand for a moment and gave it a squeeze. He was reassuring his wife just in case they were here to find out their mission together was over. He wanted to tell her everything would be okay.

Maureen gave him a look and let out her breath. Fred knew she had been wondering the same thing.

"Have a seat," said the President, waving them toward two more small chairs. "This was all we could find without more digging and we'd prefer to get this over with quickly," he said glancing back at the Secret Service agents who were also part of the Circle. "No one's too happy that I insisted on meeting the two of you in person."

Maureen and Fred exchanged a quick glance.

"I'm glad I finally get to meet Mrs. Bowers," said the President, offering his hand to shake.

"It's an honor, Sir," said Maureen, giving the President' hand a firm shake.

"Fred's pictures don't really do you justice," said the President. Maureen's eyes widened a little.

"It's probably the dark lighting in here," said Maureen. President Hayes let out a small laugh.

"You're a very lucky man," he said to Fred. "A twenty year assignment with someone else could have felt like a prison sentence."

Fred braced himself for what was coming next.

"For once, Fred, I know something before you do," said the President. "Harry Weiskopf has been removed from where we were holding him. All of the Circle operatives who were guarding him were murdered. Even worse than not knowing where Weiskopf is now, is we can't get a good idea of what use he would be to anyone."

Fred sat back a little in the small chair.

"This is not good," said President Hayes. "And it happened in almost the same timeframe as the murder of Alice Watkins. Perhaps you remember that name?" he asked. Both of the Bowers gave a small nod.

"Well, Alice knew the identity of the real Keeper, Harry's brother, Tom. A mistake that couldn't be helped, I suppose," said the President as he wearily rubbed his face. "The scene of the crime was almost pristine but her body told a different story. I've been informed that it looked like she put up quite a fight but in the end was most likely tortured. We have no way of knowing what she said but the next incident seems to say something. Harry Weiskopf was a useless human being except for two things and both of those are his brothers."

The President raised his hand as if to stop the Bowers from saying anything but they were both waiting for the rest of the story that would contain their new orders.

"Management must think we've gone soft," said President Hayes. "Like we'd risk thousands and thousands of lives in order to save one or two. I'm afraid that for us, that's not how it works. I suppose they've bought their own ideas of the good life so much they really do believe that a certain amount of mayhem is worthwhile if you can give a guarantee of the good life to just enough people." The President slapped his knee. "Enough, I'm giving a speech. Bad habit. Here's the deal."

Fred slowly balled his hand into a fist to withstand the blow and not show it on his face.

"We believe that Wallis Jones is actually the target. We need Maureen to start spending time with her to learn why they would want Wallis Jones at all."

"What?" asked Fred.

"You look surprised, Fred," said the President, giving Fred a hard tap on the shoulder. "Little surprised to find out you're not the super spy we needed this time? I'm afraid you were just the driver. We needed you to come along in order to hide our meeting with Maureen. These guys," said the President, gesturing to the two guards who stood resolute behind him, "were sure this could be handled through the usual channels. Here's the deal. Lately, everyone who hangs out with Wallis Jones for any length of time ends up dead. This mission has a high likelihood of ending up the same way. You two have served our cause and have been of great service to all of us without a complaint. Frankly, I'm not sure I could have done the same. I wanted to thank you for your service in person while a meeting was still doable at all.

The President slowly rose out of the small chair and stretched his legs. "Not as young as I used to be. Seems like I can't stand up without a good grunt to get me going," he said with a laugh. "Hand it over," he said to the agent just behind his shoulder.

The agent reached into the pouch at his feet and pulled out two rectangular black velvet boxes. The President opened them to reveal a silver key in each box. It was the highest award for service that the Circle could award anyone.

"Maureen Bowers, Fred Bowers, this medal is being given to you in recognition of twenty years of service to your country, to the Circle and to the protection of true freedom." The President handed each of them a box and shook their hand.

"Unfortunately, not only is this ceremony a little underwhelming with a lack of family, friends or even colleagues but we can't let you keep those medals in your possession, either. No, go ahead, take a good look. Hold them in your hand and see how heavy they are. That's probably brass and not silver underneath. There's a war on, after all. But understand that the sentiment is not only real but doesn't begin to convey how valuable the two of you have been to the simple idea of choice for all Americans. A humble nation is very grateful."

The President turned to an agent who was already holding up his coat and helping him into the sleeves. Fred still didn't move as Maureen gently took the box from him and handed both of them back to an agent.

"Fred, I think you actually look surprised," said the President, smiling broadly. "I never thought I'd see the day that could happen or even better, that you'd show it. Times are changing I suppose or maybe we're all just getting older, who knows. A damn war can change a lot."

Maureen put on her coat but Fred still sat there, waiting for what he was sure would get mentioned as an afterthought.

"Time to go, Fred," Maureen said gently.

"Listen to your wife," said the President, "she outranks you. Did you think there was more? No, no cake this time. It wasn't in the budget."

The agents quickly escorted the President into the tunnel as the Bowers watched them fade into the darkness. None of the tunnels were ever lit by anything more than a flashlight.

"You thought there would be more?" asked Maureen, waiting for Fred to finally button his coat so they could leave the church.

"I thought they were splitting us up," said Fred.

"Not this time. Come on," said Maureen, offering her hand. "Let's go. We can hold hands the entire way back and take our time. After all, it's our anniversary."

"A romantic walk through a dark tunnel."

"With a few dozen rats," said Maureen.

"If only your Bunco friends could see you now."

"They'd down a glass of wine and ask for details. They're good friends even if they won't ever get the chance to really know me."

Fred took Maureen's hand and gave it a tight squeeze. He leaned in and kissed his wife.

"Let's go. Maybe we can microwave that dinner in our room."

CHAPTER

It was Saturday and Wallis had signed Ned up for a kind of tween-sized survivor course that took up every Saturday morning for eight weeks. Ned was going to get the chance to climb walls, bike over rough terrain and kayak in the James River.

Wallis had come up with it as a way to try and combat his nightmares and maybe even break through the wall of silence that seemed to surround him these days.

Earlier in the year she had tried ballroom dancing and cotillion as a way to help him connect with at least his grandmother's past. Norman had rolled his eyes at the suggestion when she showed him the invitation. The entire thing was by invitation only and it was because Harriet had danced in the same group over fifty years ago that Ned was even invited.

It was clearly a Management feeder group but Wallis didn't care just this once. Too many of Ned's friends were signed up and she wanted him to feel a part of something.

The dances were held once a week at the Richmond Women's Club building on Franklin Street. The mothers who got there early enough and wanted to stay for the two hour lessons on dancing and manners could watch from an upstairs balcony. Wallis always stayed. A handful of the women from Bunco night were up there and it gave her a chance to gossip about nothing while watching Ned interact with his friends, and more importantly, girls.

The instructor was an older man who looked well over six feet with dark, wavy hair who tended to dance with the taller girls in the group. They towered over the boys their own age and Wallis could see the look of relief on their face when they got a chance to dance with Mr. Louie. It made her like the man just a little even if he was always snapping little instructions at the children.

He had an assistant, Mrs. Parker who helped him go around the room while the children were dancing and correct their moves. It just made everything seem more awkward.

Ned had done everything that was asked of him down to introducing himself to every partner. He seemed to at least be having a half-way decent time of it and kept earning the weekly red ribbons for being a gentleman but Wallis knew better.

After the stop for ice cream or a burger with the other kids and their mothers at a local Red Robin was over, Ned would stop talking and sit sullenly in the back seat, staring out the window.

He would answer if Wallis asked a direct question but only in short syllables. She was glad he seemed to be having a good time when he was with the other kids but sometimes she felt desperate to reach him for just a minute.

She wanted to see a piece of the Ned she had known before Oscar Newman had broken into their house and died on their floor.

She wanted to know why Ned blamed her for so much of what had happened but she knew better than to try and get Ned to prop up her feelings.

Besides, he was already complaining enough about everything she said to him. No need to actually hand him some ammunition.

There was still the holiday dance to go before the cotillion year was officially ended. That was when the boys were expected to wear a little tux and the girls came in formal dresses with small nosegays made up of rosebuds. The parents would get to dance with their children and there would be a live band. Wallis was hoping that Norman's presence would help lighten the entire mood and maybe they could have fun as a family for one night.

In the meantime, there was the extreme sports course to get through. Ned had already been to two of them and after the last one had gotten in the car and announced how much he hated all of it. The rock climbing wall had scared him so much that so far all he had been able to do was climb his height of just over five and a half feet before he panicked and came back down again.

When he got in the car last Saturday he had buckled himself in and quickly pronounced, "I hate you," and then turned toward the window and refused to say another word. When they got home he had hurried out of the car and run up to his room. Wallis had to call the instructor to find out the other kids had made fun of him when he had once again stopped and scrambled back down to the ground.

Ned tried to argue with Wallis about ever going again and even resorted to first bargaining about how much better he would be around the house and then looking to Norman to back him up and let him out of the whole thing.

"Sorry, buster. You're going. It's a good idea. Both your mother and I think so."

Ned had stomped out of the kitchen and gotten in the back seat of the car. Wallis heard the door slam from the kitchen.

"Sorry," said Norman. "I'd drive him but I have to check on something, I'm sure of it. The grass maybe? Walk Joe?"

"Very funny. It's okay, this was my big idea. I'll face the music."

"That's appropriate since this all feels like you're facing a very angry firing squad."

"I just want him to stop being afraid of everything. You've seen it, haven't you? He checks the doors at night to make sure they're locked and he carries his cell phone with him everywhere. I never see him on it but he makes sure he has it. He didn't use to be that way."

"He didn't use to be a teenager either. Okay, okay, some of this is from the shooting. Maybe a lot of it. But just as much is hormones combined with you trying to fix the situation. Did it ever occur to you to just let him be miserable for a while?"

Wallis didn't look up as she tried to find her keys and hurried around the kitchen looking for her phone.

"Frankly, no, and that's not like me either. Geez, I'm exhausting myself. I can't let go of this idea that people are always watching us."

"And we're not even celebrities."

"Why jokes, Norman? Is this really the best time for jokes?"

"Wow, okay, you really are wound up. Have you eaten anything?"

"I'm sorry," said Wallis, "that wasn't fair."

"What are you trying to find? Can you ask for some help?" he said in a gentle voice.

Wallis stopped in the middle of the kitchen and looked at him. "Apparently not. If it makes you feel any better, Laurel pointed out the same thing but not in such a nice way."

"I give Laurel cash on the side."

"Back to jokes."

"Sorry, I joke when my wife is testy. Reflex. What are you looking for?"

"My keys, I can't find them."

"Well, that explains why Ned palmed them on his way out the door. How did you think he could slam the car door so well? Maybe you're right. He might be mad at you but I still say it's because you have the unlucky job of being the mother to a teenager."

"It actually makes me feel better that he's actively trying to get me back for something. At least he's thinking. I was more worried when I thought he was going along with all of my ideas and just suffering."

"Spoken like you belong to this family. Pick up bagels on your way home. You and I can have something to eat while our child engages in things that are good for him that he will tell all his friends proves how stupid we are and even cost us lots of money."

"I look forward to that," said Wallis as she rushed out the door. Ned was in the back seat of the car, his usual spot when he was angry, and the car radio was blasting a song Wallis didn't recognize that she was pretty sure would still be unintelligible even if the volume was more reasonable.

"I should make Harriet drive him," Wallis said, as she opened the door and leaned in to first turn down the music.

"I was listening to that," said Ned, sounding hurt.

"And you're still listening to that," said Wallis, as she started the car, "just not at the same volume."

They drove in silence to Pump Road but Wallis noticed that Ned seemed to be choking down words.

"Your roots are showing, you know," he said, looking at her reflection in the rear view mirror.

Wallis glanced in the mirror above her visor. "You're right," she said, ducking her chin down to get a better view. "Thank you for pointing out the grey." Wallis' hair was a varying shade of auburn depending on how things turned out at the hair salon. But the roots showed that lately her real hair color was becoming white and bypassing grey altogether, despite what she had said.

Her hairdresser had said it was a sign of stress or poor nutrition.

"You used to take better care of yourself," said Ned, still looking directly at her reflection and breathing harder.

Wallis felt a pain in her chest watching how angry Ned was, without knowing what was really causing all of it beyond what they had gone through when he was younger.

"Ned, I can see that you're not very happy with me right now but I'm not going to start defending myself to you. We're not in a debate about whether or not I'm a good person."

Ned's breathing had picked up till he was practically hyperventilating.

"If you want to talk to me about something, I'd love to hear it but I'm not going to be your punching bag."

Ned seemed to crack open.

"It's all your fault," he yelled. "All of it." Tears were pouring down his face, startling Wallis. She pulled the car over to the side of the road and put it in park so she could turn around and face Ned.

"What is? What's my fault?"

"Who we are, you did this to us. I know about everything, all of it," he yelled so loudly, it came out in a growl. "I know who we are."

Wallis felt the blood rush to her face. "What do you mean?" she asked, holding her breath.

"We're part of that group that killed Mr. Blazney. We're one of them," he shouted. His nose was starting to run.

"No, no, we're not. We're not at all."

"Liar! Liar!" he screamed, his voice cracking as he strained against his seat belt toward her. "Our family started the whole thing. We are the bad guys."

Wallis had to press her nails into her palm to stop herself from crying. Ned hung his head and loud sobs came out of him as his body shook. Wallis got up on her knees on the seat and leaned across the back so she could rest her arms on his shoulders. Ned tried to shake her off but she held on tight, crawling over the seat till she was next to him, holding him tightly.

"We're not, Ned, we're not the bad guys. Bloodlines don't make you the bad guys. An accident of birth can't make you good or bad. It doesn't work that way, no matter what anyone says."

Ned stopped trying to pull away from her and his weight came to rest against Wallis' chest as she pulled him closer. He was still crying, his body shaking.

"Everybody gets to decide for themselves who they are, no matter what family they're born into. You can decide for yourself who you are, no matter what your dad or I think about what you should be. We have ideas but in the end, we want you to be happy." Wallis couldn't hold the tears back anymore. She tasted the salt as she leaned her cheek against Ned's hair.

"That's all I want, Ned. For you to be happy. I really don't care about the details. I trust you and I figure those will be alright if you're happy."

"Kids at school said I have no choice. Destiny is destiny," said Ned.

"Destiny is the excuse people use when they are afraid to just trust people a little and see what happens. I make you a promise, Ned. I'm afraid but I trust that everything will be okay and I'm going to do my best to act like that."

Ned had stopped crying and had curled up against his mother, wiping his nose on his sleeve.

"I know I haven't done the best job of being confident lately, Ned but that's going to change. Let me tell you a little something that a very wise old woman told me recently. Either God is nothing or God is everything."

"Was that Alice?"

"Yes, that was Alice Watkins." Wallis leaned back so she could see Ned's face. She smiled as she wiped the tears off of his cheek. "Alice was quite a broad, wasn't she?"

Ned nodded.

"And she definitely wouldn't want us to walk around with our heads down. She'd be yelling at us right now if she knew. Can't you just hear her?" asked Wallis.

"Mom, did she suffer? When she died, did she suffer?"

"Ned, I can't make that part better for you, I'm sorry," she said, squeezing his shoulder. "But I can tell you this, whoever it was, Alice took a piece of them with her. She didn't make it easy."

"Alice had a weird kind of faith, didn't she," asked Ned.

"Yeah, I suppose so. It was faith mixed heavily with kicking ass, when necessary. Alice had a kind of confidence that no one was going to take from her. That's a wonderful reminder, Ned. You know, we can honor her memory by refusing to let anyone tell us who we are. We get to decide, just us, and we will write our own history."

"Mom, can we please skip that class today?"

Wallis laughed and shrugged. "Why not?" she asked. "But you're going to have to try that wall again. I know you can do it Ned, even if I have to convince your father to try it with you."

"That's a good one, Mom. Dad doesn't really strap himself into anything."

"Good point. Come on, let's go get bagels. We can hang out together this morning as a family. Much better idea. Have our own little memorial for Alice."

"Much better idea, Mom."

Wallis climbed out of the back seat and went around to get back behind the wheel. She looked at Ned who seemed to look better than he had in a very long time.

"You know that dance is in just two weeks," she said.

"One miracle at a time, Mom."

Wallis laughed but felt a shiver go down her back. She pulled away from the curb, heading back toward home.

CHAPTER
①③

The sun wasn't even up yet but Mark knew he didn't have more than a half hour before the next transmission. The soldier's presence was making it an imperative for Mark to gather more information so he could tell if his family was in any real danger and needed to run.

He went into the basement to retrieve the old iPhone he had tucked into a forgotten dresser. It was meant for an extreme emergency and he had been hoping he would never need to use it.

He checked on the Sergeant in the hidden safe room who was softly snoring. Mark had stopped the bleeding that first night the best that he could with the medical supplies he was trained to keep on hand. He knew basic field medicine and could stitch someone up or set a simple bone break but he had to hope that if there were internal injuries, the Sergeant would be able to recover on his own.

Otherwise, he was going to have to bury him somewhere on the property when his children were asleep and forget he had ever seen the man. Jake would demand an explanation. Mark knew he might even need his help to hide the grave.

He was hoping none of that would happen to avoid doing one more thing to his son that couldn't be undone.

He checked the time again. Two more minutes.

The signals he was waiting for were actually ongoing in order to hide what was truly important and they were sent from a variety of locations that pinged so many times it was impossible to detect the original source. The one Mark was looking for would have started last night and the reading would be continuous in order to appear random. At the appointed time, the coded message would be read and the old phone would hopefully still be able to decode it.

The notes he was getting through the mail indicated that whoever was trying to contact him was using the last codebook he would have received before he abruptly left Richmond.

He carried the phone back up to the kitchen and plugged it in to the wall. Fortunately he had saved the old charger. It took a few minutes to get enough of a charge but the phone was ready to go before the old appointed time.

The transmission came through just like they always did, two years ago. Mark felt a sudden panic at being so easily pulled back into an operation.

"Had better be important," he muttered, half hoping it wouldn't be so he could ignore all of it and go back to a quiet life.

It was the second Article of the Constitution, Section I. 'The executive Power shall be vested in a President of the United States of America. He shall hold his Office during the Term of four Years, and, together with the Vice President, chosen for the same Term, be elected, as follows:

'Each State shall appoint, in such Manner as the Legislation thereof may direct, a Number of Electors, equal to the whole Number of Senators and Representatives to which the State may be entitled in the Congress: but no Senator or Representative, or Person holding an Office of Trust or Profit under the United Sates, shall be appointed an Elector.'

Mark felt his heart speed up and wondered for a moment if he was having a panic attack. When he was first introduced into the Circle and learned about the OTP there was one code that young recruits joked about never wanting to hear.

It was Article II, Section I that described the office of the President and meant that the Keeper was in danger of being captured. It was worse than hearing one of them was killed.

Carol Schaeffer, the previous Keeper had been caught out in the open and murdered trying to escape on a sailboat in Savannah, Georgia. She had been minutes from getting away when Management had found her and easily snapped her neck. The newspapers had reported it as an accident but Mark had learned otherwise after he met her husband, Robert and what was left of her family.

Carol had been an orphan, raised on the grounds of one of the Circle's feeder orphanages and had been such a standout that eventually she had been groomed to be at the head of the organization, while living in plain sight. Even Robert had not known her real role.

People without families usually made better Keepers because they could come and go more easily without a lot of questions but an exception had been made for Carol and for years everything went well.

That is, until Harry Weiskopf.

Carol never did understand the depth of Harry Weiskopf's insecurities or she would have realized what he was capable of doing. He was a descendant of the original twenty and the uncle to the child who was connected by blood to both Management and the Circle. She thought he could be trusted as a friend.

She never let on what her real place was in the world but she revealed enough to him and he had used it all to try and further himself in Management. To finally be recognized as somebody. In the end, it got her killed and left behind two young sons and a grieving widower.

Things only got worse as Robert ran from Management's Watchers until he somehow landed in front of Mark in downtown Richmond. It wasn't long before all of it was so tangled even Mark and his children had to flee in the middle of the night just ahead of Management, leaving behind more than a few dead bodies. Fortunately, Mark's financial plan to slowly steal from Management was able to kick in and he had gotten himself as free and clear as someone was ever able to do. Even the property in Montana had already been carefully selected and paid for before the sudden run.

It was the perfect place where other ranchers didn't care if a new family moved into the area as long as they minded their own business.

When Mark had to drop Robert and the boys, Will and Trey off at the orphanage in Iowa before he took a hard right in the direction of Montana, he wondered if Harry Weiskopf finally had any regrets. Somehow, he doubted it.

He had met the man a couple of times when Mark was first installed at the Federal Reserve. Esther had introduced them and when she had said how important Mark was to the Circle, Harry had looked like he smelled something offensive.

Mark wrote it off as a brother who had been a third wheel a little too often. He even felt a little sorry for the guy. But it all blew up in everyone's face two years ago.

"Just two years," Mark said quietly, as he sat down on the cold, cement floor. "It wasn't enough time."

"Dad?" It was Jake, standing at the top of the basement stairs. "Are you okay?"

He could hear the worry in his son's voice.

Mark wiped the tears in his eyes and stood up quickly. "Yeah, I'm fine," he said, trying to speak slowly, as if this was a normal morning like any other. "What are you doing up so early on a Saturday? You can sleep in, buddy."

"I was checking on Sergeant Kipling," said Jake.

"How did you know his name?"

"It's on the nametag sewn to his shirt, Dad."

Mark could hear the annoyance in his voice. "Of course. Guess I got a little caught up in the whole, running for safety thing and forgot to take in the details."

"Well, it's what you taught us to do. Ignore the urge to panic and pay attention."

"Good advice. I just thought it would be more about denting my car or getting caught with your girlfriend."

"Not guns and soldiers," said Jake.

"No, not guns and soldiers," said Mark, shaking his head, feeling the same regret again.

"I heard you talking to someone."

"Just myself. Your old man's a little crazy. Come on down, Jake, it's okay. Come on," he said, going to the bottom of the stairs and waving to him. "We can check on Sergeant Kipling together."

Jake came down the stairs but never took his eyes off of his father's face. When he got a little further down the stairs where Mark could see him in the dim glow from the one light that was on, he could see that Jake was carrying his shotgun.

"Were you outside?" asked Mark.

"Yeah, I took a walk around the yard with the scope. I didn't see anything. Either they've moved on or they're lying really low for the night."

"You been doing this a lot?" asked Mark.

"Yeah, every hour," said Jake.

"Since we found him?" Almost two days had passed since they had made the mad scramble through the woods carrying what had fortunately not turned out to be dead weight.

"Yep. Checking on the house and then checking on the Sergeant's breathing. So far, all is quiet and he's holding his own. I've kept notes."

"Video notes?"

Jake nodded. "It's the twenty-first century, Dad. That's kind of understood."

Mark patted his son's back. "He's lucky to have you checking on him," said Mark, ignoring the comment about the perimeter checks. He wasn't sure what to say about that just yet. "You're a real asset to this family."

"What are you doing with that old phone?"

Mark suddenly realized he was still holding the old iPhone. The news had distracted him and pulled him into a past he had spent the past two years just trying to forget.

"Looking for news," he said, telling as much of the truth as he could without worrying Jake.

"Did you find out anything?"

"No, no," said Mark, shaking his head. He was, after all still Jake's father. "We'll need to get something out of the Sergeant. Management's troops, if that's what they are, will still be in the area and could stop by at any time. We need to find out if there's something going on nearby."

"I'm not sure we can wake him up yet," said Jake. "I keep checking just to make sure he's not dead."

"That's got to be some really bad parenting on my part," said Mark, trying to lighten the mood.

"You didn't cause any of this, Dad."

"I'm not sure that's true. It's easy to say that in the short term, yeah. I didn't make anybody come look for us. That's right. I think the Sergeant was looking for me, specifically. He may have a message. But think about it, son."

"Every consequence started with a decision you made a long time ago," said Jake.

"So you are paying attention when I'm talking to you."

"Well, you've said that one so many times it was harder to miss."

"This giant clusterfuck started when I joined Management."

Jake cut him off before he could finish the storyline that went through his head at least a couple of times a week.

"You didn't choose that, your parents did. They put you in that feeder school. You had no way of knowing where all of that was headed."

"Neither did my old man," said Mark. "He thought he was giving me something he never had a chance to get. A college education."

"Then it can't be your fault either. Dad, no offense but all of your stories about how everyone else was just doing the best except for you get a little old."

"Ouch," said Mark, feeling the start of a headache coming on. "How long have you been holding that one in?"

"Well, since we moved here. You may have said it a few more times."

"I'm a crappy parent," he said and let out a deep sigh. All thoughts of the Keeper being in trouble left him for a moment.

"No, you're not that unique. You're just a parent who joined a super-secret spy group and then left that group to join another one and then left both of them to move into the wilderness with three kids," said Jake, smiling.

"That does sound ridiculous," said Mark.

"And you stole from one of those groups, I'm figuring because you're too much of a straight arrow to deal drugs or murder for hire but we could suddenly afford this kickass place so I figure you somehow stole a pile of money from one of them. My vote's on Management."

Mark said nothing and just looked at his son. He let the seconds tick by while he tried to think of something plausible to say.

"No comment," he finally mustered. "And thank you for pointing out once and for all not only that I'm not as clever as I thought but that you are really the brains of our operation."

Jake shrugged and arched an eyebrow as he shifted the gun in his hand.

"Well, I'll leave you to whatever you were doing, then. I'm going to try and go back to bed," said Jake.

"Okay, son, I love you. Hey, thanks again for watching out for us. I'll take the next few shifts. You just sleep, okay?"

He hugged his son and thought about telling him to put the gun back in the case but stopped himself. He watched Jake creep back up the stairs and heard the floor creak over his head as Jake made his way back to his room on the second floor.

If the house was suddenly breached today by people looking for the wounded soldier, or even Mark he wanted his son to be able to protect himself and his brother and sister. Maybe it was better if he slept with the gun by his bed.

Once Mark was sure that Jake was back in his room he moved the bookcase that was hiding the door to where the soldier was sleeping. It easily slid on the felt bottom that Mark had attached for just this reason.

The Sergeant was still sleeping soundly. Mark watched him for a few seconds wondering if this was a good idea until he looked at the phone that was still in his hand. He slipped it in his back pocket and knelt down beside Kipling.

He paused for a second, wondering if he could somehow stop being involved in all of this and get out of what was rolling his way. Kipling stirred and tried to roll to one side but groaned in apparent pain and settled back again.

He was still dressed in the clothes that Mark and Jake had found him in, minus the gear, the heavy jacket and his belt and shoes. He had been too wounded for them to get his shirt all the way off of him and Mark had been a little concerned about spending too much time in the small room with Kipling while his two younger children were cooling their heels in a safe room on the second floor. It didn't seem right.

Something was tucked inside of the shirt but Mark had left it alone while he had tried to stitch up the shoulder wound. The bullet had made a clean pass through the man's shoulder and appeared to have missed any bone but he was bleeding badly. There had been enough to do.

Besides, Mark didn't know when he was first trying to keep the man alive that somehow his own family was involved with the possible capture of the Keeper. If he had known that, he would have kicked Sergeant Kipling to get him to talk.

He carefully slid two fingers inside of Kipling's shirt pocket trying to pull out a small, narrow piece of paper rolled up tight like a tiny scroll. He was so focused on not dropping the scroll from between his fingers he didn't notice when Kipling's eyelids fluttered.

Suddenly, Kipling had his finger securely wrapped around Mark's wrist. Even in his weakened state he still had a tight enough grip to cause Mark some pain. His eyes were half open staring straight at Mark.

"Hello," said Mark. "Want to let go of my arm? Or I can call for my son to come and finish you off." Mark could feel himself growing angry and was trying to take deep breaths to calm down. "I'm the reason you're still alive at all."

Kipling immediately loosened his grip and Mark could feel his arm relax. He pulled his hand out, the scroll still between his fingers.

"Mark Whiting?"

"Yes," said Mark. "Were you looking for me?"

"I have a message," said Kipling. "There's a package on its way. They said you would know what it was. You're to keep it safe, no matter what. The scroll explains a little more."

Mark unfurled the small piece of paper. It was another line from the Constitution. It was from Article IV, Section II. 'A Person charged in any State with Treason, Felony, or other Crime, who shall flee from Justice, and be found in another State, shall on Demand of the executive Authority of the State from which he fled, be delivered up, to be removed to the State having jurisdiction of the Crime.'

Kipling closed his eyes and seemed to drift back to sleep.

Mark suddenly knew what was happening and he could feel the surge of anger in his gut. The Keeper was in danger because of his own brother, Harry and they were sending Tom to Montana for safekeeping. They thought Mark could keep him alive and out of harm's way.

"No one asked me if I'd do it," said Mark.

"You've been drafted," said Kipling. "Whatever it is, it's in play and there's a lot of people who are very interested."

"That squad that was chasing you. They know where you were headed?"

"No sir. That was part of the mission. To not lead them here."

"Well, small victories. So far, no one's openly approached the house. How do you know they've completely passed us by?"

"I don't."

"How do your superiors know you got the message through?"

"I had your boy make a phone call for me."

Mark practically lifted Kipling off of the bed by his shirt. He was surprised at just how violent he could become and with a wounded soldier.

"You did what?" he said, his spit hitting Kipling's face that was now just inches from his own. He was breathing hard and didn't care about the pain he could see building across the other man's face.

"I had him make a call. It had to be done. He didn't have to say anything. Just had to call and wait for an answer and then hang up. It had to be done from your house phone so that they'd know I reached you. I tried to get your boy to bring me the phone but he insisted on doing it himself."

Mark let go as Kipling dropped back to the cot with a small bounce, unable to break his own fall. He grimaced and grit his teeth as he tried to straighten out his arms. Mark covered his face with his hands and tried to think for a moment.

He looked back at Kipling.

"Was that the entire message?"

"Yes, sir."

"They risked your life for that short message?" asked Mark.

"They risked mine and my entire squad's life for that message. I'm just the only one who lived to get the message through."

Mark gasped trying to take in what Kipling was telling him.

"Are they all dead somewhere out there in the woods?" Mark was thinking of Jake and that this could turn out to be his breaking point.

"No, they died a lot closer to the Canadian border. No one near here will find a pile of bodies. By now, someone has gathered the bodies for burials. We don't leave anyone behind."

"I thought that was the Marines," said Mark.

Kipling looked agitated and started trying to sit up.

"A good soldier never leaves his fellows behind. It's just the way it is. Besides, I think the Rangers came up with that one."

"Sorry," said Mark. "Did they give you any other information, like a timeline?"

"No. You know, they tried to reach you in other ways but there was no response and things apparently took a more urgent course for some reason. The message had to be delivered."

"Then, I'm going to assume the package will be delivered very soon."

"That's probably reasonable," said Kipling. "As long as the area is clear of combatants."

"Why aren't they out looking for your remains? No offense."

"None taken, it's a good question. They probably think I'm not dead and still moving. You finding me and covering my tracks so quickly did us both a favor. There's no reason for them to head all the way up to a civilian's house. It would risk too much exposure."

"We have Jake to thank for that. My son. He spotted you."

"He's been checking on me."

"Yeah, I know. He's a good kid."

"Was he in Management's system?"

Mark shuddered at the suggestion and answered a little more strongly than he had intended. "No, no, he wasn't. Never in anyone's system. He's just like that." Mark looked away, trying to push down the regrets.

"My dad was a hero, at least that's what they tell me," said Kipling. "I had a brother, Dennis but he died on a similar kind of mission."

"He died trying to get here?" asked Mark. "How many people have been trying to make their way here?"

"No, he's been dead for a couple of years. He died trying to keep the last Keeper alive but it didn't work."

"I'm sorry," whispered Mark. "That must be hard. You have any family left?"

"Not to speak of. But I'm a Mercy Man. You'd have to be from Chi-town to know what that means but it does mean something. I have a rather large family that I can rely on at any time."

"That's good," said Mark. "How old are you, anyway?" he asked.

"Twenty-six, hoping to be get to twenty-seven in another month."

"You're not dead so your odds are good, at least from these wounds, anyway. How much do you know about this mission?"

"I know the Keeper is coming and if they've gone to all of this trouble I know he's in trouble, just like the last Keeper. I just don't know why. It's not good for any of us to know too many details. Can't get out of me what I never knew to begin with," he said, shutting his eyes.

"I'll let you rest," said Mark. "The kids should be asleep for at least a couple more hours. It's Saturday. Didn't know if you were aware that a few days have already passed, which is a good sign. There's been nothing out of the ordinary."

"Except the Keeper hasn't arrived yet."

"Yeah, that's true. That can't be good," said Mark.

"You need to go to town for an errand," said Kipling, his eyes still shut.

"You in much pain? I can give you some more meds for that."

"No, I can't afford to be knocked out. Look, you need to be seen doing something normal. Keep an eye out for anyone you don't recognize. Try and notice any out of town license plates or just cars that look too clean or just don't fit in. Bring back the information."

"I'll bring it back as long as we have an agreement that none of my kids do your bidding, for any reason, ever again."

Kipling opened his eyes. "Deal. I leave your kids alone."

"Go back to sleep. When everyone is up and settled into their day, I'll ride into town. I know how to spot a Watcher. Years of practice ought to come back to me fairly easily." Mark felt his shoulders tighten.

"I'm sorry," said Kipling. "You were famous for getting out of this business altogether. I'm sorry."

"So am I," said Mark. "It wasn't long enough."

CHAPTER

The President's reelection campaign was making a stop in Iowa. The election was growing close and he was still ahead in the polls but President Hayes and the money that supported him weren't taking any chances. The plan was to make a winding trip through the middle of the country on a private train, running alongside the path the war was taking, and make private stops to visit the troops.

No one wanted the general electorate catching on that the trip had two purposes. Several of his aides had done their best to talk him out of the idea but Hayes was determined to see how things were going for himself.

"Sir, we can arrange a press conference during prime time. Reach far more people with a lot less risk." They had tried every argument.

He had looked up at his senior aides, flanked by their junior assistants and for a moment wondered just how out of touch he might be with the real world. But then he remembered something he learned in his first year in the Circle. Reality is a very shaky proposition.

The weight of trying to figure out what was the right thing to do was with President Hayes all of the time. It wasn't right to put logistics ahead of gathering enough information so he could get as clear a picture as possible. Things were so complicated that he knew getting the information from anyone else would make that more difficult. Nothing was going to get him to stay home.

It was true that there had already been several attempts on his life. It would be next to impossible to protect him on the road. If, God forbid, something did happen to him then the certainty of holding the White House would be in jeopardy.

The Episcopal Bishop of Virginia had even sent in Fred to try and convince him to stay where he was until the war was more decided. Surely, this couldn't go on for much longer. Eventually, the middle class would start to put things together, and no one wanted that to happen.

"If you're going to order young people into harm's way, you had better at least have the good sense to go and see what's going on for yourself. Second-hand intelligence is not going to cut it," he had shouted in exasperation.

"It's hard enough to run a country with so many different forces pulling strings. Imagine trying to win a damn war where the people don't even know they're on the battlefield."

It wasn't going to be easy to get the President in front of large groups of people without the general media noticing but Hayes had made up his mind. They were being billed as visits with local business leaders, which was partially true. Many of the officers were directors and vice presidents in their jobs just a few states away.

But calling them fundraisers would give the Hayes campaign the excuse it needed to keep the meetings private and allow the enlisted men and women to be in the room without their faces being in the background of photos.

That would have been close to impossible to explain and would have broadcast to Management exactly who was in the Circle and where they were encamped.

Most of the larger battles were still closer to the Canadian and Montana border but small skirmishes had spilled over making a wide red line that zigzagged down the middle of America, cutting through parts of Iowa.

The campaign was stopping in picturesque Pella, Iowa. The storefronts all looked like something out of an upscale Western. An old Dutch windmill in nearby Central Park, in honor of the town's founders, was now being used as an information booth and was only adding to the small town charm.

It even helped that the area was filled with local hunters who wouldn't take to kindly to having their gun rights restricted. The chances of anyone bringing up what looked like an uptick in gun violence along that red line were low. As long as no one got the idea to start any kind of investigation, there was a better chance of no one connecting the battlefield like little dots on a map and seeing the bigger picture.

The town was perfect as a backdrop for a Presidential stop along an American tour de force for a lot of reasons.

There were less than 11,000 residents of Pella on any given day, which also made it easier on the Secret Service to do a general background search. The Service was not only looking for possible felons or people with a grudge against America but any Management operatives who might be living in the area.

Pella turned out to be the perfect place for President Hayes to give a speech and shake hands and return home in one piece.

The media turned out in two large buses that were leased at the Des Moines airport, the closest big city to Pella and they packed Franklin Street, making a u-shape of three packed rows in front of Mooi's Diner, open till ten pm every day but Sunday, when they closed at seven.

Secret Service made up another layer between the media and the diner standing quietly with their hands folded in front of them, constantly scanning the crowd. Several more plainclothes officers were scattered in the crowd, constantly moving around to check for anything out of the ordinary in a small Midwestern town.

Other Secret Service were camped out on top of nearby buildings and in the park keeping an eye on anyone coming and going. Others had set up computers in a nearby accountant's office to keep track of the war and ensure that nothing moved in their direction. The accountant was given a story about being of service to his country and gladly vacated the premises for the day. He was given a good seat at Mooi's and had memorized his question. Just in case he got close enough to the President to ask him something, he wanted it to count.

Pella was the safest place to be in America that day.

The President's advance team had cleared the drop-in with Mooi's owner, John Earp, a distant relative of Wyatt Earp who had grown up in Pella in the 1800's. Everyone in the diner that morning was hand-picked, vetted and had their carefully crafted question ready to ask the President when he stopped to ask how they were doing. It was the usual routine.

The team had even helped a lot of them with what to say to the media if the tables were turned and they suddenly found themselves in the spotlight. Nothing could go wrong.

"How many times can the media start a story with Wyatt Earp?" asked an exasperated aide who was staring out the plate glass window.

The President turned around and gave him a quick look that everyone on his team had seen plenty of times. A quick shorthand to stop talking. The aide gave a nervous smile and turned away to take a phone call. The President turned back and smiled at the elderly couple sitting with him.

"Wonderful town, Pella. You've lived here all your lives, I understand."

The couple smiled nervously and at first said nothing as an awkward pause went on for seconds till a junior assistant gently tapped one of the file cards in his hand, reminding the elderly man what they had already rehearsed.

"What do you plan to do to keep Social Security going?" the man asked, a small tremor in his voice. His wife smiled and ducked her chin down.

It was a slow start but the President was a veteran of the meet and greets and started off slowly with a story about how Social Security had helped him out after his father had died when he was just a boy. Hayes watched the man's shoulders drop just a little.

This is going to be an easy day, he thought. Long, but routine.

Hayes had told this story so many times he could recite it without even thinking about the details. The entire tour had become more like a one-man show and he was just the actor with a lot of people working behind the scenes.

"Our older citizens have been of service to their country throughout the years." The President heard his voice drone on as his he glanced out the window at the photographers and journalists all staring in his direction.

For a moment it all struck him as ridiculous that anyone could care this much what one man was doing in a small town in Iowa on any given day. Then he smiled and gave a small wave toward them and waited for the flash of cameras as they all got their picture. The couple across from him turned and smiled as well. Everyone loves their moment of fame, no matter what they might say later.

Long, but routine, he thought, thank goodness.

"Perfect weather you're having," he said, only slightly off-script. "Indian summer. Just marvelous and on such a clear, sunny day. My favorite weather."

He could see heads bobbing in agreement all around him.

After a brief exchange Hayes thanked the couple for their support and shook the husband's hand before moving on to the next table. It was never good to have the people move and the President sit still. It looked too much like people paying homage to a ruler or at the least like a lazy President.

Hayes worked his way around the room, guessing which topic would come up next just to pass the time. Taxes, jobs, support for farmers. He ticked them off in his head wondering if there would be one surprise in the bunch and someone would ask a question they came up with themselves. No one did.

Every question was delivered the way it was rehearsed with a few personal anecdotes about the town or their family thrown in for good measure. The President played his part and gave the answers his team of writers had already come up with for him last night on the train. Just enough of the material was familiar to the media that they would repeat his agenda once again on the nightly news, mixed with a few tweaks to keep it fresh.

Everyone was just putting in a day at their job, including President Hayes.

Hayes made a point of thanking John Earp and getting a picture with him by the counter that the owner of Mooi's could frame and hang on the wall.

He then waved at the crowd, giving a big smile that showed most of his teeth just like the media trainer had shown him in all those hours of filming as he took two steps back toward the door, flanked by his Secret Service agents who were busy talking into their respective sleeves.

A path was cut in the center of the crowd outside as a black Lincoln Continental with darkened windows pulled up close to the entrance, agents walking alongside, keeping pace.

The President kept walking and smiling, calling out to reporters and photographers that he recognized, making a point of raising his arm high to wave. Another tip from the media trainer to make him appear taller and in command of the crowd.

Everything was playing out exactly as it was supposed to and would later be replayed on every news channel for the minute it took to cover what everyone already knew, along with a spin that either supported or deflated the President, or just poked fun at him. There was nothing new in American politics, thought Hayes as he made a point to shake an older reporter's hand, giving him a moment on camera. The man had always tried to play it fair and Hayes had noticed it did nothing for his career. Still, he was still in front of a camera long after a few others had faded into other jobs in smaller markets.

Hayes reached the door of the Lincoln and was about to duck down when he heard a small rush of air that he realized a moment later was someone gasping and the bright light from a sunny day bounce off of something pointed in his direction. He wondered who was straying from their carefully orchestrated morning. It seemed so off-script that it was taking him a moment to realize what was happening.

Two large hands were on his shoulders, pushing him down and shoving him unceremoniously into the back of the Lincoln, shoving his legs inside. Just as he went head first into the back seat he saw one of his aides drop to the ground and another, a young assistant crumple behind him.

"Is someone shooting at us? Is someone shooting?" he yelled at the agent, who was quickly shoving him in further as he got in next to him and slammed the door.

"Go! Go! Go!" yelled the agent as the agent in front hit the gas and the car came perilously close to mowing down some of Pella's citizens and a few reporters.

The President was still shouting, "What happened, what happened?" as he tried to sit up but the agent next to him kept shoving him back down on the seat. He felt his head start to swim and tried to push the agent off so he could get his bearings.

"Who's hit, dammit? Who is hurt?" he growled. "What the hell happened?"

"You are, sir. You've been hit," said the agent, as he kept the pressure on the President's shoulder.

It took a moment for President Hayes to comprehend what the agent was telling him. The sudden rush of adrenaline had made his heart pound till that was all he was aware of but slowly the pain in his shoulder was growing.

"What the hell?" asked the President, trying once again to sit up.

"Stay down, stay down," barked the agent. "Pella Regional, now," the agent yelled out.

The driver nodded his head and kept his foot on the gas. Hayes could hear the engine whine as they pushed the speed limit but his head was still below the line of sight to be able to see out of a window.

"Is anyone else hurt?" asked the President, no longer trying to sit up and instead, twisting so he could get some support against the back of the seat. His long body was folded between the floor and the seat.

"Three, sir. An agent and two aides, along with a reporter. My focus is on you right now. They are all being tended to at this moment."

"I want to know their status as soon as possible. That's not a request," said Hayes.

"Understood, sir," said the agent, maintaining tight pressure, while continuously looking out the car windows in different directions. They had left the other agents who usually accompanied them in the car back at Mooi's. There wasn't time to get them in the car before they had left the scene.

The car came to a sudden halt and in one swift movement the agent backed himself out of the car while keeping a hand on the President's shoulder. Hayes could hear another car pulling up quickly behind them and tried, once again to sit up. This time the agent helped him and pulled him up so quickly the blood rushed from his head. He wondered for a moment if he was about to pass out.

It would not have mattered. Hands reached out to him and moved him along without saying a word. No one was asking him what he wanted to do or if he could move by himself. Circumstances were taking over from him.

Arms dressed in pale green were suddenly poking him and peeling back his expensive suit, cutting off his shirt altogether as he was laid on a gurney that appeared beside him. His feet had only touched the ground for a moment before he found himself being wheeled quickly into the trauma center and rushing down a hallway. Time felt like it was speeding up but for once no one was asking for his help or his guidance or even a comment.

It had been years since that had happened and he found himself slipping into a quiet, tired feeling that he welcomed.

"Am I dying," he asked, and a few anxious faces turned toward him but no one answered as they kept moving quickly, jerking the gurney into a surgical bay.

"One, two, three," someone counted, and he was lifted at his head, shoulders and feet onto a flat surface and the large, round light just above him came on, and was immediately adjusted toward his shoulder.

A needle was inserted into his arm and he felt himself drifting further away.

"Where's the Vice President," someone asked. "Is he secure?"

It was the last thing President Hayes heard before he drifted off to a drugged sleep.

Already agents were swarming the halls, securing the area and moving any unnecessary employees or any other patients off of the floor. Behind them doctors were scrambling to take the President's vital signs and determine just how much damage was done to see if his life was actually in danger of being over.

Everyone in the room was a known Circle operative who had been on stand-by as a precaution in the unexpected event something like this happened. No one had been expected to be called into service that day.

Mooi's had become controlled chaos.

The people who were inside of Mooi's who had been enjoying an historic moment they expected to be telling their family about later, suddenly found themselves locked inside and an agent barking at them to sit still, don't move.

A man had been tackled to the ground on the edge of what they could see and the man was covered by several large agents who were pinning him to the ground. Another agent was quickly going through the pockets, pulling out the man's wallet and retreating back a few steps from the shooter.

Another black Lincoln Continental that looked identical to the one that had whisked away the President pulled up and the agents stuffed the suspect, now handcuffed, into the back, an agent on either side of him. Another agent slammed the door and pounded on the roof as the car pulled away just as quickly as the President's car.

An agent on the roof across from Mooi's kept watch on the scene below as he spoke into his radio, "We have the suspect. The scene is secure. Send in the ambulances. Mission accomplished." He folded the rifle's scope and prepared to leave the scene with no trace that the team had ever been up there. It was standard protocol and particularly when there was an incident.

The people inside Mooi's could see out the large, front windows that there were three bodies on the ground with a crowd of men in suits, crouched over them, and yelling orders in different directions.

The crowd behind them was being pushed slowly back as cameras kept flashing from every angle.

"Is anyone we know hurt?" asked one of the residents. Someone closer to the front of Mooi's shook their head, no but no one was really sure.

Eventually, ambulances showed up and took three people away, scooping them up and driving off. It had all taken just minutes but to the spectators wondering what had just happened, it seemed so much longer.

The Vice President, Ellen Reese was quickly located at her residence at the Naval Observatory and was moved to the White House. Phone calls were made and key members of the President's Cabinet started showing up at the East entrance, quickly making their way to the West Wing, to the long Cabinet room by the Rose Garden. Each one had a seat that was made just for them when they were first appointed, molded to their body and posture. It made it easier to get everyone to take their seat and not build resentments over who got to sit where at any given time.

The Vice President took her usual seat, her name on the brass plaque on the back, not even glancing at President Hayes chair. She was not about to signal to anyone that things might be changing.

Once everyone was seated the Vice President opened the meeting. Less than half of the Cabinet had been invited to the meeting, along with the Senate leader, a Circle operative of many years.

"The mission was successful and the threat has been eliminated," said the Vice President.

"I'm still not entirely comfortable with our methods," said the Senator, an older man who had been named the Leader of the Senate regardless of whether the Republicans or Democrats were in the majority. As long as the Circle was able to hold on to an edge, they kept appointing him. His integrity was his best quality but could get in the way of backroom deals sometimes.

"Duly noted," said the Vice President. "Someone ought to be, but it changes nothing. We could not afford to draw any attention to what we were doing."

"What became of the shooter?" asked the Secretary of State, an old friend of the President's.

"He's been moved to a secure location and after enough time will be declared insane. We'll get him through the channels and eventually release him with a new identity. No one will ever know that he was following orders."

"Does the President know yet?"

"No, he's still in surgery. He'll know soon enough. The wound was a little more dramatic than we anticipated but the President will be fine, in the end."

"Who will tell him?" asked the Senator.

"We have a protocol set up for the more difficult news," said the Vice President. "We don't discuss the details, as you are well aware. Gentlemen," she said, looking at each of them as she spoke, "we are too far in to be quaking at the means. The young aide is dead. He has been taken care of and a very dangerous threat is gone. We are very fortunate to have found out we had someone from Management growing in our midst before he was able to do any real damage.

"We still don't know that's actually true," said the Secretary of State.

"No, we don't know, not completely but we will find out. For now, the mole is dead, and the others, including the President will recover. Well done, gentleman, and with no one in Management realizing we have a mole of our own. This was the only way if we were going to accomplish both tasks."

"What now?" asked the Senator.

"Now, we feed the other side a little misinformation to keep the idea of chaos going for as long as possible. Until we can detect who is in that super cell within Management that's trying to take over, none of this is done. Not even close," said Reese. "We still have a long road ahead of us if we're going to restore some kind of balance."

"Is that the best we can hope for?" asked the Senator.

"That is the game," said the Secretary, "and today we made sure we were still in it."

"If our person on the inside is still alive by tomorrow then we'll know for sure that it has all worked," said Reese.

"What a horrible game," said the Senator. "May God forgive us all."

CHAPTER 15

"*Your mom coming to get you?*" asked the coach. Ned Weiskopf stood on the green turf of the lacrosse field next to his gym bag and backpack, wondering if at last he had found something he might be good at doing that was considered a legitimate sport.

He was one of the smaller seventh grade boys and had not yet turned thirteen, officially making him a teenager. He saw those as two large marks against his chances of at least making a few more friends before he got to high school next year. These days that was what he wanted more than anything.

"Yeah, she should be here any minute. Sometimes she gets caught in court." Ned looked around nervously. He wasn't worried that Wallis wasn't coming as much as he wanted to make a good impression on the coach and he wasn't sure in this moment exactly how to do that. He rolled his lacrosse stick in his hands, nervously pulling at the leather straps, trying to remember if that was the right way to tighten the pocket where a round, hard white ball could be cradled.

The coach turned in a circle, scratching the back of his head.

"Maybe we should give her a call," said the coach. "Pickup was supposed to be a half hour ago and I have to go lock up. I don't like leaving kids out here alone." Ned started to protest but the coach cut him off. "I know you guys are getting bigger and can take care of yourselves, probably better than I can now that I got this bum knee. But you see, you're my responsibility and I kind of like you, kid."

Ned felt his face flush at the compliment.

"I'll be okay for a few minutes, coach. It's okay, you can lock up here. We're in the suburbs, what could go wrong?"

"Yeah, right," laughed the coach. "Well, I shouldn't be long," he said as he started to walk backwards, waving his clipboard. "You got your cell phone, right? Don't move from this spot, even for your mother, without coming to tell me. You got a lot of potential, kid. We don't want to waste that on something tragic this early in the year, you understand?"

Ned nodded and tried to stand up straighter, still rolling the stick in his hands.

"Practice actually cradling the ball while you're waiting," said the coach, "like I showed you." Ned watched him disappear into the building. He turned and looked out toward the street, shading his eyes to see if he could spot his mother at the stoplight far in the distance.

Other cars came in and passed the field, heading for the parking lot closer to the building. Ned noticed a black SUV up the hill in the elementary school parking lot next door. From his vantage point he could see it idling on the edge of the property.

After the coach walked away the car finally pulled out into traffic and neatly turned into the middle school's driveway, pulling up alongside the large, open field.

Ned felt his muscles tense as he gripped the stick harder. Something wasn't right.

He looked toward the door where the coach had just entered and down at his bag where his cell phone was buried, mixed in with his books. He thought about grabbing his phone but didn't want to have to explain to his parents that he wasn't scared, even if he was a lot of the time.

Once something really bad happens, it's a lot harder to act like it couldn't happen again.

He tried to look like he could be menacing and at the same time not in a panic as he watched the backseat door open.

"Uncle Harry!" he yelled in surprise. He felt his body relax just a little. "What are you doing here?" He took a couple of steps toward the car. "You're supposed to be dead?" Ned felt his head lighten as he tried to figure out how his dead uncle had just appeared in front of him.

Harry got out and waved at Ned as he looked over toward the street and then back in the car. Ned saw him vigorously nod his head and turn back to face him.

"Hey, Ned, how's my favorite nephew?" asked Harry.

"Do Mom and Dad know you're alive? Where have you been?"

They were both having to shout a little to be heard over the width of the field.

"You know all that nonsense from two years ago," said Harry. Ned felt the anxiety rise in his throat.

"I got caught up in it and was kidnapped, held this whole time in some little prison. I just got out, came straight here. Came to pick you up. Your mother said she would be too late. Everyone's all excited to get together."

"You were kidnapped? By who?"

Ned remembered how confusing everything was two years ago. Nothing that happened seemed normal or real. His uncle's death had seemed just another part of a horrible time. Seeing him again made Ned think for just a moment that maybe something good was about to happen.

"Why didn't Dad come with you?" asked Ned.

"You ask a lot of questions, Ned," said Harry. "I got answers but you're gonna' have to give me a little time. I haven't been exactly hanging around a lot of people lately," he said a little louder.

Harry started waving at Ned to come closer as he glanced toward the street again. Ned followed his gaze wondering what he was looking for down the street.

"Is someone else coming?" asked Ned, still not moving any closer.

"No, no," said Harry, trying to laugh.

"Who else is in the car?" asked Ned, trying to look into the dark backseat from where he was standing but he couldn't see anything. The sun was starting to set and the car was too far away.

"Some lawyers looking into a case for me. I'm thinking of suing a few people. They said they'd give us a ride on their way to dinner. Come on, Ned, don't want to hold them up, do you?" said Harry, giving a nervous hiccup.

Ned always thought of his uncle as a nervous sort.

"Okay, hold on, I have to tell the coach," he said gesturing toward the school. "He said to let him know when I was leaving."

Harry hesitated like he was listening to another conversation in the car.

"Sure, sure, let's ride over there. It'll save us time. Come on, we can run over and tell him and then get on our way. Bring your stuff. We have a lot of catching up to do. Come on, come on."

Ned looked around at the school and then the street. He thought about making the coach wait even longer and how much he wanted to stay in the coach's good graces.

"Okay, sure," he said, bending down to get his backpack. Sitting just inside the open backpack was his phone. He pulled it out and slipped it into one of the pockets on the leg of his pants and lifted the backpack, all at once. "Can you help me with the gym bag?" he asked, wondering why no one was getting out to help him with all of his stuff.

"It's a lot of stuff," he said, as Harry walked toward him and gave him a quick hug, and Ned tried to hang on just a little longer. Harry let go after just a moment and passed him, walking toward the bag still on the ground.

"Go get in the car, I'm coming," said Harry, without turning around to look at Ned.

Ned got closer to the car and the front door quietly slide open and a tall man in a suit and dark shades quickly got out and tried to take the backpack from him. Ned knew there was something wrong the moment he saw the expensive suit and shades, and how confidently he moved. No one like that had ever hung around his Uncle Harry.

He tried to pull the strap of his backpack out of the man's hand and had thoughts of yelling or running toward the building. The coach could be trusted. He would help him out, Ned was sure of it.

But the man used Ned's grip on the backpack against him and gave a hard tug, pulling Ned closer and practically lifting him off of his feet as he shoved him in the back seat. Ned saw his Uncle Harry running back toward the car, the gym bag sitting abandoned in the field.

"Get in," the man barked at Harry, who gingerly pushed at Ned's leg to make room for himself as he got in and shut the door. The SUV made a donut in the grass as the tires squealed and Ned heard the sound of four doors automatically locking all at once.

He tried to twist around and caught a glimpse of the coach running toward them, waving his arms frantically. Ned thought it was really nice of the guy to run on that painful knee just to try and save him.

He turned back around and looked at the other men in the car. There were three other men, all dressed in similar suits and his Uncle Harry in a typically, ill-fitting suit that always looked like it could fit at least one more man inside of the jacket.

"Now, Ned," said Harry, gently tapping Ned's knee, "we're just going for a ride and then we'll drop you off at home. There are some very important people who've been wanting to talk to you about some pretty big stuff." Harry practically stuttered as he got out the words.

"Uncle Harry, what are you talking about? You're supposed to be dead but you're not. You say you were kidnapped and you want to go meet some people. This doesn't make any sense."

Ned could see that he was sweating profusely even though the temperature was quickly dropping and there was a chill in the air.

"Uncle Harry, what are you doing?" asked Ned. His voice came out in almost a squeak. He wasn't sure if he should be afraid or annoyed.

"I don't know what your dad has told you but we haven't been getting along very well these past few years," said Harry. The man in the front passenger seat looked back at Harry.

"I know you," said Ned. "You're Mr. Bach. You're Leslie's dad. Where's Leslie?"

The driver turned and looked at the passenger who shrugged.

"Ned, Ned," said Harry, "look at me. We're going to just have a talk. Richard Bach is one of the lawyers on one of those cases I mentioned."

"You left my bag back at the field," said Ned, getting angry. "My dad is not going to like this at all. What do you mean, past few years? Dad thought you were dead. That makes it hard to get along with anybody. Does Mom even know you were picking me up?" The words all spilled out quickly.

"Your parents don't want to tell you the truth, Ned. At least, not all of it and you're getting older. You should be able to decide for yourself. It's not fair. They shouldn't get to make all of your choices for you. I know what that's like," whined Harry, patting his chest. "I've had a lifetime of it."

Ned could see that the car was turning away from the direction of his house.

"You're not taking me home. Where are we going?" he asked, trying to twist around in his seat. The large man next to him put a hand on his shoulder, twisting him back around to the front.

"There are some people who want to meet you. There's a meeting nearby with a lot of people gathered and they all want to meet you. They're very excited. Just relax, we're almost there."

Ned elbowed the man next to him and felt a shock of pain in his arm as the tip of his elbow knocked against something metal.

In that moment, he realized the man had a gun and something had gone very wrong. He slowly turned toward his uncle and looked at how nervous he was.

"You don't want to be doing this," said Ned. It was more a statement of fact than a plea.

Ned tried to reach over his uncle for the door but the other man pulled him back hard and shoved him against the seat.

"No roughing up the kid," yelled Richard Bach. "Clemente won't like it and I'll make sure he knows it was you."

The man let go of Ned's arm. Ned sat back and tried to take in what was happening.

"Are you kidnapping me?" he asked quietly. Harry gave a small nervous laugh and kept looking out the window, not looking at his nephew at all.

Ned wondered if he was going to live through the day. He thought about the lacrosse bag back at the field and everything he was still trying to figure out, as his shoulders sagged against the leather seat.

It wasn't like when he was in elementary school and everyone was surprised at how quickly he caught on to computers or how well he could take something apart and put it back together. Now, most of the other guys just said it was weird and the girls ignored him for someone taller.

Ned felt himself tear up at the thought that he'd never get to prove everyone wrong. He rubbed his eyes and tried to focus on where the car was going, counting the seconds between turns but he kept slipping back into thoughts of what he was about to lose.

No one at school really likes me, he thought, but they would have, eventually. He was sure of it.

It didn't help that everyone talked about him behind his back, pointing at him for two solid years as the kid whose grandmother killed some rogue cop. Ned was sure that if he'd been cool to begin with then that would have just made him seem more romantic but as it was, it seemed to make him a bad luck charm.

This proves it, he thought, as the car turned again. One Mississippi, two Mississippi, three. He kept counting in his head, trying to sort through his life for something good to hold onto and believe things sometimes turn out okay.

Even his old friends were a little reluctant to sit with him at lunchtime, like something just might rub off and rob them of whatever fragile social standing they had been able to put together.

His old friend, Paul Whittaker still stuck by him. That was something at least.

Ned tried to look out the window to get a better idea of where they were going. He had lived in Richmond all of his life.

The man next to him was blocking his view. He kept counting and wondered if his dad would be mad that he didn't even try to make sure no one took the lacrosse bag. The equipment had been expensive.

He thought about his dad and bit his lip, willing himself not to cry.

The lacrosse had been his father's idea, which made Ned a little more open to the idea. Lately, his mother had been signing him up for things left and right without even asking him if he wanted to do it. The wall climbing was the worst of it but the welding class wasn't too far behind.

Just because he had once mentioned that welding together car parts would make a good totem pole. "Why," asked Wallis.

"Native Americans worship totem poles, we worship cars," he had said, daydreaming as he looked out the window. He wished he was back in the car with his mother.

By the next week, Wallis had found a community college class that let younger kids sign up and Ned was registered and had a pair of heavy gloves and a welder's mask all his own.

After that he tried to say less and less to his mother. He felt a pang in his chest.

He hadn't even been paying that much attention when he let that story slip. He was really thinking about Leslie Thomas' birthday party and whether or not he'd get an invitation. It was one of the first parties that would include boys and girls at night with no games. Just music, dancing and standing around talking.

He wanted to go that party just as much as he was hoping he could avoid the whole thing. Ned knew that just because he got an invitation didn't mean being at the party would go well.

It didn't matter. He never got an invite and instead had spent the night at the movies with Paul, stuffing himself with popcorn. He told his dad about what happened and Norman said that Weiskopf men were late bloomers but when they finally got their act together, everything came together pretty easily.

"Someday, a lot of those kids will work for you," said Norman, "and the rest will want to know if you also want fries. You'll see. In the meantime, your mother has a point."

Ned rolled his eyes and got up to go work on homework.

"Now, hold on, she does, hear me out. Have I ever steered you wrong? Okay, there were those madras pants but I swear they were cool when I was your age. Times change, so sue me," said Norman, giving his son a nudge. "No smile, just a little one? Around the corners?"

Ned felt the low level of resentment he walked around with these days recede just a little. His dad had a way of doing that for him.

"Your mom is trying to help you navigate waters that neither one of you have been in before."

"Exactly," shouted Ned.

Norman waved a hand at Ned, his usual signal to just calm down. Ned had seen him do that since he was three and was upset over what he was sure was an unfair rule about not being able to decide what he would eat for himself.

"Except, your mother does know what is waiting for you out there," said Norman, pointing at the back door. "You mom has a very good idea of how tough it can be to navigate through a day and how many wonderful options you will have, if only you catch on to that idea. She sees it as her job to get you to want to go find out more," said Norman, getting off the kitchen stool and walking over to hug his son. "And she's willing to let you hate her for a while if that's what it takes for you to be happy for a long, long time."

"We're here," said Richard Bach. "It'll be okay, Ned. Your uncle was telling the truth. It's just a meeting. We want you to meet a lot of people who are very excited to meet you."

"You couldn't just call my house?" asked Ned, anger returning as he started to believe he might just live to see another day.

Richard Bach gave a chuckle. "You're a lot like your mother, Ned. Apple doesn't fall far, I suppose. That's what everyone in here is hoping, anyway. No, couldn't call your house. Your parents have made that very clear. Come on, you meet everyone, hear what they have to say and decide for yourself. That's all."

All of the doors to the SUV opened and everyone slid out, leaving Ned still sitting in the middle of the back seat, wondering what to do next. He looked out the door and realized he wasn't that far from home.

They were in the parking lot of Baldwin's Funeral Home along Parham Road. The parking lot was filled to capacity and more cars were still pulling in, pulling up on the grass to park.

"They're all here to see you," said his uncle, smiling nervously at Ned.

Ned looked around at all of the faces who were looking at Ned and whispering to each other as they headed for the front door.

"Come on, we'd better get moving along. We don't have a lot of time," said Richard. "Your mom will be here to pick you up before you know it. She's a clever one."

Richard quickly led them into the funeral home through a side door and down a long hallway, working their way back toward the large group of people who had all entered through a different door. Ned could hear the excited voices all talking at once.

"They're here to see me?" he asked Richard.

"Yes," said Richard, straightening his tie. "That they are. Hello, Mr. Clemente, I'd like to introduce you to Ned Weiskopf."

Richard Bach stood to the side as an older man with thick, dark hair came forward with his arms stretched forward, smiling broadly, showing off yellowed teeth. Ned tried to step back but a large hand suddenly shoved him making him take a step forward to catch his balance. George Clemente stepped forward and grasped Ned's face in his hands.

Ned felt the dry skin rub against his face and tried not to look afraid. Panic started to bubble up inside of him again.

"At last," said Clemente. "At long last, such a treasure. I trust you got here safely?" he asked, looking at Ned and then at the other men surrounding him. Ned just stared back at him.

"Nothing to say?" asked Clemente, letting out a deep, booming laugh. "So be it, for now. Was it nice seeing your dead uncle again? You are surprised, right? The lies you have been told, my boy, they would make your head spin. And on top of that what you haven't been told. Tsk, tsk."

"Mr. Clemente, there's movement at the house," said a woman in a blue skirt and jacket, her blonde hair in a short, nondescript bob.

"Thank you. Well, time to let the people get what they want," said Clemente, smiling and letting out a deep sigh. "Ned, I've wanted this for you for a long time. Come and meet your people."

Clemente opened the narrow side door and Ned saw that it was a large chapel with rows and rows of chairs facing a small altar. The chairs were filled with men and women in dark suits and neat ties, similar haircuts and sensible leather shoes. Every lapel had a gold enameled pin with an American flag prominently displayed.

The buzz in the room was deafening as people caught up with each other talking about work and how their kids were doing, until someone spotted Ned and stood up, clapping loudly. Suddenly the entire room turned to look at Ned and erupted into loud applause as they all jumped to their feet.

"This is all for you," said Clemente, as he pushed Ned toward the front of the room.

"Why?" asked Ned, leaning toward Clemente so he could hear the answer.

"It's a wonderful secret that's been kept from you long enough. You are our legacy, our prodigal son."

Clemente backed up without saying anything else. Ned looked at him but the old man was already taking a phone call while smiling and waving at the crowd.

Ned turned slowly and tried to take in what was happening. He recognized some of the faces. They were parents of kids he went to school with who never spoke to him, never sat with him at lunch.

He wondered what this wonderful secret was and why anyone would keep such good news from him. "I'm popular," he whispered. A small worry came over him that this could all be taken away just as suddenly as it happened.

Ned gave a shy smile at the crowd and turned back again to look for Clemente. Clemente waved to Richard Bach to come join Ned on stage and Richard scuttled quickly to take a place right next to Ned, slipping his arm around Ned's shoulders.

"Why are they all so excited?" asked Ned, looking up at Richard.

"You'll see," said Richard, as he waved to the crowd to settle down.

"There's not much time," said Richard, "so we need to move this along. Ned Weiskopf, I know you don't know why all of these nice people are gathered in this room. Well, a long time ago your ancestor, William Reitling looked around and noticed that there was no system to help an industrious young man move ahead in the world and secure a nice future for his family. If you weren't born into money or power it was nearly impossible to change your circumstances. William wanted to do something about that," said Richard, smiling at the crowd, who all nodded in unison.

Ned realized most of the people in the audience must have heard this story a thousand times before. They were nodding and getting excited before Richard could get out parts of the story. Tucked into a far corner was his uncle, Harry nervously watching the crowd and occasionally giving a wink to Ned.

"William brought the world into a new system of leadership. He devised a way for people who have ambition, accountability and a good work ethic to enter into a step by step program that would offer reward in return for effort. He helped build what was probably the world's first middle class and he put in place a way of living that would ensure it would all be there for generations to come. That was your ancestor. You are the last descendant of William Reitling."

The crowd stood up again and started to cheer as if Ned had won something big. He started to feel lightheaded again and he wondered if he might throw up on his shoes.

"What does that mean?" he asked Richard, yelling over the crowd so Richard could hear him.

Richard leaned down so just Ned could hear him. "It means you were born to lead. This is what your great, great, great, great grandfather had in mind for you, all of those years ago. We've been holding a spot just for you."

"I'm only twelve," said Ned, thinking that should have been obvious. "I ran for office once but I didn't win," he added, thinking it was important to really come clean.

George Clemente stepped up and held his arm out toward the crowd. "That is the genius of what William started, Ned. There is an entire system in place to train you, and especially you, so that when you are really ready, you can take your place at the front of the line."

"What the hell do you think you're doing?" someone screamed from the back of the crowded room. Ned couldn't see her but he knew that was his mother's voice and he winced at the sound. It was the one she saved for special occasions when things were really going south.

An aisle started to form as Wallis pushed her way to the front of the room. She pushed and shoved at anyone who didn't move fast enough till she got to where she could see Harry who was trying to press himself even further into the corner. Wallis' face turned ashen.

"You," she shouted, "you did this." Wallis turned toward Ned, and marched up to the edge of the altar.

"Now."

It was all she said in a low growl, raising her eyebrows and not looking at anyone but Ned.

He had never heard her speak to anyone like that, especially him and at first he froze, not sure what to do. Wallis took a step forward, breathing hard and Ned startled back a step before moving quickly toward his mother. Wallis took his hand, squeezing it hard and pulled him through the crowd.

"My backpack," he said, trying to pull back from his mother a little.

"We'll get you another one," said Wallis, pulling harder. She stopped when they came closer to Harry. "I will make sure and tell Norman you say, hello," Wallis yelled over the crowd, still breathing hard. She stared at Harry until he turned his face to the wall and then she started plowing through the crowd again, pulling Ned along behind her.

Faces in the crowd looked startled but were still trying to smile as Ned passed them, patting him on the back, saying, "Looking forward to seeing you again," and "Till the next time."

"Don't count on it," snapped Wallis.

Wallis kept pulling him along till they got to the car and she opened the door.

"Get in," she barked. He could tell she was trying to control herself. There was a hand print on his arm from where she had held on so tight. He slid in to the car without looking his mother directly in the eye.

"Seat belt," said Wallis, curling her hands into fists and then stretching them out, over and over again. "Hands in," she said crisply and slammed the door, marching around to the driver's side. Ned had never seen his mother that close to exploding in his entire life. He wasn't sure she was even that angry when Oscar Newman had broken into their home. Then she seemed more scared but just as determined.

"You mad at me?" he asked, suddenly wondering if he might start crying.

Wallis looked at him and he could see that some of her anger immediately left her.

"No," she said, quietly. "I don't know."

"They said I was born to lead them," said Ned.

Wallis hit the brakes hard, sending them both against their seatbelts.

"I'm sorry, I'm sorry," said Ned, over and over again. "I didn't mean to make you mad again." Tears started to pour down his cheeks and he sobbed into his mother's shoulder as she pulled him close and hugged him so tightly it was hard to breathe.

"I thought they had taken you away forever, Ned," said Wallis.

He looked up and saw that his mother was crying. "I'm not angry at you, Ned, you understand? None of this is your fault. When I got to the field and the police were there and they said some black SUV took you away by force." She let the rest of the words go and wrapped her arms back around Ned. "I thought you were gone," she whispered into his hair.

"How did you know where to find me?"

"Your Uncle Harry called me."

Ned leaned back so he could see his mother's face. "Well, that's good news, right? Harry's still alive."

CHAPTER

It was a strange invitation to begin with and Wallis knew it but she was out of other ideas.

Besides, after what happened she no longer cared.

She sat at her formal dining room table looking across at her mother at one end of the table and Esther at the other as they both tried to act like they didn't see each other.

For just a moment, Wallis wondered if this was a bad idea.

"We're going to have to figure out how to work together," she blurted out, feeling her face flush red. "Otherwise it's going to be two years ago all over again and I'm not going to let that happen. However, I don't believe I can do that without some help," she said, looking at the two older women.

They had been arguing and talking over each other since they arrived. Wallis had tried to wait them out but was starting to realize they could go on like that for hours. Ned was safely tucked into his parent's bed watching TV and eating fried chicken. Wallis had never let him do that before but tonight she didn't care about rules.

She had stood in the doorway of her room for a moment, looking at her son happily biting down on a chicken leg, dripping grease onto her comforter and she felt how close she had come to not seeing him again.

Before she had come downstairs she had found one of his old baby monitors and taken a battery out of the smoke alarm in the hallway. The other monitor was clenched in her hand and she could hear the faint, scratchy drone of Japanese cartoons.

"This is one of your worst ideas yet, young lady," said Harriet. "Worse than really, anything I can think of at the moment. You're usually so sensible."

"If I'd known why you called me here," said Esther, looking as angry as Wallis had ever seen her look. "I'm not staying here," she said, dramatically rolling her r's and rising from her chair, gathering her things.

Wallis slammed her palm down on the table so hard her fingers went numb for just a moment. The solid oak table shook for a moment and the sound echoed through the wood.

"Shut the fuck up, both of you," she screamed. "Enough of your goddamn rules. Enough. Enough of how things ought to be. They took my son and you both are going to help me figure out what to do next or so help me, God, I will start shooting someone." Wallis leaned over the table menacingly at her mother and Esther. "I don't really care anymore," she hissed, "and your age or your relationship to me will mean nothing. They took my son," she said, pounding again on the table.

There were tears in her eyes as she said the last words slowly, "and Alice is already dead. I will not wait for any of you to figure out what the hell is protocol. From now on, I'm your goddamn protocol."

Esther slowly sat back down and both women kept on mumbling at a low hum.

Wallis straightened up and took in a deep breath.

"Ned wants answers and we will give those to him. Some of them at least. Enough not to give him more nightmares." Harriet looked like she wanted to say something but Wallis held up her hand. "I'll let you know when you can dive in and it better be with a good idea, so you might want to be thinking about that while you're sitting there."

"Walter would be proud of you," said Harriet.

Esther drew her mouth into a pucker and narrowed her eyes. "How unfortunate that it's a dead man and not her mother right in front of her." Esther looked at Wallis and leaned over the table, pleading, "I am proud of you," she said, putting a hand to her chest, "every day."

"That's not what I meant," said Harriet, "and it's not a contest," she said, looking hurt.

"Oh. My. God," said Wallis, putting her face in her hands for a moment. She shook her head in exasperation. "It's like a disease for you people."

"What people?" asked Esther.

"All of you," said Wallis. "Every last one of you. You can't let anything go long enough to look for a solution. You'd rather keep score no matter what."

The front door flew open, the large brass handle banging hard against the wall as Norman ran into the room, wild-eyed. "Where's Ned?" he yelled, looking at each of the women in the room.

"It's okay, he's in our room," said Wallis.

Norman ran out of the room and they listened to the sound of his footsteps leaping up the stairs, skipping steps. Moments later they could hear him hurrying back down the room. Harriet and Esther exchanged glances. "Now you decide to be quiet," said Wallis. "Great."

Norman came running back into the room. He was still wearing a suit, his tie loosened but he looked as if he was headed to court except for the look of panic that was still on his face.

"What the hell happened? Somebody had better start talking?"

Reverend Donald came through the open front door and looked around for a moment at everyone in the dining room. He was dressed in his rabat and collar and looked far more relaxed than anyone else. "You're in the dining room. Huh, I don't think I've ever seen you use this room before. Hello Esther, Harriet, good to see you again."

"Not this time, Donald," said Wallis. "We're not doing the distraction thing. If that's all you got, go on home."

"Alright, I can see there's already an Indian chief at this meeting," he said, taking a chair.

"You know the Watcher outside must be buzzing about all of this," said Harriet, looking over her shoulder.

"There's only one item on our agenda, today," said Wallis, holding up one finger, "and that's all we're going to focus on, no matter what. How do we get them to leave us all the hell alone. I don't care about your other topics, not today, maybe never again."

"Hold on, hold on," said Norman, holding up his hands. "I'm going to need a few other answers first before we move on to actually taking any kind of action. What happened today? I was in court and a deputy comes up to me to tell me he's heard over the radio that my son was kidnapped." His voice started to rise.

"That isn't even the most interesting part," said Esther, who saw the look of anger flash across Wallis' face. "Alright, I'm sorry," she said, as she sat back. "My mistake. But Ned is safely back at home. It would seem that the news that your brother, Harry is not only still alive but hanging around town would rank right up there too."

Norman's mouth made a perfect o but no sound came out.

"That's right, Harry is in town for a visit."

"Where was he seen?" asked Reverend Donald, who looked a little less relaxed.

"At the funeral home up on Parham with a few hundred of his new friends. You know the place."

"That's where they took Ned," said Wallis. "They were showing him off like some grand prize when I got there. They were telling him that he belonged with them," said Wallis, trying to swallow hard to stop herself from letting out a sob. The image of Ned who had looked so small up on the stage standing next to Richard Bach had made everything that had happened flash back in her mind.

Richard Bach had chased them across Virginia the last time people had started dying, and had led that murderous woman, Robin Spingler, his boss in Management right to where they were hiding at the Episcopal Seminary in Alexandria, Virginia. All to gain a thumb drive. But Richard's own ineptitude led to him accidentally killing Spingler and he ended up having to give up the drive he had been fighting so hard to take back.

Wallis had made sure that the Circle had gotten back the thumb drive and it disappeared into the network of agents. She didn't ask about it after that, grateful it was finally out of her hands and back to its rightful owners.

After that, they had all come to an uneasy truce and given each other as wide a berth as possible. Wallis only saw him in courtrooms and that was when he didn't recuse himself from the case. He seemed to want to be around her even less. Suddenly, for some reason he had changed his mind.

"I'm not having this conversation as long as that woman is here," said Esther, sneering at Harriet. "I know who you are."

"And believe it or not, I know exactly who you are," she said, looking at Esther. "Don't look so surprised, not one of you. I'm not that stupid after all," said Harriet. "I know. Schmetterling," she said, curling her lip, looking at Esther. She crossed her arms in front of her chest. "You too. You and your brothers," she said, waving a hand dismissively at Norman.

"I didn't always know, you did a pretty good job and thankfully, Walter never knew. That would have been a much bigger problem. He was the one who was the direct descendent."

"When did you figure it out?" asked Norman, sitting down hard across the table from his mother in law.

"Don't you think I would have been just a little curious after so many people in Management were watching this house, and one of them even tried to run down my daughter? That's right, I knew that too." Harriet pointed a finger at Norman. "I told you, no one messes with my kin. And the rest of you, you have your heads so far up your ass all you can see is brown."

"Mom," said Wallis, "we're getting off track again."

"No, we're not, we're not at all. No one ever wants to listen to me but maybe you'll have to now. You better decide if this is the hill you want to die on. You think the way to deal with all of this is to avoid them all as much as possible. Act like none of it exists and go back to the way things used to be. I'd love to, myself but that's not going to happen. You don't get back the life you used to have. You just get another chance to work with what is, and what is, is Ned is Walter's grandson. That is a big prize to those fools."

"Stop it, Harriet Jones," said Esther.

"I'm not going to use my son," said Wallis.

"And I'm not suggesting that you do, Wallis. I'm suggesting you use the way they all feel about that little fact. I don't know why you two don't seem more shocked to find out that Norman's oldest brother is still alive but we can put a pin in that for now. You had best mind your elders on this one. I have lived as far inside of Management about as much as a body can and along the way I have learned a few, very interesting things."

Esther shifted in her chair. "This is not the right place for a discussion like this. There are too many people listening, inside and out," she said, turning to look out the window.

"The Watchers can't hear inside of this house. Don't you know, Esther?" asked Harriet, as she pointed up at the crown molding. "Norman buried a unique sound system in the ceiling of every room a long time ago, when the house was built. Makes it impossible to pick up on a conversation even if you managed to get a bug inside of the house. What, he didn't tell you either?" asked Harriet, looking at her daughter.

"It was a precaution," said Norman, "and frankly, one that I forgot about."

"After you failed to mention it," said Harriet.

"Not your business, Mother, not that part."

"Fair enough," said Harriet. "But I'll bet Esther already knew. Thick as thieves, all of you. Esther's not really worried about the Watcher out there, are you?"

Esther looked down into her lap and seemed to be weighing whether or not she was going to say something.

Wallis found herself pulling up a chair to get a little closer. It was one of the first times she could remember that her mother wasn't trying to talk about celebrities or dead monarchs or dish towels.

"I know you don't think much of me," said Harriet, patting Wallis' hand with her carefully manicured fingers. They were always bright red, no matter the season.

"But having a strong opinion doesn't mean you're right. And you would pay to remember, Esther Ackerman that I kept my only child out of the Management limelight. You didn't see her attending a debutante ball or joining the Junior League. You think she just told me no and I was such a featherweight I threw my hands up and said, okay? There was a price to be paid to give Wallis her freedom and I paid it," said Harriet, clicking her nails on the hard surface of the table.

"The family secret, yet again," said Wallis.

"Oh, Harriet, not again," said Norman. "Not after the day we've had."

Harriet lifted her chin, defiantly.

"You said you'd kill me first," said Wallis, in a whisper. "That summer when I was only three. You held a pillow over my face. I remember. They dragged you away before you could really do anything."

Norman stood up slowly and said, "I'm going to need a drink. We're going down the rabbit hole, clearly."

"She never tried it again," said Wallis, looking at her mother, "besides, you weren't really trying all those years ago, were you? That would explain a few things, like why Dad ever left me alone with you again."

"At last, someone is thinking for themselves," said Harriet. "Of course not. I knew your father and some of his cronies were about to come through that door."

"Aunt Lisa said I was unconscious when they did."

"Aunt Lisa is soft in the head and yes, you were unconscious. You don't take half measures with Management unless you'd like to find yourself tucked away in some corner living out the life they designed for you."

"Or dead," said Esther, leveling her gaze at Harriet.

"Or dead, true. You know, I wasn't sure you remembered at first, Wallis. Of course, once you were a teenager you brought it up rather regularly. But I had to make sure they knew I would do anything to have my way."

"Agreed," said Norman, as he came back into the room carrying a bottle of Bowman Brothers small batch bourbon and paper cups.

"Fortunately, your father wasn't strong enough to just get rid of me, either. I won that one. The fact that you were a girl helped back then, just a little. I knew they were waiting to see if maybe they'd get a boy. I made sure that wouldn't happen either."

"But then Ned came along," said Father Donald.

"That's right, then Ned came along and with a new wrinkle. His father's family is in the Circle. It was a good obstacle to throw in their way. I liked it."

"Why didn't they just kill you off at some point?" asked Reverend Donald.

"Sure, the minister thinks up that one," said Norman, pouring the minister two fingers worth of bourbon in the small paper cup.

"Are these Dixie cups from your bathroom?" asked Reverend Donald, as he took a sip and smiled. "Sorry, I interrupted you. Why are you still among the living?"

"Because I know their oldest secret," said Harriet, smiling as she held out her hand for a paper cup.

"Enough," yelled Esther. "Enough of this nonsense." She got up to leave and edged her way around the table. "You have said too much already," she said, pointing a finger at Harriet.

"Leaving won't stop me from telling them what I know," said Harriet.

"I know I don't like it when she gets that smile," said Norman.

Wallis looked at her mother and realized she had only seen that look once before in her life. When Harriet had sat next to a dying, Oscar Newman and whispered something in his ear just before he died. The man had looked shocked and he had looked like he was in some kind of twisted pain that was separate from the hole in his gut.

Wallis had decided that she didn't want to know. Everything that happened was a dark enough memory without having to know exactly what her mother was capable of doing to a dying man, no matter how much she may have hated him too.

Esther stopped moving around the table and instead, placed both hands on the top, leaning across the wide, dark expanse toward Harriet.

"You say this and there will be no coming back from it. Not ever."

"What possible thing could my mother know that you are afraid of as well?" asked Wallis. "You two can't possibly have anything in common."

"Oh, but we do," said Harriet. "We both want a balance to be maintained. There's a difference though in what we're willing to do to keep that balance. Esther may not have a limit but I do. No one messes with my family."

"More riddles," said Norman, pouring himself another drink.

"Mother, focus. Not another drop till you tell me what you're talking about. Why did Management let you live?"

"I know something about their beloved founder, William Reitling, your ancestor, Wallis. I know a secret about him that none of the royalty in Management or even the Circle wants anyone to know about. If it got out, everything would change."

"Like a genie out of a bottle," said Esther, frowning.

"Now, you're talking," said Reverend Donald, as he pulled up a chair and held his cup out to get just a little more to drink. "I always love a good story and in my profession I've found that the origin ones are always the best."

CHAPTER 17

"*William Reitling never lived,*" said Harriet, slowly.

"I have to say, I did not see that coming," said Reverend Donald, sitting back and crossing his legs. "Do go on."

"Who is William Reitling?" asked Harriet.

"You really have done an odd job of raising your daughter," said Esther, more carefully eyeing Harriet.

"I have my reasons," said Harriet. "It's not easy to break a chain."

"If you felt like this whole thing was just chains, why did you marry Dad?" asked Wallis. She could feel a headache starting and shut her eyes for a moment, trying to calm down.

"Hold on, hold on," said Norman. "What the hell do you mean, William Reitling never lived?"

Wallis didn't know what they were talking about but she could see from Norman's face that something had happened, something important.

"Anyone want to fill me in?"

Norman looked at Wallis and shook his head as he started pacing the room.

"It's the foundation of this entire fight, dear," said Esther, letting out a deep sigh as she sagged back against her chair. "He's an idea that started a way of life that made the Circle a necessity and has led us all to this moment and those idiots sitting outside your house."

"Mother, what is Esther talking about? Spill."

"Go ahead," said Esther, "it's out now. You may as well fill in the details. I'm curious to know how you knew the story too."

"I am just curious," said Reverend Donald, "about all of this. It's like watching a puzzle suddenly put itself together."

Harriet sat up straighter, looking excited, like she had finally gotten the attention she deserved.

"It sounds like a ridiculous way to start something that is that important," said Harriet, smiling, "but a long time ago, a group of merchants in Germany gathered together."

"You were never supposed to tell this" hissed Esther.

"As usual, you have it just slightly wrong, but enough to change the meaning," said Harriet. "I was never to tell anyone unless certain events happened first and they appear to be happening."

"Of course, Germany," said Reverend Donald, smiling at Harriet, "where every good plot used to begin. Now, it would have to be the Middle East or maybe Russia."

"Stop interrupting," said Norman, "this is supposed to be Harriet's moment." He finally took a seat and sat back. "I've heard this story before but it always sounded more like what somebody wanted to be true. I never believed that it could be. Did you know?" he asked, looking at Esther.

"I knew the story."

"Enough," said Wallis, an edge to her voice. She was afraid of her mother losing her nerve or just getting annoyed and leaving without telling all of the details. "Let my mother speak."

"That is a sentence I never expected to hear," said Norman, as he patted Wallis' hand.

Harriet gave a small harrumph but cleared her throat and started over again.

"These men all owned businesses that were doing well. Each of them was making more than enough money to take care of their families and they lived better than most of the people around them. But that wasn't enough. They didn't control the power. That was all still in the hands of a few who inherited it because of their family names. That's not something you can just earn or create. You're either born with it or you're not."

"So they hatched a plan," said Esther. Harriet's mouth drew into a thin line. "Sorry, go on," said Esther.

"Why do you two seem to be more like frenemies," said Norman, looking at the two women.

"That's right," said Harriet, ignoring him. "They came up with a way to make themselves seem like they ought to make decisions, at least to the rest of the world."

"Why didn't their village just call them out as liars? I mean, if they all owned businesses in the same town then they had been there awhile and everyone would have known everything about them," said Wallis.

"Good question, dear," said her mother.

"Like a good attorney," said Reverend Donald, who still looked amused by the whole thing.

"They were willing to take their time. They started with a society they named simply, die Geschäftsleitung or the Management."

"I wondered how they got that name," said Wallis.

"They wanted something that described not only how they saw themselves but their true intention. They thought that because they had actually owned businesses, managed people, kept track of capital that they knew better how to run a town than someone who got it simply because of a birthright."

"Good Lord, it actually makes sense," said Reverend Donald.

"Well, of course it does," said Harriet. "If it didn't make sense the whole thing would have collapsed at the very start."

"And we all would have been better off for it," said Esther.

"Not really," said Harriet. "They didn't want to build a monarchy. Their dream was to build a middle class that stretched across countries and could rule itself."

"Kind of like an early version of the ninety-nine percent if we could rule the world," said Norman.

"That's not too far off of the mark. They wanted to be able to rule themselves and they wanted to give that same gift to everyone else who was just like them. A way up and a way out. From where they sat, they did all of the work but at any moment, they would have to suddenly answer to a king or an emperor who really knew nothing about their lives. So, they started the Management and they created everything that ought to go with a society, all of the trappings. They understood their audience very well. Rules, costumes, rituals and most of all, secrecy."

"Sounds a lot like a religion," said Norman.

"I can't say that he's wrong," said Reverend Donald, "except for the part about who's in charge."

"They saw themselves as divinely guided. They saw their new society as what we might even call a democracy these days. They thought that being a leader should be something that someone earns and not handed to them."

"All of that sounds really noble," said Wallis. "What went wrong? When did they turn murderous?"

Harriet ignored the question and kept talking as if she didn't hear it.

"One of the founders believed that all of that wasn't enough. That one man convinced the others that no one would believe in them enough to give them power if they didn't have a legend, as well. All of man's history up to that point told stories of great founders who went on to rule their people. There were no stories yet about someone who rose to greatness and was elected. No one would have even understood what that really meant. People knew how to pledge their fealty, even to a dead man but they didn't have a clue how to just pick someone amongst them and let him lead for a while."

"So they came up with William Reitling," said Norman in a whisper.

"Yes, they came up with a legend named, William Reitling, who supposedly lived a hundred years before them in a town a distance away. That gave them the ability to write the story themselves without worrying about anyone doing any successful fact-checking. Family histories were told to the next generation, not written down. No one owned books in those days, except the very wealthy or the Church. William Reitling was a common name so that made it easier for the fictitious man to fade into the past. They included a detail that in order to join the Management back then, you had to be a descendant of Reitling and the original group all somehow created a branch of their family tree that led back to William Reitling. They all became unique."

"We are all just suckers waiting to be fleeced," said Norman, leaning on his elbows. "Someone tells us about something we can't be a part of it, throws in a scepter or even a talking stick, and we'll do just about anything to join."

"That wasn't enough," said Harriet. "That would have only gotten you the Masons. They were after far more than that. They were trying to create a middle class and at the time, nothing like that really existed. Not the way they envisioned it at least. In order to make that happen, they had to be able to promise something more to anyone who joined. A decent life."

Reverend Donald knocked a large ring he was wearing against the table. Wallis couldn't help looking over to see if there was a ding in the wood. She noticed the large gold signet ring that had two keys forming an 'x' in the center and wondered why she had never noticed it before now. It took up most of his knuckle.

"It's genius!" he said. In his excitement he didn't seem to notice Wallis looking at him or the table.

"Think about it. People who weren't born into royalty or the ruling class had lives that were unpredictable and harsh with no chance of moving up into a different class. Their entire identity was set. And then along comes this secret group that says, if you can figure out a way to join us, we can help you improve your lot in life, this life."

"As opposed to the next life," said Norman.

"Good point," said Reverend Donald. "In those days, a pastor like myself would have been talking more about the next life than this one. Even they knew that saying God would intervene in the present was a hard sell. What a brilliant idea."

"But you had to be a descendant of William Reitling in order to join. That would have kept people out, defeating the bigger intention," said Wallis.

"You'd have thought so," said Harriet. "But they weren't trying to keep people out. They were really trying to set up a form of selection that would weed out the people who were only interested in being part of the society but not willing to contribute. Everyone who suited their purposes, the worker bees, those they helped to find a connection somewhere in their past to Reitling. After all, they were all from the same village and many of them were already related anyway. At the time, they weren't as concerned with going beyond their own borders. They were trying to change just their part of the world."

Suddenly, Ned started to call out for Wallis from upstairs. "Mom? Mom."

"I'll go," said Norman, "you stay here."

"No, I'll go but not another word about this story till I get back," said Wallis, pointing at her mother. "Find something else to talk about till then."

"Have I ever told you about how the Episcopal Church started," asked Reverend Donald, patting Norman on the back.

"How is it, you can make jokes even now?" asked Norman.

"Human beings love to take everything very seriously. But eventually, we all end up as worm food. It's very humbling and somewhat humorous."

Wallis had to smile as she took the stairs two at a time. The pastor was right but it didn't stop her from worrying about making it through this life.

She found Ned standing in the doorway of her room, looking anxious.

"What is it, Ned?" she asked, smoothing a piece of hair off of his forehead. "Why didn't you come downstairs?"

"I did. I heard what you guys were talking about, William Reitling. I'm just a fake," he said, lowering his head as his voice caught. "All of those people at that meeting thought I was special. I'm not at all."

Wallis gripped her son's small shoulders. "Ned, you're special to the people who matter, for all the right reasons. You don't need to be something wonderful to a room full of strangers."

Ned lifted his face, his eyes were full of tears. "I want to be. I'm special to you and Dad and Grandma but not to anyone at school. No one cares that I'm smart and I'm not good at the stuff they do care about like a sport."

Wallis felt like she was arguing with her son that he was worth something. Her headache was getting worse. "This stuff changes all the time. Next year it will be something else. After school, there's an entirely new set and it will have nothing to do with sports. That's when the balance of power usually shifts in the other direction."

"What if they all find out that none of it's true?" asked Ned. He looked afraid.

"I don't know. It doesn't matter," said Wallis, shaking her head. "None of it matters. It's just a truth they've been carrying around that turns out to have a few holes in it. But your dad and I will figure this out together and we'll make sure you're protected. That's what matters. Ned, I want you to get this," said Wallis, holding his face in her hands. "Who you are has nothing at all to do with who you're related to or what anyone else has done. That even goes for your father and myself. It's just about you and what kind of man you become, from the inside out."

A loud, sharp bang pierced the air, interrupting what Wallis was saying and made her shake all over, for just a moment. It was a gunshot.

Another bang rang out and she could hear chairs scraping the floor downstairs and the front door being flung open.

"You stay here," she said to Ned, emphasizing each word. "You stay in this room and get down on the floor."

Ned nodded and dropped to the floor, crawling into a corner of the room.

"I will be back very soon," said Wallis, as she shut the door to her bedroom. Not again, she thought.

She ran down the stairs, trying not to imagine what she would find and found the dining room empty and the front door wide open.

"Norman? Norman!" she yelled, as she ran into the front yard and tried to adjust to the darkness. There were no streetlights out in the suburbs. People liked it that way.

She heard Norman yelling at someone toward the far end of the driveway. He sounded like he was near the backdoor and she ran around the side of the house to find Harriet holding a pistol down by her side and Norman yelling at her.

"Where are Esther and Reverend Donald?" asked Wallis, looking around for anyone who might be wounded.

"They went after the guy who was in our bushes." Norman spat it out, angry. "Someone was listening at our window and your mother spotted him and claimed she was going outside for a little air while we waited for you."

Reverend Donald came jogging down the sloping driveway, slightly out of breath. "I eat far too much bacon to be running after anyone," he said. "Is everyone here okay?"

"We're all just fine," said Harriet. "Did you catch him?"

"No, he had someone else waiting in the car and they sped off. It was one of those black SUV's. They must buy those by the dozen. Not very subtle."

"I think that's the point," said Harriet. "Management is not worried about subtle. It's low on their list."

"Why were you shooting, Mother? The neighbors were bound to have heard that and have called the police."

"Good! We have nothing to hide. I shot at a trespasser. I didn't hit him," said Harriet, sounding exasperated. "Clearly, I was only warning him. He can go back and tell the others. But you had better let me finish this story because if he heard anything it won't be long before the word spreads and then you'll know what real trouble really is."

"Ned," said Wallis, as she turned and ran back into the house. Norman was right on her heels.

Ned was still curled up and had dragged the bat Norman kept in his closet over to the corner. He was holding it in front of himself like more of a wall between himself and whatever was coming than a weapon.

"Oh Ned," Wallis said softly as she quickly crouched down in front of him and hugged him tightly, the bat still between them. "I'm so sorry."

"Is someone dead?" asked Ned, his voice shaking.

"No, everyone is alright," she said, her cheek resting against his hair.

"What was that?" His hands were still tightly gripping the bat. Wallis eased away and sat down on the floor next to him. Norman sat down in front of them and gently took the bat out of Ned's hands.

"Good thinking, buddy. You were scared and got something to protect yourself. That was a good job," he said.

"Who was shooting?" asked Ned. "Were they shooting at us?"

Wallis and Norman looked at each other. She mouthed, I'm sorry, to Norman, wanting to apologize for Harriet even being her mother. Norman gave a small shrug.

"No, buddy that was your grandmother shooting off her gun in the yard. Sometimes that happens when someone gets older."

"Was she shooting at anything?"

"Nothing in particular," said Norman, holding on to the bat.

It was the first time Wallis could remember Norman so openly lying to

Ned. It had to be killing him inside, she thought.

"The police are on their way and they'll be talking to your grandmother about shooting off a firearm in our neighborhood," said Norman, "and hopefully disarming her. It's all okay. Families are weird, you know that." Wallis knew that Norman was trying to keep his voice calm and sound like he wasn't thrown at all by his mother in law shooting off a gun in his yard. He was trying to make this all as normal as possible for Ned. Not another intruder wandering around, just the boy's grandmother with not enough hobbies.

"Really weird," said Ned, as his shoulders relaxed just a little and his body gave a shudder that rippled from his head to his legs.

"You were really scared, weren't you?" asked Norman, ruffling Ned's hair. "Me too. I was wondering who was taking potshots at the squirrels. Turned out to be a nut," said Norman, smiling at Ned.

"We need to go check on your grandmother," said Wallis, patting Ned's leg. "How about we put you back up on the bed."

Norman helped Ned to his feet, giving him his hand and pulling him up till he was steady on his feet. "You going to be okay up here by yourself for a little while?"

"Yeah, I'm okay. You come back up and hang out with me for a while?"

"Kind of have to," said Norman, smiling as he tucked Ned in under the covers. "You're in my room, after all."

Ned giggled and grabbed the remote as Wallis grabbed Norman's hand and gave it a squeeze. They backed their way out of the room, still watching Ned who was busy flipping through the channels.

"Nothing we wouldn't normally let you watch, Ned. Just because there was gunfire doesn't mean the rules are relaxed," said Norman. Ned giggled again and smiled at his father. Wallis felt her throat ache and squeezed Norman's hand again.

She stopped Norman midway down the stairs. "You have got to be one of the best fathers ever. I'm sorry about Harriet."

"What, because I can make jokes during a gunfight? You're not responsible for what Harriet decides to do. And I knew who your family was before I married you. I knew more than you did, if you'll remember. I think you and I have done enough apologizing to each other for our family histories. I know where we stand and we're good. It's okay. Right now, we need to get Harriet to tell us everything she knows. Information is going to be power and if your mother is right and that guy, whoever he was, heard anything, we may be in serious trouble."

"What do you mean? More trouble than usual?"

"Maybe. This is going to sound kind of nuts."

"Not really, whatever it is. The boundary for crazy is a moving target in our family."

"Apparently, the war is now going on right in front of our noses. It's here, in Richmond. Troops, officers, battle plans, the whole deal and they're going to just fight their way across North America."

"That is crazy," hissed Wallis. "Where are they fighting? I haven't noticed any tanks rolling into town."

"That's very old school. There's more. They've had to move Tom to a safe location, which isn't easy, especially if they know to look for him. And if there's some kind of war going on, then moving Tom is like moving your commander in chief through battle lines."

"If something happens to him now, it's even worse. Norman, I don't think they know about Tom. If they did, they would have come after us."

"How do you know they didn't? That little stunt with Ned tells me they're stepping up their game. Is that because of the war or is that because they know his uncle is the real Keeper?"

Wallis hesitated trying to think of a reasonable explanation for all of this. Norman gave her a hug, wrapping his arms around her.

"Right or wrong, this is why I didn't want you to ever know about any of this. It's a maze and it only gets worse the deeper you go into it," he said. "Nothing is actually as it seems so it's nearly impossible to do anything about any of it."

Wallis let out the breath she was holding in and started down the stairs again. "We have to keep facing this, Norman. They're not going away and like you said, knowledge is going to be power. I may not be able to solve it but I'll be damned if I just throw in the towel. I still believe we can do something and that should count for something."

Norman smiled gently at his wife. "Why I love you so much," he said, following her down the stairs. "You have some kind of faith that can also kick ass."

By the time they got down the stairs and outside, the police were just finishing up with Harriet. The patrolman was flipping his small notebook shut and Reverend Donald was shaking the other officer's hand.

"Thank you, officer. We'll keep an eye out," said the pastor, waving at the officers as they retreated up the driveway.

"They didn't need to speak to us?" asked Norman. "How did you pull that off?"

"We told them that we didn't see anything and that you were upstairs calming down your son. Esther reminded them of what he had lived through a couple of years ago. The fact that Harriet didn't hit a living thing helped quite a lot as well."

"Did they take your gun away?" asked Wallis.

"No," said Harriet, who was patting her purse, "just told me to put it away. I have a license you know. Come on, we don't have forever," she said, as she walked by them on her way back inside the house.

"She gives new meaning to the phrase, pistol-packing momma," said Reverend Donald, as he followed Harriet inside.

"You are nothing like your mother," said Norman, as he watched Harriet disappear inside of the house.

"I'm not always so sure," said Wallis.

Esther finally came back down the driveway without saying a word and followed them all inside. Wallis noticed that she had been gone a little while but decided not to ask the older woman about it, just yet.

They all gathered back around the dining room table as Wallis thought to pull the heavy curtains shut across the window. She couldn't remember when she had ever done that since they had lived in the house.

"We won't be able to see who's at the window if you do that," said Harriet.

"A bonus," said Wallis, as she took her seat. "I have a question about the story you were telling us. I get the first part and it even makes sense that it got some traction. But this Management, it's huge and from what I've been told, it's been widespread for quite some time. How in an era when nothing travelled well, did that happen? Do you know?"

"Well," said Harriet, her purse in her lap, "success can help anything gain a bigger foothold and if it involves money or power then multiply the speed by at least ten. That's what happened. Management was able to gain real power away from the ruling class in their area by claiming they were really of the same type of bloodlines. The upper crust didn't want to believe them and tried to refute it, even tried to put some of them on trial but it didn't work. The merchants were shrewd and they had already started to put their main plan into action. They were making sure that the benefits of a better life were already spreading out to those who were willing to put their backs into it. By the time a trial got underway, no one was backing the ruling powers that be and a minor revolt was underway."

"If I didn't know what came later, I'd think all of this was a good idea," said Wallis.

"It was a good idea," said Harriet. "Just because there were a few bends in the road doesn't mean it wasn't."

"A few bends in the road," hissed Esther, angrily. "That benevolent organization eventually killed millions of people, slaughtered them," she said between clenched teeth.

"All of that came later," said Harriet, a whine in her voice. "That's the mistake everyone always makes. Mixing up hundreds of years till the truth is muddled into one saying. Management has to be bad. Well, that wasn't always true, not true at all. There was a time when they were the ones saving the world."

"None of this really matters," said Norman, "because without proof we can only cause some to doubt the organization but if they believe their lives are better they won't risk losing what they have. It's just like when it all started."

"That's right," said Harriet, "except there is proof. Some of the founding fathers wrote letters and kept diaries that detailed what had happened. One even wrote out a directive that said exactly how to handle the tale when recruiting new members, especially after Management began to spread across the countryside."

"Like franchises," said Reverend Donald.

"Yes, like franchises," said Harriet. "You understand, don't you? Most of those documents were destroyed to cover their tracks but not all of them."

"I'm not following. Someone kept proof that the organization they were in, didn't really have a basis to it," said Norman.

"And you know where it is," said Wallis. "This is good news, then. We're not unique, after all."

"You two work as a team most of the time," said Harriet, sighing. "I suppose that's not all bad. Yes, yes, someone did and I know how to get access to it," she said. Wallis thought she saw her mother looking over at Reverend Donald. "And, Wallis, wrong on the last count. You see, there was never a William Reitling but there were founding fathers, simple merchants. Those men did exist and they risked everything, really, to try and create something better for themselves, their families and even their neighbors. They were worth celebrating, but no one knew that because everyone was focused on the legend of William Reitling."

"Your father," said Norman, a sound of surprise in his voice. "Walter is the key."

Harriet sat back, still holding her purse, a satisfied smile on her face. "That's right. Everyone in Management thinks that Ned is the last known male descendant of William Reitling but he can't be because Reitling never existed. However, he is the last known heir to the original merchants and he happens to be in the line that thought it best if someday someone knew the truth. His family line were the historians charged with keeping the real story of Management safe and sound till the day came that the world could know and an order could be brought out into the open."

"Which you decided was today," said Norman.

"Why are you here?" asked Wallis, turning on Reverend Donald. "I mean, you're Norman's best friend, I get that. But why are you in the middle of this?"

"Wallis," said Norman.

"No, it's a valid question. I want to know."

Reverend Donald fell somber for the first time that night and got up to leave. "I am here, I suppose as a representative of the Episcopal Church. And, the answer to your other question is that we seem to have always been in the middle of this."

Wallis thought she caught another look between her mother and Reverend Donald. It was just for a moment but he seemed to be trying to tell her something. Wallis looked more carefully at her mother.

"Whose side are you really playing on?" she asked. "Tell me where the proof is actually hidden."

"If I really knew that piece of it, I would have published it already," said Harriet.

There it was again. Reverend Donald took a moment just as he was sliding in his coat.

"I don't believe you," she said, looking from one to the other. Reverend Donald rushed out without saying another word.

"You know," said Esther, standing up and putting on her coat. "It took less than a hundred years for all of this to go sour. No one is ever elected in Management. Promoted, yes, elected, no. And like it or not," she said, rounding the table and kissing Wallis on the cheek as she passed, "promotions are not that far away from monarchies. It's still someone deciding for the group at their leisure." Esther stopped at the door and looked at Harriet. "They had a good idea, a great idea, even. And maybe you're right that no one would have even understood the concept of democracy back then, who knows. But that's not true now. Their truth has come to resemble the very people they were trying to bring down."

Harriet started to say something but Esther waved her hand and turned to leave before Harriet could say a word.

"You notice, she doesn't mention why she never told you the story," said Harriet, quietly. "The Circle has always known all of this and even if Esther didn't know there was proof she could have told you the myths, and she didn't. Without Management, there's no reason for the Circle. Another truth is that any large organization covets power, even if it's for everyone's so-called good. It's inevitable. They despise it but they need us to push against and like it or not, we do a lot of good."

"For anyone you let live," said Norman.

Harriet looked like she wanted to say something but thought better of it.

Wallis got up to follow Esther outside. She had to run a little to catch her by the mailbox at the top of the driveway. She was glad to see that there were no cars along the street. She glanced back at the old Blazney house and saw that their porch light was still on and the newly green door shone in the small light.

"Why didn't you ever tell me any of this? Even just two years ago? It would have made a difference. I thought we were friends."

"It's not just about you and me. Think of what happened to the Syrian government or the Egyptians after the Arab Spring. The younger people using smartphones and other connected devices started broadcasting their version of the news on what the regimes were doing. It all seemed like such good news. Surely, the birth of freedom was good news, till it wasn't." Esther shivered in the cold. Wallis realized the older woman was only wearing a light coat.

"I used to really love this street. Everything about it," said Wallis. "There was no place I felt safer."

"Wallis, it's important that you think of your family and their well-being, especially your family. But there's a bigger picture that can't be ignored. If Harriet is telling the truth that a diary exists, and that's still in question no matter what she says, then who controls that diary and decides when to tell it will control the way things could turn."

"You should go, it's late and you're cold," said Wallis. She waited till Esther had driven away to walk back to the house. She wanted a moment to herself and to look up at how bright the stars could be on such a dark night. Besides, she knew Harriet never lied and somewhere was proof that might help set them all free.

CHAPTER

They all fell back into a routine for a few days, despite what they knew and mostly because no matter what Wallis tried, she wasn't able to get her mother to tell her where the diary was hidden. All she would say was, "I said I had access and no, I won't tell you."

Apparently, Harriet still had limits.

Wallis was out of ideas and Ned seemed too unnerved. She wanted him to be able to feel like he could plan his and what would happen in it and that none of it would include a car chase or a gun going off. After his abrupt departure from the lacrosse field the coach insisted that one of his parents actually be there during practice and Norman and Wallis had been taking turns. It was a good idea anyway. Ned was actually getting the hang of the sport and seemed to enjoy having someone there that he knew for sure was on his side.

Wallis took it as an opportunity to get to know some of the other mothers a little better. Middle School had mixed up the roster of the usual faces and Wallis hadn't found the time to volunteer as much. She didn't know who anyone was and found herself having to start over in her own neighborhood with a simple introduction.

It was kind of refreshing after all of the attention from the Watchers to find out there were still a lot of people in town who had no idea who she was and could form their own impressions.

When it was Norman's turn, he decided to cut through all of the formalities and awkwardness and brought a large box of coffee from the local doughnut shop, along with doughnuts. The women loved him.

Wallis laughed when she found out what he'd been doing.

"Bribing women with food and coffee. You are a brilliant lawyer," she said to him, one night in bed as they curled up together.

"Well, if you can win over the jury before the trial even starts, you're more than halfway home," he said, cupping a hand around Wallis' backside.

"Is the door locked?" she asked, letting out a laugh.

"Yep, made sure, twice," said Norman, as he threw the covers over their head.

The next morning she had sat at the island in the kitchen, smiling to herself while she sipped coffee.

"What's so funny, Mom?" asked Ned. He had caught her daydreaming.

"Nothing in particular, just happy," she said, wondering when was the last time she had felt that way for no particular reason. "You ready to go?"

"Are you going to let me go to Andrew's birthday party? It's at Busch Gardens, remember? We're going there this Saturday at night to ride all of the roller coasters."

He was saying it really fast and was leaning half over the island at her. Wallis smiled at him to let him know it was okay.

"Of course I am. Andrew's parents are going, right?" It was a big deal.

Andrew played on the lacrosse team and was one of the first new friends Ned had finally made at the school. Getting an invitation to his party was taking up all of Ned's world this week.

Wallis was determined not to build a wall around him, even as she worried about what Management might be planning. It was hard to find the balance.

She was glad that it was Bunco night again and she could go spend time with her oldest friends in the world, eat too much candy and laugh about nothing that mattered.

"Anybody home?" asked Helmut Khroll, as he strolled into the kitchen through the backdoor. Ned was used to seeing him from time to time and saw him as another uncle with a heavy accent who showed up without warning with presents from faraway places.

"Why is it you never knock?" asked Wallis.

"Is that a thing now?" asked Helmut, "Hello, little man," he said, shaking Ned's hand. "What's been going on?"

Wallis held her breath for a moment wondering how Ned would take the question but he launched into an excited description about lacrosse and Busch Gardens and roller coasters.

"You are a very busy man," laughed Helmut, patting Ned on the back.

"Will you still be here after I get out of school?"

"That's the plan."

"Come on, Mom, I need to get going," said Ned, gathering up his backpack, still trying to talk to Helmut as he backed himself out of the door. "You bring me anything from Africa this time? What country were you in? West Africa?"

"That's more of a region than a country, you know that. I was in Angola and yes, there will be bribes. You seem a bit happier. As a matter of fact, everyone does," said Helmut, taking a longer look at Wallis. Ned had disappeared out the door as Wallis put her arm through one sleeve of her jacket and tried to pick up her briefcase.

Helmut came over to help her into the other sleeve. "Something happen I don't know about yet?"

"More like, nothing has happened yet. I know, fool's paradise. It's ridiculous but I have a new teenager and when he's happy it's like the rest of us can be happy too." Wallis made a face. "I know that sounds awful. We're letting the junior member run the household but you have no idea what it's like to try and raise a teenager."

"I can't imagine," said Helmut. "You heading to the office after you drop off Ned?"

Wallis felt a piece of her mood quickly drop away. "Why, did you need to see me? Has something happened and as usual, we were the ones who didn't know?" That familiar weight she had felt for such a long stretch was right there for her to put back on and drag through the day.

"Esther called me. She told me what happened."

"She's not very happy with any of us right now, is she?" asked Wallis.

Helmut smiled. "It's not that so much. There's a lot that hangs on such a simple little lie. Letting it out could end up causing harm that we haven't even contemplated."

Wallis felt a surge of anger that surprised her and she fought to keep it out of her voice. "Maybe, and maybe not. Everyone has an idea of how things ought to go and they are more than happy to tell me. There's no shortage of prophets and all of the predictions are dire. No good ones, not a one," she said, waving her hand.

Helmut held up his hands in front of him. "I understand, more than most probably. Usually, I'm the one everyone is trying to direct somewhere else or to just shut up. Have you been able to get anything out of Harriet about where this proof is?"

"Not a word," said Wallis. They could hear Ned calling from the driveway. He sounded anxious.

"I have to go," said Wallis. "If you want you can find me at the office later in the afternoon. Laurel will know my schedule."

"No, that was all I had to say. I'll let it go," said Helmut. "Norman still here?"

"He left early. My guess would be he stopped to see his friend, the good Reverend. Those two are thick as thieves. Come on, I'm not leaving you in here you know," she said holding the door open for him.

As Helmut stepped in front of her to leave he said, "It's possible to learn to live within all of it, you know. It's doable."

"Maybe I don't want to," said Wallis. "Maybe I want to feel like I'm choosing for myself."

"You are truly a Southern woman. Eventually, you'll let it be known that they can't tell you what to do."

"That's not normally what they call me," she said, "God, I hate that name, Black Widow. Look, can we have just a little more faith, just a little. Can we just try to believe that our efforts could add up to something? Is that possible?" she asked as she locked the back door. Ned was waiting by the car and Wallis could tell he was trying to listen to their conversation.

She let her shoulders drop down and relax and smiled at him. So much of their routine together had become hard and in the past few days all of that had disappeared. She wasn't willing to give that up, for anything.

"Do you know what it's really like to try and raise a teenager in the middle of all of this? A child that everyone sees as a prize?" she asked in a low voice, trying to keep the tears out of her eyes, even though she was smiling. "It's damn near impossible and every day it feels like Ned slips away from me just a little and I have to ask myself, would it be like this if we were any other family?"

Helmut tried to reach out for her arm but Wallis pulled away. "Don't. It's not necessary. Look, you go back and tell everyone that I no longer care what they want, what they think or how this ought to go. I'm done, over and finished. I can't believe I'm going to say this, but I'm taking a page out of my mother's book and I'm going to do things my way. You don't like it then shoot me."

Wallis let out a shudder as she walked toward the car and pushed the button to unlock the door for Ned. "Is everything alright?"

"Yes, of course," said Wallis, not looking back to see what Helmut was doing. "We were just catching up."

Our short reprieve is over, thought Wallis, as she pulled out of the driveway.

"I've been thinking of going back to repairing computers," said Ned, looking out the front window and not directly at Wallis. "To make some extra money."

"You need some extra money?" asked Wallis, trying to sound casual. She wanted to ask him what he wanted to buy, more out of curiosity to get an idea of where he was these days. But she knew that would leave him feeling like she was finding it lacking. Sometimes she would forget and casually let something slip out.

Ned's drop in tone would suddenly remind her that he wasn't the little boy she used to know who would go on about every detail of his life and asked her anything. This Ned had plenty of secrets.

Wallis was fine with that because she knew most of it would eventually pass. But Ned was being dragged into something that had Wallis awake at night staring at the ceiling, praying for an answer.

"Yeah, I want to earn some money and I think computers will be the way to go. Can you take me by the store this weekend?" he asked, finally looking over at Wallis. He looked so hopeful and yet, like he expected her to say no.

When Ned was younger he was able to repair anything and used to fix computers for the local big box computer store, free of charge. The deal was that they didn't have to pay him but they couldn't complain if the computers didn't work in a new way when he was done with them. That never happened.

Ned knew from a very early age how to dismantle anything and then put it back together with spare parts from other things and create something new. Norman kept saying they needed to file for patents. Ned was their ticket into the really good assisted living places.

Wallis realized that Ned wasn't really opening up to her. He needed a favor from her and was only imparting information. Her throat ached from what she wanted to say to him but she knew that would only make it worse.

"Sure, Ned, we can do that. I'm sure they'll be happy to see you again.

You were the best IT guy they ever had," she said, smiling in Ned's direction, even though he had gone back to looking out the window.

"Remember when I used to bet you a quarter that you couldn't hold still and be really, really quiet till we were all the way home?" she asked, trying to start another conversation with him.

She knew it was pointless. This had never worked but she found herself trying occasionally, anyway. "I kept giving you more chances. You always got the quarter," she said, trying to laugh.

"That was a long time ago, Mom. I'm not a little kid anymore. I need to make my own money." He had taken it as an insult, she thought. Her entire chest now ached from the effort of trying to talk to Ned.

She had been kidding herself to think that the mood from the past few days could last. Even something like tween hormones could trip her up. She wondered what chance she could possibly have against what Ned wanted mixed with what everyone else insisted they wanted.

She dropped Ned off in the large parking lot next to the lacrosse field and felt the pain only intensify as she looked at the place where she had found his lacrosse bag sitting by itself with the coach looking like he was going to have a heart attack.

Wallis had to yell at him to get him to calm down long enough to tell her what had happened. She had heard herself saying, "No, no, no, no," as he kept talking and the rest of the world seemed to suddenly be moving past her at a faster pace than she could handle.

"Did you call the police?" she blurted out, trying to get him to stop telling her over and over again that he had tried to stop them. As soon as the coach had said a dark SUV, Wallis knew anyway who had her son.

"Yeah, of course I did, first thing," he said, "I have two boys of my own."

He looked like he needed comforting but Wallis couldn't care less in that moment. Her son was missing and in the hands of Management. Just before the police had pulled up she had gotten the call. When she heard Harry's voice she had to take a moment to remember why he sounded so familiar.

"Hello Wallis. I know where Ned is," he had said, and given her the address. It was that simple. She didn't ask for an explanation about any of it. She didn't care. And she didn't offer one to the coach either. Wallis sped off, leaving him standing there, still waving his arms, yelling at her as she pulled out of the parking lot, tires squealing.

Ned had looked so small on the stage and worse, so happy. Soaking in all of that adulation like he was the little prince. It was too much to take in and know what to do with all of it.

Add all of that to this young boy trying to become a young man and Wallis worried where the breaking point might be. She caught a glimpse of him as he turned into the building. He was talking to another boy and laughing. That was something, she thought. He's made a friend.

It still didn't stop her from wondering how long it would be before Ned wanted to talk to her again.

Wallis pulled away from the middle school, intending to head for the office but found herself turning corners till she was sitting in the parking lot of the Baptist Church, gripping the steering wheel. Pastor Adler was parking his car and saw her sitting there. He came over and tapped on the passenger side window. Wallis startled butunlocked the car.

"We meet again," he said, sliding into the seat and shutting the door. "You keep stopping by like this and I'll have to put you to work. There's always a lot of polishing of something to do," he said, smiling.

"I feel like I can't breathe," said Wallis. "Just this morning I was happy and thinking maybe things were getting better. And nothing really happened. Nothing. And here I am again."

Her body started to shake as she tried to hold back the tears. "I can't fix him. I can't fix what's happening. I can't fix anything." She was shaking her head as if she could will it all away.

"Well, it would appear that you have made this life very hard on yourself. Let me give you a very simple piece of advice. Get down off of the cross. Somebody already did that and they did it better than you."

"Oh, God, my mother does this to me," she saying rubbing her face. "No offense but I've never really been able to get these sayings."

The older minister laughed and said, "Is being in control working out for you, plain and simple?"

"No, not at all," said Wallis, blowing her nose into a Kleenex she found in her purse.

"Then stop."

"What if people die?"

"Then they do."

"That's really not going to fly for me."

"I get it, I truly do. But until you can be okay with whatever is about to come you're going to try and control it. It'll make you miserable, every time."

"I can't do it, not today, I'm sorry," said Wallis.

"It's okay," said Reverend Adler, his Appalachian accent stretching out the 'a'. "Fortunately for you, God has this really long perspective, so there's time. Take all the time you need," he said, opening the car door. "Me on the other hand. I have to get to work. Church boards wait for no one even if a meeting can feel like it's sapping the very will to live out of you. There's a smile, good girl. I knew we could get just a one out of you."

Wallis glanced in her rear view mirror just in time to see the white van glide down the street behind them.

Reverend Adler glanced over his shoulder and looked in the direction of where Wallis had been watching. "Ah, I see our friends are back."

"You know them?" asked Wallis.

"Little bird, I have been around this town for a very long time."

"Why can't they watch everybody from satellites like they do on TV?" asked Wallis.

"I'm afraid that's probably more like the Jetsons than real warfare."

"You think we're at war?"

"Don't you?" asked the Reverend.

"How much do you know?"

"In the end, very little," he said, smiling. "It all shall pass, Wallis, even this. I tell you, this may be a small, Southern town but we have a nice little cottage industry going on here. You know, it's easier to hide something big in a small place. Nobody is thinking that Richmond, Virginia is the center of the world. Well, except for me, maybe."

Wallis gave a weary smile. "I need to go too. Thank you for never looking like you want to panic. I think that's why I come here when I've had enough. You never get ruffled."

"You see enough, you pray enough, you try to fix it yourself enough and eventually you catch on to which one is working. You'll find out," he said, as he gently closed the car door and gave Wallis a wave.

The van was still idling at the end of the street. Wallis was about to pass them when she decided to stop and park behind them. She got out and went to her trunk, taking out the crow bar from the well. She marched to the back of the van, planted her feet and started banging on the door with her fist.

"Open up! I'm not going away till you open the damn door!"

Finally the windowless door on the back opened up and a surprised man in the familiar dark blue suit Wallis was getting used to seeing on Watchers, held onto the door like he was going to slam it again at any moment. He kept looking back and forth between Wallis and the crow bar.

"You tell your bosses, whoever or whatever they are, I'm not playing anymore. The Black Widow is going to do whatever it takes to get you all to back the hell off my family. Whatever it takes," she said, swinging the crowbar up into her arms. The man abruptly slammed the door.

It popped back open again in a moment and Wallis could see he was sweating heavily and had a gun in his hands.

"Shoot me and a lot of hell comes down on you. I don't know if you've met the older version of me yet but she's twice as frightening. Either shoot me or put it away," said Wallis. "You know who I am, already, and you know nobody wants me dead or I have a feeling I would be already. So either go away or shoot me." The door slammed shut again.

Wallis lifted the crowbar over her head and started swinging, denting the back as the van revved its engine and peeled away.

Wallis walked back to her car and tossed the crowbar on the seat next to her. "I'm done playing it your way," she yelled inside of her car where no one could hear her. She screamed until her throat hurt. "No one cares anyway," she whispered.

CHAPTER 19

Harriet had wandered deep into Hollywood Cemetery by herself. She was running an errand. It didn't matter that it was well after the evening news, which she rarely missed. Her car was parked out on Cherry Street that wound down one side of the vast cemetery. The rolling grounds covered one hundred and thirty acres of what was originally known as Harvie's Woods, another old Virginia family name. On the far side were now other, smaller and lesser-known cemeteries for johnny-come-lately's who didn't have space in Hollywood passed to them by family but wanted to get as close as they could to what was prime real estate for the dead.

It didn't matter to Harriet that she would have to walk well over a mile to get to her destination. She was visiting family and was appropriately dressed in low heels, a dress and family pearls. What Harriet liked to call the icing on the cake.

She firmly believed no lady would ever go anywhere without just the right amount of icing. Too much though and it was just as nauseating as too much icing. Too little and it was just as disappointing as dry cake. Harriet loved the image.

The cemetery was dreamed of in 1847 as a place grand enough for the South's most valiant sons and daughters.

The acreage was split up along gentle hills with a winding road that continually doubled back on itself, creating what was hoped to be a bucolic setting. It was also a fitting place to stand guard over dangerous secrets.

Harriet could feel the pinch in her shoes as she made her way down Clark Springs Road, on the northern side, just inside the cemetery. She knew better than to try and take a shortcut on any of the smaller roads that ran across the cemetery. None of them wove a straight line but made endless loops instead and would have been at least twice as long to cross.

A couple of times she thought she heard something and stopped to listen carefully but then the air would hang still and dense with the wet cold and only the sound of the trees groaning from the wind in the top branches.

A possum crossed the road ahead and made her gasp, grabbing the pearls at her throat and counting them like rosary beads. They looked so much like over-sized rats but Harriet knew they meant her no harm.

Her destination was almost to the far side where she also knew there were nearly eighteen thousand Confederate Soldiers lying peacefully in their graves at a low end of the cemetery. A ninety-foot pyramid made of large, hand-made bricks stood in the middle of the soldiers that always reminded Harriet more of the Masons than of a Confederacy.

The lines, even then were more divided by who belonged to Management and who belonged to fledgling groups that were trying to push them out or at least balance the power, than they did to North and South. That war had been the first time families were divided down the middle and chose sides that caused generations to stop speaking and eventually lose touch with each other.

Harriet knew all about the divisions that splintered different generations that had come before hers and she was determined to never let that happen to her. Her only child may have chosen a mate that didn't fit what Harriet had envisioned but she would be damned to hell before she'd let even her beliefs separate her from her flesh and blood forever.

Family was everything to Harriet, even if she never spoke a word about her own side of things. Once she had accepted her role, she knew that her past would have to disappear.

Wallis occasionally would ask for stories about Harriet's side of the family or what her childhood had been like in Georgia. Every time, Harriet's mood would instantly grow darker and she would give a short answer with an edge to her voice. Anything to get Wallis to stop asking.

If anyone else thought to ask, Harriet would give a vague answer and quickly change the topic by asking them about themselves. Everyone loved to tell their own stories more than listen, anyway. Eventually they stopped asking and most people assumed Harriet was from Virginia after a while. The truth was, Harriet had not set foot in Virginia till college when she entered the College of William and Mary and learned a thing or two about the places where family lines and American history intersect into the present day.

She met Walter Jones in her junior year when he was returning from the Korean War as a young soldier. He had served as a radio engineer and didn't see much action but he still seemed worldly to Harriet.

There was one large hiccup in their courtship. It was Walter's mother, Mary who objected to Walter marrying outside of what she saw as their kind. Harriet's family was not in Management and never had been invited to be within the ranks. They were not only not of Virginia's bluebloods, they weren't from the finest Georgia families either. They were what others in the South would call scrub. Hard-working people who made a living but never a name for themselves.

Walter's mother was sure it would bring ruin on the entire line and Mary knew the secret of the Jones' line. She thought that their future had an element of destiny that had to be preserved. Too much dilution of the family bloodlines would make it more of a gamble that future generations would know what to do just because it was in their bones.

What she didn't know was how much Harriet wanted to rise above the opinions of others and become something more than Southern scrub. Harriet wanted to erase her past, erase her childhood stories, even from her own memory until all that was remembered was that she was a Jones and deserved respect.

No one needed to know any other truth. It's what was necessary if she was going to preserve her cover. The Circle knew what they were doing when they had recruited Harriet in college and gotten her in front of Walter Jones. She was the perfect blend of shallow chatter and cold-blooded efficiency to get the secret out of him and eventually steal part of it.

It's also what brought her out on a cold Richmond night to wander through a hilly cemetery. Fortunately, the stars were out again, the moon was full and it was easy to see the path ahead of her. She passed Midvale Avenue and knew she was more than halfway there but the urgency made her feel like she needed to rush even though no one else knew anything about what she was doing.

She knew in her heart that her part of the secret had to still be safe but she needed to see it again with her own eyes. Management was getting antsy, taking Ned along for a ride like that and then having that man Harriet had despised from the get-go, Harry, show up at a meeting. There was no predicting what they might do next.

She rounded the next curve and saw the beginning of the Confederate soldiers' graves and took a sudden right toward the river and down a grassy hill. The grass was wet from an evening mist and she had to move more slowly to prevent herself from slipping and injuring an ankle. Then it would be almost impossible to explain what an old lady was doing in the middle of a cemetery late at night, so far away from her family's plots.

She knew she would have to just claim she suddenly missed her dear, late husband who was buried in another section and she had become confused in the dark and the late hour about the right road to take to find his final resting place. Not everyone would believe the story, though and that would cause some danger.

The wrong people would start to speculate about where she was found.

MARTHA RANDOLPH CARR 223

Better to slow down a little and ensure she got there safely and then departed in one piece.

She calmed herself down figuring out where the landmarks were, nearby. Somewhere close were twenty-five Confederate generals and two United States Presidents.

The entire cemetery was built on one of the prettiest hills in the city, thought Harriet. Perhaps it was a waste of good real estate but the way they felt the need to chop down a tree and building something in its place these days made Harriet think that somehow it had all turned out for the best. Richmond was known as the City of Seven Hills, even though there were far more than seven and no one had ever been able to agree on which seven the founders had intended to designate.

One of the most prominent was Oregon Hill, which included Hollywood Hill where the cemetery sat, surrounded on one side by the James River, rolling past spots that were deep and cool, while other places suddenly grew rocky. The entire river was dangerous to swimmers and had signs everywhere that entering the river was forbidden, even though people occasionally tried, sometimes with the predicted disastrous results.

The other long side of Hollywood Cemetery used to but up against mostly working class bungalows but those were being quickly eaten up by the encroaching school, Virginia Commonwealth University. The university had started out as a small adjunct to another college but had grown into an enormous campus that never seemed to stop growing.

Harriet crossed over two more, smaller roads till she came to Westvale Avenue where she took a moment to gather herself and take a deep breath. Her shoes were soaked through and her feet were growing icy cold but she was close and it would all soon be over. The time had come for her to turn over her part of the secret. The war had convinced her of that fact. The balance between the two powers was threatened and it needed to be restored, no matter the cost.

The night was cold by Richmond standards with a sharp wind that swept through the cemetery just often enough to make Harriet wish she had given in and gotten one of those puffy coats she saw women wearing in Martin's grocery store. So far, she had refused to follow along and was wearing a long, wool coat with a matching sash around the center. The further she went, the heavier the coat felt but it didn't sway her at all from where she was headed.

Along the far side of Westvale Avenue was a mausoleum tucked into a hillside so that the entrance was the only part still visible, making it almost disappear into its surroundings. English boxwoods near the entrance helped further to tuck the marble entrance back till it seemed like too much trouble for tourists to come close and take a look.

Harriet stopped in front of the door and took a look around to see if it was even possible that someone else might be nearby, even at that time of night. She knew she was taking a great risk and she needed to be careful.

She pulled an oversized iron key out of her purse and put it in the lock, turning the key with effort till she heard the distinctive click. It was fortunate that she went through this exercise at least once a year, just in case, but usually under better circumstances.

She grabbed hold of the blackened metal ring and pulled back, using her body weight as she leaned back to pull the door open just enough to let her slide inside. Once inside, she slipped the key back into her purse. If it was ever lost that would be the end, she thought. There would be too much explaining to do to try and make a replacement.

When Walter was still alive there had been a groundskeeper, Mann that Walter knew was an old family friend. Harriet had never heard Walter use his last name and it never occurred to her to ask. He would have known what to do. She was sorry now that she didn't know his family name so she could go looking for others to see if he had a son, someone who would be willing to take over and help Harriet.

But Mann had died years ago, not too long after Walter, and was buried in a cemetery somewhere clear across town. There was no one left that Harriet knew of anyway, who would do her bidding, no questions asked. She missed that part of her life with Walter most of all.

The tomb looked undisturbed. That was good, thought Harriet. She stopped to take in the scene and remember Walter for a moment. It was her usual habit. There was time to look for what she had come all this way to see. She wanted to remember her old life for just a moment longer when Walter was alive and the community gave its respect to her so easily. Even Wallis made a point of seeing her more often in those days. It was hard to last longer than a purpose for being, thought Harriet. It was as if her expiration date had come and gone and now she was just supposed to exist till further notice. Even this part of her life, this mission was ending. So be it.

At least protecting this secret, even if it wasn't hers by birth, gave some meaning to her days. The Circle has its Keeper, she thought, smiling in the darkness. She was yet another Keeper, responsible for protecting the balance, whether many knew it or not.

Outside in the darkness, Rodney Parrish watched Harriet Jones pull something large enough to catch the moonlight and put it into the door of the vault. He marveled at such a small woman being so determined against such a large stone door. That wouldn't matter in the end. He was here to do a job and he had a reputation to maintain if he wanted to keep getting paid to do it.

The mausoleum was in a tight area and would make it difficult to kill Harriet Jones neatly, which was after all Parrish' calling card. He could wait until she finished her business and easily catch her up on the road back toward her car. There was time and he was a patient man.

Inside the vault, Harriet finally gathered her sensibilities and took the key back out of her purse. It was time.

She found the ledge underneath the name plates on the far western side of the wall and felt along underneath with a gloved hand until she could feel the slot. She knew she'd have to wash the gloves later and just hoped the grime would come out of her good cotton gloves, once again.

She oriented the key until it fit, long-ways into the carved-out hold and she could gently push up until it fit neatly into the slot and caused small tumblers to fall into place, dropping yet another key that was almost identical, into her hands. The other half of the Episcopal mark of the saltire had dropped out of its resting place and into Harriet Jones hands. The keys were well over 200 years old and were hammered out of iron by an early member of the Circle as symbols of the group in their earliest days. One key symbolized excommunication, the other that was now in her hands, for absolution.

How ironic, she thought, that this key was the symbol of absolution but could lead to so much hell if it was ever used by the wrong hands. Even better, that they had become useful to someone who was thought to be part of Management, thought Harriet, letting out a laugh that in the quiet enclosed tomb sounded louder than it was. Given enough time, ownership of just about everything changes, thought Harriet and memories can be rewritten.

Isn't that what Walter was always going on about? History is written by the winners but winners eventually die and are replaced by others who may see things differently. Family is everything, thought Harriet and I won't let anything happen to them.

Thank goodness Walter trusted her so much that he had let her in on his duties, just as the Circle had predicted. That's when a better resting place for the second key was created and suddenly, for the first time, the Circle held both parts of Management's history.

Quickly, she inserted the first key of excommunication to leave in place of the one she was taking with her. She pushed gently till the stone lever rolled forward again and everything would look undisturbed.

She put the key she had come to retrieve in her purse and got ready to leave the final resting place of the Randolph family, long supporters of the Circle movement who had no idea what interesting secrets their family burial grounds held and never visited except to inter another member. They held a similar key to the mausoleum but were unaware that it was the only spare key of excommunication left in the world and they should treat it with reverence. Usually, it sat on their mantel in plain view as a piece of Southern tchotchke gathering dust till someone else died and they'd bring it out again.

Harriet knew there was only one space left and eventually they would all stop coming and the key would lose all meaning for them.

That would be just fine with her, she thought, as she slid out the way she came and then leaned against the door with her shoulder till it slid back into place. Then, maybe someone who knew a little more about its origins could buy the key at a garage sale and Harriet could stop worrying so much about watching over keys. After all, she was getting on in years and was starting to feel it.

A few select others knew she had the key, they had to because they held the second part of all of this that led to the proof of the real origin of Management. The diary. But they were all getting old too and no one had been able to agree about who to pass the burden onto in the next generation. Harriet had quickly vetoed the idea of Wallis or Norman. She wanted something better for her family.

The war came along at a convenient time and only reinforced what Harriet had decided. It was time to bring out the diary and reveal the truth. No more keys.

Parrish saw Harriet come out and push the door close. He stood still, not moving at all as he watched her straighten her coat and start to walk across the wet grass, back the way she came. He waited until she got just far enough ahead of him that he could still see her in the bright moonlight but not hear him tracking behind her.

He wasn't worried.

He followed Harriet Jones, closing in on her and biding his time till she passed New Avenue inside of the cemetery and only another mile or so to go till she was outside of the grounds. She was easy to track. He could hear the rhythmic click-click of her solid heels on the pavement.

It was time. He put his briefcase quickly on the ground and snapped it open, making the birds nearby flutter for a moment at the sound. He pulled out a small trowel, along with some rags to clean himself off afterward, just in case, and the knife he was planning to use. It was one of his favorites. He slipped the hilt into his hands, feeling the comfortable balance of the hand-tooled knife and congratulated himself once again about being so accountable to his work. Good tools mattered to achieve a positive outcome. He left the briefcase in the bushes to retrieve in a few minutes.

None of this would take very long.

He started moving faster toward his target. It wasn't difficult to close the distance between them and he kept to the mossy grounds closer to the older trees to ensure that she wouldn't hear his approach. He could feel the familiar rush of adrenaline as he got close enough to see the color of her purse, a deep red and thought he could smell a hint of magnolias, trailing behind her.

Parrish could feel the muscles in his arm tensing as he gripped the handle of the knife just so; tight enough to make a firm incision in one sweeping gesture, but not so tight it could catch and cause a jagged line. He knew what he was doing.

He took larger strides, closing in as he came up the hill. There was only a few yards left between them and if he didn't hurry she would soon sense he was there and might turn to see him. That would complicate things. He hated complications.

For a moment he thought about his hardest assignment, Alice Watkins who had given him a run for his money. She had fought back and left him with bruises. The beating he took at the hands of those cops the same day didn't help things at all.

He put it out of his mind. This was not the time to get distracted by anything. If he could just let the energy flow, the assignment would go smoothly and he would be back at the combinating room before anyone missed him. There would be payoffs to deliver and collections to get to by sunup. Mac would not care about his reasons for being late.

"Stop," someone hissed, just off to his side. "Parrish, stop." It was Richard Bach, breathing hard, coming up through the bushes around a family grouping of headstones, making a racket. Parrish saw Harriet turn around and grow frightened as she picked up her pace and practically took on a run toward the exit.

He swore quietly under his breath and let his arm relax. Parrish might have considered killing Richard Bach instead and then seeing if it was still possible to complete his assignment and find Harriet. That is, if it hadn't been Bach who had hired him in the first place.

"You're a little late to be trying to give new orders," Parrish whispered loudly, angry. The adrenaline still had his heart beating faster.

Richard Bach was sweating profusely, particularly given the cold air but he had hurried to the cemetery wondering if he was too late. Someone he feared more than his deceased boss, Robin Spingler, had warned him to leave Harriet Jones alone.

Richard had been thrilled when Robin had died right in front of him, thinking that his troubles in Management had ended and he'd be able to finally move up in the ranks. He had no way of knowing that there was someone worse, George Clemente who would soon be invading his space.

Richard felt a shudder go through him when he realized how close he had come to planting a bulls eye on himself that he was sure would have Clemente aiming at his demise. There had been a board meeting earlier in the night of the local Management's top seeds and Clemente had railed over the group how they were failing him. Their task was so simple, he shouted as he beat on the conference table with both fists.

Another angerholic, thought Richard trying to look sufficiently attentive and frightened to not catch Clemente's attention. He was really sitting there thinking about what had to be happening just across town, right about now and was finding it difficult not to look smug. Another loophole finally closed.

Surely, when others found out they would eventually thank him.

It wasn't until after the meeting that Clemente had cornered him, pressing the tip of his finger into the soft spot in Richard's shoulder where the pain was almost unbearable and leaning in so close Richard couldn't escape the stale, hot breath as Clemente spit out the words.

"If anything happens to anyone in Wallis Jones family without my direct order I will hold you personally responsible," he said, "and you will end up begging me to finally finish you off."

Richard had felt the blood drain from his face and he had hoped that Clemente had taken his look of shock as just fear at being so close to the man's angry face. He wouldn't have been completely wrong.

"I have my own plans for that damn woman," Clemente had spit out. "And no one is getting in the way of them. I've gone to great lengths to make sure it's done right this time and you," he said, stabbing each word into Richard's shoulder, "will not take this away from me."

It was all Richard could do to back calmly out of his parking spot and leave with the other cars in an orderly line. Richmonders never even honked at traffic lights. If someone didn't move, after a while someone got out of their car to make sure the driver was okay. Honking would have just started a round of gossip.

It wasn't until he was at the next light that he could turn the corner and push his foot against the gas pedal to get all the way across town as fast as his car would carry him. It was just luck that it was late at night in a town where everyone went to bed after the news except for a few revelers down in Shockoe Bottom who didn't have sense or family or were transplants from the North.

He could barrel down the streets, wondering if he could say a prayer that a murder he had ordered and paid for out of his own pocket wasn't over with yet.

He took it as some kind of odd sign when he saw Parrish creeping up on Harriet Jones who was still very much alive. Thank God, he had insisted Parrish call him when he located the woman and tell him where it was going to happen. Otherwise, he would have been trying to take his family to where Clemente couldn't find them and he wasn't sure such a spot even existed.

"What the hell?" stammered Parrish, who rarely lost his cool but no one had ever interrupted a job so close to its completion before and risked his exposure. He thought about still killing Bach and keeping the down payment. No one would know.

"It's been called off," Richard said, still out of breath.

"By who? I thought you were the one paying for this event."

"It's been called off. That's all you need to know. Keep the money," he said, waving at Parrish as he leaned over, trying not to throw up.

"You still owe me the balance," said Parrish, lifting the knife to where it could be seen in the moonlight. Richard saw the glint of metal.

"Sure, sure," he said, wondering how often his life would be threatened this week. "I'll get it to you tomorrow, just like we planned. But this job is called off. You don't go anywhere near that woman. We understand each other?"

"We do," said Parrish, nodding his head. "You pay me as we planned, you call the shots. Mind telling me, though what's changed?"

"There's new Management in town and he has a different idea about things."

Detective Arnold Biggs took small sips of air, trying not to make a noise as he listened to Bach and Parrish only a few feet away from where he was hidden behind an oversized marble statue of an angel with a small child sitting by its feet.

Buster was waiting in their car back near the entrance. His only comment when the detective got out to follow Richard Bach was, "this reminds me of a certain children's story about the dog following the cat who was following the mouse."

Detective Biggs ignored him and quietly shut the car door. They had been following Parrish for days since he was let out of lockup without being formally charged with anything. Buster wanted it on the record that it was possibly futile but Biggs had insisted and in the end, they were partners.

"Why do you think Parrish is at a cemetery in the middle of the night? All of his potential victims are already dead," said Buster. They were planning to wait till he came back out the other side but when Richard Bach had walked close enough by them to see in their car if he had only looked, Detective Biggs decided to follow him.

"That's too weird," said Buster.

"You stay here. It'll be hard enough to get close to them without them noticing as it is," said Biggs.

"Suit yourself."

The detective had caught up to Bach in time to see an older woman walking on the road above them and he realized that Parrish had a target all along. A surge of anger came over him as he realized that if they had sat there waiting for Parrish to exit the cemetery he would have left a deposit for the gravediggers.

He found a hiding place behind the oversized marble angel and crouched down, his gun drawn, ready to shoot anyone who looked like they were about to kill someone. The woman quickly disappeared out of sight as the two men in front of him argued over calling off the hit and new management being in charge.

Detective Biggs wondered if a new crime syndicate had moved into town and did Mac know anything about it. Mac was a lot of things but he wasn't a killer by nature and just tolerated Parrish as a necessary evil. He was sure that Mac would know who they were talking about and would be willing to give up information to stop Richmond from being taken over by a rough crowd.

After all, that would at some point lead to someone trying to cut into Mac's business. That's how certain parts of the city kept itself in check.

Mac took in too much cash for others not to eventually try to take some of it and that's where Mac drew a very deadly line.

Harriet had heard the two men in the bushes and the fear of God had gone through her very soul. This late at night in a cemetery, even one as nice as Hollywood could not mean anything good.

She had broken into as fast a run as she could manage, realizing this was not the time to worry about what anyone else thought about what she was doing and ran for the exit as fast as she could manage in wet leather shoes.

She thought she heard them still following behind her and in a panic got off of the road, thinking that she'd have a better chance of hiding for a while, maybe till the sun rose when a groundskeeper would arrive for the first shift.

The side of the road was crumbling at the edges and Harriet almost turned an ankle taking a small leap across a dip in the hillside and pushing through bushes that scratched at her arms and face till she was well out of sight of the road.

It wasn't until she was on the other side of the shrubbery that she realized what part of the cemetery she was in and then it seemed only natural that she would go find solace in one of the few places she was able to for so many years. Walter was buried nearby. She could sit with him and chat till the sun came up and the daylight would make everything seem safe again.

This assignment didn't used to scare her so easily, she thought. I am getting too old for this nonsense.

She knew this part of the cemetery as well as she knew the road where her house stood. She had been here so many times to sit with Walter and tell him how things were going in what she still saw as their lives and not just hers, alone. That thought, the solitary nature, was too much for her.

She had placed a stone bench right by his headstone so she could sit and talk to him without having to stand for so long and now it seemed like divine order that it was there for her to rest after such an ordeal.

The night had been too much for her in the cold air and the damp grass and then the excitement of thugs chasing her down the road. Just retrieving the key was enough drama, she thought, as she settled herself on the bench, still holding her purse close to her chest.

"Walter," she started to say, but the word came out in a slur. That surprised her. She tried again. "You won't believe."

That's what she could hear in her head but the words didn't sound anything like that when they came out. They made no sense. Her purse started to slip from her grasp and she felt the panic return again. The key was in her purse. She tried to hold on tighter but that only seemed to make her arm grow more heavy and useless until it slumped in her lap and the purse rolled to the ground.

Harriet looked at the purse on the ground at her feet, marveling that she had all the will in the world but couldn't make her body move an inch. Slowly, the stars above faded for her till there was complete darkness and she slumped over on the bench, her mouth hanging open in a way that would have embarrassed her, if Harriet Jones had only known where she was anymore.

Parrish and Bach hurried down the road toward the exit and Biggs followed them to ensure they didn't take up the trail of the elderly woman he had seen and change their minds about her well-being. But at the entrance the two men parted ways and quickly walked in different directions.

He made his way back to the car and signaled to Buster to put down the window.

"Did you see an old woman pass by here? About five feet, dressed pretty nice?"

"No, just saw Parrish pass by pretty quickly. No one else. Why, what's wrong?"

"Parrish had a target. She would have had to go right by here. You would have seen her."

Something was wrong. Biggs had calculated how fast the old woman was walking and he knew she should still be visible somewhere along the path or at least on the street.

"I'm going to go back in and look around."

"Okay, let me know if you need back up. I'll call you know if anyone goes by out here."

Detective Biggs walked swiftly on the outside road, scanning the sides for any sign of someone just passing through there. He was wondering if he had somehow missed something and Parrish had finished off another old woman right under his nose. His frustration at Parrish only grew with each step.

Just where the boundaries of the cemetery cut in sharply the detective spotted the broken bushes and followed the trail till he came upon the stone bench and the woman on her side. He rushed over and put two fingers against her neck, feeling for a pulse.

"Buster, I found her. Looks like she had a stroke or something. Call for a tanker," he said.

"She still alive?"

"It was barely there but she's still alive. Better hurry though, if we want to keep her that way."

"Any ID on her?"

"Yeah, her license says her name is Harriet Jones. Hold on, her phone is here. Most of the phone calls are to a Wallis Jones."

"Isn't that the woman we saw outside of Alice Watkins murder?" asked Buster.

"Yeah, it was," said Biggs. "We may need to ask Wallis Jones a few questions."

CHAPTER

$\mathcal{A}$ small squad of just six Management soldiers moved through the Richmond neighborhood without notice. That was their job. Warfare was hard enough but this war had insisted that American soldiers learn how to fight on their home turf in areas that resembled their own suburban backyards.

Tonight was no exception.

They had left their van at Deep Run Park and walked out to John Rolfe Parkway, waiting for a later hour when there would be fewer people on the road. The park closed at sundown and a Management operative dressed as a park official chased off the few lovebirds and teenagers who were still hanging around till they were sure the park was empty.

They were deep into a neighborhood full of known Circle operatives and they knew it but they were given orders to find and execute a target.

No one asked them how they felt about it, or cared.

At the appointed hour, the street lights there were would go dim and they knew they only had ten minutes to hustle up the street, past all of the dark Colonials and ranchers till they got to Pump Road where they would be closing in on their target.

The Sergeant in charge of the squad gave the signal to get ready. It was almost time.

The rest of the neighborhood was watching TV, tucking their kids into bed and reading them stories or laughing over dinner with friends in their dining rooms, just off their kitchens. Some of the families that lived there knew there was a war going on but the battles were supposed to all be to the far north and Midwest. Nothing had come this close, yet.

They all felt safe this far into their own territory. Everyone in the West End of Richmond, in some of the better neighborhoods, were just going about their business with no idea that a small piece of the war was drawing close to them.

Wallis had walked over to Bunco night from her house, grateful that it was so close tonight. The air was a little cold but the short walk did her some good. She got a little fresh air walking the short distance while she admired the bright stars overhead.

There were no streetlights along her street but the moon made it possible to see everything. She was really looking forward to tonight.

Bunco was at Sandra Wilkins house that night. The women in Wallis' neighborhood had been getting together for a regular Bunco game since their children were still in diapers. Mostly it was an excuse to eat candy, drink wine and share the best gossip about the neighbors who weren't in the room.

There had been a little chatter about doing something like a book club but Julia, always one of the louder voices in the room, always said that a book club was too much effort and guilt. Effort to go get the book and guilt when no one read it before the meeting. "It would just turn into a drama club instead," she had said with a snort.

Bunco just involved a few dice, a lot of food and a few halfway decent prizes.

The group had started with sixteen women whose children were all in the kindergarten class from the nearby public elementary school. In the last couple of years some of the children had been selected to attend Sutler, the local private school while others were divided up among the public middle schools and their lives were not as interconnected as they used to be.

The private school had all of the amenities that any parent would hope for to help their child succeed and maybe even do better than they had, with a little something extra. It was the local feeder school for Management. Getting accepted to Sutler, whether the parents really understood it or not, meant they were making a lifelong contract to follow Management's ideas about a lot of the details of their life.

Wallis knew the hard way that sometimes it ended in a premature death. She had tried to warn Sharon not to send Ned's best friend, Paul there and so far, she was successful. But at least once every few months Sharon brought up the fancy school again, wondering if she was cheating Paul out of something better. Sutler offered large scholarships that covered almost all of the expenses and Sharon's ex, David Whittaker, wasn't about to help out with one more dollar than he was ordered to by the courts.

Sharon was barely getting by and Wallis knew she was worried about getting him through high school, much less figuring out college.

She convinced her to hold off by pointing out that David was on the board and he rarely joined anything that was completely legal. He was firmly ensconced in Management's ranks, even if Sharon didn't know it and had been a violent and angry husband.

Wallis wondered if even Management was sorry they had once offered a scholarship to a young David and were now stuck with him.

Others in the group, though had taken Sutler's offer and their children appeared to be on a trajectory out of the middle class struggle of their parents. One of them was Roger, Julia's son and another friend of Ned's.

Julia was always talking about the opportunities that Roger was getting that she could have never given him. "He's taking piano lessons. I couldn't do that on my salary, not without Sutler." It was all Wallis could do not to start asking her pointed questions to lead her to a different conclusion. She wanted to warn her to get Roger off the tracks in front of a train none of them seemed capable of seeing.

But Norman had pointed out more than once that nobody was asking for her help. Wallis liked Julia though and wanted to help her friend.

Julia was a fun, oversized blonde who was usually in matching velour that she even wore to work. "The rules say no jeans. There is nothing about velour."

Tonight she was wearing a pale green set with matching suede clogs. Julia was usually in some color that wasn't too far off of a shade that reminded Wallis of an Easter basket.

Wallis appreciated the attention to detail.

"Where's the caramel cake, Sandra?" Bridget, a lanky brunette, yelled toward the kitchen. The cake was a southern delicacy and almost impossible to get the icing just right. It was all a bit mystical. Women from her church were always trying to make the cake just so and they got the consistency right about one time out of ten.

"It's coming," said Sandra, as she came out carrying her claim to fame on a milk glass cake platter. "Have I ever missed a Bunco night?" she asked. She was new to the group and had only been invited to a handful so far but she was right. The cake had appeared at every one of them.

Her accent was old Richmond with rounded words that sounded like she was about to start singing at any moment. Wallis smelled the familiar Chanel Number Five as she passed by mixed with the sweet caramel from the cake. The combination was so familiar to the women she had known as a child. It always made her feel like she was home.

Sandra was the oldest woman in their group and the newest member. She had moved into the neighborhood not too long ago from the Raleigh area. She said she needed a fresh start.

Her marriage had ended and along with it, her catering business but she was determined to start over and was decorating cakes for a local bakery. What she really needed, she said, was some new friends she could count on that were local. Wallis knew exactly what she meant. Everyone in their Bunco group did.

After their friend, Yvette Campbell was murdered in what still looked like a random poisoning, the group had stopped meeting for well over a year.

It started as a few phone calls with someone suggesting they could use a break. No one really wanted to talk about what happened. A friend had died and no one could explain why or even who did it.

One month turned into two until a year had passed.

But eventually Maureen Bowers started calling all of the members and said she missed her friends.

When they had taken a break, there were only twelve women who still met regularly, all from the neighborhood. Now, after Yvette, they were down to eleven who would get together for Bunco night.

They needed another player. Julia quickly started a round of phone calls to insist they should try someone new to the area. She apparently didn't care for a couple of the other regular's friends that came as occasional substitutes, and said so, somewhere in each phone call. Everyone knew it would be easier to just find a new face than live with Julia's sighs and comments for the next year.

Besides, she had a point. Lucy usually brought a friend, and much like Lucy, they complained about their lot in life. It was a little much.

Wallis volunteered and took it upon herself to go knock on the old Blazney house and use Bunco night as a good excuse to let go of even more ghosts and meet her new neighbor. Sandra had answered the door and invited Wallis in for a piece of cake. Wallis knew she would fit right in with the others.

"Have you ever heard of Bunco?" she had asked her.

"Why, yes," said Sandra, the words sounding like she was about to sing at any moment.

Angie Estaver had insisted on hosting that first night back and her husband, Hector grilled out back with all of the husbands in tow. Their dog, Ralph was yipping at Hector the entire time he was turning the chicken.

Yvette's husband was the only one missing. He had moved back to somewhere in Colorado not too long after the funeral to be closer to his family.

At first it was an awkward night.

Everyone had a little too much to drink and for a while, people wanted to sit around and tell stories about Yvette, and memories of when they all were younger.

Hector noticed the mood taking a turn for the somber and turned up the music. He tugged at his wife's arm and kept cooing at her to join him on the dance floor. He got Norman to help him move the coffee table out of the way and eventually, everyone kicked off their shoes and started dancing. Even Wallis managed to join in and forget everything for a little while.

Bunco never really got started that night. Maybe that was the point.

It did the trick though, and reminded everyone of why they tried to get together all the time. They were all more like family to each other. Sandra Wilkins was just the newest member.

The next time they played was at Wallis' house, it was her turn and she made sure to get Norman and Ned to make every cookie they knew how to bake. They were the cooks in the family. Wallis had been asked a long time ago by both Norman and Ned to stop trying.

The last straw had been the recipe she got out of a woman's magazine for a quiche that had so many eggs the consistency was more like a gelatinous custard.

To make matters worse, Wallis had been distracted by a phone call from a client. She was pouring the mixture into the ready-made crust while trying to comfort a worried mother asking about custody arrangements for the third time.

It wasn't until dinner with Norman and Ned looking on anxiously, when she tried to cut into the quiche at the table that she realized she had left the wax paper in the bottom of the crust.

Norman and Ned had tried not to laugh but a snicker out of Ned led to an outright guffaw from Norman till even Wallis found herself giggling over her cooking skills.

But that was years ago.

The memory used to be one of Wallis' favorite. Lately, every happy memory with Ned had a little bit of doubt and regret attached.

As a family court attorney, Wallis had seen countless families pass through her office or the court room. She had seen her share of moody teenagers who were living ordinary lives and she knew that most of them eventually passed through the phase and became happy adults who still talked to their mother.

But Ned was having a different kind of childhood. She couldn't be sure that the same rules applied to him anymore.

"Put down whatever that store bought dip is that you brought, Wallis and come sit by me," said Bridget.

"It's actually snickerdoodles," said Wallis. "Don't worry, I used my ringer. Norman made them and he sends his love, as well."

"You have got to be the luckiest woman in this room, Wallis Jones," said Julia, "outside of maybe, Angie and that's just because Hector is hot and kind. Or maybe Maureen because Fred is the strong and silent type. You've got a man who's easy on the eyes and can cook."

"And has a decent job," said Bridget.

"A hat trick," said Julia.

"Come on, start at my table," said Bridget. "I'll even let you ring the bell and start the game. You can put the cookies down, right here," she said, laughing, as Wallis took a seat at a square card table covered in a pale green and gold checked tablecloth that puddled on the ground. The table was barely big enough to fit four people around it. One more table just like that one was set up next to them in what was the living room and there were four seats set up at the nearby dining room table.

Maureen quickly took the seat next to Wallis and gently patted her hand as she sat down next to her.

"I'm so glad we get to start out next to each other," said Maureen.

"Yeah, I know. I'm sorry we haven't been able to figure out a time to get together. You've been so good about keeping in touch," said Wallis.

She had always liked Maureen and Fred Bowers. They were such a good couple. They always spoke well of each other and seemed to have a strong marriage based on friendship. It's what Wallis hoped she had built with Norman.

Besides, Maureen was the least likely, besides Wallis to start a round robin of gossip over the phone just to get her way.

Maureen always seemed to Wallis like she was happy to go along with whatever came next, which made it easier to get along with this group. There were already so many strong-willed women who had a few ideas about what everyone should be doing.

"Here you go, I'm a woman of my word," said Bridget. "You get to ring the bell," she said, pushing the hand bell in Wallis direction. Wallis smiled and forgot about her troubles for a moment as she lifted the bell and gave it a hardy shake, laughing at Julia blowing on her dice at the table next to hers.

"Y'all make it so easy to take a deep breath," said Wallis, smiling.

"I know what you mean, honey. Come on ones," yelled Julia with a whoop as two of the dice delivered what she wanted. "Wahoo," she yelled.

The women kept rolling the dice, laughing and drinking wine and eating until late into the night. Wallis took a break when she realized the hour and called Norman to let him know she was fine and was still playing. He laughed and asked if she had some hot dice and she said no, but there was also the prize for most losses and she was definitely in the home stretch for that one.

"You okay to drive?" he asked.

"Yeah, I'm fine, especially since I walked here from just a block away, thank you very much. I'm mostly eating chocolate by the handful but that doesn't usually impair my driving skills. However, the couple of glasses might have done something if I had to drive."

Norman laughed. "Hurry home, I'll try to wait up."

"You're an 'effin liar," said Wallis, laughing, "but I'll wake you up when I get there. Promise."

"Deal," he said.

She had gone back to the game and quickly won a few rounds wondering if she had blown her chances at the coasters with Irish symbols on them that was the booby prize that night. It was one of the first times she could remember having so much fun for an entire night without wondering what it all meant or how everyone was doing. She laughed out loud when she realized she was surprised to just be having fun. That was it. No underlying conspiracy or someone wanting to know something or dropping some large secret on her head.

She looked around at the women and felt gratitude for their friendships. Wallis had no sisters of her own and these women were the closest thing she had to siblings who held her history in a way that no one else would ever be able to again.

Besides, for the most part they all seemed so good at being happy. Julia got up and danced around the room like she was a cowboy riding a bull when she realized she was going to win the grand prize for the night. Wallis leaned back and let out a belly laugh till tears came to her eyes. She thought Julia might rip the velour pants if she kept gyrating and kicking up her leg, whooping loud enough to bother the neighbors next door.

She was trying to get a peek at Maureen's chit sheet when she suddenly realized her phone was buzzing. She was slow to pick it up but by the time she did it was buzzing again and it was Norman, trying to explain that something had happened.

Harriet was in the hospital. She had been found in a cemetery and the doctors said she had suffered a stroke. Wallis should hurry to Medical College of Virginia downtown, near where she had been found. Norman was already there and a neighbor had come over to stay with Ned who was sleeping in his room, unaware that anything was wrong.

Wallis stood up, shaking and dropped her phone onto the table, trying to decide what to do next.

"Wallis, what is it?" asked Julia. "You look awful."

"It's my mother, she's had a stroke."

"Oh dear, come on, game called on account of family emergency," said

Bridget. "Let's get you to the hospital. Where'd they take her? Julia, can you drive her?"

"She's at MCV," said Wallis, turning slowly in a circle, trying to decide what to do next.

"All the way down there? How did that happen," said Sandra.

"I'll drive her. I haven't had anything to drink. I can call y'all when I know anything." It was Maureen, sounding steady and calm as she put her arm around Wallis waist and led her toward the door.

"You sure, honey? You don't want us to come with?" asked Julia, looking around at the others. Wallis looked at them as well and saw how concerned they were for her.

"It's okay. It's a work night," she said, suddenly feeling closed in by all of the faces turned toward her. "There's probably not that much to do just yet and we can call you when we get there."

"Maureen, you make sure and call us the second y'all know anything, you hear?" said Sandra.

Maureen was helping Wallis into the car when they both noticed the streetlights on Pump Road just a block away blink off. Wallis barely took note. The electricity was constantly going out all over the city for one reason or another. The system was all above ground and if it wasn't the weather, it was a drunk driver running into one of the transformers that dotted the landscape.

"What are you doing?" she yelled through the door. She tried to open the door but Maureen kept pushing the door closed again, while scanning the horizon.

She turned and gave Wallis a look she had never seen on Maureen before that reminded her a little of Harriet.

"Stay here," she said, in a stern, clipped tone. "Get down and do not get out of this car. Do not even lift your head. Do you understand?"

Wallis looked at Maureen and just nodded her head as she slid off of the front seat and curled up against the dashboard. Seconds passed and she couldn't hear anything and somewhere out there her mother might be dying. She thought about her resolution to quit taking orders from everyone.

Besides, she wasn't going to stay on the floor of her car forever. Not so close to home where Ned was still sleeping. If something was going that wrong, she had to get home and protect her son.

She pulled the handle slowly and crawled out of the car without lifting her head. It wasn't going to help Ned if something happened to her before she even got away from the car and she wasn't even sure what the danger out there was. There had been no signs of Watchers in the neighborhood since Harriet had tried to shoot one but that was only days ago and didn't mean they weren't watching.

Wallis knew a few of her neighbors might have been in Management and she would have no way of knowing who was being friendly and who had orders.

She looked around the front fender of the car and could see Maureen a yard away moving along the edge of the street, staying low with a gun in her hand.

"Is everyone I know armed?" she whispered.

Wallis didn't have long to think about it because small flashes of light shone in the street and with each one she could see what looked like a small group of people dressed in dark uniforms, pointing weapons in their general direction, firing.

Maureen was returning fire but there was only one of her against what looked like five or six well-armed people. Wallis stripped off her light tan coat that made her more visible in the darkness and felt a little gratitude that she had decided to wear the dark turtleneck tonight.

She ran along the short tree line that separated the two yards to give herself more cover. She was just inside the trees when there was another spatter of what sounded like harmless pops but Wallis knew was automatic fire and she heard Maureen make a small moan. She could see the edge of her house but Wallis couldn't leave her friend lying in the street.

"Oh, Norman," she whispered, wondering if she would see him again as she ran in a crouch by the trees toward where she had last seen Maureen.

She got to Maureen who was lying by the curb and saw that she had been shot almost in the very center of her body and was bleeding badly. She pulled her into her lap as best she could and cradled her face, cooing to her.

"Maureen, it's me. It's Wallis, I'm here," she said, not sure what more there was to say.

"Wallis," Maureen mumbled, opening her eyes slowly. "No, you shouldn't be out here. No."

Wallis heard the click before she saw the gun and looked up in time to see a little red light appear on her chest. She peered into the darkness and saw a small group not too far in the distance all looking their way.

"One Mississippi, two Mississippi," she whispered, waiting for the shot.

It came, but when it did the soldier in the front of the group fell and the rest of them raised their guns over Wallis' head toward a house down the street. The front door of the house was wide open with a light on in the hallway but whoever was shooting was in the front yard and it was difficult to see them with the light coming from the house behind them.

The sharp high-pitched sound of a succession of whistles passed over Wallis' head and she realized that more someone was shooting at the group from behind her. Wallis tried to turn around to see who it was, after all that was in the direction of the house she had just left and all of her friends.

Maureen let out a soft groan and Wallis realized her friend was dying. Suddenly, nothing else mattered in that moment to her except Maureen. Maureen was trying to say something but when she tried she made a gurgling noise and spit up more blood.

"You're not alone, my friend. I'm here."

"Fred," said Maureen, in between gurgles. "Fred. Tell Fred I love him."

"Sure, yes, I will, Maureen, I'll be sure and tell him." Wallis wasn't even going to try and act like Maureen would survive to tell him, herself. She knew it wouldn't happen.

"They're not after Ned," Maureen gurgled. "Not Ned."

"What? What about Ned?"

"It's you they want dead. It's you. You're in the way."

"The way of what?" Wallis felt the tears running down her cheeks and tried to press her hands over the wound to slow down the blood loss. The soldiers were backing up, away from Wallis as gunfire continued around her, all firing over her head in the direction of the squad.

The whistling sound continued but was pulling off to her side. The squad returned fire and a bullet whizzed by Wallis, leaving her ears ringing but she didn't move from where she was holding Maureen. She wasn't going to let her die in the street by herself.

"In the way of what?" she asked, leaning down to hear Maureen over the noise that was now all around her with people running forward and shouting to each other. There seemed to be a flow of people who all poured out of nearby homes knowing what to do and they were all armed.

"They think you're the real Keeper. The other one. That you're the Keeper no one has talked about for generations. The one who guards the secrets. They think it's you and you're in the way. They want to take over and as long as you're alive, it will always be more difficult. You're the balance."

"I know the real Keeper and he's nowhere near here," said Wallis, thinking of Tom and everything he had told her about being named to the top cell of the Circle that really only had one member known only to a very small group of people.

"No, I know who you mean and it's not Tom," she said, coughing. "He's the one that's out front, giving orders and making sure things move forward. But there's another one that guards the secrets and has been around far longer."

"Maureen, it's okay. You can rest. This isn't important anymore."

"No, you have to know. That Keeper was given only one mission for their entire life."

"Why do they think it's me? What secrets?"

"The secret of how this all really started. You are at the very center of it all. You were born to keep the balance."

"I'm not, I'm from Management's bloodlines. I know all about this. Maureen, this isn't important. Not now. They think Ned is the new savior."

"It is important, Wallis. Listen to me. Not a savior. The balance. Not Ned. You." The words came out haltingly. "Your father was from the original line of the merchants who founded Management and his line are the historians, you know that part."

Wallis heard shouting from the direction of Sandra's house. Her friends were trying to get across the yard to where she was laying with Maureen but they were being held back and were shouting angrily at whoever it was.

"But your mother, haven't you ever wondered about her childhood, her history? She probably says very little and turns the conversation away from herself, all the time. Have you ever noticed?"

Wallis felt her face crumple as she held onto Maureen and her chest shook from the sobs rising up her throat. "Your mother is one of the original twenty. Your mother," coughed Maureen, spitting out a thick stream of blood and mucus, "is one of the best agents I have ever seen. She was determined to create peace. She picked out your father before he knew who she really was and got him into marriage and then along came you, her ultimate prize. Only problem was, she never expected to love you so much. It nearly spoiled everything for her."

"No, no, no," said Wallis, rocking Maureen in her lap.

"It's true," said Maureen, smiling, her teeth coated in blood. "All those years she let you think that her only desire in life was to dress well and try to get you to do the same thing. I suppose that was part of it but really, she wanted you to live long enough to maybe change the world. I think she may have been right."

"Maureen, I'm sorry," said Wallis, brushing the hair off of Maureen's face.

"Don't be. This was my mission, to protect you and I did it willingly. Protect your mother, Wallis. Protect the Keeper." Maureen let out a large gasp and died. It happened in a moment and surprised Wallis. She looked at Maureen's still body, wondering if there was more.

Wallis finally gently shut her eyes with a shaking hand and was still holding her when the people she had thought were ordinary neighbors hurried over to help.

They tried to get her to go home and change and she listened to them talk among themselves about moving her and Ned to a safe house but she insisted on being taken to the hospital. She would not be stopping at home and scaring Ned.

"Can someone guard my house till morning?" she asked. She wasn't even going to question them about what they were all doing out here armed with semi-automatic weapons.

Someone brought out a towel and a jacket for her and said they'd sit with Maureen's body till the ambulance could get there. "It's better if you're not here to answer questions, anyway," said a young woman, Wallis knew she was one half of a young couple that both worked in finance in a nearby office park on Broad Street. Wallis had gone to one of their talks on retirement. All of the new information to take in was making her nauseous.

"Get me to my mother," she said, pulling her hair back and straightening her blood-soaked shirt, still holding Maureen's lifeless hand.

"I'll take her." It was Sandra Wilkins, calmly giving orders to the others to look for shells, make sure the area was put back to order and then quickly go back to their houses. She told the young couple to go stay at Wallis' house and asked who was already there watching Ned.

"Good, she's a crack shot. Probably been ready since the lights all dimmed. Come on, Wallis, we need to get going. We're attracting too much attention and there's already way too much to explain to the others. I know, I know," she said, pulling Wallis away from Maureen's body and making her stand on her feet.

"I promise you, we will not leave her alone. We need to go," she said, pulling her toward a car.

"Her shoe isn't on right," said Wallis, pointing at the brown leather shoe that was halfway off of Maureen's foot.

"Okay, we'll make sure she's taken care of, I promise," said Sandra. "I promise."

On the way to the hospital Wallis stared out of the passenger side window. She had no idea what to say to Sandra and she was either going to start screaming at her about a million things or save it all for later. She chose to stay quiet.

Sandra pulled them up to the emergency room door that was closer to the ICU where Harriet had been moved. MCV was really a hive of different hospitals and stretched out over a long block. It could take a lot of running to go from the public parking lot to the ICU and all of it with Wallis in blood-soaked clothes.

The doctors and nurses who saw her coming tried to slow her down and speak to her gently as they quickly scanned her for injuries even though she kept saying, "It's not me, it's my mother."

Sandra had left the car parked in the turn-around in front of the emergency room doors and was right behind Wallis, gently pushing her along, telling everyone that she wasn't injured, just needed to get to ICU. She didn't give any further explanation, knowing that the dramatic entrance would actually help them part the crowd.

Norman was waiting outside of the little room that was part of a circle of rooms surrounding a large nurse's station. Detective Biggs and Buster were standing next to him. Wallis recognized them from when she had seen them at the courthouse. She stopped for a moment, trying to remember if she had seen them outside of Alice Watkins' house the day she was murdered. It didn't matter now. Alice was beyond help. She needed to get to her mother who was still alive.

Each of the small rooms had a partial, glass wall making them visible to everyone in the center.

Reverend Donald was inside of the room and Wallis started running toward them, thinking he was giving Harriet last rites. She wanted to blurt out that her mother was really Jewish and it was just one more lie she had been saying all of her life but she wasn't sure of anything.

Instead she pushed past Norman who was trying to stop her from going in the room. He kept saying, "Are you alright? What happened?"

Wallis didn't answer him. She just wanted to get to her mother.

"Get out," she said to Reverend Donald, tears in her eyes.

"I was reading a prayer."

"Get out," she said, pulling on his arm and pushing him toward the door. "All of you stay out till I tell you otherwise," she said, looking at Norman and Reverend Donald.

Norman nodded his head. "We'll be here," he said, trying to sound like he was steady but his voice shook too much to really pull it off.

Wallis held up both hands to stop them from saying anything else. She saw for a moment how the blood had pooled around her fingernails and was drying in streaks all over her hands and arms. It was her friend's blood.

She pulled a chair close to her mother's bed and gently took Harriet's hand into hers. Harriet was unconscious and there was the constant sound of a heart monitor steadily beeping in the background. Wallis noticed she was breathing on her own without a ventilator but there were other tubes going into her arms and all of Harriet's right side seemed to be sagging under the pull of gravity.

Her purse was sitting open on the small table next to the bed and Wallis glanced in to see that her mother's wallet, reading glasses, spare tissues and gum were all in there. Her usual supply. She snapped the purse closed.

She took a deep breath and wondered where to start but the words came out in a rush.

"I'm sorry," she whispered close to her mother's ear. She wanted to make sure Harriet heard her and that no one else in the hall was a part of their conversation.

"I'm sorry," she said again. "I was so selfish that I never noticed anything about you. I took it for granted that you liked things the way they were. I was so angry at you for what you tried to do to me." Wallis stopped for a moment and held her mother's soft cool hand to her forehead and sobbed quietly.

She sat up straighter and breathed in, wiping the snot off of her face with her sleeve, leaving a small streak of blood across the bridge of her nose.

She leaned in and started again. "I'm sorry that you never thought you could tell me the truth. I know that's not all on me but some of it is. I made it harder for you and I'm sorry. A good friend of mine died tonight, Mom. She died trying to protect me. She said it was her duty and she was glad to do it."

Wallis couldn't stop a loud sob from escaping her throat. Everyone in the hallway stirred but she didn't look directly at them. Instead, she kept whispering to her mother.

"Now, I find out that you have always been doing the same thing. You were doing the one thing I have always wanted to do but you were doing it a lot better than I think I even know how. You were protecting your family against all of the monsters out there. And you did it without anyone telling you, good job. Well, that all changes tonight," she whispered. "Good job, Mom. I love you and now it's my turn. I'm going to keep watch over you. I'm going to watch over the Keeper." Tears filled her eyes, making it difficult for her to see.

Harriet slowly opened her left eye. Her right eye was taped shut to help her close it all the way. She slowly looked over at Wallis and held her gaze for a moment before shutting it again.

Out in the hall, Reverend Donald watched the reunion and marveled at the turn in events. He had been nagging Harriet Jones for years to tell her daughter the truth but without success. He patted his pocket gently one more time to reassure himself the key was still there.

There was time. He could tell Wallis all about what the key could do, later.

CHAPTER

Sergeant Leonard Kipling's wounds were healing and he was able to move around the house on his own, even if he needed a makeshift cane and shuffled more than walked. The squad that was chasing him eventually circled back knocking on doors and they stopped at the Whiting door one afternoon just before dinner.

Jake saw them approaching with his telescope and went to warn his father and the Sergeant. They hid the Sergeant in the safe room behind the bookcase and put Ruthie in there with him. She was too little for them to be sure she wouldn't give them all away and it was easy enough to explain her absence by saying she was at a friend's house for a sleepover. Peter was not as steady as Jake but he knew enough to stay close to his brother and say nothing at all.

Mark answered the door and only one of them had come up onto his porch, flashing what looked like an official badge of some sort. The rest stood down below, gently holding their weapons in front of them. They were all dressed in white, easily hidden against the snow unless you were looking for them with a sensitive telescope from the small room at the top of the house, like Jake was doing when he saw them come over the ridge.

The small flag with the family crest was already flying at the very top of the house, signaling that the enemy was nearby and holding off the Keeper if he was trying to approach. That was Circle training and the flag had been raised days ago just in case. Mark was not taking any chances until he was sure that Management's squad had moved on to another territory.

He was relieved that the flag was still up there, whipping in the wind, when Jake came to tell him that soldiers were approaching.

Jake had spotted the patrol and quickly left his post and locked the door to the tiny room before he came down the stairs. By the time the soldiers came to the door the boys were in the middle of a video game, making a lot of noise and laughing. There was a warm pizza in front of them, some of the pieces already gone, hidden at the bottom of the trash can.

"Can I help you gentlemen?" he asked, opening the door only far enough to show his two sons, smiling and pushing each other as they kept right on playing. "Is there something wrong?"

"My name is Lieutenant Radford. We are tracking a fugitive who escaped across the Canadian border. Have you seen anything suspicious on your property?" Mark gauged the man's age to be about the same as his own and he wondered where he was really from and if he had an entirely different job when he wasn't on patrol, stalking his neighbors.

"No, haven't seen a thing. Is this fugitive dangerous? Should we be worried?"

"Yes sir, he's considered armed and dangerous and at this point desperate. If you should notice anyone, please give me a call," he said, handing Mark a card. Mark glanced down at it, knowing that's what anyone would normally do in a situation like this. He had been trained years ago on what to do if something like this ever happened when he had originally been with Management. No one had anticipated that he'd be using it all against them in the mountains of Montana years later.

"I'll be sure to call you. Are you with a Federal Agency?" he asked. It was pushing things a little but to never ask was suspicious and besides he wanted to hear how they'd explain what they were doing out here in the middle of nowhere.

"Yes sir, we're with the Military Police, with the U.S. Army," he said, tapping the card.

"Oh yeah, the MP's," said Mark, looking down at the card. "The fugitive is with the Army?"

"Yes, he was a Sergeant so he's trained with a gun and highly skilled. Be very careful."

"What did he do?"

"He killed a few good men and betrayed his country," said the Lieutenant. "We'd like to take him in alive, if possible. That's where information from people like you could be very helpful."

Mark smiled at the compliment. The lieutenant was following protocol, making friendly with the locals to get information. He would shoot Mark and his entire family if necessary for the mission. "Thank you, these are good people around here. Will do."

Mark went to shut the door and the lieutenant held it open for a moment. Mark slowly turned back like he was annoyed but not rushed. "Was there something else?"

"Do you mind if we take a look around your property? Make sure he's not hiding anywhere? You have kind of a big spread."

"Sure, no problem. I'd prefer if you were gone by sundown though. I don't like the idea of so many guns roaming around near the house. I have children in here, you know. But take a look. I'd like to know we're all safe in here too."

"You have a basement or any exterior sheds where someone could easily gain entrance?"

"The basement is shut tight. That's not a problem. There's a shed out back about thirty yards behind the house that's full of storage. You're welcome to take a look, we don't lock it but someone would be hard pressed to squeeze in there. We've stocked it pretty full of junk."

"Thank you," said the lieutenant, nodding. Mark slowly shut the door again, but this time kept looking at the group until the door was shut completely. He slowly walked away from the door like he had something ordinary to do and headed for the kitchen to get the boys something to drink.

He knew the squad would watch the house more than search the grounds, at least at first, to see what Mark did next. A rookie mistake was to suddenly try to run and tell anyone what had just happened or watch the squad out of a window. Jake and Peter knew that too and kept right on playing their games. It would be at least a couple of hours before he would dare go check on Ruthie and Sergeant Kipling.

The next day there were tracks in the snow all over the property from where the lieutenant and his men had tromped around looking for Sergeant Kipling. It was clear to Mark that they were making a show of doing a good job and he wondered if they were still watching him from a long way's away.

He went down into town for supplies and to sit around the diner to see if anyone else had met the squad. If they had, that was good news and meant that the Management team really did believe Mark's story and that the Sergeant could be anywhere. If no one had seen a thing then Mark was targeted and they would have to keep the pennant flag flying for a lot longer.

Any sudden change would attract attention and removing the pennant could invite disaster. If the Keeper tried to move across the glare of the snow toward the house with anyone watching he would be spotted and it was a sure bet that everyone in the house would be slaughtered, leaving no witnesses.

Training had also taught him to set up routines that might prove useful later, no matter how much time they took up even if they never came in handy. One of them was going into the local diner on a regular basis and sitting at the counter having a chat with whoever wandered close enough for him to ask a question.

Locals at first were a little put off by the stranger who kept smiling and engaging them in conversation but eventually they got to know him well enough to chalk it up to him being from the South. He never invited any of them up the mountain to his place but that wasn't too unusual for these parts. People were friendly but no one thought it was a good idea to get that far into anyone's business. The local temperament suited Mark's purposes just fine.

"Hey Sam. Hi Luke. How's it going?" Mark called out as he came into the diner, stomping his feet to get rid of some of the snow before he walked across the linoleum.

"Doing well, come sit over here with us," said Sam. "Hey, you're up on that ridge. You see them fellas in their fancy outdoor suits traipsing all over creation? They 'bout near scared my wife to death talking about some fugitive and flashing badges. They come by your place?"

Mark wanted to hug him but knew he needed to maintain the same amount of annoyance because in the end, anyone could be an operative. It didn't matter that he was up in the mountains. After all, he had played for both sides and here he was sitting on a stool, trying to act natural.

"Yeah, they came by yesterday. Told me the same story and took a look around the place. Don't think they found much, though because they left like they came and I haven't seen them since."

"I heard they was staying at the B and B one town over. Millie's sister owns the place and said they came in toting weapons and shaking off snow, making a big fuss. They said they were going to be there for a few days but she's trying to get them to leave faster. Not good for business, all those dangerous looking weapons. One thing to have hunters around but not this."

"I see what you mean," said Mark, sipping his coffee. "Hopefully, they'll get their man and keep going. We can get back to normal peace and quiet."

"Amen," said Sam, holding his mug up in a toast. "Amen."

Mark stayed for an hour and talked about the long winter and the price of fuel before saying he needed to go get supplies and head back up the mountain before his kids tore up the place or ate him out of house and home. Just a week ago he had trusted these people and was willing to believe that not a one of them had ever heard of Management or the Circle and didn't care, anyway. Now, he found he wasn't sure and he knew he never would be able to really relax again.

As he drove up the long driveway to the house he tried to look around for signs of anyone else on his property. If the lieutenant saw him he knew he could always say he was keeping an eye out for intruders, which was true. He was also trying to make sure he didn't see signs of a third group moving in a forward direction toward his home.

Once he got inside he went looking for Sergeant Kipling and found him playing checkers with Ruthie in the safe room.

"I haven't really left this room," said Kipling.

"Do you think they know you're trying to move the Keeper?" asked Mark.

"They? You mean that squad out there? No, I don't. I think they know something important is happening but I don't believe they have a clue. Otherwise," he said, covering Ruthie's ears for a moment, "they would have burned the house down just to be sure there was no place to go," he whispered, taking his hands down. "Your move," he said to Ruthie, smiling.

"King me," she shouted in glee, smiling.

"Aw, you're too good. That's like three in a row."

That night Mark waited till everyone was asleep and he turned on the ham radio he had set up in one of the spare bedrooms. He turned it on at least once a month and chatted with mostly old men who were retired and enjoying a hobby. They had a lot of interesting stories to tell about the lives they used to lead but nothing more than that.

Mark was establishing another routine.

He searched around for one of the familiar handles and found a regular in Winston-Salem, North Carolina who wanted to know how much snow Mark was getting. Weather was always a big topic with the retired set and it gave Mark an easy topic when he couldn't think of anything to share. So much of his life wasn't supposed to exist anymore. It could make starting conversations a little awkward.

Just as he was about to sign off, thinking that his idea wasn't panning out, a new voice came across the airwaves. It was a handle from Petersburg, Virginia addressing him by his handle as if they had chatted many times before that night.

Mark had the out of date OTP by his side and waited to hear the first bit of conversation.

The man immediately started talking about his marriage, like they had just left off a conversation. "Couldn't have formed a more perfect union." It was the connection. Mark kept track of the words he used. Sprinkled in the sentences that seemed to meander all over the place were the words Full, Faith and Credit. "The Creator sure knew what he was doing, in the course of things. Don't you agree?"

It was the request for an affirmative that he would take in the Keeper. He knew it was coming and had resigned himself to the answer. "I definitely do. If I could meet the right woman, I think I'd take the same course of action."

"We've been married just on forty-five years this coming May third with three kids and four grandkids. It's a good life."

There was a party of four and the Keeper coming his way and they were already in the area. They would wait five more days but then would have to either turn back or come up the mountain.

Something had gone wrong and the Keeper had only been able to give them partial information. The sender was letting him know that things might get hairy, quickly and he should be prepared. Mark thought about his kids and wondered what he could do to ensure their safety. There weren't many options at this point. It was too late to make a run for it to someplace else. They might get caught on the open road with too many questions from an armed military squad that could be watching them.

He couldn't just force Sergeant Kipling to leave without similar results. He would have to play it out to the conclusion. There was one last piece of code that came through and made no sense at all to Mark. It translated to, 'the proof is safe but the Keeper is not.'

"No kidding," he mumbled to himself. "Tell me something about the Keeper I don't know." He had no idea what they meant by proof but decided to let it go. There was enough to worry about and he wasn't going to start sending coded messages back to try and clear it up.

If the radio chatter was to be believed, it would be a few days before he would get his chance. Mark, Kipling and Jake had started taking shifts so that there was always someone who was awake and watching the grounds for any unexpected arrival, whether friend or foe.

Three days later, Mark was drinking strong coffee watching the snow gently falling at three in the morning wondering how he had so easily slipped back inside of the Circle when he noticed movement among the trees.

The pennant was still flying at the top of the house, so he wondered if the squad was making a reconnaissance at night to see if they could catch everyone with their guard down and finally discover where the missing Sergeant was hiding.

He felt for the rifle by his side and held it up to his shoulder to look through the scope. He knew not to look down at the ground but train the scope on the tops of the pines and watch them sway in a way that would tell him if a group of people were moving through them. It was also easier that way to know which direction they were heading.

There it was again. There was definite movement and they were headed in a curve in a general direction toward the house. He put down the gun and ran into Jake's room, gently shaking his shoulder and putting a hand over his son's mouth so he wouldn't make a sudden noise and wake his brother.

Jake's eyes popped open and he tried to sit up but Mark stopped him and gave him a signal to be quiet and follow him out of the room.

"Someone's coming," Mark whispered, once they were in the hallway. "Carry your sister down to the safe room and put her with the Sergeant. Do the usual protocol and make sure you don't leave any pattern in the dust on the floor. They'll be here in just a few minutes or less, so you have to hurry."

Mark said everything as calmly as he could but he could hear his pulse beating in his ears. This was not the life he wanted for his family and he had taken great risks to protect them from something exactly like this. None of it, in the end, had worked.

Jake quickly gathered up his sleeping sister in his arms, and Mark watched how gently he carried her down the stairs. He ran back to the window and picked up the gun so he could see how close they were getting to the house.

He looked through the scope but couldn't see anything. For a moment, he wondered if he had imagined the whole thing. Maybe he was just tired and overwrought.

But Jake came running up the stairs and whispered in an excited voice. "They're here. The Keeper has made it. They knocked on the basement door, just like you said they would. They knew the right code."

Mark followed them downstairs and found everyone sitting in the safe room. All of the lights throughout the house were still off in case someone was watching, even from miles away. A single light would look too suspicious at that time of night.

The group was gathered in the small safe room and Ruthie was now awake, rubbing her eyes and sitting in the Sergeant's lap. Ruthie always made friends easily.

"You must be Mark Whiting. My name is Tom Weiskopf. I've heard a lot of good things about you."

Mark took his hand to shake it, wondering what it must be like to be the head of such a large organization without any of the trappings that normally came with such a post. Tom Weiskopf had all of the burdens without any of the pleasures.

"I have a message for you," said Mark, remembering the odd postscript that had been added to the transmission.

"Already. They've been busy, I see," said Tom, smiling but Mark could see the exhaustion around his eyes.

"Yes, the message was 'the proof is safe'. I don't know what that means, though. I'm hoping that has some meaning for you."

Tom Weiskopf sat down on the edge of the bed and took a deep breath.

"Was that the entire message?" he asked. "There had to be more."

"There was one other thing but you're here so that can't be useful. It was just that the Keeper is not. We already knew you were in trouble. You're safe here, at least for now."

Tom looked at one of the men who had arrived with him. His face had turned ashen. "We can't stay here. We will have to move again as soon as we can. The Keeper isn't safe and we have to get to Richmond or die trying. Esther has sent a message. Everything hangs on it."

CHAPTER

22

Fred was surprised that he could feel that much anger and still function. It was a new sensation. He was sleeping when Norman came to his door. It was almost dawn and Norman looked like a man who had seen too much and didn't know what to do with all of it. His face was drawn and he looked far older than his forties as he tried to explain what had happened that night.

"Can I come in?" he asked, standing on the doorstep. At first, Fred thought about saying no. He knew what was coming. There was only one reason someone stood on your doorstep like that and it wasn't a good one. Norman and Fred weren't close enough friends for it to be someone in Norman's family. There were too many other doorsteps Norman would have been standing at if it was Wallis or Ned.

But Maureen and Wallis are friends, thought Fred. And Maureen was ordered by the President, no less, to protect Wallis by any means necessary.

How long ago was that, thought Fred. Just a couple of weeks, no maybe a month by now.

He was still holding the door open with one hand, almost leaning on it now. He still hadn't said a word to Norman except for 'hello', trying to hold off the inevitable.

In this moment, nothing bad had happened yet. No one was hurt or worse, dead. No one was missing. He didn't have to live with the loss, forever.

Norman looked around nervously and repeated the question. "Okay if I come in?" he asked. Fred moved back a little to give Norman room and he slid past him, looking Fred in the eye as he held out his arm to gesture toward the formal living room that no one ever really used.

That's where information like this was usually spilled out. In a room that was a little uncomfortable, a little too formal that was hardly ever sat in by anyone. That way, when the dust has settled and the routines have returned, no one has to go in there, ever again. No one has to face sitting in the same spot remembering what was said there, what was suddenly lost when they weren't looking.

No one has to think about all of the regrets over what they could have done differently, if only they'd thought about this conversation, in this room, that came way too soon.

Fred watched Norman wind around him but he stayed by the door for a few minutes longer, looking out at the front yard and the small bit of his neighborhood that he could see in the morning light.

Everything looked normal, just where he had left it when he went to bed. His car was parked in the driveway with room for Maureen to get by so she could have the space in the garage. The Richmond Times Dispatch was sitting on front stoops of the houses that still got a newspaper and wanted to see the local scores and read about the small city politics.

The recycle bins were neatly stacked by everyone's curb, waiting for the truck that would be there shortly. His lawn still needed mowing sometime today even though the morning air was cold. It took a lot to get his lawn to shut off for the winter.

He held onto those images, watching them slowly, trying to memorize them before he would be willing to follow Norman into the living room and listen to what he had to say. Into his and Maureen's living room, that Maureen had decorated.

He lifted his chin and reminded himself that this was all an assignment, not a life he had chosen. There were certain outcomes that were always a possibility.

It's just that he thought the deadly outcomes belonged to him. He had always thought that Maureen would be the one standing at the front door on a beautiful Saturday morning, listening to a blue jay even in the late fall, wondering how things could have changed when he wasn't looking.

That's what really got to him. He was trained to scan situations and take in possible outcomes so that he could do whatever was possible to bring about a different ending. Last night, when Maureen was leaving for Bunco night he didn't do a thing but kiss her goodbye.

Nothing more had occurred to him.

The wave of anger washed over him again, making him crumple, just a little right in the center as he gripped the door for support.

He knew what her assignment was and that Wallis would be at Bunco night, after all this was the neighborhood's version of Ladies Night and yet, he didn't even sense the possibility of anything going wrong beyond too much drinking and eating or telling too many secrets.

But Norman was here looking like he'd rather be anywhere else, inviting Fred into his own living room to sit on the edge of a couch that was too hard and too small to ever really be comfortable.

Maureen had found it in an antique shop and insisted they get it and reupholster it themselves. It could be a project they could do together. Besides, the Circle only gave them so much of a budget to decorate and his salary from being an accountant mostly went toward their retirement. That was a recent decision that they had not mentioned to anyone.

It was against protocol to build a mutual retirement with someone who was assigned on a detail with you. It compromised the integrity of the relationship according to the training manual. An operative couldn't be relied on to keep to their singleness of purpose if they were authentically invested in the relationship.

"To hell with that," Maureen had said. "We've made it this far. I'm too used to you now. And if we don't start saving, when we're forced out to pasture we won't have enough to finally travel without our weapons." He had laughed and given in to her plans.

It wasn't too long after that they had spotted the couch and she had taken another step toward being a real couple and convinced him to buy something because they wanted it and not because they had an item on their list that needed to be filled. They wanted the couch just for them.

This would even help their cover, she had said, beaming at him in the store.

He dreaded the idea of figuring out the right way to upholster the fussy piece of furniture so that they didn't ruin it but he couldn't resist the look on Maureen's face. That was happening to him a lot more, lately. He didn't care anymore. For her, he would finally let his guard down.

"I love you," she had said when he kissed her goodbye. Her voice was like an echo in his head. Norman hadn't told him yet but he knew and her voice was already just a step away in his head. He wondered how long before it would get harder to really hear how she sounded. Where was her phone, he thought. If he could get to it first he could capture her reply on voicemail before the Circle erased all of the data so that Maureen Bowers ceased to exist.

Fred started to shake, making the front door rattle as he held on even tighter. Norman got up from where he was perched and came slowly over to Fred to help him gently let go of the door.

Fred let Norman help him. He was trying to remember something. "I know why you're here," he said, not looking at Norman. He was focusing on the small, uncomfortable couch. He sat down slowly and slid back against the upholstered back that was topped by an elaborate wood carving, stretching across the entire back of the couch and repeated along the front of the arms. The wood carving always poked whoever was sitting there in the back, making the whole experience even worse. Fred sat back and let the curlicues dig into his shoulder while he tried to remember something.

"Fred," Norman started, as he sat down in the wing chair next to Fred, leaning forward till their knees almost touched. "Something has happened to Maureen." Norman looked like he was struggling to get out the words. "There was a gun battle." Fred cut him off.

"I'm trying to remember something." Fred was trying to contain his anger. It threatened to spill out onto everything, including Norman. After all, Maureen's assignment was to protect Norman's wife and Fred was having trouble remembering why Wallis was more important than his Maureen. He heard the echo of her voice again. 'I love you.'

"I can't quite remember," he said, choking back the first wave of nausea to hit him. "What did I say to Maureen before she left last night? I remember what she said to me. It was I love you." He held up his hand to stop Norman from speaking. He didn't want to hear the words yet. Then everything would change and it would all have to be dealt with and he would have to show Norman out and move to protocol. His training would insist on it.

But if he could hold off those words for just a few more moment he could be Maureen's husband for just a little longer and grieve for the woman he had learned how to love despite the way the operation had started.

"I can't remember what I said to her. Did I say, I love you, back to Maureen? Did I? I'm not sure," he said, through gritted teeth.

Norman waited a moment and started again.

"There was a gun battle and Maureen was shot. She died at the scene. I'm very sorry. I'm very sorry." Norman looked like he was waiting for Fred to say something, maybe ask him questions but it wasn't necessary.

Fred knew that Norman would only know part of the story and would get some of it wrong. Better to wait for the official report. Fred's clearance was high enough up that he would see the report before most of it was redacted and Maureen Bowers would be honored before fading into memory.

What was her real name? It was something they never talked about even when they were alone. They couldn't be certain that no one was listening from Management or the Circle. He wished he knew. He wished he had figured out a way to tell her his real name was actually Fred. He was named for an uncle. She would have found that funny.

Fred showed Norman to the door. He turned down the offer of help with any arrangements and said he would be sure to get in touch once he knew anything more. Fred knew the Circle would insist on setting up everything and would use another operative. Both of them had occasionally mentioned relatives who lived in another state to establish the roles for a situation just like this. More protocol, more training.

An older woman around their age who would be cast in the role of Maureen's sister and would even bear somewhat of a resemblance. She would come in from out of town and help Fred set up all of the arrangements. Maureen would be cremated so that no corpse was left behind to dig up later to look at how she died or test DNA against anyone else. There would be no loose ends.

If Maureen had managed to protect her real role in the neighborhood, right until the end, Fred knew he could be expected to continue in his assignment. They might move him to get him out of the role of grieving husband so that he could better do his job but even that was not for sure.

The reality was, he was a valuable asset right where he was in Richmond. Close enough to D.C. to have immediate access to the President without being seen around the Capital and becoming a familiar face to anyone.

He watched Norman pull away from the curb and then he took a last look at his neighborhood before shutting the door. He went to his go bag that was kept on a shelf in the garage behind the leftover paint cans and took it inside to check the contents. It was a process he went through every few months like clockwork, only this time he planned to use what was in it.

There was a passport with a new name, Jeff Monaghan, a nice Irish name to go with his fair looks and close to a hundred grand in cash. That was what Maureen and Fred had decided should be their retirement account. Trust, but verify Maureen had said, laughing. They would take a note from Ronald Reagan and keep their assets under their own roof.

That way, if something happened they could get out of town together and for a while at least, survive off of the grid. It was a ridiculous plan, he had thought at the time. He would not have left the President unprotected and just disappear unless the government had ceased to exist and then the money would have probably been useless.

He didn't realize there was another possible scenario.

At the bottom of the bag was a burner phone that contained information in its directory that Fred had been collecting steadily over the years. A list of known Management operatives in the area.

He reported them, as he was instructed but he also kept a list with their names, addresses and titles in the phone. That part was not protocol.

Fred retrieved the phone and charged it. It took less than an hour. The phone was a smart phone that he had converted so that it couldn't connect to any wifi and stayed off of the grid. There were a few more burners in his bag just like this one, all designed to keep him off of the grid in the case of an extreme emergency.

He saw that there were almost a hundred names on the list. Mid-level managers who were thought to be rising stars in Management. Others who he suspected were now commanders in the field and had taken sabbaticals from their jobs but still returned home on most weekends to keep up appearances of a normal suburban life. Still others who were leaders in their business or in politics and all reported to some other cell within Management.

There wouldn't be time to get to all of them. He would need to choose the ones that were most likely in the squad that he knew had come for Wallis Jones last night. Even if he was wrong about some of them, he knew that he'd be able to pick out a few. The rest would be selected for their strategic role in Management and their absence would cause the most harm to the organization.

At the least, it would really piss off a lot of people. That was enough for Fred.

All of them had notes in the directory under their names that included their regular routines during the week. Fred had been monitoring them for years, as instructed, but siphoning off the information.

Fred checked his weapons. There was a shallow closet built behind the walk-in closet in the master bedroom. It was just big enough for a rack on the wall that held enough firearms of various sizes to start a battle, not just a fight.

Fred chose carefully and laid everything out on the kitchen table. He went outside and backed his car into the garage and shut the door. He loaded the weapons onto the backseat and covered them with a blanket, keeping a Heckler and Koch .45 caliber special operations command pistols next to him on the front seat.

The go bag with a change of clothes, the new identity and the money was in the trunk.

He opened the door to the garage and slowly pulled out onto the street. The anger was making his chest hurt but he put it aside.

There were a few things to take care of first and time to let it all go, later.

The first name on the list was a woman who he suspected was in Special Forces for Management. There was a good possibility she had been one of the shooters last night. He started with her name and drove to the Martin's on John Rolfe Parkway. The woman was a creature of habit and would be just getting to the store as it opened. She liked to get in and out before the store got busy with shoppers and the good produced was picked over.

Fred had made a point with each name on his list to run into them somewhere along their route and start a conversation, gather information. It had taken years but he was patient. A lot of what he gathered seemed innocuous. Even though each of these people was a trained agent they didn't understand they were being mined for details that could prove useful to the Circle and eventually, Fred.

When he got to the parking lot he saw the woman parking in her usual area, a little ways from the store. She had a nice car, an early model silver Urban, and he watched how careful she was with it. She didn't want the doors to get dinged.

He waited till she had taken a few steps away from her car and he lifted the gun, aiming carefully and shot her down with just one bullet. It was easy and quiet. The gun gave off no noise and she had dropped so quickly, so close to the edge of the parking lot it would take some time for anyone to notice she was out there, lying on the ground.

He had rehearsed what would happen a few times before this morning, just in case. His own protocol.

He didn't know what might cause hunting down Management operatives to be necessary but there was a war going on and he knew all along it was a possibility. He had assumed, though that someone would have given him an order. This was okay, though.

The war was just spreading out into the suburbs of Richmond, Virginia.

He knew what his actions would bring down on himself and even on the Circle. Management would want to fight back and there was the likelihood that the Circle would try and beat them to it.

He deleted the woman from the phone and looked up the next one. He knew he needed to hurry. There were almost twenty people on his list and it wouldn't take long for someone to connect the dots and figure out that someone was hunting Management. Then they would institute their own protocol and this would all get more difficult.

Maureen's death might even point back to him and Fred's face would appear on a lot of Management screens. There wasn't much time.

The next name on the list was an older man who had risen through the ranks to become a vice-president in a commercial real estate firm. He was close to retirement.

Fred had watched his coming and going lately and knew he was probably in charge of troop movements for the mid-Atlantic region. He would have passed down the order to hunt down Wallis. Fred drove to the golf course in Goochland where the man spent a lot of his Saturday mornings. It was a good way to keep his visibility in the community and catch a little down time from the machinations of the war.

Fred found him on the ninth hole, playing with a few younger Management operatives, all most likely officers in the war. He shot them all, leaving them lying around the tee-off. None of them had time to pull out the weapons that were secured in their golf bags. During wartime no one went anywhere unarmed. That was to be expected. But this was Richmond and no one believed that a sniper would bring the war to their doorsteps, even after last night.

Wallis was the target, after all and Norman was a known recluse from whatever the Circle was doing. Casualties were to be expected. Vengeance is not normally a part of conflict. It brings too many unknown factors.

Fred noted on his phone that one of the men at the golf course was number eleven on his list. He deleted that name too.

Less than an hour had passed since he had pulled out of his driveway. He calculated that he had until one o'clock at best before he needed to leave whether he had gotten to his entire list or not.

The next name on the list was a lawyer. This one would be harder to catch out in the open. He turned the car toward Patterson Avenue and headed for Route 288 and the Veterans Memorial Bridge to the Southside. He needed to hurry. 'I love you.' He heard himself saying it in his head. Surely, he answered her.

Fred was right. It was early afternoon when word was sent through secure channels to Tom Weiskopf in Montana. Someone was hunting Management operatives in Richmond, Virginia and they were being very selective about who they chose. Tom already knew about the botched attempt on his sister in law's life and he knew that Maureen Bowers had died.

"Shit," he whispered, realizing that a very well-trained operative, Fred Bowers, had decided to change the game plan.

Fred was one of the few people entrusted with the next phase of the war plan. He was read in because he was believed to be someone who would not slip and give away details, even under pressure.

Tom had to admire that even though Fred was completely off the reservation, he was still working within a Circle operation. This wasn't just a random act of violence. It was an act of armed conflict, part of a battle plan that had been carefully weighed and thought out among advisors.

He was just forcing their hand in order to exact a little payback. Tom knew that Fred was already in the wind. He would have planned this part out as well and cleaners were sent to his residence to make sure no evidence of Fred's real background was left behind.

Every square inch would be searched to make sure there were no hidden compartments or closets that still had weapons or caches of money or secrets left for someone else to find.

Then they would start the new backstory that Fred had decided to bury Maureen's ashes near her fictional sister. The funeral home would say, if anyone asked, that Fred had been there to make the arrangements himself and had taken the ashes with him. He was already on a plane.

Pieces of the story would be spread out in the neighborhood at the appropriate time till everyone slowly forgot about Fred and Maureen Bowers, except at the occasional backyard cookout. Maureen's official cause of death was hit and run. There was no mention of bullet holes or gunfire. The EMT's who picked up the body were with the Circle and had taken her body straight to a designated funeral home where she disappeared into the system.

Everything was neatly handled and the coroner signed off, making it official. The women who had been at Bunco night were kept apart from each other. The Circle agents who had spilled out of nearby houses and were on the scene made sure of that. The women were to be questioned all night, wearing them down, while having an alternate story suggested to them, till they thought it was really what they must have seen.

The detectives assigned to the case were part of the Circle and made sure that the case made a nice loop back on itself, answering all of the questions except for who might have been driving the car that hit poor Maureen. Must have been a drunk driver, how awful.

Most of the people who lived around Wallis Jones and her family were Circle operatives, put in place to watch over the family and keep out prying eyes. They had tolerated the Watchers who parked on their street because of orders to not give away their positions.

They all knew what to do if there was ever an attack on the family and they had all played their parts well, even Maureen. By the time the night was over there wasn't a trace of a gun battle but there was evidence of a car accident and broken windshield glass left behind for others to see and draw their own conclusions. Poor Maureen. She probably never even saw it coming. Thank goodness, Wallis got out of the way. Did you hear her mother had a stroke?

Tom Weiskopf gave the order that he knew Fred was forcing him to, the failsafe, and found he wasn't even annoyed. It was all inevitable anyway. Somehow, this made it a little easier. He had wondered when the plan was devised if he'd have the stomach to do it. Now it was here.

The Circle One battalion with almost a thousand men and women was activated. The companies that made up the battalion were sent out over all of the surrounding counties. Soldiers were fanned out in squads in every direction to finish Fred's work.

None of the Circle One battalion was from the Richmond area. This battalion came from the Northwest and were loaded onto a transport plane, arriving by dinnertime. The soldiers were hunting down Management operatives in an American suburban setting. They needed to at least not be able to recognize their target or know their life's story.

There needed to be some separation so that everyone had at least a shot of being able to ever sleep peacefully again.

Management was also starting to gather information and knew there would be more trouble. It didn't take them long to understand that the war had suddenly moved to Richmond. Local commanders were warned and soldiers were called up to the area but before the planes could take off, headed for Richmond, a vicious battle broke out along the Canadian front.

The Circle had started a human wave attack on the northern border, sending a massive wall of soldiers to overrun a known Management base, capturing prisoners who were sent even deeper into Canada to be interrogated.

Another wave started simultaneously in Texas, pushing into Mexico and another in the west, in the Bay area. They were all distractions, meant to keep Management from concentrating troops in the Richmond, Virginia area.

The Circle had designs on the Federal Reserve in Richmond that was currently staffed mostly by Management operatives. That portion of the Reserve was set aside for the entire system's software and was the brain of the U.S. banking system and therefore, Management's banking system.

The Circle wanted to take it all over but in order to do so they needed to get some people out of the way. None of it was going to be easy but in the end, the Keeper and his advisors, along with President Hayes and his aides had all decided it was necessary. The Keeper gave the order. The battles shortly got underway.

Some of them were portrayed in that evening's news cycle as police operations in suspect neighborhoods, trolling through looking for gang leaders. Others were random violence that was shocking and unexplainable and would require a little national mourning to deal with before everyone could get back to their routines.

Several of the Management operatives went on the run and spread out through Church Hill, just across from Mosby Court, another public housing complex that sat on a hill neatly overlooking what there was of the Richmond skyline.

The fighting became close-range. Circle soldiers ran through the streets in what might pass for casual weekend dress for a long hike with heavy backpacks, looking for their targets who were scurrying just ahead of them. One target was found just as he took the corner by St. John's Church but he didn't make it any further. A van pulled up quickly and took away the body before anyone could take notice.

The Circle squads were doing their best to push the Management targets toward Mosby Court. The Management operatives were running for the highway just beyond Mosby Court where there would most likely be transportation vehicles prepared to take them away to safety.

Between them and the highway lay Accommodation Street and hunkered down all along the edges of the road for at least a mile were Circle soldiers waiting for their orders. Once the targets were all running in the same direction and too close to successfully turn back, the soldiers rose up and marched forward, all in local police uniforms, looking as if they were playing out a drug sweep, picking up everyone who got caught in their net.

The locals who were caught up in the net would get released later that day, a few the next day if they were caught with illegal weapons or too much illegal drugs to ignore, while the rest would never make it to Accommodation Street or anywhere else.

The mission was thought to be a success by the Circle and when the day was over the Federal Reserve and a few other key businesses in the area had openings that needed to be filled.

Norman stood in his kitchen and watched the news, wondering how all of it got started.

CHAPTER

Maurel Samonte understood her new orders perfectly and sent the orders to the pharmacists who were operating as moles for the Circle on the mail order floor of Westin Fullerton. The next phase of the Keeper's plan was put into motion. It was decided that enough personal health information about key Management players had been collected and Maurel was too valuable to leave in place much longer.

Once the second phase was well underway she was to depart for the Midwest. It was good news. Maurel was returning to her last assignment and becoming a Mother Superior once again.

When the time was right, Maurel was to finish the job and unleash a virus into the Kroton system that would eat up all remaining space and permanently scramble all of the stored information whether it was legitimate or not. This would accomplish two goals.

It would be almost impossible for Management to find out what the Circle had collected on who and for how long and it would cripple one of their bigger cash cows, Westin Fullerton. It would take days, maybe even weeks for the company to be fully operational again and it would cost Management millions of dollars as well as put a nice dent in the company's sterling reputation.

All it took was three pharmacists in the right places at the different mail order locations to complete the Keeper's project. They had been planted a long time ago before there was ever a reason to worry and did nothing over the years but be good employees, slowly getting cost of living pay raises and small promotions.

Each facility looked almost identical. They were non-descript, wide-open warehouses that covered areas as big as a few football fields. Inside, the noise was deafening and everyone who worked on the floor wore headphones to cut out the noise. Pharmacists had small cubicles where they checked medications against the prescriptions to make sure everyone was getting the right medicine and the right amount. They even checked to make sure that there was no toxic combination just because someone took the right dose for their order.

They were the last guardian against anything going wrong and took their jobs very seriously.

Most patients ordered the same medications at just about the same time, every few months. Everyone loves a routine.

That made it easier to select certain prominent figures from all over the country based on the information that Maurel Samonte had gathered from her post, glean what they were taking and therefore what condition they were suffering from.

From there it was easy to create a plan to poison them.

It was the simplest kind of warfare that could reach out anywhere, started long before a war was even thought of by anyone except an overly-cautious Keeper. He had grown up hearing the stories from his father about what Management had done just two generations ago to millions of people.

The uppermost cell had devised the plan and were the only ones who knew about it. Those who worked at Westin Fullerton, including Maurel, only knew pieces of the plan.

The selection of who would die was always changing as time passed but the intent was still the same. They would not go after the uppermost tier of people because they were usually older and closer to retirement.

The real targets would be their replacements, the mid-level managers and vice-presidents who were still young enough to have years left but had developed chronic conditions that could be exploited.

It wasn't an easy plan for Tom Weiskopf or any of his advisors to stomach but it was only meant as the failsafe in the event that circumstances became dire.

The day had arrived.

The war was growing worse and harder to contain. If it was all true. If Management's aim was to create enough havoc in the country to bring the presidential election's outcome into question. If there really was an inner cell that had burrowed itself into a place where they could cause a war in order to change Management's top level and take over from them.

If that cell had enough resources to not only find Harry Weiskopf but take him away from the comfortable prison.

Then it was time.

This would be the Circle's atom bomb to end the war before too many more people were hurt or before an even darker force than anyone was used to managed to take over control of an organization that had almost endless resources.

The medications came to the pharmacist, the Circle mole and with a sleight of hand the prescription was switched out for pills that looked exactly the same to anyone but a professional who was looking for a mistake. Even then, it would have been close to impossible. Once they successfully left the pharmacist's cubicle the contents would be sealed and not reopened until they were in the hands of the customer.

The next step in the process, the medication was labeled and put in a small green tub two feet by two feet and placed on the rolling assembly line that wound around the top till the contents came to the other side of the room where they spilled into a plain, greyish-white padded bag, ready for shipping.

It was a simple, transparent process with checks and balances everywhere to make sure nothing went wrong. After all, fouling up the medication could lead to deadly results. Everyone knew that and it was why anyone standing above on the glassed-in catwalk could easily see what anyone down below was doing.

It was another way of keeping everyone honest.

No system is perfect.

A long time ago, an employee who delivered the mail and walked the floor of one of the plants every day, pushing a cart, had spotted the hole in their system and reported it back to the Circle. The idea was simple and only required enough time and patience.

Each of the pharmacists had been recruited in a group of children when they were still in middle school growing up on a children's home and showed a proclivity for math and science. Slowly, they were groomed and over time, some decided to stay with the Circle and devote their lives to the service of the organization.

Just as many decided they wanted out of all of it and moved away to start a life without answering to anyone but their boss or their spouse. They wanted to forget they ever knew there were really two giant powers going at it, all the time behind the scenes.

That was the difference between the two groups. The Circle wanted their recruits to stay a part of their system but once someone had decided they were leaving, no one stopped them. There was a guarantee that no one would threaten them or their family in order to get them to stay.

It was true that the Circle couldn't always offer the highest reaches of the business or political world like Management could but anyone who opted for the Circle held on to something even more precious than an upper middle class life, if they only understood it. They could always choose something different.

This was the day, though that being in Management's upper reaches turned out to truly be a career move without enough options.

Each pharmacist had slowly over the years put themselves in such a place of trust that they had access to all of the orders that came through the facility.

In order to block out the noise of the machinery overhead, most of the people who worked at the plant had purchased their own noise-killing headphones that could also play music. The pharmacists were no exception.

They streamed music all day long that randomly selected songs from the internet.

Each day at precise times throughout the day the songs that were chosen contained key words that let them know all was well.

Once they were home, they received coded messages over their iPhone that were quickly decoded with the current OTP, telling them what playlists to expect if all was well the next week. There was a different selection if something changed and their reason for being there was suddenly put into play.

They were expected to memorize both lists every week.

No one in the small group brought the iPhone to work with them. They all used a different phone at work that they had purchased on their own and was setup like everyone else's.

Their lives, these three pharmacists, were to be as normal as possible with the usual birthday celebrations for their kids at Chuck E. Cheese's and trips to the dentist and worries about car repairs or the weather. They were to blend right in with everyone else till they became invisible because they just did their jobs and went home to their families. This had been going on for almost a generation, waiting for different orders.

The day the playlist suddenly changed over to the alternate list, each of them knew that their assignments were coming to an end. It was part of the original agreement.

Their families would be relocated with them and given entirely new identities. They would have to start over in new professions that didn't leave a trail back to pharmaceuticals in any way. It wasn't because the Circle was trying to keep them entangled but because if Management ever figured out what they had done, they wouldn't stop searching for them. Their families would be tortured for information and destroyed. That was common knowledge.

This was the failsafe operation and each of them had been groomed so that once things were put into play they wouldn't hesitate. There was no backup plan and if one of them hesitated, it would mean that an entire third of the targets would escape unharmed and possibly lead to failure for the entire idea.

The Circle had to be sure these three people would act swiftly the moment they heard the music change and begin to manipulate the correct orders. They would only have days to infiltrate the system before the mail orders would reach their destinations. There would even be days before the deaths would be attributed to the medicine and more time before someone would realize there was a pattern.

By then, the three pharmacists would be gone and every trace of them wiped away by the cleaners. Management would be left to marvel at the patience of the Circle.

That is the one thing the smaller dog who bears all of the scars has when going into a fight. If they want to survive, they learn to be patient.

The operation started on a Monday and by Wednesday afternoon the three pharmacists, one at a facility not too far from Maurel, one in Texas near the gulf and one in Colorado, all left for lunch and never came back. They all mentioned doctor's appointments that might run long and asked their backups to take over for them, just in case.

No one missed them till the next morning. By then, they were on planes bound for other locations, spread across the world with entirely new lives waiting for them.

To buy more time for the medications to do what they needed to do, each of them called in sick. No one would be alarmed by three employees in three different areas who had always been model workers calling in sick. It would be routine. It happened so rarely. They hoped to be back on Friday.

By Monday, the operation was reaching its logical conclusion. Someone was found on their bathroom floor, foam around their mouth, their body contorted by the last moments when they had gasped for air.

Someone else was found still, lying in their bed and it was assumed at first that they had died peacefully in their sleep. Only a few were at work where there were witnesses who saw how quickly they seemed to be deteriorating until they found it harder to breathe or to talk. Ambulances were called and doctors tried valiantly to save them but without an idea of what was causing this, it was all too late.

This went on for a week.

Maurel kept coming into work every day, doing her job, chatting with her coworkers, waiting for the order to execute the virus. Finally, on the following Monday the order came through.

She waited until everyone was taking their lunch to key in the code that would unlock the virus from where it had been waiting in the system. It didn't take long for Kroton to start to freeze and then stored documents to crumble like sand as if they were real instead of virtual.

Maurel called the IT department and reported a problem. They said they would be there as soon as possible. They had a few other problems of their own but it wouldn't take more than an hour. "Okay, then I'm going to lunch," she said.

She put her communicator on 'away' and took only her jacket and purse, as if she was headed out to grab a bite to eat. The rest would have to stay behind for the Management cronies to sift through for clues. They wouldn't find any.

By the time November was over, there were hundreds of deaths all over the country. Even some that were being reported worldwide. The national news was abuzz about the South African businessmen who suddenly dropped dead in Angola but the media quickly tied it to the rebels.

George Clemente knew what was happening. He could see that there were leaks throughout Management and they somehow added up to his careful plan to take over failing on a catastrophic level. He wasn't about to let that happen.

CHAPTER 24

George Clemente was tired of taking phone calls from worried Commanders who were reporting that they had lost too many officers to continue in the field. A mild annoyance had taken over his mood and stayed. It had never occurred to him that the Circle was capable of an unprovoked assault and it left him feeling energized and frustrated, till it formed an anger that was taking over his ability to think clearly.

His first thought was to take out the entire neighborhood surrounding Wallis Jones and her family and send a message to Circle operatives everywhere. But that would only incite fear among the outsiders who knew nothing of the Circle or Management. He would be pegged as a terrorist and it would only make it easier for the Circle to leak that George Clemente was a long-suspected terrorist responsible for everything the Circle had actually done.

It would tie everything up for them rather neatly. It was the only thing stopping him from giving out the order to retaliate.

Of course he had known that the Jones house was surrounded by Circle agents. He wasn't sure who they were or where they lived but it was to be expected. It would have been the first thing he would have done under the circumstances. There was too much to protect to leave it to chance and it would have been too difficult to keep track of the family without living next door.

Management had tried to move into the neighborhood but without luck, further confirming what he suspected about the area.

Ironically, it made it easier for him to give the order to storm the house and kill Wallis Jones, knowing that there would be few or no witnesses who would report a gun battle to anyone but their superiors. Both sides were still trying to maintain a veil of anonymity, even if it was in the middle of a war.

Clemente had to calm down, think for a moment and let his emotions drain out of him till he could see just the information being presented.

He wanted to see his strategy win out more than he wanted revenge. Truth was, he didn't care who had been killed, only that their death jeopardized his goals. Given a little time and some luck, he wouldn't even remember their names. They were soldiers after all.

The attempt on Wallis Jones' life had ended badly. Not only was she still alive and without a scratch but he had lost two of his best snipers. The whole thing seemed to have set off the Circle but Clemente couldn't be sure what exactly it was that had set things in motion and led to such a deadly assault.

Wallis had become a target the moment he found out that the proof they had sought of their organization's true start was known by her entire family. They could dismantle most of Management just by leaking the truth if they had proof that William Reitling never existed.

It was worse than learning that the brat, Ned Weiskopf was the last known descendant.

In the end, Clemente knew that he could use Ned for his own means, just like he was using Harry and get some pleasure out of knowing that the Circle had a part in destroying themselves. Wallis Jones was going to be another story.

If only he could see past this temporary glitch.

He had to take into account that the Circle apparently had a good bead all along on the mid-level superiors within Management. His arrogance at thinking Management was so invulnerable had made them lax at keeping a low profile. Clemente couldn't say the same thing about the Circle and knew that it would be impossible to identify enough people in similar positions in the opposition.

Killing a lot of people to affect change wouldn't work, so figuring out the one person that might do the same would have to be just as effective. Clemente settled on Ned Weiskopf.

His own people would object but he would explain to them that it would appear as if someone within Ned's own family had pulled the trigger. His uncle, Harry Weiskopf.

Key members within the Circle would be thrown and hesitate while Management would see it as a rallying cry. It was so simple, thought Clemente as he smiled.

Thank goodness the grandmother was in the hospital. She was the only one who had the right idea, thought Clemente and was always on guard for intruders. The rest of them were so busy trying to maintain a normal lifestyle that they left holes that could be filled with opportunities. Clemente planned to use one of those. Perhaps he would just get lucky and be able to kill Wallis Jones, the Black Widow at the same time.

Tom Weiskopf was worrying over the same problems as George Clemente but from an entirely different angle.

He knew that their bold move would bring some kind of retaliation but given all of the circumstances it would not be an obvious twist. He had actually come to the same conclusion as Clemente and knew the most vulnerable target.

"I have to get to Richmond," he said to the detail that had accompanied him to Mark's house in in the mountains of Montana. "Now."

Mark was glad to hear him say he was leaving. It would mean his family was safer and he could get back to what was left of the life he was trying to build.

"We can get a message to the right people," one of them said, "and they can carry out your order. It's too risky to try and move you again, much less head straight into the worst of the battle."

Tom sat down on the cot set up in the hidden safe room. "Give me the room," he said. He needed to think. Everyone filed out quietly, following orders, except for Mark. He hesitated at the door.

"I have another idea, if you're open to hearing it," Mark said. He was used to having to find solutions that didn't follow the usual routes in order to keep someone he loved, safe.

"Let me start with, you can't stay here. I'm sorry but my family comes first and every day you're here, you threaten their existence and that can't happen."

Tom didn't answer him but just nodded, looking weary.

"But there is someplace else you could go that they wouldn't be looking for you or Ned and might provide the necessary cover." Mark thought about the route he had taken out of Richmond when he had made his own flight ahead of Management to try and stay alive.

"We both know that the Episcopal Church maintains a kind of modern underground railroad to get people out of harm's way. You could go into it and head for the Midwest. It could work. No one is looking for you, specifically. There's a squad out there hunting for the Sergeant because they believe he has important information but they don't seem to know exactly what it is."

He paused and took in a deep breath, letting it out slowly. He knew how important this was to everyone, even if he didn't want to be a part of the Circle anymore. A certain balance had to be maintained and as long as there was Management, there needed to be something like the Circle.

If they were all to survive, then for now, this man had to survive.

"They don't know who you are, either. You're the Keeper," Mark whispered. He said it with a certain amount of reverence. There were always stories about the existence of a Keeper at the top of the food chain and who it might be, or at least what they might be doing. Some insisted that there was more than one and they divided up the roles but no one was sure.

"You are, aren't you?" he asked.

Tom rose slowly, grunting from all of the travel over rough terrain and the lack of sleep. He put a hand on Mark's shoulder. "I want to thank you for giving us shelter. I'm afraid we took advantage of you, clearly, by presenting you with a problem that you couldn't turn away. But you're right, we can't stay here. That's the beginning of a good idea."

"But has a few flaws, I know," said Mark, noticing that Tom never answered his question.

"This part of Management, they appear to be very determined. Just disappearing won't make them stop looking for us. And even though they don't know they're looking for me," he said, giving Mark a wink. "They will be looking for Ned, my nephew. He is the one that I need to protect. He's my family," said Tom, trying not to think about his older brother. "They also have another asset we need to reclaim," he said. "My brother, Harry."

"I thought he was dead. It's what I had heard. You must be relieved," said Mark.

"Not exactly. We were the ones holding him. Harry is the one who almost got you killed. He betrayed us all."

Mark felt a burst of anger and clenched his fists. "Why was he still alive? You would never have let someone else cause so much death and then walk away," he snarled. All of the respect he had felt just a moment ago was gone.

The guards who were always with the Keeper appeared at the door but Tom waved them away. "I'm alright, please leave us alone," he said. "You're right but we didn't exactly let him walk away. I'm sorry. I'm human too. I couldn't bring myself to kill my brother so we locked him up in what we thought was a secure prison that no one knew about but the uppermost cell."

"Then you have a leak."

"Clearly. That's part of the problem we're facing right now. Who to trust so that we can get out of here and successfully move Ned and his parents. This isn't Harry, you know. He's not this smart, I'm sad to say, I suppose. He's weak. All of the harm that he seems to constantly cause, it's because he's weak and selfish and trusts whoever promises him what he wants."

"Which is?"

"To feel like he matters," said Tom, "and sadly, he keeps looking for a way to matter from other people. In a way, that has led us all here. Fortunately, Harry doesn't know the identity of the Keeper," said Tom, trying to manage a smile. "But he could be used and he needs to be retrieved, if possible." Tom tried not to wince as he said it, knowing that Harry had to disappear again, even if this time it meant his death. Too many other good people had died in his place already.

"But first things first. I need to find a way to get to one of our children's homes. It's a good idea. Ned will blend right in while we try and pinpoint this poisonous cell and destroy them. How do we do that?" he asked, looking at Mark.

"You'll need a diversion. Something to distract them away from this goal long enough to move Ned and so they don't pick up on the trail." Mark thought of Robert Schaeffer and his boys that he had deposited at the children's home in the Midwest and he wasn't willing to just lead Management straight to their door and put all of them in danger.

"Do you even have an idea about who it is in Management that has started this war?" asked Mark.

"I have an idea, a very good one, which also gives me the start of a solution."

Reverend Michael was an elderly minister who had been part of the Episcopalian underground transport for as long as he had been ordained. He had been recruited from the start and groomed to be a part of an old Order. His assignment was always in the South where he was born and raised, making it easier for him to blend in with a crowd and his movement to go relatively unnoticed.

Southerners don't take well to outsiders who have no family ties in the area and would always wonder what someone was up to, creating exposure. Reverend Michael had been moved around different parts of the South till he witnessed the last Keeper, Carol Schaeffer's death in Savannah. He nearly died as well from the beating he took from George

Clemente.

After that, his Order, the Episcopal Order of the White Rose gave him a lighter load. They were also keeping an eye on the growing war and when the Keeper sent the order to help him and his nephew move safely across the States, they reactivated more of the underground that moved through a select number of homes and older Episcopal churches and seminaries. That also meant calling on Reverend Michael to rejoin the fight. He was glad to get the news.

Reverend Michael had his suspicions about who was behind the new mayhem in Management and he had voiced his opinion more than once to his bishop.

"It's George Clemente," he said. "He's still alive and he's trying to take over. God help us all if he succeeds," he said, shaking with anger and fear. His bishop had given him a glass of water and told him to calm down. There was no proof that Clemente had ultimately survived that day in Georgia when the Reverend had fought him off with the only thing he had been holding, a 1928 Book of Common Prayer.

Reverend Michael still used the prayer book every day, despite the broken spine and stains. It was to remind him of the dangers that awaited all of them if they ever dropped their guard again.

"It's George Clemente," he repeated. "Please, I am begging you, tell the others along the chain. The only way to kill this snake is if we hunt him first." The Reverend's right hand spasmed in pain along the ropey scars and the inflamed knuckles where Clemente had managed to almost cripple him. He could barely hold a fork in that hand anymore but it was worth it. Clemente had to be stopped.

The bishop had not been as sure as Reverend Michael. After all, the hospital had said that George Clemente didn't survive his wounds. He hesitated, not wanting to embarrass the older minister who had served them for so long and so well. There was plenty of time to pass on the message if things got worse.

"It will be alright," the Bishop said to Reverend Michael, trying to comfort him. "God is in charge of all of us."

"That doesn't mean the evil among us cannot cause great harm."

The Reverend knew what Clemente was capable of doing and wasn't willing to wait and trust that everything would turn out alright this time. There had been too many close calls and too many people like Carol Schaeffer who didn't survive the Church waiting for the natural order to restore itself.

When he asked for a brief sabbatical to go and visit family, the Bishop reluctantly gave permission and even said it was a good idea. It had been much too long since the Reverend had taken any kind of vacation and family was just what he needed. The war could let go of one of its oldest servants and they could talk more when he got back.

Reverend Michael was never a fan of lying and tried to comfort himself with the notion that the Weiskopfs were the family at the center of the Circle that he had sworn to protect. He didn't agree with the Bishop's last statement but instead, thanked him for letting him go. The Reverend wasn't anticipating a return trip this time. He knew it would take everything he had to locate Clemente and finish him off and he didn't expect he'd survive the effort.

It would be alright, though. He'd lived a good, long life of service and this would be his last act even if no one else but God accompanied him on the journey.

He packed a small bag and took a taxi to the airport so that no one would see his plane was not heading to his sister's house in Florida. He would be in Richmond before dinnertime. The two men had tangled enough times for Reverend Michael to know exactly what Clemente would try to do to next.

"It's George Clemente," he said quietly, massaging his hand. "I know it is, and he will be near the boy." He took his seat on the plane and shut his eyes. He would need his rest if he was going to track down George Clemente and finish things, once and for all.

Wallis Jones looked out of her bedroom window at the quiet street.

"I won't do it," she said. "We are not running." She turned to look at Norman. "It goes against everything we have been trying to do," she pleaded. It wasn't like her. But once again, she was not sure of what she wanted to do next.

"It's become too dangerous," said Norman. "Tom would never ask us to do this if he didn't believe it. I'm not risking Ned's welfare. Not again, I'm sorry. We need to move quickly and get him out of harm's way, just for a little while. I need you to go along with this so that he doesn't think it's worse than it is."

"You mean, that we are not a team."

"Yes. That we don't agree. Even if we don't, you and I know that somehow we'd work all of that out later, but Ned doesn't. We can say that we're visiting for a little while."

"As we drive like hell down the highway, switch cars, meet people we've never seen before and stay on a campus full of children who don't really have an intact family. This will fool Ned into thinking what?"

"Look, I'm sorry, it's all I've got," said Norman, his hands out to his sides as if he was arguing his case in court. "I want to be damned sure we get to fight another day. I know Tom. This is real and he said there's no time to waste. We either leave quickly now with no one right on our heels or we end up with a worse scenario. I'm not willing to take that chance."

Wallis' eyes filled with tears. "How do we tell him? And my mother?"

Norman pulled her close. "Your mother has guards outside her door at all times. No one can get to her."

"But she'll wonder where we are."

"No, we'll make sure someone tells Harriet and if anyone understands, it will be Ned's grandmother who has shot off a gun twice in our vicinity, to protect him. We will tell Ned to get in the car. A long explanation is just not a good idea for a newly minted teenager."

"He is going to hate us for a long time to come," said Wallis. "We haven't even told him about his grandmother. This isn't how we usually do things. Just when it seemed like he was thawing just a little."

"May he have a very long time to hate us, then," said Norman. "But for now, we have to go."

There really wasn't much time.

George Clemente wanted to make sure he had everything he needed before he made his move this time. He was tired of all of the recent failures so close to what should have been the final steps and his claim at last to lead all of Management.

He already had a stranglehold on Management's finances, worldwide, and that had taken him years to do, siphoning money into different accounts. Now, he needed to win the hearts of the people and Harry Weiskopf, the unwitting fool was going to help him do it.

After the boy was dead, George could finally kill Harry and take credit for killing the traitor himself. He would claim that Harry had faked his own death and out of bitterness and half-crazy had killed his nephew in order to claim himself as a force to be recognized. That would all be reported posthumously. Harry's family would never believe he was capable of any of it but that didn't matter. Millions of people who wore the small flag pin to show they were proud of being a part of Management would believe the story till it became a fable of sorts.

And this time Clemente would make sure that Harry Weiskopf was really dead.

But not till he served his purpose. "Come on, Harry," said Clemente, smiling and putting an arm gently around Harry's back. "Your brother called. He wants to hear your side of things, give you a chance. Seems your family has a real soft spot for you."

Harry smiled and let Clemente lead him out to the car. After all, it was all he really wanted, someone to understand.

CHAPTER 25

Reverend Donald drove as fast as he could toward East Broad Street and left his car in one of the Medical College's parking lots that was intended for physicians, hoping that someone would recognize the familiar gold cursive lettering of his name beneath the driver's side handle on his black Lincoln Continental and give him a pass.

At this point, it didn't matter. He needed to get to the church that was snugly tucked between several of the medical school buildings before anyone else did.

Monumental Church sat between Twelfth and College Street, facing what had been H Street and was now called East Broad Street. The church was built as a tribute to the first great urban disaster of the new country. In 1811, the Richmond Theatre was a glorious, brick structure with several stories broken up into three layers of box seats and balconies that entertained some of the greatest names of the barely minted, United States of America. The plays were always well attended and the new theater could hold well over five hundred people. After the fire, the church had replaced the theater as a tribute to the dead.

Some of the city's founders who had helped build the new church had known all about the true origins of Management and that was when a deal was struck with Management. The Circle was tasked with watching over their part of the secrets, no matter the cost. The church had seemed like a natural resting place for an old diary.

Reverend Donald ran the last block toward the church, the heavy, iron key in his jacket pocket pulling his coat on one side as the other side of his jacket flapped in the wind. Several people stopped and looked as if they wanted to say something to the minister.

Southerners were easily worried by over the top displays and particularly from their clergy. They would assume that something terrible must have happened and want to come to the Reverend's assistance.

But there wasn't time to reassure them that everything was fine. He stopped, though when he got to the steps at the front of the Episcopal Church and could see that the three-foot high monument shaped like an urn that sat in front of the stone porch was missing.

He tried to take a few deep breaths and waved at the people who were still watching him. They were prepared to jump in and help out if he would only give them instructions.

That was all they needed. A few made comments as they turned away about clergy and how much things had changed, but they all looked relieved to be left to their day.

Reverend Donald felt his knees shake a little as he started to walk up the stone stairs and got closer to the empty space where the stone urn had sat, just yesterday in tribute to the seventy-two people, mostly women who had died in the fire of 1811.

Just a year after the new theater had been built, one day after Christmas and a delay, a packed house had come to see a popular actor and were all in a jovial mood. The governor of Virginia was there, along with his family, as well as several other well-known politicians and local bluebloods, first families of Virginia.

Many of them had met in the new theater to discuss forming a committee to talk about how to deal with this rapidly growing power that was migrating from Europe and called itself Management. Some of those in attendance that night were even known to be a part of Management and had come to the Circle to talk about a deal.

That night, the audience was overflowing with nearly six hundred people, eighty of them children. Everyone had come to the theater to relax and wind down after the festivities from Christmas. There were people from every age and background packing the house along every level and every balcony.

The good mood continued just after the first act when the curtain came down to signal an intermission, and backstage a boy raised a chandelier, still lit, toward the ceiling entangling the ropes, catching scenery that was hoisted near the roof on fire. No one in the audience was aware for a bit longer that there was a problem. The curtains were hiding the growing emergency.

Panic struck when the roof caught fire and the building was quickly engulfed. The narrow doors quickly became clogged with people.

Most of the Management in attendance survived and the negotiations continued with the Circle as they tried to create a balance that would stop anyone from every turning America into a monarchy. Even Management was more interested in democracy in the early days.

One of the Circle members at the table was a new Episcopal minister and a member of the Order of the White Rose, sworn to assist the new Circle.

The Order quickly offered to take over the protection of the diary. They recognized how ingrained Management already was in society and they feared what Management might someday become if there was nothing to keep them in their rightful place. Their message of a middle class as a ruling force was intoxicating and it was clear that saying anything against Management or how they did business would only cause people to turn away and stop listening.

It became necessary to keep the diary hidden, until a different time came when they might know better what to do with the truth.

Reverend Donald walked around where the large stone urn that was nearly three feet tall had sat and toward the front door of the church. The door was unlocked. He was already too late. He felt for the outsized key in his pocket and wondered how he would tell the others.

He went in and moved more slowly down the middle aisle of the empty church, stepping gingerly across the thick red carpet. There were white footprints in the carpet that looked like several men had tramped up and back several times. It was not a good sign.

At the altar he knelt for a moment and asked for help, whispering, "If it's your will, I'll follow you," he said, trying to gather his courage.

At the back of the altar was a narrow door that led to a small anteroom where the minister would have one last moment to pause and take a deep breath before heading out in front of the congregation. The room had a small Persian carpet, placed there in order to hush the sound of shoes clicking across the wood planks while everyone was sitting in pews out front. The carpet was still pristine. "Please God," he whispered.

Reverend Donald peeled back the carpet and pulled up the trap door underneath. It led to a walkway that stretched underneath most of the church and held the remains of the Richmond Theatre and the brick pilings that had survived the fire. The ground underneath was a mixture of Virginia clay and ash preserved by the new building overhead.

The minister pulled out a large rag, neatly folded from inside his coat pocket and carefully folded back the edges, removing the iron key and dropping the rag onto the floor. He held onto the key as he lowered himself into the space and dropped the last few feet, steadying himself for a moment as he landed.

He was in the tallest part of the cavernous space and felt a certain reverence for what had happened on the grounds. First the fire that took so many lives and then only months later another decision was made that would eventually be passed down to him.

He pulled a small flashlight out of his pocket that shown a thin light he could follow till he found another trapdoor that led to the resting place of fifty-four women and eighteen men.

The trapdoor was impossible to see unless someone knew where they were looking. Two hundred years of settling dust had obscured most of the original floor from the Richmond Theatre.

Reverend Donald hesitated for a moment as he shown the flashlight in different directions, taking in what was still preserved from that night. The red brick pilings were still mostly intact and showed the original foundation of the theater.

Outside the temperature was dropping but in the deepest parts of the church, the air was close and hot and the minister had to wipe sweat from his face as he pulled up the trapdoor and set aside the panel. Underneath was the marble crypt that held the remains of everyone who had died trying to get away from the flames.

He pulled out the large key that Harriet had gotten from its resting place at Hollywood Cemetery by using the first key that she had been entrusted to guard. The two keys that made up the mark of the saltire and the Order of the Rose Resistance.

He got down on his knees and rested a hand on top of the crypt as he leaned over to the right side and felt along what was by now familiar to him. He had been appointed to be the one in charge of watching over the diary for well over thirty years and had on regular occasions over time make sure that everything was in working order.

The minister had to lean in to the right, balancing himself with his hand, as he got at an angle where he could insert the key and gain enough leverage. He turned the key, listening to the sound of the tumblers scraping until there were three distinct clicks. A panel that was two feet long and six inches tall fell forward on hinges, revealing an old, worn circular leather pouch that fit neatly in the space. Reverend Donald pulled out the pouch and opened it up to see that the diary written by Wallis Jones' ancestor revealing the truth about the origins of the group that came to be known simply as Management was still intact.

He sat back on his heels and felt his first wave of relief.

As he suspected, Management had believed that the proof was hidden in the monumental urn outside and had taken the entire thing away in the night when everyone would be safely tucked in bed.

Then they could crack it open like an egg and find out what mysteries were inside the stone. Fortunately, there would be nothing to find.

Reverend Donald quickly put the top back on the leather canister and leaned back down to replace the thin, marble front piece, putting the key back into the lock and fixing everything back in its place. He put the trapdoor back into its place as well, gently pushing down till it was all level with the floor and retraced his steps back to the other opening.

He hoisted himself up, grunting from the effort and scraping his wrist, thinking that this used to be a lot easier when he was younger, as he finally lifted himself to where he was sitting on the edge, his legs still dangling in the opening.

He leaned over for the rag he had left behind and carefully wiped off his clothing and his shoes till the old clay dust was removed and would leave no trace of where he had been on the carpets.

The key was wrapped back in the rag and put back in his pocket as he rolled over onto his knees and pulled himself upright.

A flurry of sound suddenly came from what must have been the front door of the church and was quickly getting closer. Reverend Donald stood still, listening and instinctively felt for the key in his pocket. Several voices arguing about something as they came toward where he was standing.

The minister had been trained for moments like this and knew it was best to keep moving in an orderly fashion and get it right than panic and try to force the trapdoor back into place. It would never work. It was designed to fit snugly in only one direction and took a small amount of patience to do just right. Reverend Donald looked at the piece of floor in his hands and at the pattern of the floorboards and took two steps gingerly across the opening till he was holding it just right and placed it in the opening, pushing down with some effort.

He rolled the carpet back into place and listened again for a moment, trying to figure out exactly where the voices were coming from so he could make his escape.

"There was nothing in it, so does it really matter what you thought?" demanded an angry male voice. Reverend Donald thought it sounded like an older man, and he knew at once what they were arguing about, as he tightened his grip on the leather pouch.

"It has to be in this church somewhere and we are not leaving until we find it, even if we have to tear this place apart to find it," yelled the man.

Reverend Donald quietly moved toward the far door that led into a narrow hallway and ended by an exit that could take him out into the alley. He had almost made it to the outside but had to stop when he realized that the intruders were heading straight for him. They had not walked straight up to the altar but were circling around and were right in his path.

He turned back toward the small anteroom and wondered if he should hide the pouch to delay its exposure when the door from the altar popped open and he felt his second wave of relief that day.

"Reverend Michael," he whispered as loudly as he dared. "What are you doing here?" he asked. The elderly minister was a long way from his region.

"There's not enough time to explain. Keep moving," he said, pulling on the younger minister's sleeve. "You need to get out of here. Take the side door on the Gospel side of the church. There's a car waiting for you out there. I'll hold them off."

"You will?" The thought of leaving an elderly minister behind to hold off what sounded like several men stopped Reverend Donald in his tracks for just a moment.

"Get out of here," hissed Reverend Michael. "Now! There are more important things and you will have to trust that I know what I'm doing."

Reverend Donald looked at him for a moment as he passed him in the doorway near the altar of Monumental Church and tried to think of something to say. "God be with you," he whispered, knowing that the minister was doing what they had all pledged to do when they joined the Order.

"Now, go," said Reverend Michael as he swung the door shut in Reverend Donald's face and he could hear the door on the other side of the room bang open with some considerable force. There was no time to linger and find out what happened. He quickly closed the space between himself and the far side of the church and found a waiting car with two more ministers from the Order sitting inside with the car idling. They left without looking back.

Reverend Donald kept mumbling prayers under his breath for the elderly minister he had left behind, as he held the pouch and its contents close. The diary was still safe in the hands of the Circle.

Reverend Michael had shut the door to the altar as quietly as he could and braced himself against the door. The first one through the other door was exactly who he had expected.

"Good afternoon George, we meet again," he said to George Clemente's angry face, beet red with frustration.

"Where the hell is it?" yelled Clemente. Reverend Michael could see what looked like a large thug behind Clemente and a very worried older man that Reverend Michael recognized as the missing Harry Weiskopf.

Harry seemed to want to be somewhere else. They were an unusual grouping to come to fetch two hundred year old proof of a conspiracy.

Reverend Michael was counting in his head, calculating how much time Reverend Donald needed to get safely out of the church and then to get away in the car. He wanted to give him enough time to deposit the leather pouch with the next messenger so that Clemente would lose the trail completely, again.

"I noticed that the church is missing something out front. Don't you already have what you came for?"

Clemente shoved the minister hard, making him bounce off of the door he was leaning against and shouted, "Give it to me. This is a waste of time. We will find it anyway."

"There is nothing here to find," hissed Reverend Michael, "except salvation, if you were so inclined."

One of the larger men rushed at the older priest but Clemente held him back and came at Reverend Michael himself, ready to strike him across the face. The priest ducked and caught only a glancing blow as he struck his toe hard against Clemente's knee, making him squeal in pain. He toppled onto Reverend Michael who used the opportunity to pull his keys from his pocket and slash Clemente across the face with the side of his keys, making him scream even louder in pain.

The larger man with Clemente started to reach out and separate the two older men but was stopped by a ceramic table lamp that came crashing down on his head, making him wobble on first one foot and then the other. Harry Weiskopf stood behind him, looking just as startled, holding the remains of the lamp.

He seemed to be waiting to see what the man did and when he finally toppled over, Harry moved and wrapped the electric cord around Clemente's neck, and pulled as he listened to Clemente gurgle as he tried to claw at the cord and Harry's hands as they all slowly sank further along the floor.

He finally elbowed Harry hard in the ribs and loosened the grip of the cord, slipping it over his head. It was all of the time that he needed.

Clemente had wanted to torture his old enemy, Reverend Michael but he was prepared to just end things if that became necessary. Even though he was dizzy and there were deep, red lines around his throat he still had enough presence to reach down to his legs that were splayed out on the floor and remove the small pistol he always kept there.

Harry looked startled when the gun went off in his face. He died making a small noise and fell back from where he was sitting on the floor, with a small thud, staining the Persian carpet.

Reverend Michael didn't hesitate though and fought back, biting Clemente's arm as hard as he could, trying to get the gun away from him.

A loud bang could be heard out on the sidewalk, followed by two more bangs as people pulled out cell phones and called for help.

Several, braver souls rushed into the church and toward what remained of the noise bursting into the room where they found the elderly priest barely alive with a gunshot in his shoulder. Harry was dead, still staring up at the ceiling and Clemente was nowhere to be found.

The rescuers thought they heard the elderly priest praying but one of them said, "No, he was counting something. I'm sure of it. He kept saying, just long enough, just long enough."

Reverend Donald had made it to back to St. Stephen's in record time, wondering about the outcome at Monumental Church as he waited for Norman Weiskopf and his family, ready to pass on the leather pouch.

Norman and Wallis were standing in the front office of Ned's school trying to look relaxed as they waited for someone to fetch their son.

"Where are we going?" asked Ned. The hall monitor had shown up in his class and the teacher had motioned for him to get his things and follow the student. His parents were waiting for him in the office.

"Okay, good," said his dad, seeming to ignore Ned's question. They had all walked outside with Ned following behind them, still asking the same question as his frustration only grew and his voice took on a certain amount of whining.

"I have lacrosse practice," he said, gesturing toward the field. "Coach said if we miss a practice, we miss a game."

Ned stopped at the car and refused to get in, planting his feet. "I can't go yet. What's going on? I deserve an answer," he shouted, finally getting his mother to look him in the eye. "Why are you taking me out of school? What's gone wrong now?"

Wallis looked like she'd been punched in the gut and couldn't get a deep breath. She forced herself to keep trying and take the moment to think about what to say. Ned turned to head back toward the school as Norman stepped in front of him and blocked his way.

Ned tried to push past him, a look of determination on his face but Norman grabbed him by the arms and stopped him again, without saying a word. Ned started to yell at Norman as loud as he could, inches from his father's face.

"I hate you! I hate you!"

Wallis knew it had all gone too far. They were making Harriet's mistakes and it was too much.

"Stop! Stop!" she yelled, trying to be heard over Ned's screams. Ned let out one last, long scream of sound like he was in some deep pain. Norman grabbed his son in a tight hug and refused to let go no matter how much Ned pushed and pulled, trying to break free.

The assistant principal came running out of the door they had just exited, carrying a walkie talkie and looking very concerned. A guard was right on his heels.

Ned finally stopped yelling and Norman held on to him, more gently and rubbed his son's back. Wallis tried to look calm as she waved at the men.

"We're okay. A little family drama but we're okay. Sorry." It sounded so melodramatic and she wasn't sure anyone would buy it but the men stopped and glanced at each other before they slowly turned and went back inside.

Wallis wondered if they saw a version of this kind of family story all the time. In her practice, Wallis did and she vowed often that she would never be a part of it. Things change, sometimes when we're not looking, she thought.

"We owe him an explanation, Norman," she said, quietly.

Norman tried to shake his head, no but Wallis said, "We have to start acting as a family and that means we trust each other. Like we always have."

Ned pushed away from his father and turned around to face his mother. He wiped his face on his shirt and looked like he was waiting for something.

"We should have done this sooner, Ned. I'm sorry. This is going to sound lame but when you're a parent you do what you think is right and it's only later that you can tell what was a good decision and what was a really wrong turn." Wallis thought of Harriet and wondered for a moment what it must have been like trying to decide if she could trust Wallis enough to tell her such enormous secrets.

Wallis let her shoulders drop and found herself feeling an odd sense of peace. It was like she had come to a stretch in the road where at least she didn't have to wonder if this was the right thing to do.

"There are a few things we haven't told you," Wallis started.

"You lied to me," said Ned, nodding his head. There were tears in his eyes.

Wallis hesitated for a moment. Norman looked like he had been slapped. He was standing behind his son, holding very still, not saying anything. Wallis wasn't sure if that was good or bad.

"Okay, I can see why you'd say that. We didn't set out to…to lie to you. We were trying to protect you. Like I said, seems pretty lame now. Look, there's a lot of ground to cover and it's going to take a while. I'm going to hope that you still trust me just enough to make a deal with me. If you'll get in the car, we'll tell you everything."

Norman looked like he was about to object again.

"Everything," Wallis repeated. "If you start to feel overwhelmed, we'll stop but we'll let you decide. We'll stop making that judgment call for you. Okay?" she asked, looking at both Ned and Norman.

"Where are we going," asked Ned. He wasn't asking so much as stating something.

His curls were matted down in places from his struggle with his dad and his face had a sheen of sweat. He looked so young to Wallis. She grimaced, remembering the little boy who would run at her down a long hallway every time she picked him up at preschool. Somehow that road had led them here.

"We are hitting the road and heading for the Midwest, I think," said Wallis. Ned started to protest.

"Wait, wait," said Wallis, holding up her hand like she was trying to protect him. "I'm not trying to hide anything. I'm admitting that we don't exactly know either. A few things have happened and we're going to get help from Reverend Donald and his friends to get out of town. Unfortunately, they don't tell you more than you need to know to get from Point A to Point B."

"What's Point A and Point B, then?"

Wallis smiled, grateful that Ned was trying to work with her at all.

"We start at St. Stephen's and get our instructions from there."

"Is this like when you helped Will and Trey get out of town?" asked Ned, referring to the Schaeffer boys. "Are we going to see them?"

"I honestly have no idea," said Wallis. "But I'm actually hoping. A familiar face or two would be a comfort. All I know is we need to get moving, and fast. There are a few people that may be looking for us that don't have our best interests at heart."

"That man from the big meeting, the auditorium. From where I saw Uncle Harry. That's who you mean, don't you?"

"I do," said Wallis, nodding, taking a step toward her son. Everything between them was so cautious these days. Wallis found herself overthinking every movement. It all used to be so easy. Once again, she wondered how much of this was the horrible reality that had become their lives, and how much of it was really just her fault.

"Well, then, we better get going," said Ned, ducking under Wallis' arm. He made his way to the car and opened the back door and got in, without ever turning back to look at them. Just as quietly, he shut the door and Wallis could see him putting on his seat belt, and sitting back against the seat. She wasn't sure if this was all a good sign or not and she started to cry. Norman rubbed her arm as he tried to give her a small nudge toward the car.

"You do realize that there is nothing about my life that is where I left it, again." Wallis stopped walking and pushed away Norman's arm. "I used to have so much confidence about things. I knew right from wrong and I judged everyone, myself, my mother, based on what I knew."

"You know, you and Ned are a lot more alike than you realize," said Norman, trying to get Wallis moving but without success.

"Norman, stop for a moment. This may be the last moment we have together, alone, for a week or more and I can't walk around with these thoughts swirling in my head, anymore."

"Okay, but you only have a minute. We can't get caught out in the open just because you had to tell me how you felt. No offense, love of my life," he said, making an effort at a small smile.

It only made Wallis cry a little harder. "Duly noted," she said, wiping her eyes with the back of her hand. "God, I'm so full of self-pity. All I really want to know is if I have screwed up everything, like that needs to be settled right now."

"Wallis," Norman whispered, lovingly as he took his wife's hand. "We do the best we can, all the time and sometimes we really make a mess of things. Add in a family or two that loves to keep some pretty big, hairy secrets and you can see that our operating instructions were faulty to begin with. Look, for right now, we need to go with, it is what it is, because it's all too much to take in but we have to so that we can keep moving."

He started to push his wife toward the car again.

"I'm sorry, I know you're hurting and need to talk. I know Ned is hurting. I know Harriet needs us to sit by her side and just talk to her about the day so she hears a friendly voice. It's not ideal that none of that is going to happen, yet. But I'm going to make damn sure that we all live long enough to hash it out later, no matter how painful all of that turns out to be. Okay?"

Wallis relented and opened the passenger side door. "I always thought that Ned got his determination from you," she said.

"Hmmm, no," said Norman, as he waited till his wife was safely tucked inside and he shut the door, hurrying around the car. He took a quick look around to see if he could see anything suspicious, anyone suddenly pulling into the school's parking lot before he got in and started the car.

Reverend Donald was waiting for them when they got to St. Stephen's and wasted no time giving them the next stop along the Episcopal Church's idea of an escape route.

"Your mother was a faithful servant watching over this pouch for most of her life. It seems only fitting that you should carry on that legacy, at least for a little while," said Reverend Donald, as he carefully laid the pouch in Wallis' hands.

"What do I do with it?" she asked.

"When you get to your final stop where you'll be staying till things can calm down here and we can figure out what to do next, you'll know. Someone will be waiting there for you. Now go."

CHAPTER 26

The squad that had been hunting for Sergeant Kipling wasn't anywhere to be found. They seemed to have moved on to another area and the time had come.

Tom waited until closer to dawn to give the order for all of them to move out by foot. They were taking Sergeant Kipling with them. Mark woke up Jake so he could say goodbye. The teenager had tried to stay awake but had dozed off and was sitting up in a chair by the window at the top of the house, his head resting on his arm against the ledge of the window.

"Hey, Jake," he said softly, "it's time. They're getting ready to go. Did you want to come see them off?"

Jake roused from his sleep and startled awake. "What? Are they gone?" he asked suddenly standing upright, almost knocking over the chair.

"No, they're waiting to say goodbye. It's okay. You have a moment. Come on, let's go say goodbye."

They found the small band of men standing with Ruthie and Peter, smiling and watching Ruthie entertain them with her idea of dancing.

Sergeant Kipling stepped out from the group and extended his hand to Jake. "You saved my life," he said, "and probably everyone else's life here. You were a very brave soldier."

Mark bristled at hearing his son called a soldier but stayed quiet when he saw Jake smile and grab the Sergeant's hand to give it a vigorous shake.

"Not so hard," said the Sergeant, smiling. "Still recovering and we have a lot of terrain to cover in the snow on foot."

"Sorry," said Jake, letting go of his hand.

"Not a problem, you have a good grip there. Your dad must be really proud of you."

Jake looked back at Mark who smiled at him, trying to get the worry off of his face.

"Management has lost the war," said Tom. "Something happened in Virginia that set off a chain of events. That's probably why that squad has disappeared. For now, things are going to quiet down, we hope. But the Sergeant is right, Jake. You and your family made it possible for us to get to this point. Without you, the orders to move forward wouldn't have been given because I wouldn't still be alive. We owe you a debt of gratitude that we may never be able to repay."

"Leave us in peace, that's all we ask," said Mark.

"Dad," started Jake, surprised. He turned back to Tom. "I was thinking of coming with you."

"No," said Mark, shaking his head vigorously, "Not a chance. You will be going to school and then college before you make those kinds of choices."

"It's alright, Jake. Your dad is right. He's a good man," said Tom. "Listen to him. Taking care of your family and creating a life with those you love right around you is all that matters. Not all of us get that choice. If you're one of the lucky ones, hold onto it. Otherwise, everyone else's sacrifice has a little less meaning."

Everyone gathered their gear and were heading out into the night as the sun barely started to rise over the far peak. Mark pulled Tom aside for a moment, away from the others.

"Are you sure the war is ending?" he asked.

"There is every indication. You know, there will never be a formal surrender like in other wars. This was never an official war. There will never be an official end. But they've lost too many key people to continue and something has happened to whoever was pulling the string from within Management. Everyone is headed home, from both sides. Now, we all have to learn to live as neighbors again and go back to what's left of our lives."

"How do you do that?"

"That is what the Circle is about to find out. There are ideas about how to be the group in charge and we will finally get the chance to put them into action. That's where we will really find out if we're any different from Management and can lead without having to take away choices. We will see."

"Try not to ever bother us again, okay?" said Mark, putting out his hand to say goodbye.

Tom laughed and said, "I will do my best. There's so much to do when I get back. I wish you were coming with us. The Circle will get the chance to fill a lot of key roles all over the country and you could write your own ticket. That last operation left a lot of empty Management slots and they don't have replacements, but we do."

"No, thank you. I've been on that merry go round and I'm not getting back on at any price. Besides, you saw my son, Jake. He wants to be a part of the action too much. I'd prefer to change his mind in the time that I have left."

The group slipped away quietly, Jake still trying to negotiate at least crossing the woods with them to show them the quickest route. Mark never relented and Jake watched from the top window for as long as he could, telling himself that someday he was going to be the one to lead the expedition.

The election came and went and President Hayes won, as expected with a wide margin as the waves of violence that rolled across the country simmered down. Everyone started to feel better about keeping things just the way they were. A mood of general optimism hit the country.

Fred Bowers was still in the wind and the upper cells of the Circle had talked about sending out teams to try and locate him. He knew too much.

But President Hayes had said that being President ought to count for something and in the end ordered everyone to stand down and leave Fred Bowers alone. He trusted the man with his life and knew they had more to fear from chasing him than from letting him disappear.

There were still bigger worries.

Reverend Michael had barely survived his wounds this time but the nursing staff at Henrico Doctors Hospital found it difficult to keep the old man quiet and in his bed. He was insistent on speaking

Even though he was on pain killers that should have knocked him out cold, he kept insisting instead that he had to speak to someone he kept calling a keeper.

"Keeper of what?" asked a nurse.

Tom Weiskopf made his way to Reverend Michael's bedside as quickly as he could where the minister told the Keeper about the death of his brother, Harry. Tom had felt a mixture of relief and regret. At least in the end, Harry was a hero and he would make sure to tell Norman that when he had to break the news.

The elderly priest though was more insistent about his other piece of news.

"It was George Clemente. I was right. The scourge still lives and he will be back. You have to hunt him down." The staff at the hospital interrupted them when Reverend Michael's heartbeat got to be too fast and they were worried about him making it out of ICU.

Tom was not as sure that one violent man could have wreaked so much havoc across so much territory and two large organizations. He thought it was too dangerous to assume that much and gave orders that different cells be assigned to investigate different angles, independent of each other. Tom was more certain that there were still moles within the Circle but he was also convinced that they would find them.

Wallis and Norman arrived safe and sound at a children's home in the

Midwest after travelling for days between different homes and churches till their trail grew cold. The Keeper may not have been convinced that George Clemente was that powerful and seeking revenge but the Church did not share that opinion.

The Order of the White Rose was assigned to serve and protect the balance between the two groups and they knew that keeping Wallis and her family safe was part of their assignment.

The other part of their mission that had been suddenly foisted on Wallis Jones, ended when they were greeted at the home. Wallis knew the moment she saw who was there to greet them as they got out of the car.

"Mother Superior," said Wallis, smiling despite how tired she felt after all of the sleepless hours on the road. "I didn't know if I'd ever see you again."

The woman who went by many names, the most recent one, Maurel Samonte, hugged her old friend.

"I hear you have something for me," she said. "Not the first time you have helped keep the order of things straight," said the Mother Superior as she took the leather pouch. "We will see to it that it stays safe and is placed somewhere equally as difficult to access. Although replacing Harriet Jones as a Keeper of the diary will be far more difficult."

"How is my mother? I've called the nurses station a few times but that doesn't really tell me anything. They said she's out of the woods but she's not really speaking yet and until I hear my mother nagging me about something."

"Esther Ackerman is sitting with her. That's right, Esther. Those two are old friends of sorts, you know, until for a long time, they weren't. Mostly over who Harriet chose to marry. Esther said it was too dangerous, especially given Harriet's assignment but you know your mother."

"No, I don't," said Wallis, "but I'd like to change that and get to know her."

"Well, you're in luck because there's time. Don't worry. Esther is just as cagey and tough as your mother and she will watch over her till you can return."

"When is that, exactly?"

"The Church is busy looking for someone named, George Clemente. He seems to be the only one who actively cares about your welfare, or lack of it. Reports are coming in that he has fled the country and is headed for Angola. You have dear Helmut to thank for that bit of news."

"How is he?"

"He has taken off to track Clemente and to follow a few other leads and is not here, I'm afraid. In the meantime, see this as a vacation. Sleep in, walk around the grounds and we'll talk about what comes next. Perhaps it's time we read you in more."

"There's more?" asked Wallis, but the Mother Superior was already walking away, quietly giving orders to a gaggle of young nuns. Wallis tried to see if she could recognize any of their faces from the ones she had last seen with the Mother Superior in Richmond two years ago but no one looked familiar.

She found Norman sitting by himself in the meditation room, which got her to laugh out loud and garner a few looks from others sitting in the quiet room.

"Sorry," whispered Wallis, which made them all look up again.

Norman smiled and got up to follow his wife outside.

"Don't cause trouble. We're on the run and can't afford to get kicked out of our safe house."

"Well, I know you're feeling better. Already with the jokes," said Wallis, as Norman grabbed her around the waist and kissed her. "Where's Ned?"

"He's gone off to talk to the Schaeffer boys. I think he was glad to see a couple of familiar faces. I could be wrong but I thought I saw him talking to a girl."

"Norman, one problem at a time."

"We have to talk about how we can do things differently," said Norman. "Given our unusual family, our parenting skills may need to include a few extra categories."

"Like how to clean your weapon properly?"

"Ha. Well, that and how to learn to be careful and have a life without going crazy."

"You actually know how to do that one? Why have you been keeping that one to yourself?" asked Wallis.

"No, I don't but, now don't grow violent, your mother might. Okay, okay, or Esther or Reverend Donald. They all seem to have a lot of practice. Maybe between all of them we can figure out how to do this better. Ned deserves the effort, don't you think?"

"I think we do too. It's a good idea. I heard about Harry. Are you okay?"

Norman stopped smiling and let out a deep sigh. "No, not at all but it's easier knowing Harry really did figure out the right thing to do in the end. That's all he ever wanted, you know. He was just so screwed up about the definition of the right thing. Usually it involved whatever was best for Harry. In the end, though, he saved the day."

"We'll have to quietly bury him this time."

"When we get back to Richmond."

"I thought about whether we should just move," said Wallis, "but then I realized two things. This would all just follow us wherever we went."

"True."

"And that's our home. Our friends are there and our roots are there. We'll make our stand there and learn how to be happy, despite all of this."

"So, we're good," said Norman.

"We're good," said Wallis, "and Ned will learn how to be."

Halfway across the world, Fred Bowers sat in a small coffee shop in Luanda, the capitol of Angola waiting for his connection. The place could barely be called a shop and was more of a tin shack that charged for burned coffee. It was a simple place for a meet.

"Good evening, Helmut. I trust you didn't have any trouble getting here."

"No, I've been here often enough. Thank you for coming. I'm going to need your help."

"You agree to my terms?"

"I do. We'll do things your way as long as the goal is the same."

"Then let's get started. The sooner we do, the sooner we can stop George Clemente."

"Is he here?"

"There are rumors he's licking his wounds here but no confirmed sightings. You think if he's alive he'll head back to Richmond?"

"He will try. Whether or not he gets there, well, I plan to make sure he doesn't get the chance," said Fred. "I intend to kill the bastard for what he did to my wife."

"I'll take the motivation if that's what gets you going but you realize that he still has the remains of a network?"

Fred ran his hand over his closely cropped hair. "To Maureen," he said, raising the cracked coffee mug with faded blue cornflowers on it.

"You realize we can never say her name again, or for that matter your old name. Okay, okay, to Maureen," said Helmut, raising his cup.

"Let's get started," said Fred. "I don't like to leave loose ends. Is the mole we left near Clemente traveling with him?"

"Yes and from what we can tell, his real identity is still unknown to Management."

"Good, then George Clemente will never see me coming."

About the Author:

Martha Carr (Chicago, IL) is the author of four previous works, including The List, the First Book in the Wallis Jones Series. She is a national columnist, a persistent but slow runner, melanoma cancer survivor, former tap dancer & Girl Scout, national speaker and a Southerner in a big city where she lives near her son, Louie and his wonderful Katie.

Carr is currently at work on the third thriller in The Wallis Simpson Series, The Circle, due out in June 2015.

For more information or to get updates by email go to www.WallisJones.com. Tweet the author at MarthaRCarr or at Google+ at +Martha Carr. Become a regular fan and like the author at www.Facebook.com/MarthaRCarr or sign up for blog posts at www.WallisJones.com.

Praise for other Works by Martha Carr:

In The List, Martha Carr has crafted a slick political thriller that navigates a world laid bare with the quest for power and control. Once you pick it up you won't be able to put it down.
James Eddy, Producer

The List is a rip-roaring read from start to finish, filled with unexpected twists and narrow escapes and a tremendously satisfying payoff that I never saw coming!
Tom Purcell, Nationally Syndicated Columnist and Author

From page one through the last chapter Carr takes the reader on a quick-paced and easy-flowing tour of murder, suspense and steamy romance. Be prepared to stay up past your bedtime with this one.
Library Journal

Every bit as good as Mary Higgins Clark's highly successful novels of psychological suspense. Suspenseful and entertaining.
The Chattanooga Free Press

Simply enjoy being in the hands of an accomplished writer like Carr, whose lively characters and inviting descriptions of family life and love are the hallmarks of a gifted writer.
Grand Rapids Press

Carr's book should touch hearts and open minds.
Publishers Weekly

Wired is the best novel I have read in years.
I'll never look at malls the same way.
Susan Thompson, Little Professor Book Center, Ashland, Kentucky

WIRED, will join other first novels, like TIME TO KILL and GONE, BUT NOT FORGOTTEN as the creator of a new cult following for Carr. We anxiously await her next endeavor.
Mike Cullis, Little Professor Book Center, Middletown, NJ

Martha Carr is the new voice for Middle America using insight, humor and a common sense approach to spirituality. She's the one to watch.
Cari Dawson Bartley, Cagle Cartoons, Inc.

Martha Carr invites the reader to a journey through the 'change stories'.
You will see parallels in your own life's victories.
Bob Danzig, former CEO, Hearst Newspapers, author and speaker